Praise for BIG MUSIC

'Insight and intrigue behind the concert curtain. Big Music is a riveting read.'
–Laura Boon, editor and author of *Tips from a Book Publishing Industry Insider*

'Funny and beguiling. In Big Music, Wills reveals the egos, passions, and deep humanity behind the teaching of music. The character of Beat is a triumph.'
–Kristina Olsson, author of *Boy, Lost* and *Shell*

'Pulses with experience of the music world, fired by an intriguing imagination.'
–Piers Lane AO, a London-based Australian concert pianist

'A musical masterpiece by a master wordsmith – sensitive, insightful, and moving.'
–Karin Schauup, internationally acclaimed classical guitarist

'Funny and intriguing, the story resonates with the music world. A truly joyous read.'
–Dr Donna Hewitt, vocalist, electronic music composer, and instrument designer

'Witty and pacy, *Big Music* captures the emotional turmoil of academic life.'
–John Dale, author of *Huckstepp*, and *The Faculty*

'A literary masterpiece. A gripping journey through heartbreak, triumph, and self-discovery. A must-read for anyone interested in a story that resonates both intellectually and emotionally.'
–Lara McCormack, reviewer

Big Music

Gillian Wills

HAWKEYE
PUBLISHING

First published in Australia in 2024 by Hawkeye Publishing.

Copyright © Gillian Wills

Cover Design by Lakshmi Dasi
Cover art is a detail from *Piano*, a painting by Mostyn Bramley-Moore

All rights reserved. No part of this book may be reproduced, stored in a retrieval system, or transmitted, in any form or by any means, without the prior permission in writing of the publisher, nor be otherwise circulated in any form of binding or cover other than that in which it is published and without a similar condition including this condition being imposed on the subsequent purchaser.

This is a work of fiction. Unless otherwise indicated, all the names, characters, and incidents in this book are either the product of the author's imagination or used in a fictitious manner. Any resemblance to actual persons, living or dead, or actual events, is purely coincidental.

A catalogue record of this book is available from the National Library of Australia.

ISBN 9781923105287
Proudly printed in Australia.

www.hawkeyebooks.com.au

For Mira & Alma

Human speech is like a cracked kettle on which we tap rhythms for bears to dance to, while we long to make music that will melt the stars.
Gustave Flaubert.

1

PERFORMANCE

BEATRICE stood on the steps of an old green Queenslander, a wooden house on stilts. The blue sky's early morning tinge of lilac had paled, bleached by an unrelenting Australian sun. She mopped her dripping forehead, flicked a mosquito off her arm, stared at the smear of blood on her skin. It was steamy, airless, a cloying summer's day. Melody, Theo, and Georgy were finalists in the Byron Bay Music Competition and on their way to give a recital. Nervously, they waited by a white minibus glinting in the harsh light. Dreamy-eyed, a chestnut horse ripped at the grass, watched by a kookaburra on the yard's wooden fence.

'Luggage goes in here.' The driver tapped the vehicle's trailer.

'Exactly. But this,' Melody pointed at her large yellow cello case, 'is not luggage.' She took off her sunglasses and glared. 'Putting it in your trailer in this heat would be like locking a toddler in an unventilated car.'

Melody drew her forefinger across her neck as if it was a knife. A flock of noisy white corellas wheeling overhead drew Beatrice's eye and she reprimanded herself for letting her thoughts drift. If today's venture was to succeed, it needed all her attention. She looked on, ready to step in if the exchange between Melody and the driver became too intense. Clearly, he had no idea how protective musicians were towards their instruments. She could tell him how some believed a violin or cello had a soul, others thought a string instrument stored a player's emotions in the wood.

He flicked through the company's dog-eared regulations and read out loud, 'Golf clubs, suitcases, backpacks, animal cages, and *musical instruments* are classified as luggage.'

'If the 200-year-old glue melts and the seams come unstuck the repair costs will break you.' Melody propped the cello in front of her like a shield.

'Is it yours?'

'No, it's on loan from Turalong Arts.'

The driver checked his phone. Shook his head. Dropped his cigarette and ground it under his boot.

'We're running late. Take it on with you,' he sneered, dismissing Melody with a flick of his hand.

~

On board, the air-conditioned interior offered relief from the heat. Beatrice stared through the tinted window as the van cruised past a yard jammed with rusty cars, dismembered machinery, and a solitary goat. Farmland studded with pale brahman cattle silvered in the harsh light made her smile. But she looked away from the crows tearing furry strips off a rotting kangaroo carcass on the lip of the road.

Beatrice began to feel cold, and exposure to dry, chilly air could make Melody's valuable instrument crack. She wrapped her arms around her to demonstrate how cold she was and asked the driver to raise the temperature. He didn't need to know it was another instance of cello coddling. With his eyes fixed on the road ahead, the driver nodded, adjusted the temperature, and turned on the radio. A famous singer's silky vocals, vintage synth, and 90's back beat wafted through the cabin. Returning to her seat, Beat noticed Georgy, the pianist, asleep, mouth open, her head propped on a folded sweater pressed against the window. Theo adjusted his noise-cancelling headphones. Melody hummed along, bopping to the pop anthem's groove.

Beatrice was on the brink of nodding off when Melody tapped her shoulder.

'Beat. We forgot the sheet music,' she said. Her panicky blue eyes peered through rivulets of blond hair. The van braked abruptly as the driver slowed to accommodate the crawl of bumper-to-bumper cars ahead. Melody was thrown forward.

'For today's concert?' Beat asked wearily.

'Yes. Can we go back?'

'No,' Beat sighed. 'We don't have time. Let's hope the competition organisers have spares.'

~

She should have asked whether they had the music, but she hadn't wanted to patronise them. After all, they were adults. Instead, she'd chewed on a strand of hair, fidgeted, checked and rechecked the content of her shoulder bag while each one remembered yet another item they needed for the trip and ran back into the house to retrieve it. They had fussed. Joked. Dawdled.

Progress had been pitifully slow, the traffic congested until just past Dreamworld, the Gold Coast theme park, but over the Queensland border the vehicle reached maximum speed along the highway slicing between sloping plains of golden, sun-washed hills. Purple mountains loomed in the distance, the wavy, undulating silhouettes like knuckles on a fist.

Beat fretted. Despite the North Coast's beckoning spirit, she worried about what lay ahead. When she'd agreed to coach the trio, she knew their talent was matched by scatty behaviour. Practice sessions hadn't been smooth sailing. Theo, the violinist had regularly stormed out, and after each indignant departure, Melody carefully placed the cello on its side and ran after him. First, she let him rant, then hooked her fingers through his and gently, fondly escorted him back.

Rock groups play by ear. Sheet music isn't essential. But classical trios are judged on how imaginatively and accurately they can spirit an existing piece of music into life. The crucial pages on which she and Georgy, the pianist, had scribbled prompts: when to quicken, brake, blend, whisper, and which player leads, were in Brisbane, marooned on her pine, kitchen table among a rubble of congealed egg and half-nibbled toast.

'But it's not a catastrophe?' Melody probed. Her muscley fingers and broad hands, ideal for a cellist, scooped her hair into a tight ponytail.

'It doesn't get much worse unless you use your iPad readers.'

Melody shook her head. 'Theo told us not to bring them.'

~

Abruptly, the driver accelerated to overtake an old Land Rover laden with bicycles and camping gear and Beat was sickened by the stench of Theo's liberally applied citrus deodorant mingled with disinfectant in the scrubbed interior. If only she could open a window.

Georgy sat up, 'Stop! I'm going to be...'

The driver swerved into a layby. Theo jumped out and opened the sliding door for Georgy, who hitched up her crumpled skirt and dashed behind a thicket of scrub swarming with flies. She moaned. Retched. Black Angus cows in the paddock beyond lifted their heads to stare. Unperturbed, the driver drew on a cigarette. His face parked in neutral like his vehicle.

'Georgy has a migraine.' Melody thumbed her phone.

'A hangover more like,' griped Theo.

Beat raised her eyebrows. 'Georgy's piano part is demanding. If she's unwell I should ring and cancel your recital.'

Theo scrunched up his face, folded his arms. 'We're in the finals. We could *win!* This competition has real kudos.'

'Yeah, but your pianist is out of sorts, and you don't have the sheet music,' Beat reminded him.

When Georgy reappeared, her clammy face was just as blanched but she was steadier on her feet. Melody handed her a bottle of water. Georgy closed her eyes, grimaced, and cautiously sipped.

~

Beat was once again absorbed by her worries as the vehicle flashed by an endless stretch of glinting sugar cane. When Theo called her name, she turned and smiled but flinched at the alarm in his slate grey eyes.

'What's wrong?'

'There's no easy way to say it.' Theo's finger toyed with a button on his ill-fitting jacket, an unwise charity shop buy, by the look of it.

Beat's jaw tightened. 'Then say it the hard way.'

'Thing is…'

'He forgot,' Melody blurted.

'What?'

'His violin.'

'No, no, surely not?' Beat closed her eyes: she couldn't bear to look at him. She waved him away. What a loser. She threaded her fingers and twisted and pulled at them. It was unbelievable. Farcical. How could he? Without his violin, Theo had no voice.

Problem solving was one of her strengths, but she had no idea how to salvage the situation. Not having his instrument was as ridiculous as a show jumper without a horse, a rally driver without a car. As they drove into Byron, she envied the hollow purpose of holiday makers. Women in batik sarongs, skinny kids hugging surfboards, lovers hand-in-hand were all heading for the sea. She longed to run along the beach, breathe in the ocean's salty air, feel the breeze mess with her hair, plough her toes through the sand. When the driver slowed to navigate the snug roundabouts in Byron's hectic centre, Georgy yawned. She put her head back, stretched her arms, sprinkled water on her face.

'How are you feeling?' Beat asked.

'Better. Yep.' Georgy lifted her sunnies and rubbed her eyes.

'Anything to eat?'

Beat rummaged through her bag. She handed Georgy a weathered but unopened packet of salt and vinegar chips.

~

All three were dressed in black and concert ready which was a blessing because the trio was due on stage in fifteen minutes. When the van pulled up at Byron's Community Centre, Beat rose to her feet and waved at Greg, the competition's artistic director who shielded his eyes and scanned the horizon like a skipper on the prow of a ship. He hadn't noticed the people mover. As soon as the driver parked, Beat leapt out. Squinting in the glary light she rushed towards Greg and pumped his hand.

'Can we do the formalities later?' She gestured at a glum Theo. 'He forgot his violin.'

Greg swivelled and raised his hands at an oncoming violinist like a policeman halting traffic.

'I need this,' he said and snatched a shocked young woman's instrument. Weaving through the gathering crowd outside the recital hall, he glanced over his shoulder to make sure she and the threesome were following and, when they reached a suite of warm-up rooms, he handed Theo the violin.

'Here, make friends with this.'

Some say it takes at least a year to coax optimal tone from an unfamiliar violin. Theo had nine minutes.

Beat put her hand on Greg's arm.

'Is there something else?' Greg said gently.

'Yes. I was hoping you might have copies of the Brahms B Major Trio and the Shostakovich in E minor?'

'Yes, but the judges are using them.'

'Then we'll have to—'

'Do it without the dots,' Georgy chipped in.

'From memory?' Greg's eyes widened in disbelief.

Melody tightened her grip around the cello's neck. 'Yes.'

Georgy, meanwhile, stared at her oversized black patent shoes.

'Have you discussed this with your violinist?' Greg frowned. 'You'll have to remember each other's parts as well as your own.' Theo's nervy fragments filtered through the practice room wall.

'It was his idea. He's keen.' Melody rubbed more rosin on her bow.

~

Georgy's introduction was brief. 'We're playing from memory. Don't clap until the end.'

Her words unleashed a ripple of commotion, someone whistled, another shouted 'go you.' Greg looked over his shoulder, scowled at the students, and the noise abated. Beat marvelled at Georgy's recovery and her composure until she shucked off her shoes which prompted laughter.

Then, joined by Theo and Melody, they stepped forward, the trio firing their quirky icebreaker, stamping in unison and shouting, 'We are...1 2 3!'

~

Georgy's first Brahmsian melody glowed. Melody joined in, closely followed by Theo whose tone was warm if not his eloquent best. Soon, the tuneful skirmishes and emotional chases ended. Random throat clearing and the rustle of lozenges being unwrapped chafed the silence. Beat reached for her phone, there was a text from Marilyn Thorne, Chief Executive Officer of Turalong Arts where Beat worked. She was surprised, but quickly turned her phone off. The next performance was about to start.

Melody bowed the high-pitched whine of Shostakovich's eerie *hello*. The cello's lament, grounded by violin, yielded to the piano's reproach. And, as all three unspooled the menace in the music's stark terrain, the composer's fury at Stalin scalded and pummelled the walls.

Now that the music was drawing to a close, the judges stopped scribbling and smiled; probably relieved they had a clear winner. Beat kneaded the knot in her neck, the day's aggravation retreating. It had all been worth it. Triumph was minutes away. But a mild tickle in someone's throat grew into a gasping, hacking cough which, in the space's swimming resonance, overwhelmed the trio's beautifully sculpted sound. Whether anyone could hear them or not wasn't an issue now the music neared the end. Beat tensed, her pulse quickening.

How many times had she told them not to stop whatever the circumstances? It was an unequivocal rule. She'd seen a conductor die from a heart attack mid performance. He'd raised his arms in the climax of Verdi's Requiem and the choir and orchestra had powered on until the conductor keeled over, dead. But Georgy's chords stopped. Theo's tone dwindled. Melody braked. The performance aborted mid-sentence. But for those unsung final seconds, 1 2 3 would have triumphed.

No one spoke, no one moved. Beat's hands nested in her lap. She fought her disappointment, the fractured hope. Greg patted her arm in sympathy. She closed her eyes against the sight of the trio's slumped defeat. Then the youthful crowd yelled out, thrilled by the trio's storytelling, the flawless memory work. She ought to have focussed on the positives too. Performing two major works so convincingly in such testy circumstances was a feather in their cap and this standing ovation was well deserved. But remembering Thorne's message, she suspected the day's rollercoaster ride wasn't over yet.

~

Beat slipped outside. Marilyn Thorne had never texted her before and she had no idea why, after five years of service, she would do so now. Turalong's managerial structure was top-down, as hierarchical as a military unit, and as a thirty-two-year-old teacher she had a lowly position. She sat underneath a jacaranda, a riot of purple blooms. These trees had strong-armed natives out of the way, but she loved their beauty. She had a similar ambivalence about the trio's program of European rather than Australian classics. Next year, she'd program Aussie works exclusively. She took a deep breath and clicked on Thorne's message.

Beatrice, Yesterday, Steven Hadley resigned from his position as dean of music. We need to talk urgently. Marilyn

~

Dan, her husband, was the only man Beatrice had ever known who cried out "no no no" at the point of orgasm. He had other quirks: he drank strong coffee before going to bed. When a rock concert ended, he waited until the venue had all but emptied before he got up to leave. Reliably unpredictable, he was a man of extremes. Overly attentive one week, remote the next. His changeable behaviour sparked enough intrigue to keep her interested and mostly content. She was the breadwinner. Dan worked from home on his PhD. Reluctantly, he looked after her horses Bolt and Storm and her greyhounds when she went away for work.

She started up the ride-on mower before setting off to trim the grass and grind her horses' manure into the ground. She travelled in straight rows but turned off the cutter when the grass was clean to leave it for the horses. A butcherbird followed her, now and again swooping at an exposed frog or insect on the shorn patches. It was a cathartic activity which allowed her to think and on this stifling morning with temperatures expected to soar even higher by the afternoon she had a great deal to think about. She had to talk to Dan, but he thought of Saturdays as newspaper time, an indulgence which rendered him unapproachable as he devoured every page of the newspapers flung over the front gate. She slowed as she approached Bolt, but in a fit of pique he threw back his head and galloped away with Storm not far behind. Annoyingly, they had gouged holes in the ground.

She was just as shocked by Steven's sudden resignation as she was by Marilyn Thorne's request for her to become dean. True, she'd taken on his duties whenever he'd toured as a solo cellist, sometimes for months at a time. It was intense and hard work, but she'd managed, and her colleagues were content that his absences didn't mean the music school's operations ground to a halt. But doing that was a far cry from stepping into his shoes officially and being accountable. Dan would need to take on extra chores which no doubt he'd grumble about. She inched forward carefully. What looked like a piece of bark could be a frilled neck lizard. When the blink of an eye confirmed her suspicion, she steered out of its way and headed back to the house. Dan waved to her from the veranda. She stopped the machine in the shade and joined him.

'Dan, we have to talk.'

'What's up?'

'I've got a tough decision. Need your input.'

'Let's see, you don't know whether to hire a farrier or a barefoot trimmer?'

'Be serious, Dan.'

When she rattled off Thorne's offer he stared at her, stony faced. Afterwards, he didn't say a word.

'Well?' she pressed.

'It's a no brainer.'

'Why?'

'You've taken on Steven's role whenever he's on tour without remuneration. As dean you'll be paid to do it.'

~

'Madison refuses to play.'

'Why on earth...?' Beat looked over her pink-framed glasses at Garrett Blue, the visiting Californian conductor, and smiled at Melody and Theo who she'd asked to run errands for him.

'Apparently, you haven't met one of Madison's conditions...' Garrett whined. The cellist and violinist looked awkward.

Beat's anxiety had intensified when she saw Garrett take the stairs, two at a time. His red mottled face and his struggle to catch his breath signalled that tonight's flagship concert, the first she'd managed since becoming dean, was as problematic as she had feared. Conductors don't leave rehearsals as a general rule unless there is an exceptional situation, a medical emergency, or a bomb scare. 'Remind me...'

Garrett snatched a cotton handkerchief from Theo to dab at his sweaty forehead. He leaned over, put his hands on his thighs, took a long, deep breath and exhaled slowly.

'Well, it's not the usual bottled water from Greenland, French champagne, and a deluxe limousine,' Garrett said. 'Tell her, Melody.'

'Madison wants garlic,' she said, biting her lip.

'I beg your pardon,' Beat said.

'You heard.'

'But I don't understand.'

The conductor folded his arms.

'Our celebrity Canadian pianist,' Garrett rolled his eyes, 'is unable to perform unless a string of garlic bulbs dangle from the Steinway's open lid.'

'That's ridiculous. Why?' Beat asked.

'The aroma protects her from bad spirits.' Garrett tapped the toe of his white sneaker. Despite the conductor's outrage, Beatrice threw back her head and laughed. Theo pulled a face. Melody smirked.

'Glad you find it funny,' he said, stony-eyed.

'No,' Beat placed her hand over her mouth to stifle her merriment. 'I'm sorry, it's anything but.'

'She won't even touch the Steinway,' Garrett said.

'Let's get the garlic happening then,' Beat gave the conductor a wry smile.

'Really? That's all you've got. It's preposterous.'

'Yes,' she sighed wearily, 'unless you've had a better idea?'

'Melody, can you and Theo go to the canteen and see if the caterers have some to spare?'

~

More than seventy-five instrumentalists were squashed into the rehearsal studio on the floor below Beat's office. Despite the air-conditioning on this hot and humid day, the room would rapidly become uncomfortable. Even so, Beat had expected to hear a mixture of noise streaming through the air vents and up the stairwell; brassy bluster, piano chords, the tuning of strings.

The ominous silence was all wrong in a school dedicated to music performance. From early morning until late at night the old, four-storey, red-brick building hummed, noise splashed from practice cells and corridors. Violins, trumpets, and electric guitars competed with singing, flutes clashed with saxophones, tubas, and undetermined sound. Sometimes the cacophony even blared from staff offices and toilets. The wild combinations excited Beat, reminding her the drab old building with its dreary, cream-painted interior, had a bold, beating heart.

Steven, her predecessor, had managed the school's high-profile orchestral concerts for many years. As a top-flight cellist in demand across the globe, he'd easily garnered respect. It didn't matter if he did or said something stupid, puzzling, or nasty, the staff's acceptance of him as dean was unconditional. Today, she had to convince everyone, especially herself, that she could effectively organise her first major event.

For three years, she'd assumed Steven's duties whenever he was away and the staff had valued her input, with the exception of Winton Thomas, the British Caribbean trumpeter who ran the rock program. Yet, now that Steven had resigned, her colleagues were not in favour of her taking on his job officially. She wasn't a star performer or a conductor, which her colleagues believed is a pre-requisite for the role. She'd majored in piano performance at Juilliard, but she couldn't muster the necessary nerves of steel, stamina, extroversion, and gruelling practice routines to be a concert pianist. With considerable relief, she'd retired her black concert dress much to the disgust of her agent who had berated her for giving up on her gift. No one had dared say it yet, but she was convinced her gender and relative youth wasn't in her favour either.

Her desk sat in front of large ceiling to floor windows, giving her an excellent view of students, staff, and visitors as they strolled past. In the middle distance she could see traffic on the busy road out front, visitors to Brisbane's arts precinct and the Botanical Gardens getting off the buses which stopped directly opposite her office. She loved to go to the Gardens in her breaks, wander off the path and breathe in the leafy, natural world.

Outside, a butcherbird thrashed a wriggling worm on the concrete path. How she envied the bird's straightforward goal. Since her promotion, the school had complicated her life at work and home. Day in and day out, she was dogged by self-doubt which disturbed her sleep and wrestled her awake at dawn. Marilyn Thorne, director of the government-funded arts institute comprised of music, art, and dance schools, had warned her that a woman had to be twice as good as a man to succeed, further escalating her anxieties. But wallowing in negativities on such a demanding day was stupid. Until she was interrupted again, she'd continue to sort the mountain of paperwork cluttering her desk. She made a start, tossing outdated fliers in the bin.

A disturbance in the outer office distracted her. The loud clattering of furniture was followed by muffled swearing and Polly her assistant crying out as something shattered on the hardwood floor. Emerging from the confusion, Garrett stormed into her office.

The last time she'd spoken to Steven, he had told her the Californian conductor was world class, the 'best in the business.' He certainly exuded glamour and youth in his over-used publicity shot. With an easy smile, all-over tan, and wind-ruffled blonde hair – as he posed with a surfboard on Malibu Beach – he looked confident and seductive. Today, he looked fraught, with streaks of noticeably greying hair. His gaunt, sun-wizened face was flushed, his neck ringed by an angry rash. Apparently, if Polly could be believed, his tense appearance was the result of too much whisky the night before, a tryst in the early hours, and to cap it all a dud rehearsal.

'Beatrice, I'm at my wit's end,' he dragged his hand down his face and neck. 'You're trying hard. You mean well, but honey, this is a specialist role. Do you really have the experience, the whatever-it-takes to do this job?'

She took a breath, locked eyes with him. There were many ways to be a musician and just as many to be a dean. 'Qualified enough to confirm your contract.'

'Okay, well... touché, I guess.' Garrett sighed, lowered his head and scratched behind his ear. He pulled his shoulders back, carefully folding his shirt cuffs over each wrist. Still smarting from his put down she wondered how he would like it if she stormed into a rehearsal to ask if he was skilled enough to conduct? She'd been stepping in and out of the dean's role for thirty-six months. And next year, she was under no obligation to invite him back as a visiting musician.

'Look, until the garlic arrives, you could rehearse Ravel's Bolero?

Garrett stood up and pressed a finger to his lips: the sign for Beat to wait while he bent each hand back for a count of ten before giving them a rigorous shake and picking up his baton. Evidently, Madison wasn't the only one with performance rituals. Having completed his routine, he resumed his rant.

'Madison is a bleating, blubbering time waster.' He brandished the baton, causing Beat to duck. 'After the demons are evicted, she'd better...'

'Steven rated her highly. She'll come through,' Beat reassured him, trying not to project her own major reservations about the pianist.

The conductor clawed his spindly fingers through his ample locks and stomped out of the office. Beat looked at the empty door for a minute, willing her mood to lift, and then returned to her administrative chores, smiling at how much unwanted paperwork filled her bin. Polly knocked and tiptoed in, teary eyed.

'He broke my cat!'

Beat knew the ceramic ornament had been a present from one of Polly's numerous Vietnamese aunts. She pondered the consequences of that as she murmured condolences. If breaking a mirror brought seven years bad luck, what would be the cost of a shattered lucky cat? Minutes later she was interrupted again.

'Madison, what's wrong?'

'I can't play.'

'Are strings of garlic hanging from the piano's lid?'

'Yes.'

'Great?'

'But, it's...'

The concert was shaping up to be a nightmare. The conductor was offside, the soloist distraught, and the rehearsal constantly interrupted. Her bittersweet experience with the disorganised piano trio in Byron a few weeks before had been a dream run by comparison.

'Steven told me the Tchaikovsky was one of your specialities.'

Madison stroked the tip of her perfectly proportioned nose, her hazel eyes pained and weary. Beat suspected Steven had hired Madison because her vulnerability had resonated with his compulsion to champion broken musicians. The former dean had hired duds before, an alcoholic guitarist with nerve-wracking memory lapses, a British pianist who had frustrated the audience with wordy, patronising prefaces to every piece she'd played, and then there had been a baby-faced, out-of-tune cellist who gambolled in dangerously fast speeds. Alarmed, the audience had squirmed and fidgeted, wondering not if, but when, the soloist would be derailed.

'I never said the Tchaikovsky Concerto was a speciality of mine, I simply meant it was special.'

'I see.'

Madison closed her eyes, and her fingers massaged her temples. 'Steven wouldn't take no for an answer. He rang and rang and pestered until, against my better judgment, I agreed. Garrett doesn't respect me. When he played the orchestral part on the piano, in our private rehearsal, he was horribly mean.'

'How upsetting. That's not...'

'His mind's made up, I'm a waste of space. He spooks me.'

'Too bad you feel so pressured.'

'It's tough, especially since I haven't performed in public... for more than...'

'Yes?' Beat winced.

'Three years.'

'That's a long time, Madison.'

'Steven told me this was a low-key affair. He insisted it could reboot my career.'

How annoying. Steven must have regarded the school's orchestral concerts as a therapeutic resource he could squander on needy, lapsed instrumentalists. Matthew, the strings convenor or Hermione, the clarinettist, could have been the soloist without all the garlicky angst and expense.

'I committed to do this, and then Steven resigned.' Madison slammed her palm on the table with such force that a container of ballpoints jumped off the edge. Beat was unable to console her. Then, in an indignant flurry, the conductor burst in.

'Take a seat, Garrett,' Beat gestured at a chair.

'Look, we're incompatible,' he said.

'Not much we can do about that.' Madison jabbed a nail-bitten forefinger at the grim-lipped Californian.

'Be-a-trice,' said Garrett, his voice murdering each syllable. 'I can't take the second movement as slowly as Madison wants. Making string players sustain notes for too long could trigger repetitive strain. You know that!'

'You're exaggerating, Garrett.'

'No. I am not.'

'Sounds like you've been chatting to Matthew. He's forever concerned about tendonitis, tennis elbow, and—'

'Regardless, the pace drags, lumbers – it's not justifiable artistically and it's all because of this, this snivelling dilettante.'

'Garrett, please, there's no need to be insulting,' Beat prompted.

'How much did you pay her? I'd want the fee reimbursed if it was up to me.'

'Well, it isn't, Garrett.'

'More than she—'

'Enough.' Beat pressed a finger to her lips.

Madison's hands trembled. It was disconcerting, like observing a brain surgeon's hands shake uncontrollably on the day of a complex neurological operation.

'Can you pick up the pace, Madison?' Beat asked gently.

The pianist blew her nose on a scrunched-up tissue. Garrett's eyes rolled with impatience. When Beat's phone rang, she knew better than to answer. It sounded shrill and complaining, like Dan. She let it ring out.

'Garrett, please negotiate a compatible tempo.'

~

Polly poked her head around the door, looking strained, still mourning for her beloved decorative cat. She softly announced Connor was waiting for her in reception.

'Can't be long. I'm in a class,' he said. 'What's up?'

According to Polly and others Connor Perkins was level-headed and generous with his time, though in her own observation he seemed aloof and cantankerous in meetings. He'd never made an appointment to see her since she'd become dean, nor previously when she'd deputised for Steven. He taught history and music theory now, but Beat knew he'd once had a successful career as a conductor, and sometimes he'd stepped into the breach in orchestral rehearsals.

'Connor, we've got an emergency. I need to ask a favour. Can you please extract yourself from whatever you're doing and take over the orchestral rehearsal?'

'Why?' he glowered. Beat made a fist and dug her nails into her palm, registering the icy blue of his eyes and his cropped dark brown hair that resembled a hogged mane. She knew better than to pull rank. Where musicians were concerned, a heavy-handed approach backfired more often than not.

'The conductor and soloist are resolving something,' Beat said.

'Which is?'

'The pacing of the—'

'Second movement?'

'Correct.'

'Deciding on a tempo should take seconds, a minute at most.'

'The situation isn't straightforward.'

Connor checked his watch, an old, stainless-steel Rolex like the one her grandfather used to wear. Who even wore a watch these days? The man was stubbornly last century. A relic. But he hadn't tried to diminish her, resent her appointment, or attack her personally like some.

'I've got a busy schedule. I didn't think I'd have to serve as a conductor's assistant. Why didn't you warn me I might have to step in?'

'Look, I had no idea the soloist would be problematic.'

'Conductors, soloists, composers, and concert masters are like old gelignite in the countdown to concerts. Sweaty and ready to blow. Always have a plan B. As far as orchestras go, I don't get involved. I've served my time where all that's concerned.'

'Look, this is a special case.'

'Special? How?' Connor leaned forward.

'The concert is tonight – the conductor and soloist are fighting and you are my plan B.'

Connor leaned back; his eyes softened.

'Okay, put it on record, this is the last time I take over a conductor's rehearsal.'

'Yep. Got it. Thanks so much.' Connor tramped off. Beatrice was thinking he wasn't such a pompous grump as she'd first thought, and quite attractive too. But after a few steps he turned back.

'Oh, and if it's not too much bother, can you tell me what I'm to rehearse? Or is that classified?'

'Tchaikovsky's *Piano Concerto Number 1.*'

'Oh great! That arthritic old warhorse is flogged into yet another airing. What you need is a chiropractor, not a conductor. Did you brush the cobwebs off?'

'How can you? That amazing beginning of blazing horns, the gorgeous theme played by the strings which the pianist takes over and that's only in the first minute.'

How disagreeable he was. Yet she had to admit she'd found their tetchy exchange refreshing. In the heat of the moment, she'd flexed authority. She'd made a stand. She allowed herself to be chuffed, if only momentarily because on the return to her office one glance at Polly's tense face signified yet another problem.

'Dan rang again.'

She keyed Dan's number into her phone.

'Beat, we really have to talk.'

She knew what that meant. He wanted to scold her for leaving the milk on the table or not hanging out the washing.

'Dan, I can't right now, things are unravelling here.'

'Nothing unusual then.'

'Don't be like that. Remember? It's that big do tonight,' Beat said.

'It's always something,' he grumbled.

'I'll phone soon. Promise.'

Back in her office, Madison and Garrett gazed at the carpet in silence. A conductor and soloist log jam, terrific. There's nothing so tiresome, thought Beat, except maybe a conductor and concertmaster deadlock, or a clash between a rock singer and a sound engineer.

Beat snapped. The softly, softly approach wasn't working and there wasn't time for a few rounds of 'he said, she said' to clear the air. Resolution was imperative.

'Garrett and Madison, I'm going to leave you for five minutes. If a compromise on a suitable speed hasn't been reached when I return, tonight's concert will be cancelled.'

She didn't look, but imagined the hurt in Madison's eyes and how Garrett's features would have crumpled and creased like a bulldog's.

Polly apologetically handed her a message.

'Ring Marilyn.'

She sat down in Polly's office, took a deep breath, counted to four and released it, slow and easy, the way Dan had taught her, and she had so often practised, and then she made the call. The CEO's warmth when she'd offered Beat the deanship a month before had inexplicably curdled into carping disdain.

'Beatrice, tonight's concert had better be great.'

'We're doing our best.'

'As you know, the university's music faculty has an event tonight which clashes with ours. That's annoying enough. But you may not have heard they've hired a dazzling singer.'

'Taylor Swift? Pink? Adele?'

'A truly awesome family star,' Thorne cooed.

'Who?' Beat was intrigued.

'Luna Madena.'

'Well, at least we're not up against Billie Eilish or Lady Gaga. You know they've deliberately arranged this clash, right?'

'Beatrice, the point is, Luna is a gem and experienced in performing with an orchestra. She'll be a huge hit with the over 60s, the very demographic you keep telling me enjoy classical concerts.'

'Yes, you're correct about that, but my goal is to lure a younger audience.'

Afterwards, Beat went outside to breathe fresh air, feel the warming sun on her face and to be reminded there were alternative worlds, just as appealing, beyond the music building. And it was just a building. Feeling calmer, she walked back to deal with Garrett and Madison. When she entered her office, the antagonistic pair were scowling at each other.

'Well?'

'I'll pick up the pace,' the pianist said.

'Great news,' Beat nodded, gratefully.

Garrett straightened his tie, took a neatly folded mauve linen handkerchief from his breast pocket, wiped his face, and left. Madison hobbled along behind him in towering, open toed heels.

Through her window, Beat watched a crowd heading towards the Botanical Gardens. Families carried blankets and picnic baskets. Excited primary-aged children jogged along mustered by anxious teachers. They were going to the alfresco big band concert organised by Winton, the rock convenor. These outdoor specials drew huge crowds.

Beat heard sobbing coming from Polly's office and when she looked it was Madison slumped in a chair. Evidently, the Canadian wasn't going to be a triumphant piano warrior. Not tonight anyway.

'I can't do it. I'm leaving. I assumed a young Aussie orchestra would be woeful and I could bluff. That was a dumb...' Madison mumbled.

'Yep,' said an exasperated Beat. 'Dumber than dumb.'

~

How could she find another soloist at such short notice? She could try a music agency. Fly in a soloist from Melbourne or Sydney? One way or another, she'd have to think of something fast.

A rude, sforzando thump on her door had to be Garrett.

Beat prepared herself mentally, she needed to be kind yet firm. When Garrett stomped in, she stepped towards him and raised her hands for him to stop. She told him Madison had pulled out. Garrett stared, open-mouthed and speechless.

'Trust me. I'll find a replacement.'

'Pianists who can deliver a decent *Tchaikovsky 1* do not grow on trees.' Garrett sneezed and blew his nose loudly, but if he wanted sympathy for his allergies triggered by Aussie pollen, he was going to be disappointed.

She glanced at her reflection in the mirror on the back of her ceiling to floor cupboard door. Tall and slender with an athletic build, a warm smile, knowing brown eyes, and straight chocolate hair nudging her shoulders, Beat had attracted male and female attention in the past and she'd enjoyed it too, but not any longer. Now, her visual appeal and femininity eclipsed the professional image she wanted to project to be plausible as dean. Her gender made her vulnerable, discrediting the diverse range of skills and managerial know how she possessed. She shunned the dresses and skirts she'd once loved to wear, pushing them to the back of her wardrobe, adopting instead a non-conformist uniform of distressed jeans, block colour shirts, and riding boots, a look not far removed from what she wore to ride and tend to her beloved horses. Not conventional optics for a director, but in these clothes, she could pretend to be steely, resilient, and faithful to her authentic self and life on Wongara, the small farm she cherished.

~

Beat googled Brisbane-based concert pianists, and there were plenty, but none with the Tchaikovsky in their repertoire. Maybe Connor was right, and the concerto was out of fashion. Then she heard a scarcely audible yet persistent knock on her door. 'Come in,' Beat called without bothering to see who it was. She continued her search. If it was Connor or Matthew or Hermione, they could all wait. When she craned her neck to look, she was taken aback to see Georgy, the pianist from 1 2 3.

'I'm pretty frantic, Georgy. How can I help?'

By way of an answer, the girl stepped forward and coyly placed a Tchaikovsky piano score on Beat's desk. At a quick glance, her shoeless feet could do with a thorough wash. Georgy had earned the nickname Barefoot because she rarely wore shoes.

'You need a soloist.' Georgy circled her big toe on the carpet.

'We sure do,' Beat sighed. Perhaps one of the Brisbane-based, professional orchestras could give her suggestions. Or maybe the orchestra could present a less demanding concerto?

'Please, please give me a go. I adore the Tchaik,' Georgy gushed. Her fingers toyed with a delicate silver necklace.

'Thank you, that's a generous offer, but stepping in...'

'It's memorised,' Georgy dropped her shoulders and raised her chin.

'Really?'

'I'm the soloist for Sunshine State Orchestra next month. The first movement's three tunes are like living souls to me. Every note, every phrase, every key change are in here.' Georgy placed both hands over her heart. 'I know it so well I can play it eyes closed.'

Beat noticed her closely bitten nails.

Then she recalled hearing about Georgy's outstanding performance of another big concerto in the finals of the Queensland Piano Competition the previous year. She'd won second place. Elvira, the piano convenor and Georgy's teacher, had brimmed with pride. Even piano-phobic Matthew, who regarded pianists with contempt, 'because the piano is nothing but a mechanical wooden box,' had agreed Georgy had an original voice and something meaningful to say.

'I can't let you, Georgy. It would be risky.'

'Risky for?'

'Everyone, but especially you.'

'Beat, please, I won't let you down. The piano part's seared into my hands.' Georgy held out her upturned palms, those slender fingers stretched and splayed.

'Even a professional would be wary about stepping in with a few hours' notice,' Beat said.

'The Tchaik sings in my head all day and in my dreams at night.'

Beat closed her laptop. What could be the harm in giving her the chance to run through it?

'Take a seat, let's talk it through.' Beat sat opposite Georgy. With her short, spiky hair, lean frame, and those big, calloused feet she hardly looked the part. Beat's biggest concern was whether Elvira would approve of her gifted student stepping in without sufficient notice. If Georgy made a mess of it, her solo career could be in tatters before it had even begun.

'Give me a moment please,' and Beat paced up and down until she realised she must have already accepted Georgy's offer because the weight of anxiety had lifted, the tension in her shoulders had gone.

'All right, Georgy, I'll give you a go. The orchestra's in session. Garrett's not the easiest and, as conductor, he'll have the final say.'

Terrifying soloists seemed to be one of Garrett's specialities but Beat recalled the young woman's courage in the Byron recital.

'Do you need to warm up?'

'I've just finished three hours practice.' The girl wiggled her fingers as if to show how supple they were.

~

When Beat broke the news to Garrett, he closed his eyes, pummelled his temples with his knuckles, hung his head, and swayed from side to side. She heard Amy Winehouse singing "no, no no." But, in a tight spot, with a potential catastrophe looming, Beat was unstoppable and the horrified Californian reluctantly consented to give Georgy a hearing.

Relieved after Garrett left her office, she unlocked the door of the dean's lounge, closed the curtains, set her mobile on mute, peeled off her boots, fluffed a cushion into shape and curled up on the sofa. She should have phoned Dan after their brief conversation, but she badly needed a moment for herself even if it meant he would take umbrage. But she needed something besides Dan to mull over or she'd never drift off.

Eyes closed, she listened to a determined harpsichordist on the floor above, whose nimble fingers navigated a path through the tuneful wrangle of a Bach fugue. A thumping bass guitar's *doof doof doof* smashed through Garrett's elegant orchestral phrasing in the studio below. Sound proofing: she'd have to fix that too. How can a musician be expected to refine and polish their sound if they can't listen to it exclusively?

Pushing those thoughts aside, she imagined tearing along the freeway to her bush property, inspired by the promise of a greener, less populated landscape. At home, she saw the massive eucalypts framing the paddock as her horses thundered towards her through sheathes of long, long grass.

~

Beat jolted awake when Polly breezed in. 'Sorry to interrupt but Tim Newton from ABC's *Drive Time* is on hold.'

Beat sat up, stretched her back, stifled a yawn and took the call.

'Can you confirm Madison Rose has pulled out of your concert tonight?' Newton, who she knew socially, was stern in professional mode.

'Yes.'

'You'll be cancelling?'

'Far from it. The replacement's an exceptional 19-year-old.'

'I want to interview you about it around lunchtime,' Tim said.

Phone down, a gleeful Beat clapped her hands together. If Garrett accepted Georgy as soloist, she could upsell the concert on air.

~

With Georgy's spiky hair, skimpy gold top, denim shorts, and naked feet, she looked better suited for a game of beach volleyball. Could this otherworldly girl climb Tchaikovsky's lofty heights and sustain the necessary stamina?

Clearly, Georgy's peers thought so because cheers and whistles greeted her as she gingerly took her place at the gleaming Steinway grand. Her hands gripped either side of the piano stool as if she might fall off. Startled by the garlic bulbs hanging from the grand's open lid, Georgy clamped a hand over her nose and for that she could be forgiven, for the stench had infiltrated the entire space. Funny how garlic's aroma in the wrong context could be unpleasant and yet, in a kitchen, sizzling in a pan, it signalled the promise of fabulous food.

Beat looked around, hoping Connor was there. She wanted to thank him for taking the rehearsal earlier. But Garrett's sour expression as he registered Georgy's naked feet distracted her. She was afraid he'd stomp off in a fit of pique. Eyes closed, the conductor ruffled his hair, as if in doing so he could replace this wisp of a player with Martha Argerich, the legendary Argentinian-born, Olympian virtuoso whose performance of Tchaikovsky's concerto had been hailed as the world's best. Georgy blinked and wiped her sweaty hands on her shorts, but her jittery apprehension was forgivable since Garrett looked ferocious. Beat turned down a trombonist's offer of a chair and leaned back against the studio's green wall, willing herself not to reveal a flicker of the anxiety stampeding in her gut.

Georgy shuffled and fidgeted, but then adopted a more convincing pose. Garrett signalled he was about to start, and Beat's anxiety eased on hearing the introductory horns. But her relief was premature, because the piano was infuriatingly, resoundingly mute. Georgy's hands were parked on her bare knees. Furious, the conductor directed the players to stop and, when they didn't, he kicked the podium hard.

Arms folded, the baton pointing towards the ceiling, he turned to Georgy. 'Was I too fast or too slow?'

Beat imagined a tiger stalking its prey, crouched low, muscles bristling, primed to spring.

Georgy mouthed sorry, shook her hands and positioned her fingers on the first chord, her frame wired like a thoroughbred in the starting trap. When the opening fired, Beat was delighted to see Georgy's hands executed the chords with an easy precision. She travelled the breadth of the keys, from the bottom to the middle, to the top, and the same again and then again.

Garrett tapped the end of the baton on the lectern and the orchestra straggled to a frayed-edge stop. Growling at the recalcitrant woodwind, frequently the last to stop in the folklore of orchestral rehearsal, Garrett yelled, 'Billy, are you familiar with this concerto?'

'It's Georgy. My name's Georgy.' Her public correction and reedy voice triggered hoots of laughter.

'And?' Garrett fumed.

'I know it inside and out.'

Garrett was old-school, believing a top performer wasn't made by encouragement, but by cruel words, parody, and critical assault. If the player, *had the goods* then, according to the likes of Garrett and Matthew, they would flourish.

Deathly pale, Georgy's long fingers trembled on the keys. Beat held her breath when Garrett commanded the orchestra to begin for a third time. The eager woodwind, brass, strings, and percussion sections pinned their eyes on the conductor. Beat couldn't watch. She nibbled on a strand of hair. Her inner critic scolded, begged her to search for a bankable professional. She could scarcely breathe, but to her immense joy, the piano bellowed, the sound colossal, thrusting through the orchestral waves.

WHAM, WHAM, WHAM!

Georgy's mighty chords had theatrical resonance. Garrett let the first movement run its course. Musically, the young woman charmed and sparkled with a quickdraw dialogue between piano and orchestra, and with a spontaneity which so many struggle to achieve. Garrett cajoled the ensemble to rise to Georgy's challenge, and when the sound died away, Garrett blew Beat a kiss.

Excited, Beat looked around to see if any of her colleagues had heard Georgy's remarkable effort, but there was no one except Polly, who beckoned to her through the glass-panelled door. It was time for her interview with Tim Newton. Beat slipped out as a cheer erupted from the elated orchestra.

2
VIRTUOSO

'YES. Nineteen-year-old Georgy Green is the soloist for tonight's performance of Tchaikovsky's Piano Concerto due to the sudden illness of the advertised Canadian virtuoso. Georgy's so brave,' Beat spun her office chair away from the window.

'Why brave?' asked Tim, live on Drive Time.

'*Tchaik 1* is scary and from a traditionalist's point of view, it's considered to be a man's concerto. Georgy stepped in a few hours ago. It will be like watching someone negotiate a tightrope across Niagara Falls. An edge-of-the-seat, nail-biter.'

'I see,' said Tim. 'And yet your concert clashes with the university's event headlined by the fabulous Luna Madena?'

'And with the long career Luna's had,' Beat's tone flatlined, 'she'll be solid. Dependable.'

'How true,' Tim agreed.

'All the Grannies and Grandpops are going to—'

'Adore her,' Tim interrupted.

'Yep. But for those craving thrilling theatre, I'm thinking the young and young-at-heart, our concert at Brisbane City Hall is the place to be tonight.'

'Folks, music lovers are spoilt for choice. Two extraordinary events in one night. I know my preference, but phone in and tell us which tickles your fancy and you could win a copy of *Luna's Greatest Hits*. Goodbye.

Play nice,' Tim gushed. 'Put those feet up and enjoy *Tropical Waves* which is balm for the soul.

Luna's crooning caressed the airways.

Disgusted, Polly switched the radio off. 'Tim's only made things worse. What a pest.'

'You mean arse?' Beat corrected.

'That too.'

'Come on, Pol, we got airtime, let's be grateful.'

'As runner-up to the faculty's superior program,' Polly whinged.

Beat looked outside. A wild duck and her seven tiny ducklings had paused in the middle of the busy road's pedestrian crossing. Heart in her mouth – she wanted to rush out and save them – but at the last possible second the traffic stopped to let them cross.

She turned to Polly. 'Some publicists swear by social media for last minute marketing. Please blitz the socials: Instagram, Threads, X, TikTok or whatever the current fads are, and, if anybody still uses Facebook, take photos of Garrett and Georgy, caption and publish.'

Polly shrugged, looked doubtful.

'What choice do we have?'

~

Elvira was reading in Polly's office when Beat got back from lunch. She slapped her forehead. How could she have forgotten to consult the piano convenor about Georgy? In music circles, not honouring a student's teacher is a grave misdemeanour. The bright, sunflower themed dress Elvira wore did nothing to lighten her glum mood. Beat unlocked her office door.

'Come in, Elvira. Take a seat. Coffee? Tea?'

'Nettle?' Elvira mumbled, not meeting Beat's eyes.

Beat shuffled through her collection of designer teas. 'We're out of Nettle, sorry. Dandelion?'

'Fine.'

Elvira sat down, lunged forward, elbows on her thighs, her temples pressed between her fingerless, black-gloved hands. The book she'd been reading fell off her lap, but either Elvira hadn't noticed or she didn't care.

Beat waited and tried to be in the moment without all the things she had to do jostling for supremacy in her brain. Then to Beat's relief the piano convenor righted herself, her shoulders pressed against the back of the chair.

'Georgy's my student.' Elvira's voice cracked. 'Why wasn't I consulted?'

Beat improvised. 'Polly called, but your mobile was switched off. It was an emergency. I had to source a replacement.'

Elvira looked at Beat for the first time with sad, pained eyes.

'I thought you, of all people, would have discussed it in your own interests, if not in hers or mine. I might have suggested a more experienced, less problematic player.'

'But I said yes to her, mostly because of you.'

'It was Georgy's idea?' Elvira looked horrified.

'Yes. And I remembered her superb performance in Byron Bay's Chamber Music Competition with 1 2 3, and the positive impression she made in last year's Queensland Piano Competition. You told me she was, "charismatic, a future star."'

'I never called her a "future star."'

Chastised by the hurt in Elvira's doleful eyes, she was struggling to find a way to console her when the door flung open so hard the steel handle cratered the wall. There was a hole from Hermione the woodwind convenor's previous dramatic entrances.

'Let's do John Williams' film music for our next bash.' Hermione's crimson lipstick complemented her dangly red earrings. 'It would be a cracker. Imagine *Jaws* and *Jurassic Park* in one program. Awesome.' Her eyes widened, she clasped her hands, and her cloud of gingery-blond feathery curls danced in the light.

'Look, I appreciate the suggestion and yes, the *Harry Potter Extravaganza* was a tremendous hit when the Melbourne, Sydney, and Tasmanian Symphony Orchestras programmed it several years back. Sorry, but we're busy.'

Beat tilted her head in the direction of Elvira. Hermione hesitated, curious. Mercifully, she took the hint, and with a finger on her crimson painted lips, backed out, closing the door gently behind her. Beat could see she'd lost ground with Elvira, who was even more downcast after Hermione's intrusion.

'Sorry about that,' Beat said.

'I don't feel valued.' A flinty edge had crept into Elvira's tone.

She'd be taken far more seriously, Beat thought uncharitably, if she didn't drape herself in cheap batik outfits plastered with floral clichés.

'You are respected, Elvira, but if you don't feel you are then I need to do something about that. In future, I promise to consult you about pianos, harpsichords, organs, piano tuners, anything keyboard related and, most definitely, your students.'

'Mmm... you're always busy. Matthew or Hermione take up much of your time.'

Elvira rippled her fingers on her knee as if it was a keyboard. Beat had to admit she had taken Elvira for granted because she wasn't as headstrong or as challenging as the others. Apart from today's sensitivities and protest, the piano convenor was on side.

'What if we had a weekly time?'

'Maybe,' mumbled Elvira, pinning her sleek black hair into a messy bun.

'How about *Poco Mosso* for lunch next week?'

'I'd prefer *The Green Bus* because it's not crammed with stuffy arts people,' said Elvira. 'I'd like to talk about me taking on a major performance project because I'm ready for the challenge now.'

'Sounds good.'

'Now, I've something I want to run by you,' Beat said.

'As in?'

'Ways of helping students plagued by nerves before a concert. I want to initiate a weekly class which teaches psychological strategies and how to channel anxiety into a performance,' Beat said.

'Sounds positive. Relevant.'

'Also, should we run meditation classes or tai chi to cultivate mindfulness in young players? The necessity to be present, in the *zone*, before they begin to play?'

'Matthew won't like it,' Elvira suggested.

'Why is that?'

'I would be asking him, in your deanly shoes,' Elvira said. 'See what he says. He's even more intimidating since Steven resigned. Those two were thick as thieves.' Elvira retrieved her book, blew some fluff off the hardback's cover.

'Do you know why Steven resigned with no notice?' Beat asked.

'Phone. Ask him.' Elvira said.

'His number's changed.'

Elvira shrugged.

'Anyhow, about tonight,' Beat said, 'can you prep Georgy? Walk her through stage protocols, how to acknowledge applause, when to take a bow. I doubt she owns a suitable dress. That black velvet number she wore in Byron is threadbare.'

Elvira nodded. 'Sure, I'll lend her one.'

'Can you fix the no shoe quirk?'

'What an absolute minefield!' Elvira sounded shrill. 'It can't be sorted in a day. Had you checked in with me, I would've warned you. Georgy could play like a dream tonight or...'

'What?' Beat was alarmed.

'As a soloist...'

'Yes?'

'She's unpredictable.'

'Really?' Beat cupped her face in her hands.

'Look, no promises but I'll do what I can.'

~

Beat checked her phone. Three missed calls from Dan. She was about to ring him but Polly walked in, Matthew in her wake.

Disdainfully, he sneered at her crowded desk and sat down, black moleskin diary in hand for documented evidence, Beat presumed. He sported a red velvet bowtie, his choice for tonight's concert. Bowties were his signature look. She hadn't seen this one before but typically he wore it crooked, which suited him, because there was nothing straightforward about Matthew. Begrudgingly, she had to admit it made a welcome change from the kitsch socks male concert pianists favoured.

'Beat, I've had the rehearsal studio booked for months.'

'Garrett needs extra time to rehearse the soloist,' Beat said.

'I heard she'd dropped out.'

'Georgy's taking her place.'

'That oddball, praying mantis?' Matthew sucked in his teeth. 'You have to start thinking outside the box.'

'What d'you mean?'

'I could have rattled off Tchaikovsky's *Violin Concerto.*'

'Matthew, where would we have got the orchestral parts at such short notice?'

'I have a full set.'

'We can use them another time,' said Beat. 'Now, where were we?'

'My ensemble has a prior claim,' said Matthew. 'Make other arrangements.'

'Why would I do that?' Beat asked.

The violinist frowned. 'Lyrebird, which I founded, is a semi-professional chamber orchestra unlike the apologetic riff raff downstairs. I've an ABC broadcast coming up. Booked the space with Steven last year.' He circled the moleskin diary above his head like a drone.

'Thing is, Matthew—' Beat began.

'That studio is unequivocally, indisputably mine.'

'No. It isn't.'

Beat recalled the camaraderie between Matthew and Steven, and her resentment about the favours Steven had bestowed on the violinist resurfaced. Matthew had played Steven almost as well as he played his Guarneri. But he had her to deal with now and it wouldn't be a cushy ride.

'Steven would have cancelled.'

'But he's gone. We have to be flexible in a tight spot.'

'Give it up, it's a lost cause. Your concert clashes with the university's classier event.'

'Not *my* concert, Matthew, *ours.*'

'You won't get an audience,' Matthew said.

'Seventy percent of Lyrebird players consists of our students, your loyalty is to the school.'

Matthew jammed the diary into his jacket pocket.

'Fine. But string students must attend my class this afternoon.'

'They'll be rehearsing.'

'Non attendees will fail,' Matthew said.

Beat reeled from his harsh tone. Though she knew his threatening tactic wouldn't survive legal scrutiny, she was reminded how much she loathed assessment being weaponised and used as a bargaining chip. But before she could bring him back to earth, he'd turned on his heels and left. A discussion about his outrageous posturing could go on the back burner for now but she made a mental note to add assessment reform to her ever expanding to-do list. As yet, her targets had been cast aside because of the concert, day-to-day practicalities, sudden flare-ups, and unexpected discord.

Emotions ran high at Turalong Arts. She was beginning to grasp that restoring the music school to its glory days was going to be a tough ride, bumpier than she'd ever imagined.

3

TEMPO

CLOCKS measure time with a mechanical precision, but in Beat's case her perception of time was puppeteered by anxiety and the arrival of the merest trickle of an audience thirty minutes before the concert's eight pm start. She had chosen Brisbane's historic City Hall as the venue because of its generous acoustic and grandeur and its ability to seat 2,500. Once the tallest building in the city, it had been constructed from luxurious materials: white marble from Italy, black from Belgium, brown from Orange, New South Wales, and sandstone from a quarry south-west of the city. What had possessed her to think she could fill so many seats? With a paltry fifty souls milling around the foyer, the building's grandeur mocked her. She walked up to Polly, elegant in a sleek, black dress.

'Beat, before you ask, everyone has posted on the socials.'

Polly picked at the wick around her already mauled nails. Beat didn't press for further detail; her assistant was already stressed enough. Polly hovered around the table she'd rearranged several times. Programs were neatly stacked. An open cash box glinted with a smattering of gold coins. To Beat's consternation, Matthew, hand-in-hand with his latest girlfriend, a doe-eyed, leggy viola player, was the first of her colleagues to walk between the Corinthian columns flanking the Hall's entrance. Gloating and superior, he shook his head at the modest audience numbers and mouthed, 'I warned you.'

She watched cellists, a cluster of violinists, and even oboe and flute players clamour around Matthew when he reached the lift to access the changing rooms. She was surprised by his popularity with the students. Perhaps, just as a humourless football coach rallies the team to defeat the opposition, his sour expression and gruff commentary spurred them on to excel.

Elvira arrived in a long, black silk dress. Her daytime wardrobe left a lot to be desired, but she owned deluxe evening wear. By 7:30 more people trickled in. When Thorne arrived, in a green off-the-shoulder evening dress, she marched over to Beat and panicky questions tripped off her tongue.

'Beatrice, have you secured a big audience? Arranged VIP seating at the front? Have you organised interval drinks?'

As a music coach she'd largely kept to herself. Occasionally, she had attended staff meetings but operated independently. In this elevated position, she found her supervisor's frequent demands a challenge. She'd always hated to be bossed about. Now, she was distracted by the sight of Dan, looking sharp in a lemon shirt and charcoal jacket. She watched as he bought a ticket from Polly. He made no secret of how much he detested classical music concerts. Why hadn't he told her he was coming? Then, she remembered he had rung her about something important and she'd fobbed him off, promising to ring back but she hadn't.

'Beatrice, I'm talking to you,' snapped Thorne, shaking her silver-beaded clutch she held in her white gloved hand. A waft of Dolce and Gabbana *Light Blue* perfume sweetened the air.

'About?'

'The VIP seating.'

'Yes. All organised.'

'In the front row?' Her supervisor whined.

'No. Because the sound is better from the twelfth.'

'Not much of a turnout.' Thorne's eyes narrowed as she looked around.

'A packed house can't be guaranteed.' Suddenly light-headed, Beat took a deep breath.

'Very well. I'll take my seat. Let the sponsors know where to find me.'

Beat nodded absently, shocked to see Georgy, head bowed as she trailed her black gloved fingers along the wall. She had the demeanour of a hospital patient, shuffling along in slippers, not a solo pianist. But Elvira locked an arm around her and led her to the changing rooms. Elvira was worth her weight in gold as a teacher, and she would tell her so next week at lunch. Next, giggling players in black op-shop garments bounded up the steps. Again, Beat looked into the concert hall and counted those seated, as if each time she checked, the numbers would have miraculously multiplied.

Winton sauntered over.

'How was the big band concert?' Beat asked.

'We drew a huge crowd to be honest. If this was a rock concert, you'd have a packed house. The resources wasted on this archaic enterprise is almost sinful.'

'Wow. I thought I exaggerated.'

'In London, if a concert wasn't going to be profitable, it was scrapped just like that.' Winton clicked his fingers.

Beat blushed, at a loss to think of anything more she could've done to attract a bigger crowd. Winton was distracted. 'Blimey,' he said craning his neck to look behind him.

Beat gasped. The longest queue she'd ever seen for a school concert snaked across King George Square, all the way to Polly's ticket table. Instantly, Beat's anxiety switched gear, from her disappointment about a meagre audience to whether they could sell tickets fast enough.

She waved Hermione over. 'Can you help Polly? Connor's over there, grab him too. Let's stick to the 8pm start.'

City Hall's maple and silky oak interior glimmered. Its spaciousness buzzed with urgency and the huge milling crowd softened the architecture drawn from Rome's Pantheon and topped by a copper dome. Ticketholders raced to find their seats. Parents, siblings, staff, council members, music lovers, and journalists sat snug, elbow-to-elbow.

Someone tapped her on the shoulder. 'I didn't want to miss your first shindig. Is it too late to buy a ticket?' pleaded Ellie, Dan's sister.

Beat hugged her. 'You can sit next to me, my row's reserved for guests. But it won't put you beside Dan, I'm afraid.'

'I'd rather keep you company.'

'Perfect.'

'But how come you're not with my brother?' Ellie unbuttoned her jacket. The players on stage adjusted music stands, fussed over scores, clarinettists and oboists sucked on reeds to moisten them. Dan sat a few rows from the front. He looked around the hall. She waved, but he hadn't seen her and his eyes returned to the stage. When Garrett claimed the podium, all thoughts of Dan were forgotten.

Garrett's direction was electrifying in Verdi's *Force of Destiny Overture* and the strings articulated the tricky reaches with sparkling clarity. When the final chord faded, the audience clapped, a few shouted 'bravo.' Oblivious to the orchestra filing off stage, a burly stagehand with a long ponytail muscled the Steinway Grand into a central position. He raised the lid to capacity, manoeuvred the stool closer to the keyboard, straightened it, leaned back to check all was in order, then lumbered off.

Beat nodded at well-wishers. A few seats away, *Nationwide's* classical music critic scribbled notes, her presence in itself a triumph because her editor had previously refused to report on the school's concerts. Her policy was not to review students. Beat had pressed the point that these 'students', as she called them were apprentices, emerging professionals, many already making a decent living through temping in professional bands and orchestras.

Restless, Beat crossed and uncrossed her legs, leaned forward, smoothed her hair and read the program Theo had written for the umpteenth time.

At last, Georgy appeared in a flattering lacy black gown. Awkwardly, she shuffled towards the piano in low-heeled, black satin pumps that glinted in the stage lights. Now seated, she chewed on her lip, stole furtive glances at the audience. Beat remembered Elvira's warning about Georgy's unpredictability and her neck tightened, her throat constricted.

Garrett sprinted across the stage, sprang onto the conductor's podium, grabbed the bronze rails, lifted his weight and swung his legs back and forth and drew a scatter of applause. When he raised his baton, silence prevailed. But a trombonist knocked her iPad reader off her stand and an ugly clatter strafed the sound-free ambience. Beat's heart pounded because she knew Garrett would have flashed a mean look and snarled at the offending player. Ellie squeezed her hand and whispered, 'don't worry.'

Beat breathed again when the horns began and yet, when the conductor signalled the pianist's entry, Georgy doubled over and removed her shoes. Beat's face burned. What was the girl thinking? How could she ignore her cue? At the piano's gaping absence in Tchaikovsky's mighty soundscape, the performance suspended, Garrett slowly lowered his outstretched arms like a Tai Chi practitioner and easefully, gracefully cradled the tension as if it was entirely normal for a soloist to miss their first entry.

The concerned orchestral players and the massive congregation endured an irritating ripple of coughs, shuffled feet, and the rustle of sweet wrappings. Slumped low in her seat, Thorne closed her eyes. Dan turned his head and waved at Beat and she managed to smile back despite the vice-like tension in her neck. The Hall held its breath, a vast chasm of suspense.

Beat could scarcely breathe, but she admired Garrett's showmanship – the way he primed the players for a second start. At last, the conductor signalled the orchestra to begin and the famous opening phrase rang out for a second time. Would Georgy sabotage another beginning? But this time she sat tall, finger-ready, eyes glued on Garrett, her bare toes perched on the pedal.

Georgy threw her weight behind the opening chords and the whopping attack resonated in the hall's interior as orchestra and pianist began a theatrical duel. Momentarily, a mistuned orchestral chord compounded by Georgy's fleeting memory lapse set Beat's teeth on edge. Very few would have noticed, Beat rationalised. Besides, Georgy's fingers packed such a punch and as she revealed her superb technical skill, a moment of forgetfulness was irrelevant. She played dangerously, quickening the pulse, forcing Garrett to follow her lead in passages of blistering virtuosity.

Impressively Georgy stayed on track and delivered a showy cadenza –without the orchestra – in which she punished, cajoled and whispered the keys with astonishing skill. Georgy's risky approach was due to Elvira, who made her students practise a variety of interpretative approaches so that, mid-performance, they could chop and change the way they shaped a piece. Elvira's foibles, hyper-sensitivity, devotion to nettle tea, and addiction to woeful batik cloth, were far outweighed by her brilliance as a coach.

Thorne, Winton, and Matthew were thrilled by Georgy's blow-your-socks-off delivery, her precise execution of treacherous virtuosity. Clarinets, flutes, oboes, trumpets, and violins flew through Georgy's roiling fingers, as if the piano was a competing orchestra. Her performance wasn't CD perfect, but more like skiing down a treacherous slope, skimming around trees, clearing snow drifts, yet somehow arriving unscathed. Her daring take on the Tchaikovsky tipped Georgy into the status of a star in the making.

Afterwards, the audience rose to their feet. Fathers lifted children in the air, friends linked arms, some whistled. An elderly woman shouted, 'You beaut, darl,' and Beat laughed as a notoriously mean music critic tossed his notebook aside to clap vigorously.

Beat worried that the mood would flat-line during Ravel's Bolero, after such a thrilling performance. Yet, when the snare began and the softly uttered slow-teasing build powered into an explosive peak, the crowd was excited all over again. String players are the foot soldiers in symphony orchestras. Always busy, they sit eyes glued to the music, sometimes weary yet always dutiful and ready to serve. On this happy occasion, the strings' tone shimmered with a joyful, spirited pride.

Afterwards, Beat enjoyed Elvira's delight, her face a wreath of smiles. Matthew begrudgingly saluted Beat, and Winton pumped her hand in passing. She darted here and there, complimenting students, shaking Garrett's hand, exhilarated as she listened to the audience's favourable comments before they bustled onto King George Square.

'We did it, Pol.' Beat hugged her assistant. 'Thank you.' Not even Thorne's speech in which she had lavished praise on Matthew, who had 'expertly steered this remarkable event,' could dent her happiness.

4

COMODO

BEAT flicked through the pages of *Queensland News*. Relieved the concert had been such a success she should be relaxed, but instead she felt wired.

'Dan, why were you so late home?'

Chuff chuff, chuff chuff – a helicopter flew overhead. Beat watched her horses bite each other's necks in a playful joust before spearing into a gallop, manes flying. Police had recently found a massive drug stash buried in the bush reserve for koalas and frill-necked lizards a couple of properties away. Her only adventures there had included a red-bellied black stretched out on the path ahead and a cyclist who rang his bell and wheeled too close to her horse on a ride. Dan groaned as he slapped at the green leather sofa to dislodge dog hair before he sat down.

Beat looked outside. The manure pile was mountainous. High time she bagged some to sell. And the dense grass around the house was a snake haven. She'd seen one the week before, in dazzling sunlight. It had taken her a few seconds to realise that a tall quivering blade of grass, was actually a highly venomous eastern brown in defence mode. She froze and when the sun ducked behind a cloud, the snake rippled away at speed.

'What happened? I woke at three and you weren't home.'

'Must you let the dogs use this couch?' He brushed hairs off his jeans.

'You know what they say,' countered Beat, 'adopt a greyhound, lose a couch.'

'Rubbish. Discipline them.'

'Well?'

'Been having problems with the Ducati lately. Not far from home, the brakes jammed. I thought of ringing you to pick me up but my phone was out of charge. Dumb, I know. I fiddled around for ages before the brakes were fixed enough to ride home.'

Beat could question him all day and all night for a week, but she'd never get a straight answer. Dan excelled at playing the elusive card.

'If you'd said you were coming, I could've given you a ticket.'

'Polly told me you need every dollar you can get. Consider my ticket money a contribution.'

The dogs woofed, bounded around the kitchen table and jumped at the back door. Beat looked out of the window to see what had excited them. A flock of Australian wood ducks had landed on the lawn.

'Seriously, Dan, we could've sat together.'

'Called you a few times. Either Polly says you're tied up, or I get you only to hear the inevitable, "Can't-talk-now."'

'You could've texted.'

'Look, this concert's run you ragged. You've been preoccupied. I thought I'd come and show support.'

'That's why you came. Really?'

'Yes.'

'Except you loathe classical music.'

'Not all of it.'

'True,' said Beat.

'I heard about it on the radio. Kinda exciting. That kid stepping up like that.'

'Did you enjoy it?' Beat asked. 'Be honest.'

'Yeah. Not that I've many classical concerts to compare it to.'

'But you're investigating *Pictures at an Exhibition* and how Mussorgsky depicts Victor Hartman's paintings for your PhD. That's classical. You listen to it a lot.'

'True. But at home. I dislike the formality of a concert hall.'

Dan's rare enthusiasm encouraged her. She put the newspaper down and reached for his hand.

'Let's do something. How about lunch in town?'

'Can't. I'm having a natter.'

'Natter?'

'Yes, my PhD supervisor's idea, not mine. Besides, the horse yard needs attention.'

He pointed at her with a full-blown smile. He could be such a charmer. She would have liked to clear the branches strewn across the yard with him, but he regarded anything to do with her horses, even the slightest chore, as her exclusive business unless she was absent because of work.

'It's been a while since we hung out,' Beat said.

'Yep. I'm busy. You're busy. You've got those pesky grazers.'

'Seriously though. We ought to do stuff.' Beat reached for a newspaper.

If she pursued the discussion, he'd retreat into his office. Wistfully, she recalled how he'd once hung off her every word.

'What are you searching for?' said Dan.

'Polly texted. *Queensland News* and *Nationwide* reviewed the concert. I haven't seen them yet.'

'Not chasing the latest world news then?' Dan rubbed at his eyes. With his ruffled hair, he had that bleary, unshaved look that had endeared him to her.

'I'll search *Nationwide*. You do *Queensland News*.' Dan took a bite of croissant.

Beat picked up the paper and reefed through the pages. She found the review on the back page, after the sports news and racing results. Not an ideal spot, but it filled more than two-thirds of the page. There was a knockout photo of a beaming Georgy, posing at the piano without her shoes and, much to her surprise, her own name tripped off the page. She hadn't expected a mention. In amazement, she read it out loud and the unexpected praise made her skin tingle.

The promotion of Beatrice Snow to the position of Dean of Turalong Arts Music School has not been without controversy. Yet, if the success of the orchestral concert on Friday is anything to go by, Ms Snow's appointment is a winner.

Beat longed for Dan to hug her, be proud of her. Something. But he hadn't been listening.

'Here it is.' Dan tapped the broadsheet. 'I've found it.'

'Dan hand it over. Come on.'

He handed her *Nationwide*. 'Not sure you'll like it because it's all about Georgy.'

Dan was wrong. She was delighted. Over the moon. '*Barefoot Champion*,' was the headline and Georgy deserved every positive word. She'd delivered: brilliantly, courageously. It's huge, thought Beat. A review of the school's concert had been published in a local and a national paper. Prideful, she remembered Steven had never managed a concert applauded in the press.

When nineteen-year-old Georgy Mellors, engaged as soloist for Tchaikovsky's Piano Concerto no. 1, missed the conductor's signal to begin, a sell-out audience gasped. Instead, Mellors ignored him and wrenched off her shoes. The conductor, Garrett Blue, carried the Concert Hall's awkward silence in his upraised arms, like Atlas holding up the world. On the second beginning, Mellors dived into the music. This time, her massive sound ricocheted around the walls and reeled in a spellbound audience. The responsive orchestra gifted the soloist with attentive support. It was easy to forget this was a novice soloist and student orchestra.

Beat could scarcely contain herself, but Dan was lost to the sports section. She wanted to break out of their rut and smash the barriers between them.

'I miss you, Dan. Come and lie down with me before you go. Can we do that?'

He kissed her, took her hand and led her to the bedroom. Undressed they lay in a loose embrace. Dan wrapped his arms around her, spooned into her back. It had been a long time, but her body danced to his lead.

She longed for intimacy. To shut out the world. She and Dan lost in the familiarity, the certainty of the home key, awakening, modulating, a percolating urgency rising to a crest, the caress of retreating waves. Dan stroked her hair, his lips brushed her neck, she arched her back and pressed closer, but abruptly he rolled away. Abandoned, humiliated, she watched him retrieve his socks from under the bed, tuck his clothes under his arm.

'Sorry.' Dan reached for her hand. 'My mind's all over the place. But I can't be late. Not today.'

Next door, the neighbour's ride-on, a noisy dust maker, growled into life. She knew he would persist until the pasture was razed mercilessly short and no longer able to shelter frogs, skinks, and insects. The grassy stubble browned after his mindless cutting, but either he didn't care, or he didn't notice. Her veranda, the table, the chairs, and window ledges would soon be coated in dust.

On the other side, Sally was more of a friend than a neighbour. She not only gave Beat's horses access to all of her land, but willingly fed and watered them and the greyhounds if she had to work late. In exchange, Beat brush cut the toxic blue-flowering weed which ran along Sally's fence line. Since Beat's unexpected promotion, they'd not seen much of each other. Beat had resorted to texting her and waving.

The smudged kitchen window, a graveyard for moths, clouded her treasured outlook, but she still looked out as she did every morning. Ernie, a lone black-winged ibis, a daily visitor, dunked his beak in the horses' water trough. She liked nothing better than to potter outside, commune with the horses and tend to the land. She never mentioned her farm at work. Her home was private, and she wanted to keep it that way.

It was hot, the glorious blue sky reminded her of an Arthur Streeton painting. She pulled on her boots to go outside but her mobile trilled – "*Somebody that I used to know,*" despite the interruption, she never tired of Gotye's bouncy groove and flippant grief.

'Hi. It's me, Hermione. Congratulations. What a stunner! Everyone's rapt. Well not our Winton, truth be told. Surprise, surprise. Same old, "Everything's better in London".' The last person Beat wanted to talk to was Hermione – without question a gifted clarinettist, but always heckling and finding fault.

'Thanks. Appreciate it. The woodwind bowled me over. Simon's clarinet solos were classy. He's in first year, isn't he? I'd no idea he was so talented,' Beat said.

'Yep, yep, yep, he's not bad.'

'Hermione, what did you think of Garrett?'

'Not much in rehearsal frankly, but last night he crushed it,' she cooed. 'How cool, the way he stretched the silence for a second start.'

'That was incredible.'

'Scratching my head about Georgy. I've never seen a soloist ignore their first entry. What on earth was that about?' Hermione asked.

'Terror?'

'There are rumours.'

'About Georgy? Like?'

'Elvira can fill you in. Now about all this showy... yes... window dressing.'

'Window dressing?' Beat's neck tensed, a pain throbbed behind her eyes.

'Concerts are one thing, but the school has to get its act together in substantial ways...'

Beat gritted her teeth, as if she wasn't already aware of how many things needed reform. 'Don't you mean in *other* substantial ways. Our mission is to train performers.'

'Point taken.'

'Sorry, Hermione. I interrupted.'

'The courses need an overhaul. Concert programs should include guitarists, singers, pianists, and...'

'Rock players need a concert, like last night's,' Beat chipped in.

'Pop bands aren't a priority.'

'Not sure Winton would agree,' Beat said.

'Stop deflecting. When will you tackle the big issues?'

'Hermione, reality check, I'm a month into the job. I inherited Steven's agenda.'

'You've certainly been… distracted' Hermione hedged.

'I'll say.'

'Anyway, the media put a positive spin on your promotion. That's what counts I guess. But dig deeper. Unpalatable elements are blocking our progress…' Hermione tailed off.

'Meaning?'

'You'll find out.'

'I intend to keep it real,' Beat deliberately used Hermione's favoured catchcry.

It wasn't a workday. No one should call her on a Saturday. How had Steven coped with the whining, the unrealistic expectations, the sense of entitlement, the politicking? Then, she recalled to her shame, she'd been just as critical of Steven as Hermione was of her.

'I'm guessing that wasn't a happy-go-lucky Saturday morning call. Who the hell were you speaking to?' Dan called out from the bathroom.

'Hermione.'

'She's got a nerve to blab about work. Did you know that discussing work on the weekend is illegal in France? The 'right to disconnect' was passed by the French Government in 2016. You'll have to whip 'em into line, or those prickly narcissists will gobble you up.' Dan emerged from the steamy bathroom energetically towel-drying his hair.

'Fat chance,' Beat raked her fingers through her matted hair. Yet, he'd touched a nerve. She was finding her new authority, a trial.

'I met this nice guy from your place at a seminar,' said Dan.

'What was his name?'

'Connor, I think. He's interrogating whether music can express anything other than itself. Is it referential? Can it portray landscapes, ships, caves, animals, people, and objects?'

'That sort of fits with your topic.'

'Yes, true. He didn't say a bad word about you or anyone else come to think of it. Why don't you chum up?'

'The long or the short answer?'

'Short, definitely.'

'He's irascible. On days of the week ending in Y, he's a spectacular pain in the butt.'

Dan laughed. 'Got it loud and clear.'

Sally's cattle dog yelped, a butcher bird chirruped on the veranda rail. Somewhere, a country music station blared Keith Urban. She tuned into the sounds around her to edit out Hermione's 'homilies' riffing in her mind. As Dan dressed, he fired instructions.

'We need milk, butter, toilet paper. Shopping list is on the fridge under the dolphin magnet.'

A fluttering curtain of leaf litter, stirred by a sudden breeze, dropped to the ground. Hadn't Dan promised to do the chores, manage the house and grounds in exchange for her paying all expenses until he'd completed his PhD? He'd sworn he'd submit the thesis within three years. Five years later, it was nowhere near completion. He barely kept the house in order, let alone the grounds, and the overhead light on the veranda had been without a new globe for months.

'It's hard to keep this place clean and the kitchen floor's mucky,' Dan said.

'Hardly an emergency. You know I looked for you when the concert ended. Ellie wanted to say goodbye,' Beat said to Dan's departing back. 'What time did you say you'll be home?' Beat had meant to sound light but neediness had crept into her tone.

'Late afternoon.'

He paused, turned to face her. 'There'll be other occasions for Ellie to annoy me.'

'What is it with you two?'

Dan shook his head and sighed, cue for subject closed. 'Beat, about today. Why don't I call in sick?'

'No. We need that PhD out of our lives. Gone. Will today's meeting push it along?'

'Yes,' he said.

'That's your answer then.'

'Beat, take a break. Forget about the chores.'

'I intend to.'

Dan came back inside, left the door ajar. 'Let's drive somewhere tomorrow. We'll have lunch and rummage in junk shops like we used to.'

The sickly scent of flowering jasmine bushes on either side of the front door wafted inside and tickled her throat. She watched as he eyed himself in the hall mirror. Pursing his lips as if taking a selfie, he shifted his head right, left, and right again, and exited. She was grateful he hadn't noticed Dora, the chunky rat scuttle down the hallway. He wasn't a fan of rural living, and it was best he had no idea there were long-tailed lodgers in the basement where he stored his precious Ducati.

5
TROPPO

BEAT was bone weary. There were no appointments, not that she knew of anyway. She checked her phone. It was 9:30 and the air was fresh, the sun inviting. She lay in an Adirondack chair in the canteen's courtyard garden, watching a couple of bees hovering around a large pot of lavender. Dan had told her about the painter John Constable, a keen observer of the sky, who coined the expression 'to sky', and today she happily skyed at a school of fish-shaped clouds. Her conscience was quiet. She was idling, but after such a success, surely no one would mind.

'Wish I had so little to do I could sunbake.' A smirking Winton took a mouthful of egg and bacon breakfast roll. Fat dribbled down his stubbled chin.

Beat wondered how long he'd been there.

'Come and do my job,' Winton said.

'In your dreams.'

'Well, you're the one twiddling your thumbs.' Winton wiped the grease off his mouth with the back of his hand.

'What did you think of the concert?'

'Before my mum moved to London to be with my dad she lived in a town called Blandford Forum. She played violin in the local orchestra and would have loved the classical feels. But remember, you're only as good as your last performance.'

'Which was last Friday.' Beat was infuriated but far worse, ashamed. She'd never let her guard down on campus before. Now that he'd seen her taking a moment to herself, Winton had something else to gripe about. She knew it wouldn't matter how many problems she solved. How many wins she chalked up. She'd always be at fault.

'Don't let me disturb you,' he said.

'You haven't.' Beat marvelled at her lie, her heart pumping hard.

'I like to do a full day's work. Poms generally do.'

'Well feeding your face with fatty food is in keeping with your British image.'

How dare he? She deserved praise, not snide, underhand remarks. What was he doing if not taking a break? She closed her eyes, but the serenity she'd enjoyed had gone. Winton's contempt hurt. She'd really have to toughen up or she wouldn't last six months. Perhaps she'd ask Thorne how she manages toxic individuals.

Beat's coffee cup toppled when Hermione slammed the score for *Jurassic Park* on the table. Beat removed her broad-brimmed hat. She must look like a punter fraternising at the Melbourne Cup. She was shocked by Hermione's ashen face.

The arch clarinettist, generally unflappable, could scarcely catch her breath.

'What's wrong?' Beat sat up, her hat forgotten.

'Remember how beautifully Simon played in *The Force of Destiny*?'

'Yes, of course.'

'He just went berserk on ABC Radio in a live performance.'

'You were on air?'

Hermione nodded, her curls bouncing. 'He dropped his clarinet, kicked a music stand over and careened around the studio mad as a cut snake.'

'The other players?'

'Shaken, but carried on, bless their hearts.'

'Shit.'

'Beatrice,' she covered her chest, 'he groped my boobs.'

'That's gross.' Beat scrambled to her feet. 'Where's he now?'

'In the foyer. I have to fly, there are auditions today,' said Hermione.

'For flute and clarinet?'

'Yep, yep, yep. Good luck. You'll need it.'

Beat snatched her bag, ignored a dance colleague who waved and wanted a chat. A ruckus greeted her in the foyer. A receptionist sobbed. Beat sympathised with the alarmed woodwind applicants cowering against the office wall. Instrument cases littered the floor, abandoned sheet music blanketed the sofa. Beat shrieked when Simon aimed a fire extinguisher at Winton as if it were an AK-47 rifle and doused him in foam.

Simon's desperate yowl of 'B-B-B-Beat' pierced her heart. Slowly, she stepped towards him and he dropped the extinguisher, which rolled to a stop.

'I'm here.'

Onlookers gasped. She could feel eyes burrowing into her back. Shocked by the student's sweat-soaked hair and unsteady gait, Beat led him down the corridor past her office towards the Dean's studio. Staggering like a drunk, he punched each of the framed portraits of past Deans. Several smashed and glassy shards strafed the hardwood floor. Polly tiptoed along behind her to see if she could help.

Beat ushered Simon into the studio. 'Sit down.' Her tone soft as a whisper.

'We can bathe in moonlight.' Simon gazed at the ceiling. 'Reach for the stars, sleep on clouds.' Eyes closed, Simon was lost to a turbulent inner world.

Beat opened a bottle of water and handed it to him, but he knocked it from her hand. Watery bubbles patterned the Scotchgarded carpet.

Simon's gibberish competed with an upbeat spin of Vivaldi's '*Flute Concerto*' upstairs. Propelled at breakneck speed, the flautist's breathless pacing militated against Beat's efforts to placate Simon. His dirty nails clawed at his arm, a skein of drool dangled from his lip. When the door opened, she was glad to see Connor.

'Can I help?'

Beat shook her head, only to regret it the moment he left. What had caused Simon's hyper state? A knock on the door made him jolt. Putting his feet on the sofa he wrapped his arms around his knees.

Winton burst in, wagging an accusatory finger. 'Wake up to yourself Simon.'

'Not. Helpful.' Beat motioned for Winton to leave. Simon sprang at the back door, wrenched it open, ripping his shirt on the balustrade as he stumbled down the concrete steps into the garden.

Beat chased him. But he was too fast. He sprinted into the main road. She watched, petrified. Shaking, she elbowed her way through the crowd. Heard the screech of brakes. Someone screamed. A car swerved. People stared as Simon lurched forward on blackened feet. Dashed between vehicles. Leaning on a Peugeot's bonnet to steady himself and echoing Winton, Simon aimed an accusing finger at the driver.

'What happened?' Beat asked a mature-aged candidate who hugged her flute to her chest as if her life depended on it.

'He was knocked down. He got up. A taxi hit him. He fell hard, but jumped up.'

Clearly, Beat needed security's help. She rummaged in her bag, her fingers rifling through receipts, keys, a hoof pick until, at last, she found her phone. She punched in the Deputy Director's number but remembered he'd taken the day off. She tried Thorne. No answer. She wanted to run. Scream. Elvira's hand touched her shoulder.

'How can I help?'

'Be with me.'

Simon shoved people aside on his way through the foyer to the stairs leading to the basement. He balanced on the balustrade. Then, jumped. Beat heard the clarinet's screamed *glissandi* at the start of Gershwin's *Rhapsody in Blue*. Whether it was real or imagined she'd no idea. Elvira grabbed her arm, and they clattered down the stairs. There was a blood stain where Simon had landed and Elvira dry retched.

Beat rang the police despite Elvira's protest. 'What if they shoot him?'

'I don't have a choice.' Beat ignored the pianist who tugged on her sleeve.

'Promise. No guns,' she told an officer.

How long she and Elvira waited for help was hard to fathom. Time moved fast and too slowly, but at last three uniformed police, two men and a woman, hoisted Simon to his feet, pinned his arms behind his back. Cuffed him.

'We've got you, mate. Don't struggle,' an officer said unnecessarily because Simon's adrenaline was spent. He hung his head, unsteady on his feet.

'Where will you take him?' Beat's voice broke.

'Hospital.' The stocky officer handed Beat his business card. 'He's in bad shape.'

In her office, dazed and weary, she closed her eyes, cradling her chin in cupped hands. She didn't hear Connor come in. 'I've brought lemon and almond biscuits and a sugary milky tea on Polly's instruction. She's tied up.'

'Not literally, I hope.' Managing a half-hearted smile, she looked up into Connor's concerned face, which gave her a warm feeling for a change. She noticed he carried a Herschel backpack.

Eagerly, she picked up the tea, but her phone rang.

'Beatrice, is it true you called the police, all because some daft kid chucked a tanty? Do you think you could have over-reacted?' Thorne complained.

'No.'

'Give me a detailed report tomorrow. Do not talk to the media.'

'No one was…'

'In. Writing.'

6
PIANGEVOLE

BEAT rushed to her front door. If she could talk to Dan, she'd feel better. It was still light. The sun didn't set for an hour, and they could have a drink on the veranda and watch it go down. Too bad the light out there didn't work, but she'd use citronella candles which would provide some light and repel mosquitoes. Fruit bats streamed across the sky. She enjoyed their metallic chittering as they roosted in a tree.

She rang the doorbell. Her dogs whined, their nails skidding on the wooden floor, but Dan didn't come. She knocked, managed a wave at her grass-murdering neighbour as he lovingly watered his precious cherry tomato plants. Corellas fluttered around the enormous ghost gum which overlooked the horse yard, the tree's branches like gnarled fingers.

Heavy-hearted, Beat let herself in, ignored the clamouring dogs, and ran up the stairs. With a hand on the banister, she yelled, 'Dan? Are you there?'

No answer. Downstairs, she looked in his office, keeping the dogs behind her – he hated them going in because his art books and papers littered the floor. He wasn't there.

A woman's coat draped over a kitchen chair. It surprised her because Dan hadn't mentioned a visitor. In the backyard, the horses stood parallel to the fence with pleading eyes, heads held high, waiting. The afternoon's bucket feed was overdue. She prepared it quickly, hoping to watch the horses consume it before darkness fell. She sat on the lower rung of the wooden fence, braving midges, as the day tipped into dusk. She never tired of the dreamy pleasure in her horses' eyes, their busy lips whittling at the feed.

Simon's haggard face popped into her head. She shivered, zipped up her jacket. If Dan didn't get back soon, she'd start on the report while her memory was fresh. Hearing the spluttered cadence of Dan's bike, she rushed to the house, the dogs powering ahead.

Indoors, abandoned cups, plates, and cutlery cluttered the kitchen table. At the sound of footsteps, she looked towards the kitchen door. Ellie, Dan's sister, wandered in, the black safety helmet with silver trim – the one Beat used when she rode pillion with Dan – under her arm. It had been over a year since she'd last gone for a spin. Dan followed her through the doorway.

'Ellie had run out of her asthma medication. I had to take her to the chemist,' Dan sighed heavily. 'Didn't expect you back yet,' he said. 'It's only five-thirty.'

'Today was unusual. Long story.'

Ellie leaned in to kiss Beat's cheek. 'I've been wondering if I should rent somewhere near you. The area has a lot to offer.'

'Dan told me you're moving to America.'

'What? No. I'm going on a holiday. Four weeks tops, an end of year treat.'

Ellie grimaced at her brother. Dan ignored her. He poured Beat a glass of wine and gave Ellie some water, then wrenched the top off a beer.

'Where in America?' Beat sipped on her wine. The day's events melted away.

'New York. I've got a friend there,' said Ellie. 'We'll check out the galleries, go to the theatre, window shop. Check out the Chelsea Hotel. Who knows?'

'Sounds fun,' Beat said.

'Yes. Two weeks off from obsessing about the future. Studying law's been great but unless I can get a clerkship with one of the big companies, the chances of working for a law firm are virtually nil,' Ellie confessed.

'It's that competitive?' asked Beat.

'Depressingly so.'

'It's hard for music graduates too,' Beat said. 'Landing a position with an Aussie orchestra is rare. Not because they're not talented enough, far from it, but the industry tends to prefer recruits from overseas.'

'That's a shame,' Ellie said.

'Did you know it was this tough before you began your degree?' Dan asked.

'No. Or I might have made other choices.'

'Ellie,' Dan leaned back in his chair, hands behind his head. 'I've got a friend, he's a partner at Spicer, Pearce and Munro.'

'I know the firm.'

'I could have a word with Oliver Munro, we're mates. No promises, but he could possibly swing a clerk's position if that would help?' Dan offered.

'That would be awesome.' Ellie rushed over to hug him, but he flinched at her touch.

Something didn't ring true about Dan's offer, but Beat couldn't put her finger on it.

'Look, it's getting late; shall I knock up dinner?' Dan deposited his empty beer bottle into the sink.

'No. Assignment deadlines are looming. Beat's shattered.'

'No different from any other night.' Dan lifted the lid off the retro green bread bin and took out a loaf.

'Don't listen to him, Ellie. The challenges were unusual today,' protested Beat.

'Oh, what kind of—' Ellie began, but Dan cut her off.

'Don't inflict that dysfunctional place on my sister.'

Ellie looked awkward. She stared out of the window and the backyard beyond.

'I'd love to visit more often, it's so peaceful here.'

'Come over whenever you like.' Beat ignored Dan's inevitable scowl. Bad feelings had flared between Ellie and Dan following the death of their aunt, who'd been a surrogate mum after their parents died in a car crash. But if she quizzed him, he always skirted around the topic.

'When my PhD is out of the way I can be social, do fun things,' Dan said.

If Dan ever submitted his PhD, he'd be far too old, Beat thought but stopped herself from making a snide remark. Ellie and Dan's relationship was tricky enough without her airing her own grievances.

'Keep in touch,' pleaded Beat.

'Have you ever considered having a tenant to help pay the bills? I know horses are expensive. I could feed them when you're at work.'

'No. But I'll give it some thought,' Beat said.

'Get your stuff Ellie. I've called an Uber,' Dan said.

Her sister-in-law cleared her throat, wrung her hands together. Beat doubted a backlog of university assignments could explain how wired she was. She blew her sister-in-law a kiss at the front door but when Ellie reached the garden gate, Beat noticed she wasn't wearing her coat. She ran back inside to fetch it but by the time she returned Ellie had gone.

Beat curled up on the sofa, patted the cushion, and the silvery-blue greyhound jumped up and snuggled beside her.

'Ellie's right, you are tired. Shall I make pasta?'

'Not hungry. Dan, can we talk?'

'About?' Dan rolled up his sleeves, reached for a hard-backed chair and sat down to face her. The dog bumped against Beat's glass in its effort to jump off the couch to escape Dan's reprimand, spilling her wine.

'I'll wipe that up,' Dan sighed.

'No. Please, just listen. A student had a psychotic turn today.'

'And?'

'I panicked.'

'No surprises there. Why?'

'I was afraid he'd hurt himself or someone else.' Beat coiled a strand of hair around her finger.

'Mmm, must you?' Dan said.

'What?'

'Chew on your hair,' Dan checked his phone.

'I rang the police.'

'Let me guess,' Dan tapped his cheek, 'Thorne wasn't impressed because she wants to improve Turalong Arts' public image?' He narrowed his eyes.

'She wants to see me first thing.'

'Spit it out. How much trouble are you in?'

On the other side of the windowpane, skirmishing geckoes competed for black flies the size of peppercorns. Beat fumed. It always boiled down to money. Nothing was more important to Dan than her capacity to earn. She hungered for syrupy comfort, his arms around her. She wanted sympathy.

'Forget it, Dan.'

'I'm sorry, if I linger, I'll be late.'

'For?' Beat sighed.

'I'm chairing the Ducati Sports meeting.'

'Didn't know you were a member,' Beat muttered.

'You don't have a monopoly on responsibilities.'

'You could cancel?' Beat suggested.

'No, I don't want to let them down.'

'Thorne wants a report about the incident. I'd value your input.'

'Nonsense. You're the most capable woman I've ever met.' Dan smiled.

He sat beside her and pulled her towards him, patting her shoulder absently as if she were one of the dogs. Abruptly, he got up, cleared the table. Popped a couple of slices of wholemeal bread in the toaster. A kookaburra cackled, offset by the percussive donk of tree frogs.

'You were the one in the eye of the storm. Thorne will respect that,' Dan said.

'Maybe.'

'I'd like to mull this over, but I made a commitment.' He spread a thick helping of peanut butter on a piece of toast. 'Blame my sister. If she hadn't out stayed her welcome, I would have had time.' Dan chewed, his mouth open as he spoke. Beat looked away.

'You're too hard on her.'

'She's angling to live here.'

'Would it be so bad for a month or two?' Beat asked.

'Yes. Ellie's a charmer on the surface but you don't know the half of it.' Dan looked as if he had something else to say, but the moment passed.

'Since Ellie's a taboo subject, how can I? You told me Oliver Munro had left Spicer, Pearce and Munro in Brisbane to work at the Townsville branch. Munro's based there isn't he?'

'What of it?'

'You raised Ellie's hopes.'

'Wanted to show support. You're always nagging me to be kinder.'

'Yes, but not if it's a lie.'

'Ellie could do worse than move to Townsville,' Dan said.

'She'd be a long way from us.'

'Exactly.'

Twice she'd caught Dan lying. He'd told her Ellie was moving to New York, and then there was the Oliver issue. She'd always known he harboured secrets, but early on her strong attraction to him had somehow made his lies irrelevant. She'd laughed about his fabrications. He hadn't refuelled the car because the petrol station was closed. He was late home because the lecture had run over time. He'd tried to call her many times when he hadn't. Now she regretted how she'd enabled his lying. Back then, his falsehoods were insignificant compared to her physical need for him. There wasn't time to badger him about untruths. After lovemaking she'd unpick Dan's fibs and they'd chuckle about it. But Beat's friends and her father found her unconditional tolerance a worry. Nowadays, although she wasn't about to broadcast it, Dan's evasions chipped away at her desire.

'I'll read the report later.'

'I'd appreciate it.' Beat stretched out on the sofa, chewed on a strand of hair.

'Stop doing that,' Dan stooped to kiss her, but Beat drew back, repelled by his peanut buttery breath.

'Give her a one pager. Ten bullet points.'

7

BRIDGE

BEAT threw her bag over her shoulder, opened her office door and almost crashed into a bemused Thorne. Her chin-length bob, one side cut longer than the other, and straight fringe, looked modish. Asymmetry suited her.

'Marilyn, I was just about to come to you.'

'But we can talk here just as well?'

'Of course. Sure.'

'I'm early, but I need a break from the non-stop calls and that damn air conditioning. I'm terrified of catching Legionnaire's disease.' Thorne pretended to shiver.

'You'd have more chance of catching Legionnaire's in a river or a creek. Oh, and through potting mix.'

'Please, Beatrice. My courtyard is crammed with potted plants, don't give me anything else to fret about. Non-stop visitors spraying germs is bad enough.' Thorne fingered the charms on her bracelet.

'About yesterday...'

Beat handed her the report she'd prepared. It had taken most of the night and in the cold light of day its stapled pages looked excessive.

'Shall I talk you through the incident?' Beat said.

'If you like.'

'I was in the canteen's garden when—'

Thorne waved her hand dismissively. 'Hermione filled me in. We were at the launch of the Queensland Chamber Music Competition at Government House last night.'

Beat felt the slight of that. Why hadn't she been invited? She'd coached 1 2 3 – the school's most gifted ensemble. Hermione, who coordinated chamber music could easily have asked for her to be invited.

'Hey, Beatrice, you've drifted. Are you listening?' Thorne slapped her hands on her lap.

'I am.' Beat sat taller, clasped her hands together.

'Hermione said you handled things remarkably during the ordeal. She's in awe of your courage. But let's park yesterday. How are things generally?'

'Fine.' Beat glanced at the report her supervisor had placed on the table. She would have to make sure Thorne took it with her when she left, although she doubted she would read it.

'Are you certain?'

'I'm just...'

'Weary?'

'Yes,' Beat said.

'Understandably. The last few days have been taxing.' Thorne took a bag of smoked almonds out of her shoulder bag and offered her some.

If she looked tired it had more to do with her staying up all night writing an overly detailed report. Next time a statement was required, it would be one page as Dan had suggested.

'It's not that so much.'

'Then what?' Thorne prompted.

'Someone troubles me,' Beat confessed.

'Who?'

'Winton.'

'How predictable,' Thorne said.

'Maybe, but he's blabbing to anyone who'll listen that I'm too young, a woman, a pianist, a fantasist, inexperienced, and—'

Thorne gestured for Beat to stop.

'Let me guess,' Thorne spoke softly, 'I bet he says, "an inappropriate appointment like this wouldn't happen in London." He's chewed my ear about it many times.'

Beat folded her arms – she loathed the dobbers and the doubters who vaulted over her head and ran to Thorne.

'Oh.' Beat frowned.

'I encourage the staff to talk to me,' Thorne said. 'How else can I keep up to date with the art, dance, and music schools?'

Beat changed tack. 'How can I get Winton on board?'

'You may not be able to. The chip on his shoulder is bigger than Blackpool Pier,' said Thorne. 'He's a misogynist with a problematic ego. And then there's the rock stream's – yada yada – vermin riddled facilities – yawn yawn. He's a nuisance. A thorn in the side. Ha ha.'

'I want to try.'

'Naysayers come with the job.'

'I suppose.' Beat looked at the floor.

'Look, have a chat over coffee. Ask him why your appointment offends him? Put him on the spot. Get him to vent.'

'I'll give it a go.'

'And, there's something else.' Thorne cupped the shorter side of her sleek hair in her hand.

'What?'

'Never expect praise. It doesn't matter what you achieve or what kindnesses you bestow, don't hanker for approval or become bitter about ingratitude.'

Beat's face flamed. Thorne had touched a nerve. She longed for a kind word, a show of appreciation and her need to be liked plagued her. She was appalled by her vulnerabilities. Dan liked her inflated salary, but was it worth it?

'Friday's concert was a triumph.'

'Thanks.'

'But the staff won't applaud you even if Carnegie Hall gifted you the venue for the orchestra to be conducted by Sir Simon Rattle, or if Georgy is signed by Decca. No one's going to pat you on the back.'

'Yes,' Beat blushed, 'I know.'

'If there's a stuff up,' she clapped her hands, 'it will be front page news, featured on a *60 Minutes'* exclusive, investigated by *Four Corners* and interrogated in Parliament.'

'You had me at front page news.'

Thorne laughed, but just as suddenly became serious.

'Great job yesterday by the way.'

Beat brightened. 'Did you get any feedback about Simon? Do you know what the trigger was?'

'He stopped taking his bipolar meds and took recreational drugs. He won't say who supplied them. And drinking too much coffee and too many energy drinks. He'd practised all night for the ABC broadcast and the result was yesterday's mad *King Lear* scene.'

'That would do it.' Beat nodded, stifling her annoyance that Thorne yet again knew more than her. 'Marilyn, can you recommend a workplace psychologist?'

Thorne looked thoughtful for a moment. 'Caroline Watson is good. Give her a call. Just a throwaway, but why not give a recital with Hermione? Building musical alliances could boost your credibility.'

'I'll think about it. Thanks.'

'Beat, that pinched look. The grim lips. Whatever is the matter?'

'Could you...'

'What?' Thorne looked in the mirror. Preened her precision cut hair.

'If Matthew or any of the other staff complain to you about something musical, could you ask if they've run it by me first?'

Thorne stared. Let herself out. Scooted down the corridor, one arm waving in the air.

8

DIVISI

THERE was a loud rap on her door. Startled, Beat turned around just as Hermione walked in. The clarinettist had never knocked until now. Her bountiful curls were pulled back from her face. She wore a full-skirted lemon and black patterned dress, the cinched waist celebrated by a tight, red belt.

'Come in.' Beat smiled, glad to see her – no one had popped in for several days. Even though she'd complained about the steady flow of colleagues into her office, she'd begun to miss the social interaction. Hermione continued to stand with her back to the open door.

'Do you want to discuss ideas for a concert?'

By way of an answer she snapped, 'You are an ice-queen.'

Beat reeled from the hurt of it.

'What do you mean?'

'You're not in touch with our concerns?'

Beat's eyes widened. 'What concerns?'

But Hermione turned and walked out gently closing the door behind her.

Now she had a brain worm. Not the hook of a song or a riff but an insult. There was something going on. When she strolled through the music building, her colleagues scuttled into offices or walked the other way. According to Thorne, the staff thought she'd handled the Simon situation well. But in the staff meeting a couple of days after the post traumatic counselling sessions, their attitude had soured.

Polly's monosyllabic responses are what hurt her most. All Beat got was 'hi,' 'bye,' 'no,' 'yes,' 'as you wish.' Her assistant had worn her hot pink comfort sweatshirt, her cat's portrait on the front, three days in a row. She had stopped fielding calls or organising the diary. The wounding distance between them was professionally counter-productive. Hurtful. Yet Beat didn't have the stamina to discuss it, because the phone never stopped. Like now. She hesitated. Its tone had a heavy edge.

'Beatrice, it's Connor. Could you please come up?'

She sighed. Her office was her safe place, an exclusion zone, but every instinct she had told her she must talk to him. Polly's eyes were glued to the screen when she left.

She'd never been to Connor's office. She still found his superior attitude exasperating. Hermione's confronting challenges and Matthew were easier to handle. Connor ignored petty politics, avoided socialising, and could barely contain his impatience in meetings. Although, she had warmed to him after he offered to help with Simon, and for delivering much-needed refreshment after the incident.

If Connor looked at her at all, it was with an absent expression, head tilted, like a water dragon soaking up the sun on Brisbane River's bank. But if he could throw any light on why everyone was upset with her, she'd be grateful. She knocked. Waited. Poked her head around the door. Connor was on the phone, but she slipped in anyway, removed a heavy set of papers from a worn leather armchair and sat down.

She liked his maroon Persian rug, unpatterned except for the emblem of a goat and the tree of life. Anything the staff did to defeat the complexion of the school's sallow walls pleased her. While the floor-to-ceiling, over-filled bookcase covered an expanse of the dreary paintwork, it was a hazard. If Hermione slammed Connor's door, it could start an avalanche of scholarly rubble. Connor hung up.

Now she had his attention she asked, 'What's up?'

'Like some water? I wanted to talk to you away from your office.' Connor's green and navy, diagonally striped tie confirmed his old-school persona. Today's black backpack, a Patagonia, perched on the corner of his desk. If only she could be observing an Andean Condor with a three-metre wingspan wheeling in the sky between South American mountain peaks, anywhere other than Connor's cloying quarters.

'You must have been pleased with the concert?'

'Turned out well. Hey, I never thanked you for helping out.'

Connor shrugged, 'Don't mention it.' He cleared his throat, swallowed.

'The staff asked me to talk to you.' He swivelled on his office chair and faced her full on.

'Sounds ominous.'

'Several... well... members of staff are bruised by the... um...' Connor's voice tailed off. He squinted at a tall essay pile. Lifted the one on top and placed it in the middle of his desk.

'How come? The incident wasn't a siege or a mass shooting.'

'Never say that in public.'

'I see.' An ACDC riff pounded downstairs. It made Beat think of Angus Young, in a school uniform, the neck of his guitar pointed ahead, his left foot upended, the right jumping across the lip of the stage.

'Beatrice, our associates are...'

'Petulant? Peeved?'

'Come on, Beatrice, how can you dismiss them like that. No. A few are distressed.' Connor poured himself more water, sculled it in one go, then leaned into the back of his chair.

'Thorne told me the staff were impressed how I handled the Simon incident.'

'True, but,' Connor took a deep breath, 'Elvira's on sick leave and—'

'Fucking hell! What're you implying? That all this unhappiness is my doing?' Beat clenched her fists.

'Your official emails cause offence,' Connor said quietly.

'Too bad. How else am I to distribute information. Should I send you all a personal postcard. Wow! What do you people want from me?' Her fist thumped the chair's arm. Was she shouting?

Head bowed, eyes closed, Connor rubbed his temples, and yet Beat couldn't stop.

'I'm sick, sick, sick of it.' Her voice ratcheted up a notch. 'Aggravated.'

'Sickened?' Connor added.

'The whispering, the sly, shirty looks, the moronic sulking. It's odious. I didn't sign up to babysit a blithering cesspool of narcissistic nut jobs or to be a target for a blame culture.'

'Beatrice, let me—'

'You've...'

'What?' said Connor.

'No. Forget it.' Beat sighed.

'I want to...'

'As for the whining, lily-livered snitches hot-footing it to Thorne, I am...' Beat stopped, shocked by her outburst. She sucked in some breath, and then another, and her mood transitioned from a strident, major tonality to a mellower minor key. She toppled into silence.

Connor handed her a glass of water. She gulped it down.

'Is there something else?' Connor sat forward.

'I arranged PTSD counselling the next day,' she croaked, her throat scratchy.

Connor lined up a batch of biodegradable pencils beneath a chorus line of blue ballpoints. Who could blame him for fidgeting? Her outburst had shocked her, let alone him. The blue, wall clock's relentless *tick-tock-tick-tock* set her teeth on edge. He poured her another glass of water.

Connor broke the silence. 'Here, take this.'

She took the cool glass and pressed it against her flaming face.

'The anger is because—'

'Anger?'

'It's pretty basic.' Connor picked up a paper clip and began to straighten it. He seemed to have lost his train of thought.

Irritated, she gestured for him to continue.

'Trouble festered when you didn't attend the debriefing sessions.'

'My choice surely,' Beat snapped.

'No. Wrong. It's really not.' He hesitated. 'A manager leads by example.'

After her outburst, Connor's level-headed decency was unsettling.

'Did you go?'

'Absolutely not.' Connor opened his desk drawer, removed a box of bulldog clips, and then met her eyes. '*I'm* not in a position of authority.'

Beat groaned. 'Yikes, is there more?'

'Yes.' Connor scratched his forehead.

'Hit me with it.'

'You've been distant in the wake of a disturbing event.'

Now Hermione's accusation made sense. Beat had to leave. Go home. 'I'm doing my best.'

'No one disputes that, but for pity's sake, don't initiate therapy sessions unless you attend yourself.'

'Got it.' She saluted him.

'Had you gone, you would have understood staff vulnerabilities.'

'All I did was send a memo wanting to clarify the regulations surrounding a student's return after an illness.'

'Yes. But people are worried about Simon coming back. What if he has another episode? If there's resistance, talk about it in person. Ask about it. Care about it. Musicians are touchy about bureaucracy.'

'How do I fix this?'

'No idea.' He shrugged. 'Your call.'

Beat groaned, she rubbed her eyes.

'Initiating counselling was smart, but not participating was...'

'Stupid?'

'I didn't say that.' He added another ball point to the chorus line. 'Open up, for goodness' sake.'

'About?'

'Your truth, your vision, your perspective.'

'Just did with Wagnerian emphasis.'

Connor smiled. 'There's a far greater issue looming over the current dysfunction.'

'Go on,' Beat said.

'Recently, you became Dean. Except, you've always stepped into Steven's shoes whenever he was away. After his shock resignation, you took over, same as always.'

'Your point?'

'Don't you realise it's different because you're not keeping Steven's seat warm, you *are* in charge and responsible. You tell us you want Turalong to become one of the top-ranking music schools in the world.'

'I do.'

'But the staff are in the dark, fearful about how you're going to achieve it. Are you going to replace them with American scholar-cum-performers like Garrett? Are you going to scrub the rock program? Unless you share your plans for the school's future, your team, in the absence of explanation, will jump to conclusions and suspect the worst.'

'During the interview, I did.'

'Yes, but the staff weren't there and after you were appointed, the orchestral concert and the Simon thing swallowed you whole.'

'Ah.' Beat sighed.

'Our colleagues are angry, baffled.'

'Yes, my bad. I'll make amends.' Exposed, embarrassed, her legs had turned hollow. She wanted to leave.

'Moving on. Did you know I play viola?'

'No, but in the words of a famous conductor, "Violas should be seen and not heard."'

Connor grinned. 'Careful now. Viola jokes could rattle my cage too. Would you perform Brahms' *Clarinet Sonatas* with me? Obviously, I mean the viola versions.'

'Funny, you're the second person to suggest something like that.'

'Could be a winning idea.'

~

She cringed when she replayed her meltdown with Connor. Her tolerance was threadbare, but splashing her ugly rage on him was unforgiveable. He'd been tactful, but she felt hijacked, shocked by her own insensitivity. She decided to leave for the day, blame it on a headache. Still edgy, she could easily snap at someone else. That her colleagues thought it her obligation to manage any situation, no matter how distressing, made her blood boil. Dan's indifference hurt too. Was she angry at him, her workmates, or both? Was she an ice queen?

Much as Turalong's challenges motivated her, she resented the way it dominated her life, it haunted her dreams, shredded her self-esteem. Worst of all, the school had become a Berlin Wall between herself and Dan.

The car park – if you could call it that – was more like a moonscape, with its mass of large and small craters. At its best, the surface was compacted soil harbouring sharp-edged rocks that deflated tires. Torrential rain which had been predicted in today's weather forecast guaranteed sucking, viscous ground. She quickened her step. Climbed into her 4WD just as swollen clouds dumped heavy rain which turned the pressed earth into mud.

Beat was unaware of Polly's frantic dash to reach her until, about to drive off, she checked her mirror and saw a bedraggled figure splash across pooling ground. Beat braked. Switched off the radio. Her tastes were broad. Not for the first time, she wondered why she loved music. It was emotion transmitted through sound. Amusing, erotic, intellectually challenging, it inspired and pumped her spirits, triggered memories, gave her courage, sent her to sleep. She could lose herself in music, it was an escape, a contemplative space where reality was suspended and she could float, idling among tonal spheres. Bach's cello suites for reflection, Taverner's misty, choral scapes when she was intense. Reggae's bouncy groove to lift her mood. Best of all, was the challenge of transforming dots on a page into a living narrative.

Beat leaned across to open the passenger door. 'Quick, get in,' and a saturated Polly hauled herself on board.

'Shame about those,' Beat pointed to her assistant's mud splattered yellow trainers.

'We have to talk.' Polly's face was grim.

'I was available most of the morning,' Beat said as kindly as she could.

'The friction is unworkable.'

'I'm aware of that, as is everybody else,' Beat agreed.

Polly gathered up a mess of papers by her feet, rolled the loose sheets into a cylindrical shape, applied an elastic band, and tossed it on the back seat. Vigorous rain pelted the windscreen.

'Let's not do this here, Polly. We'll go to a pub. My treat.'

'Good idea.'

There was a dingy hotel opposite the railway station, with a messy façade of half scraped off posters. Inside, Grubby lemon paintwork was bordered by brown trim. Amateurish paintings hung on the wall behind the bar. Had Dan been there, he would have savaged the staff and paraded his superior art knowledge to anyone within earshot. Beat pulled off her damp jacket and reached for her wine, hoping it tasted better than the awkward interior looked.

'I'm all ears,' she said.

'Ever since that crazy clarinettist—' Polly's tone was bitter.

Beat jumped in, 'You mean Simon's psychotic episode?'

'Call it what you like,' countered Polly, fiddling with her gold locket, which Beat knew contained a photo of Tosca, her prized moggie.

'You were saying,' encouraged Beat.

'Ever since Tara resigned because the Simon thing freaked her out, the office staff have been down in the dumps.'

'Due to increased workloads?'

Polly rolled her eyes, put her drink down. Musicians were setting up on a cramped corner platform. Beat pointed them out to Polly. A nervy singer tapped the mic and spouted, 'testing, one-two one-two.' To her surprise, the young woman tuning her cello was Melody. Beat waved in her direction, but she didn't notice. Beat admired her versatility. She was just as comfortable playing in a pop band as she was performing Schubert.

'Beat, that's insulting.' Polly toyed with her locket. 'Tara and I were close.'

'And you miss her?'

Polly put her drink down and nodded. 'But for heaven's sake, Pol, when can we move on?'

Beat gulped down more wine than she'd intended, which made her splutter.

Polly sighed. 'It makes no difference if what happened was three days or three years ago. Some of us are struggling.'

'Yes, so I hear, but how to fix it?'

'I was thinking an outing, something we all do together.'

Polly placed her glass of merlot parallel to the table's edge. If Beat positioned a glass the same way at home, a swinging greyhound tail would sweep it to the ground. She fought the impulse to move it.

'Bowling?'

'No,' sniped Polly. 'Sport pushes the competitive button.'

'Karaoke, swimming with dolphins at Sea World? Hiking on the Story Bridge? Tai Chi?'

'Or something you enjoy,' said Polly firmly. 'I'd like to spend time with you in your happy place.'

'Wongara's not far from the city, twenty-five minutes if you avoid peak traffic. How about a trail ride, just you and me?'

'I'm in, but what about the others?'

Beat chinked her glass with Polly's then turned to the band as Melody, her face curtained by blond hair, danced with her cello and plucked a mean riff.

'Ah.' Beat scrunched up her face, jutted her chin.

'How about a party at yours?'

Beat pulled a face, 'For Winton and the rest?'

'Yes. Why not?'

9

DISCORDANT

THE canteen was empty. The round tables and blue chairs looked as if they had been pre-arranged for a cabaret entertainment. She was tempted to buy a pastry, but consuming an apple cinnamon scroll in front of Winton could embarrass her. She checked her phone. The meeting was for 7:30. He was already ten minutes late. It was ironic how much apprehension she felt, the same intensity she suffered when going to the dentist. But there was a notable difference, her dentist didn't keep her waiting.

~

'Why don't you approve of me taking on the deanship?'

Winton sat arms folded. 'Well, I don't mind your friggin' jeans and riding boots like some. In London, people generally wear what they want. I don't even mind you are only thirty-two.'

'What is it?'

'You just don't fit the gig.' He picked up a spoon and tapped a salsa rhythm.

'Seriously?' She wished she hadn't taken Thorne's advice. An informal chat wasn't going to shift Winton's views. They were cast in stone.

'That's merely the tip of the iceberg,' he droned. 'You're not a rock player, which is of no use to me. And you're not a conductor, which doesn't impress the other mob.'

'There's more, isn't there?'

'You're a pianist. A nobody. Blimey, the friggin' rumours about how you landed the position turn my stomach.'

'That's the one where I fucked at least twelve members of the selection panel including the women.'

Winton coughed into a bunch of paper tissues.

Beat fetched a jug of water and poured him a glass. He swilled it down, stuffed the used tissues in his shirt pocket and resumed his rant. She vowed from then on to be strictly professional and stop making caring womanly gestures.

'Jeez, pianists know nothing about bands,' Winton raved.

'Let's see. Randy Newman, Tim Minchin, and Elton John.'

'There are exceptions.' Winton plucked an iPhone from his shirt pocket and began to polish its screen.

'Yes,' said Beat. 'Stevie Wonder, Ray Charles, Nora Jones, Billy Preston, John Legend, Billy Joel, Carole King...'

'Friggin' light weights,' Winton snarled.

'Alicia Keyes and Donald Fagan. Lightweights?'

Beat reached for her coffee, but it was long past drinkable. She scanned the canteen to see if anyone was eavesdropping, but she and Winton were still the only customers. A sparrow foraged under a table and soon another three swooped down. Until the doors opened, the birds were trapped.

Shrieks and squeals of laughter in the kitchen shattered the silence. She watched as employees arranged muffins and egg and bacon rolls on serving trays. The radio blared *Hard Road* by the Aussie hip hop band Hill Top Hoods. That these Aussie rappers had had great success in performing with the country's top orchestras pleased her. She reached for her shoulder bag, jaded by the awkward conversation. There was no point in going on with it. She stood.

'Beatrice, look, I'm sorry. Let's keep talking.' He scratched at a speck of congealed egg on the tabletop. She sat down.

Winton's hostility had upset her. Outwardly she radiated calm, but her body protested. Her mouth was dry, her throat so constricted she'd choke on a sip of water. A waitress wiped the canteen tables, and the cleaning agent blended with cooking smells made her queasy. She watched a caterer open the doors and, to her relief, the birds flew out and reached for the sky. Winton tugged at the cuffs of his black shirt and rolled up each sleeve as he always did before he played the trumpet. Whenever he or Matthew or Hermione gave a sublime performance, their annoying foibles became insignificant.

'You've got a this, that, and the other from Juilliard – you'd have us believe – but you haven't earned your stripes as a performer. A concert pianist you ain't!' He slammed the knife, he'd been absently rotating in his fingers, down. If cutlery could speak it would have shouted game, set, and match.

'There are many ways to be a musician,' she said quietly.

Brass players arrived and generated laughter and rowdy banter. They sat down and soon a moat of chunky instrument cases surrounded their table.

'The budgetary distribution isn't fair,' Winton said.

'Agreed. And you need better accommodation.'

'And a whole lotta respect,' Winton glared.

'Same goes for me.'

'Try being black.' Winton narrowed his eyes and sat forward. 'There's one scholarship for rock students, twelve for classical. On official occasions, when the platitudes flow, you've not once mentioned rock. You brag about the classical stream's success stories, but Turalong's rock stars don't get a look in.'

'What? I've presided over one formal occasion as yet and there were no public speeches.' She wanted to tell him her goal was to address the inequalities and to dissolve borders between the rock and high art genres, but he wouldn't believe her.

'It was shoddy, damn shoddy, you applied.'

'I didn't just apply. I was appointed. Someone has to do the job. It's not the easiest. I chase paper trails, monitor budgets, attend endless meetings, sort out messes, and cop flack from everyone. Do you think you'd be any better?'

Winton wasn't listening. She watched the brass players fool around. She enjoyed their camaraderie, the playfulness. Beams of light streamed through the ceiling to floor window which afforded views of the canteen garden. She liked the potted lavender, the banksia's crimson hues.

'No, not at all,' Winton rolled his eyes. 'The job should have been advertised. I've got contacts in the UK. I could have made some good suggestions.' Winton slapped at a mosquito.

'Never mind. Can you work with me?'

'The alternative is?'

'Go back to London.'

'That's uncalled for.' Winton shook his head and his dread locks danced.

'I want you...' Beat had his full attention now.

'To?'

'Not take any issue about our school to Thorne unless you've run it by me first.'

'Paranoia's kicking in.'

'Can you promise?'

But Winton never answered because Polly sidled up. Beat could have hugged her. Winton brightened too. 'You're looking stunning as always.' Polly beamed. Without even a cursory nod at Beat, the trumpeter stomped off. Beat couldn't help herself, 'Randy Newman! Leon Russell! Bill Evans!' she said to his back.

'Tense?' Polly asked.

'You have no idea.'

'Melody's waiting for you. To discuss discrimination. Remember?'

Polly was good value but, she could be annoying, the way she stated the obvious and always so prim and proper. Beat had never liked being told what to do. Never mind, the clear blue sky suggested a walk in the Botanical Gardens, and she'd have a badly needed moment to herself.

'How could I forget?' Beat moaned, grabbed a tissue and blew her nose.

'Avoid sympathising with Mel too much,' Polly said. 'I don't need to remind you, do I?'

10

VERISMO

BEAT dashed into the dean's studio. The cellist's orange and pink striped top was an eye-popper. She would have to be tactful, because she suspected the session could easily sour.

Beat knew that fully fledged solos didn't often come Melody's way. Backing singers, trombonists, and lower-stringed instrumentalists like double bassists often contribute a bass line, depth, texture, and colour in a performance, but the chances for them, and cellists, to shine were few and far between. Cellists, like trombonists, often rose to the crest of the music world by swapping their instrumental voice for a political one. Beat wondered if Melody's visit was a cry for attention but dismissed the thought as churlish. She'd have to be careful not to carry over the unpleasant vibe from her chat with Winton into this meeting. Polly's tray of tempting pastries and fresh coffee was as yet untouched.

'Polly's taking notes.' Beat gestured to her assistant.

Melody nodded approvingly. 'I'm here to represent female students.'

'Thanks for doing so,' Beat said.

'It's kinda ironic you're the dean because Turalong Arts sanctions gender bias.'

Winton's '*You just don't fit the gig*' popped into Beat's head.

'Say whatever you need to.'

'Yeah, well, the culture doesn't support women. I'm the only classical-cum-rock cellist.'

'I enjoyed hearing you in the pub the other night,' Beat said.

'I'd no idea you were there, but thanks,' Melody mumbled. 'I've got a thick hide. Mostly I cope.'

'With what?' Beat leant forward.

'Intimidating bullshit like, "We'll go belly up with a girl improvising solos."'

'How is it in rehearsals?'

'I vamp a tune on the rare occasion I'm asked, and the guys drown me out. It's tough to spin a lick, because I can't hear what I'm doing.'

'How soul destroying.' Beat copped a warning look from Polly because she'd promised her assistant she'd be impartial.

'Have you analysed the ratio between male and female applications?' Melody enquired, helping herself to a blueberry pastry.

'No, but it sounds like I'd better start,' said Beat. The school's courses were outmoded and to cap it all, there was embedded prejudice against women. With such colossal deficits, how could she rebuild, let alone transform, the school's reputation?

'Last year,' continued Melody, 'four hundred and eleven people applied to do rock. 270 were female, and 141 were male. And yet, seventy of the successful candidates were male, and only ten were female.'

'How did you come by those figures?' Beat asked.

'From the student rep on the school board.'

Hermione burst in, startling everyone.

'Let's program *Quartet for The End of Time* for a lunchtime concert! Messiaen wrote it in a concentration camp after he was captured by the Germans in the Second World War. It was the first time he braided birdsong into his music.'

Exasperated, Beat clapped her hands to underpin her words. 'Not. Now.'

Hermione stared at Melody quizzically and left. Polly closed the door. 'Melody, go on please.'

'As women are not represented on rock's audition panels, the shortfall of female places is hardly surprising.'

'Meaning?'

'The chair says ignorant things.'

'Like?' Beat was appalled. The applicants paid a hefty audition fee.

'There's nothing worse than women on campus.'

Beat was flustered, deciding what issue to tackle first, when the cellist began to read from her notes with all the gravitas of a prosecutor in a murder trial.

'Winton teaches history classes. He's compelling, knowledgeable, but fails to mention female players, bandleaders, songwriters, conductors, composers, and soloists. When I commented on this he said, "Women have babies. They're not creative."'

'Unbelievable,' Beat said.

'Yes. Peggy Glanville-Hicks, Billie Holiday, Diana Krall, Patti Smith, and Taylor Swift don't get a mention.'

Melody frowned at the carpet. Beat resolved to inspect that patch of carpet everyone gawped at. Were there fleas? Was it a portal into another world? Because now would be the perfect time for her to escape through it. Polly's foot nudged Beat's boot, an agreed upon signal if her mind wandered.

'... Then he said, "The problem is we've got students with," and he drew musical pause signs upside down to look like breasts on the white board. The guys honked. Hooted. Executed drum rolls on the tables. When I got up to leave, a bloke jeered, "Can't you lot take a joke?"'

'How insulting. How...'

Polly's eyebrows pinched together.

'And take a look at last year's visiting musicians.' Melody handed Beat a list. 'Great players, all men.'

'True.' Beat's eyes opened wide.

'When a woman is appointed, she's a dud like Madison.'

'A bit harsh Melody but I agree. Women need role models too.'

'But what are you going to do about it?'

Polly stiffened. Beat dared not look at her, knowing how she loathed disrespect from students. If her assistant was a cattle dog, she'd have bared her teeth, ready to spring.

'Ms Snow will need time to reflect on what you've told us this morning before she decides upon the best course of action,' said Polly.

~

'Pol, did I tell you about the retreat?'

'No.'

'Basically, it's an opportunity to talk about my goals and my intention to gender-proof our courses and concerts.'

Polly closed her laptop. 'Not everybody's reconciled to your promotion. If you pull the gender card too soon it could backfire.'

'Legally, we're obliged to offer optimal learning conditions for all students. Clearly, we're failing,' said Beat, regretting how stuffy and formal she sounded.

'Maybe but... be cautious.'

She'd also have to find a cunning way to bring the classical and rock streams together. Steven had failed to do this, as had his predecessors. The week before, Matthew stomped out of a meeting just because Winton arrived.

A wren outside her window balanced on a swaying pink hydrangea bloom. She'd read that the petal colour changed according to the soil's acidity. For blue flowers, the soil had to be acidic, pink blooms came from alkaline earth. If only it was that easy to change Matthew or Winton's mindset.

~

It was gusty and surprisingly chilly for late summer, not that Beat could feel it in her hermetically sealed office, but she could see it. Dislodged hats rolled along the pavement. Dozens of parents pushed buggies towards the Botanical Gardens. A few stopped to zip up their children's jackets. She ought to thank Winton for all the alfresco concerts he presented – they drew large crowds.

Winton referred to the classical stream as "the ruling class". She knew why, and she sympathised with him – she was possibly the only non-rock musician who did. Rock personnel taught in demountable classrooms which were unbearably hot in summer and too cold in winter. Classical staff argued rock players didn't need tuned pianos, air-conditioning, or sound-proofed practice rooms. Decent facilities were wasted on them. Deep in thought, Beat was unaware Connor stood at the doorway.

'Can I have a word? I heard about the retreat.'

'Come in then.' Polly must have told him about it which was irritating and a breach of trust.

'Our school is no different from a small village,' Connor explained. 'Whatever you think, quite apart from what you say, spreads like wildfire.'

'Connor, why are you here?'

'To warn you – it'll be confronting. Steven didn't do sleepovers.'

'You make it sound like a romp. This will be anything but. Besides, higher education retreats have been standard for decades.'

Connor said nothing. She dropped the tiniest portion of fish flakes into the tank. She liked seeing the goldfish surface with rude, gulping mouths.

'Connor, you urged me to share my vision.'

'But not in a stayaway scenario.'

'People want change. There's much to discuss.'

'Hardly a softly, tread lightly approach. You'll regret it.'

'Yes, if I take all the sessions. But Hermione will steer a session on diversifying concert programs. You can kickstart the debate about updating our courses.'

'Why me?' Connor frowned.

'Why not you?'

'It's not something I care to do.'

'Last time I checked, it's in your duty statement.'

'Discrimination will also be on the agenda.'

'Not again? That's old news,' Connor protested, his eyes fixed on the goldfish.

'Public opinion and legislation have moved on and yet here we are stuck in a sexist time warp.' Beat smiled.

Connor scratched his head. 'You're either brave or...'

'Nuts,' Beat affirmed. 'And you're a...'

'Stick in the mud?'

'You said it, not me.' Beat scribbled notes.

'Any thoughts about the Brahms?' Connor sounded defensive.

'Not yet.'

'A performance could be a circuit breaker,' Connor said.

How would she find time for that? Besides, she doubted she and Connor would have any rapport.

When Connor left, Beat had a bold idea. She'd need an affordable centre, not too far from Brisbane, and flexible enough to accommodate her horses.

11
MESTO

SUNLIGHT licked the green pasture. Dazzling white light crowned the treetops. She heard a guitarist play the introductory *twang twang twang* of Powderfinger's *(Baby I've Got You) On My Mind*, but the rhythm wasn't quite right. Her neighbour stooped to pick up fallen branches, a sure sign he was about to mow. His yapping fox terriers circled each other. She knew it wouldn't be long before his ride-on stirred swirls of dust. She turned away from the kitchen's picture window.

'Dan?'

'What now?'

Beat hated Dan's exasperation, the tone of martyred patience, as if she not only wasted his time, she *was* a waste of time.

'I'm getting nowhere.'

'Where do you want to get to?' Yawning, Dan brushed crumbs off the table.

'Anywhere other than where I'm in charge of recalcitrant misogynists.'

There was a sickening bang on the kitchen window. A territorial kookaburra had crashed into the glass mistaking his own reflection for a competitor.

'Should I cover the window with newspaper again?' Dan volunteered.

'Please. If he keeps doing that, he'll be a goner.'

Dan penned a note on an envelope.

'I could resign,' she said. It was spiteful of her, but she savoured Dan's discomfort about the threat to his lifestyle.

'You can't be serious.'

'Never more so.'

'Have a heart. Let's not go there today.'

A sulphur-crested cockatoo, head angled to the side, shuffled its feet along the veranda railing. Another landed on the table in a flash of white. Fascinated, she watched the newcomer preen its open wing.

'What's got into you?' Dan's tone had menace.

Now she had his full attention. Another cockatoo settled on the back of a chair. Cockies were her favourite birds, except when they nipped the heads off sunflowers she'd grown from seed.

'I'm over it, Dan.'

'We depend on your income.'

'Don't.'

'There's the mortgage, the car, those animals and...'

'You.' Beat added.

'Buying acreage was your idea.' Dan sat back.

At least he looked her square in the eyes.

'That place stresses me,' she said.

Dan breathed in deeply. 'What doesn't? Buy a horsey colouring book or a squeezy stress ball. Join a flipping yoga class like the rest of the Australian work force.' Dan eyed his reading matter, fury in his eyes. Then he looked contrite.

'I'm sorry for what I just said.'

'Apology accepted.'

'Beat, I admire your dedication and if you resign before achieving at least a few of the challenges you've set yourself, you'll fret.'

'How do you know?'

'Because I know you.' He closed his book about Mussorgsky. 'Incidentally, did you find out about Steven's resignation?'

'No.'

'Aren't you curious?'

'Sure, but I'll never get to the bottom of it. Thorne isn't telling anybody.'

'I smell a rat,' said Dan. 'Maybe getting to the bottom of Steven's exit could bolster your own efforts.'

'Possibly.'

Dan nodded. 'You've got clear goals. Funky ideas. Maybe you're in too much of a hurry. Threatening the status quo. Strikes me resistance is inevitable.'

'I could find another job.'

'Because you're afraid to...'

'What?'

'Exert leadership.'

Beat fought the constriction in her throat. Outside, the cockies had flown. Dan stood up, tucked his book and laptop under his arm and rested a hand on her shoulder.

'What's brought this on?' Dan's eyes softened. 'Resignation isn't an option.'

'Says who?'

'Cheer up. You've a day off tomorrow,' Dan said.

'That doesn't change anything.'

'Let's go shopping. Freshen you up. I'm convinced it could help if you looked the part.'

'Not even Winton is fussed about the way I look.'

'Who's he?'

'A British-Caribbean trumpeter. He's the rock specialist with a chip on his shoulder as tall as the London Shard.'

Dan laughed, squeezed her arm. Headed to his office. Door and subject closed.

~

Beat slipped between the rails of the wooden fence into the horses' yard. A butcherbird flew onto the fence beside her. She watched a team of ibis comb the grass for insects. She haltered Bolt and groomed him, teased spidery knots out of his tail. She ran her hand down each leg to check for inflammation. Lifting each hoof in turn, she picked out stones and dried mud. Next door, her neighbour's brush cutter whirred into life and a wild-eyed Bolt snatched his hoof from her hands.

If Dan was the breadwinner, the power dynamics would shift and if she were honest it wouldn't be in her favour. He'd hassle her about horse-related expenses. Surely the pressure would ease the more she got the musos onside. Meanwhile, she'd keep an eye out for another job. She didn't need to tell Dan about it. He'd never approve. No, he didn't have to know anything until she had a suitable offer in hand. Why did she want his permission? She didn't need it. The accented octave chords which fire the Finale of Chopin's *Piano Sonata in B minor* chimed in her head and stiffened her resolve.

12

MARCATO

'SHIT. I've overslept.' Beat kicked off the cover.

'You've got a day off, remember?'

'Yes. But I'm going for a ride.'

Dan squinted at the alarm clock. 'Fuck. At 5am?'

'I've got stuff to organise.'

'You're impossible.' Dan gathered the quilt around him and cocooned himself in its warmth.

'Charming, you mean.'

'No. Overly responsible.'

Beat ran into the kitchen, closely followed by the greyhounds. Before seeing to the horses, she gave each dog a bowl of kibble with a sprinkle of grated cheese and dollops of yoghurt. It was pitch black, but unless she fed the horses now, they'd still be grinding on hay when Polly arrived. She guessed there would be heaps of manure scattered across the yard. Her horses doubled their deposits whenever there was a full moon. She picked up the pitchfork and made a start on clearing the yard. The butcherbird that shadowed her outside was primed to catch exposed insects. Once she found the groove: scrape – scoop – scrape – scoop – dump, the yard would soon be spick and span.

Polly would be early. She was a stickler about time, which in her book meant turning up at least fifteen minutes too early.

The tacked-up horses were tied to the fence. She was happy, a tentative friendship had flared since she'd chatted to Polly in the pub that rainy afternoon. Would her assistant be surprised by her Wongara self, where her happiness sprung from the soil, keeping the paddocks clear of fallen branches, the sight of egrets perched on her horses' backs?

~

Back in the kitchen, she found Dan surly, brewing coffee, his wavy hair matted at the back. Dan's sulky silences set her teeth on edge. His brooding permeated the entire house and lasted anything from a day to a week or a month.

'D'you want me out of the way when Polly comes?'

'No. Seriously Dan, she's a gem, but you already know that from the night of Georgy's concert. Apart from Elvira, she's the only one I trust.'

'I bet she's unpopular.'

Dan opened a cupboard to find the sugar.

'Why?'

'Because she's the ultimate gatekeeper, she's like Cerberus, the multi-headed dog, guarding the gates of hell. Honestly, the way she parrots, "Beat is unavailable. I'll let her know you called," chills the soul.'

'Why haven't you told me this before?'

'You mean you don't know?' Dan scoffed, stared at her in disbelief.

Connor had implied as much. How did he put it exactly? "You've become inaccessible, office bound." Since then, she'd wandered through the building at a different time each day and stopped to talk to as many people as she could.

'Shall I sort out some morning tea? How long will the ride take?'

'About an hour. Refreshments would be great but don't go to any trouble. Got to rush.'

Beat checked her phone; it was six forty-five. She hurried downstairs. Under the house she bundled the saddles, bridles, and riding helmets into the peacock blue wheelbarrow, a gift from Dan, which juddered as she trundled it into the yard. Car wheels crunched on the gravelled driveway. Polly arrived just as she tightened Storm's girth.

'Don't tell me. I'm early,' said Polly.

'Yes. But it doesn't matter.'

A massive branch smashed to the ground. Bolt skittered sideways, pulled back hard snapping the pink twine which tied him to the wooden fence.

'Please, tell me I'm not...' Polly looked aghast and pointed at Bolt, 'riding him?'

'No. Bolt's way too forward. You're riding dear old Storm. He's kindly, a plodder.'

~

They rode through unkempt grass, past a neighbour's yard of white and tan Boer goats, the air had a salty tang, the horses' breathing audible in the stillness of the bush reserve. For Beat, the land framed by mangrove swamps and accessible through her own and her neighbour's back paddocks, was a haven, not just for koalas and frilled neck lizards but for her. Dan had dampened her mood, but she shooed him from her mind. Riding here was a gift she treasured. But she had forgotten about her assistant who looked far from happy as she gripped the reins in white-knuckled fear.

'I know it's hard, Pol, but if you're fearful or if you tense, Storm will think he's in danger, and he'll be more inclined to freak.'

Polly exhaled, dropped her shoulders and leaned back.

'How's this? Better?'

'Yes. Now, loosen the reins.'

'Like this?'

'Yes.'

They rode in silence, but the bush had plenty to say: the crackle of bark under hoof, a territorial koala growling, a magpie's throaty song. Storm paced in concert with Bolt, mimicking the horse's gait, the roll of his hips, his stride. Polly's hands softened.

'How d'you feel?'

'Better.'

'That's the way,' Beat encouraged. 'I don't want to talk about work, but for one thing.' She merely wanted to distract Polly because her voice would calm the horses.

'Go on then,' Polly said.

'Am I office bound?'

'In your shoes, I'd lock the door and throw away the key.' Polly pushed loose strands of hair under her helmet.

'Seriously, am I?'

'I don't think so.'

'Hermione thinks I'm chained to my desk.'

'Come to think of it, some do get cranky if I say you're unavailable,' Polly said.

'Like?'

'Guess.'

'Matthew?' Beat said.

'Yep.'

'How about whenever Matthew comes along you say go right in, she'll be keen to see you.'

'That wouldn't be true,' Polly protested.

'No, but it's a strategy, a way to promote better morale.'

'Right.'

'The following week we do the same but with Hermione or Winton.'

'How will you get the paperwork done?'

'I'll take more home.'

'I think...' Polly began, just as a massive goanna, a reptilian missile, skimmed the scrub at lightning speed. Bolt shifted his weight into his hindquarters and sprung forward into a gallop. Beat tried to pull him up but was unsuccessful and to her horror Storm sprinted in his wake. She looked back. Polly tugged on the reins which put her too far forward in the saddle and it gave Beat's retired racer the chance to grab the bit and fly.

'Polly,' Beat shouted. 'Loosen the reins, loosen them.'

'Can't,' shrieked Polly.

'Sit back, that's the way, he's going to—'

Storm braked, a *subito,* finite, authoritative stop worthy of the Aussie conductor Simone Young. Beat's face flamed as Polly vaulted over the horse's head and lay flat on prickly scrub, the reins in her hands.

Unfazed, Storm nibbled the grass. Polly was still, silent. Beat jumped off, tied Bolt to a tree and ran to her assistant, whose white face and rag doll sprawl terrified her.

'Are you okay?' Beat took hold of Polly's wrist and took her pulse. When Ellie had ridden Storm, he had trundled along like an old riding school nag.

'Speak to me, Polly. Any harm done?'

'I'm... winded. Can we wait here for a bit?'

'Yes. There's no hurry, take your time.'

Beat took her arm and slowly helped her to sit up.

'I've never been so scared.'

'That makes two of us.' Beat brushed prickles and dusty debris off Polly's pink shirt.

'Shall we head back? We could walk the horses in hand?'

'No. Help me get back up,' said Polly. 'Do the circuit as planned.'

Beat opened her phone to tell Dan they would be late, but there was no reception.

Minutes later, Polly was back in the saddle. Shards of bark clung to her clothes, but her colour had improved.

Neither spoke, but Beat drew comfort from the briny mangrove smell and the goshawks winging thermals in the sunny sky.

'Nearly home now.'

'That's a relief. But on another matter...'

'Yes.'

'Connor lurks around the office a lot these days,' Polly said.

'Lurks? You make him sound like a flasher.'

'I hardly ever saw Connor when Steven occupied your office.'

'He doesn't come and see me as much as Matthew or Hermione,' Beat protested.

'But he's keener. In step. Involved. I can feel it.'

Beat sat back to shift her weight into the back of the saddle and slow Bolt down.

'Really?'

'Yes, really. He used to fly all over the world conducting. Europe, North America. Everywhere. Johnny regularly booked him to conduct the State Orchestra.'

'Steven alluded to it, but I never knew the full picture because I'm not from Brisbane.'

'But you do know about him and...'

'I have to confess, I don't.'

'I'll tell you back at the house.'

~

Beat unsaddled the horses, fetched the hose, sluiced sweat off their steaming flanks. She looked back at the house. Dan was watching.

'How was the ride?' He had made cheese and tomato sandwiches with roughly sliced sourdough bread and too much butter. She hoped they tasted better than they looked.

'Great, until I fell off,' Polly smiled.

'Shall I ring for a doctor?'

'No. I'm fine, Dan.'

'I made morning tea. Had no idea you'd be gone for over two hours.'

'Everything all right?' asked Beat.

'You said an hour,' Dan said.

'It would have been had Polly not fallen off. I had to make sure she had recovered enough to ride back.'

'Excuse me, I need to freshen up.' Polly left the kitchen.

'Down the corridor, second left,' Beat called after her. With Polly out of earshot, she apologised, 'I'm sorry Dan. Can we hang out?'

'No. I'm going for a burn on the Ducati.'

'Stay. You'll like Polly when you get to know her.'

Beat turned to the sink and poured herself some water. She didn't want to fight in front of Polly. Heavy-hearted, she cast her eye around the kitchen. How shabby it looked, the scuffed green paintwork, the grimy surfaces, motorcycle magazines littered the floor, her green velvet couch, blitzed with dog hair. When Polly returned, Beat was ill at ease, ashamed of her grubby kitchen.

Dan sprang from his chair. 'Sorry, got to go. I hadn't realised how late it was.'

'Me too, actually.' Beat's assistant collected her things.

'Isn't it always the way?' said Dan. 'By the time you decide what to do, the day's half over.'

Polly blew Beat a kiss and left, but before the front door closed, she yelled, 'See you tomorrow.'

'Why did you arrange this on your day off?' Dan asked.

'Trail riding relaxes me. And Polly's a friend. I wanted the ride to be a bonding activity.' Beat chewed at the inside of her mouth, fought back tears. 'I've never had someone I work with here. But today wasn't about work.'

'We could have gone shopping,' Dan said.

'For what?'

'New clothes.'

'What's wrong with how I look?'

'The jeans, the daggy riding tops,' Dan said.

A heaviness – a C minor gloom– descended.

'I'm out of here.' Dan snatched his keys from the kitchen table.

'Don't go, please.' Beat made a move towards him, but he stepped away.

'If you bring someone here to ride again – and I suggest you don't – make them sign a disclaimer.' He struggled into his bulky safety jacket, picked up his helmet.

'Why?' Beat said.

'If Polly had been injured, she could have sued, and we'd have to sell up to pay the legal costs.'

Dan stomped off down the hall. She heard the clamour of discord capped by a strident timpani strike when the front door slammed.

13
ORCHESTRA

BEAT would not be bullied, not today. Enough was enough. Matthew was nudging fifty, but he looked thirty-something with his thick, boyish curls and eager manner.

'Come in.' Beat grinned in welcome, leaving her desk to sit opposite Matthew, primed to ignore his belittling sideswipes. It would be a choppy half hour, but she wouldn't be derailed.

'I know how busy you are,' Matthew drawled with a sarcastic accent on *busy,* 'but I had to see you out of loyalty.'

'Because?'

'Morale is rock bottom.'

'Tell me more.'

'Hermione drones on about how "staid" the last orchestral program was.'

'The Verdi, Tchaikovsky and—'

'Ravel. Yes.' Matthew confirmed.

'Really? Did you know that Steven selected those works against his better judgement because Hermione badgered him to program them.'

Matthew combed his bushy eyebrow with his finger and hesitated. 'Well, she's also upset her students' talents aren't sufficiently showcased in the works chosen for the orchestra to perform.

'I see.'

'My apologies for her turn of phrase but she insists that orchestral planning needs, "a bomb up its arse."'

'Matt, I couldn't agree more.'

The violinist frowned, his eyes narrowed. He detested any shortening of his Christian name.

'Also, there's grumbling about a certain American's exorbitant conducting fee,' said Matthew.

'Garrett's remuneration falls a long way short of that and he's taking several performance classes, lecturing, and teaching the piano.'

'But is it an appropriate use of funds, given we have an exceptional conductor on staff?' Today's fuchsia bowtie heightened Matthew's ruddy complexion, he looked unhealthy. Foppish.

'You mean Connor?'

'I do.'

'A variety of conductors is ideal,' Beat said. 'Because it mirrors the reality our graduates encounter in the profession. But I'm also in favour of player-led orchestras like the Australian Chamber Orchestra and London's Academy of St Martin in the Fields. Next year, I may not appoint a conductor at all.'

'The money saved by using Connor could be put to better use, like the purchase of superb instruments.' With a toss of his head, he flicked his plentiful fringe out of his eyes. Matthew's persistent idea of buying a Stradivarius or Amati violin to boost the school's modest instrument collection wasn't remotely achievable. The budget was already stretched to capacity. Such a treasure would have to be gifted.

'Connor told me he never wanted to conduct again,' Beat said. 'I can't force him.'

Matthew picked up the handbook and skimmed the pages until he reached a photo of himself in the strings section. 'Have you ever had a conversation about it?'

'Yes, I have.'

'Seems to me you must have misunderstood him.'

The silence gathered between them.

'Now, where were we?' he said at last.

'I'm attending the next orchestral meeting.' Beat said.

'No. Stay in your own lane. The orchestra isn't your concern.'

'But low morale most definitely is and I'm the only one who can action changes.'

Once he'd gone, the elusive fundraising idea she'd been chasing for days shone like a beacon and her exasperation evaporated.

~

Beat arrived early the next day to run her idea past Polly.

'Don't you look good in red,' Polly said.

'I was looking for a lost shoe. Instead, I found this jacket in the back of the wardrobe.'

'Look in your wardrobe more often then.'

'Maybe.' Beat smiled, hands behind her head. 'I've got an idea. If all goes to plan, it could stop Winton grizzling.'

'Cats meow, horses neigh, Winton moans.' Polly smiled. 'You hinted you were dreaming up a special project, so spill.'

'I'm thinking of an event starring Sian Williams the opera-trained pop singer and a combined school orchestra and backing group coached by Winton.'

'What a cocktail! But isn't Sian an overreach? She's a superstar and her fee must be astronomical.'

'She's an alumnus,' Beat countered. 'I'm going to persuade her to do it pro-bono.'

'Hopefully.' Polly looked doubtful. 'Would you want her to do aerial tricks?'

'I hadn't thought about it.'

'Wouldn't that add even more appeal?'

'Yes, it's a good idea. Now all I have to do is make it happen.'

'How?'

'First, I lobby the head of the Arts Centre for a reduced or a waived fee for the concert hall. He's on the Turalong Council after all.'

Polly brightened and gestured for Beat to continue.

'Next, I persuade Johnny Wood to foot the bill for a conductor?'

'Good luck with that.'

'I know he's creepy.'

'You could always use Connor?' Polly volunteered.

'No. He's... pompous, stuffy.'

'But in front of an orchestra he's electric.'

'Not sexy.'

'But a gem, a true believer once you get to know him. Students take to him. Scrubs up well too.' Polly clammed up.

'About the general idea?' Beat had heard enough about Connor. She noticed a stain on the red jacket's sleeve and rolled up her cuff.

'Great if you can pull it off,' said Polly cautiously. 'I'll make those appointments. Sounds Best have sponsored the school in the past. Should I arrange a time with the managing director?'

'Please. Thanks, Pol. Best I see them today.'

Brass, whipped by wild percussion, rhythm guitar, and a booming bass with soul feels sparked in her head and spurred her on. She ought to canvass the idea with her colleagues and Thorne first, but she couldn't wait until the afternoon or tomorrow because her mood could flatline. She was inspired now. Reckless, outgoing, fizzing with intention.

'You're firing on all cylinders today,' her assistant said. 'I think it's the jacket.'

~

Beat decided to walk, but she hadn't known drenching rain was expected. The sky darkened. Torrential rain fell on the concreted landscape. Waiting at an intersection, close to the curb to cross the road, the wheels of a truck ploughed through pooling water and splashed her jeans and jacket. She looked down at her saturated outfit. Dan's jibe about her not looking the part crossed her mind. She quickened her pace, pushing the intrusive thought away.

In the Arts Centre, she waited on a plush, plum sofa outside Nicholas Barker, the CEO's, office, her mind blank. Her ideas flowed when she hadn't prepared what to say. She'd learned the hard way it was better for her to improvise, to gauge the mood, and shape her tone to suit the energies of her audience. Then, she could be convincing. But when she was ushered into a grand Tasmanian oak-floored office, Beat's courage waned.

Nicholas Barker, the sixty-something CEO was a silver fox, charm incarnate and by all accounts, devilishly canny. He sat at his expensive, lustrous wooden desk, a panoramic cityscape behind him.

'How can I help?' Barker said.

'I'm following up on my email,' Beat said.

'When was it sent?'

'This morning.'

'Remind me.' He pushed his blue-framed glasses further up his nose. Had he chosen them because, putting the deep blue colour aside, they resembled the black specs of the beleaguered Shostakovich?

'It's about a major fundraiser with a world-famous headliner.' She was uncomfortable in her cold, damp jeans in the chilling air-conditioned office. 'But there's no point if...'

'What?'

'We have to track a venue with a big seating capacity. We'll need to generate enough box office to offset costs.'

'I'm guessing the surplus is to purchase a Stradivarius?' Barker said.

How annoying. Matthew had been in his ear too.

'No, it's to go towards a bespoke building for our rock stream.'

Barker's friendly expression darkened.

'Beatrice, there's no such thing as a fundraiser. Even the Australian Chamber Orchestra runs at a loss, or at best breaks even, on national tours. I'm sure you know that.'

'Yes, I do,' she admitted.

'What's the draw card?'

'Not the same old Bach and Brahms.'

Amusement glinted in the CEO's eyes. He leaned forward, elbows planted on the burnished redgum desk.

She scanned the paintings on the fresh white walls: Deborah Walker, William Robinson, Mostyn Bramley-Moore, Elisabeth Cummings, and a photo-realist horse portrait by Michael Zavros.

'Who then?'

'Sian Williams.'

'Interesting. Yes, I know her. Very woke, all about climate change and the extinction crisis. My kids adore her. She flies across boundaries and blows-them-up. Her operatic range is extraordinary like last century's Nina Hagen.'

'What d'you think?'

'Splendid choice, Beatrice. But aren't these mixed-genre concerts old hat now?'

'You're right, which is why I'm going to give it an innovative spin,' she said.

'I won't ask you what this spin consists of because I don't think you'll tell me. My first thought is, can you...?'

'I've negotiated a mate's rate. She's one of ours,' Beat said. It wasn't technically true as yet, but it bolstered her pitch to this formidable operator.

'Good, but she'll be controversial with her preachy lyrics.'

The CEO opened up his diary.

'True. But Sian can bind the rock and classical streams together,' explained Beat. 'Without these opposite forces bonding, the school can't reach its full potential.'

'Remember the mega-moneyed high-brow are not low-brow tolerant.'

'True, but I'll be targeting a younger set.'

'There'd have to be something in it for us. I could offer you a reduced fee for the concert hall if—'

A smart-suited, stern woman opened the door, pointed at the jumbo pseudo railway clock and left.

'What do you have in mind?' Beat asked.

'I want State Orchestra members to mentor your youngsters and play alongside them on the night,' he said. 'Ours is the only Australian orchestra I'm aware of missing out on a special financial loading for contributing to the training of future orchestral players.'

Beat wrinkled her nose. 'Frankly, it would be easier to climb Mount Everest in stilettos.'

'You have a point,' Barker laughed at his pun.

'Johnny Wood detests mentoring schemes.'

'But that's my driver,' he said. 'If you can swing that, I'll waive the fee. How does that sound?' His phone rang. 'Got to take this I'm sorry. What've you got to lose, Beatrice?'

She nodded, glad to leave his fortress with its strategically placed showy brochures and the grandest desk she'd ever seen. Outside, a gusty wind blew her hair across her face. Beat hugged her folder tight as she walked to the ABC building. She reached the ceiling to floor glass walls at Southbank and walked through the revolving doors into a sunny, light-streamed reception. A receptionist handed her an iPad and asked for her signature.

'Who are you here for?'

'Johnny Wood.'

'What time were you to meet?'

'Now.'

'Ms Snow, take a seat.'

Time passed and many visitors had approached the desk since she'd arrived, and each one had been given a security tag and told to take the escalator to the suite of offices upstairs. She knew Johnny played games. No doubt keeping visitors waiting was one of them. Some kind of power play. She approached the receptionist again after fifteen minutes.

'Still waiting?' Muttering under his breath, he dialled Johnny's extension.

'He's been held up. Won't be long.'

Beat yawned. If she wasn't careful, she'd fall asleep. But Hermione's shrill greeting jolted her awake.

'Funny you're here. I've been in a rehearsal. What's your excuse?'

'I'm seeing Johnny.'

'What about?' Hermione looked chic in a black trench coat, red pants, and towering black heels. The foyer cowered in her formidable presence.

'I want to talk to him about it first.'

'Buckle up,' she shrugged, 'He roared at the clarinets in rehearsal. Turned puce.'

When Johnny swaggered towards Beat with a toothy grin he cut Hermione dead. 'Come up. But make it quick.' Then he ran up the escalator, flashing his whiter than white trainers. Beat struggled to keep up.

'Sit there,' he pointed to a retro green armchair with wooden arms in his office. 'What brings you here sweetie?'

'An opportunity.' Recoiling at his saccharine endearment, she sat taller. Willed herself not to fidget, not to play with her hair.

'I read your email. You want to get down and dirty with Sian I'm listening.' Johnny cupped his ears.

Beat opened her mouth to reply but the telephone rang. Johnny picked up.

'Absolutely not.' Johnny slammed the receiver down.

If he'd been speaking to Nicholas, his mood would worsen. Her palms prickled with sweat.

'Shoot.' Johnny glowered at her.

'I've got a proposition.'

'Which is?' he spoke softly but with a menacing edge while scraping dirt from under his fingernail with a paper clip.

Beat breathed deeply. She'd best be quick and get out of there. 'For your orchestra to perform with our classical and rock musicians.'

'Isn't that just the tastiest.' Johnny's forehead wrinkled, his fingers drummed the chair's arm. He paused. Flicked each of his fingertips against his thumb. She doubled her efforts to look composed.

'Who put you up to this?' Johnny's eyes narrowed.

'No one. I want to offer our students a rewarding experience.'

'Right.'

Beat spoke fast fearing he was on the verge of an ugly outburst. 'By enlisting professionals to join us in a genre crossing event.'

'You've got a bloody nerve,' Johnny tapped his foot. 'The answer's no.'

'I wanted you to have first option.' Beat's mouth was dry. Her eyes found the jug of water and two glasses on a nearby cupboard. Out of reach.

Johnny grabbed a paper tissue, twisted a corner into a point and poked around in his cavernous nostrils as if he was alone. Disgusted, her fists tensed into angry balls. She considered walking out.

'How considerate Beatrice. But it's still a big fat no.'

'Then, I'll take my offer to Orchestra Queensland.'

'You've a bloody nerve.' Johnny stomped across the room, hands clasped behind his back.

'As you know Johnny, orchestras who mentor young players can apply to government for financial remuneration.'

'I am sick and tired of Nicholas Barker pestering me about this. He wants us to dance to his tune.'

Johnny grabbed a blue watering can and, with his back towards her, he over-watered the pots of aspidistra and peace lilies perched on the window ledge. Excess water trickled down the wall. She waited. The more aggressive he became, the steelier she would be. She had residual anger left over from yesterday's exchange with Dan.

'Now, you listen to me,' Johnny yelled, jabbing his finger at Beat.

'Don't. I loathe shouters.'

'Yeah, yeah. Gotcha.' To her amazement, Johnny sighed and flopped into a chair.

'Tell me all.'

'Nick Barker offered us the Concert Hall for free if...'

'I smell a rat.' Johnny tapped his nose. 'What does wily Mr Barker want in return?'

'Nothing much, except for your players to combine with ours.' Beat sat back, determined not to look flustered.

'I've serious reservations.'

'Yes, you said.'

'It's demeaning for pros to pair with amateurs.'

'Thing is, Johnny, your players are already doing that,' said Beat.

'What are you implying?'

'The school's musos are emerging professionals. The very same you hire to boost the orchestra for works with huge instrumentation. I'm thinking Berlioz' Symphonie Fantastique and Mahler Symphonies. Theo, an exceptional violin student pays his rent by guesting for you.'

'This stuff does my head in.'

'Fine. I'm leaving.'

'Wait,' Johnny grinned. 'Not so fast. We'll do it.'

Beat waited a moment. 'And can you lend us one of your visiting conductors as a freebie?'

~

Grey clouds clogged the sky as she bustled towards Sounds Best's premises in Adelaide Street. From the glass lift ascending to the eighth floor, she caught glimpses of sales assistants idling in showrooms. She marvelled at a fleet of gleaming Yamaha Grands on the sixth floor. On the seventh, she waved at guitar students browsing through sheet music.

When the lift stopped a tall, elderly man had been waiting for her and welcomed Beat into his office. A glass cabinet contained gold and silver trophies. On the walls, were numerous identical gold plaques from consecutive years inscribed with "Best Music Store".

Christopher's much younger, trophy wife flashed an earnest toothy welcome from the framed photo on his desk. Beat wouldn't be surprised if her teeth glowed in the dark and he could read by them.

'How can I help?' Christopher steepled his sun-spotted hands.

'Do you believe Turalong's music students should be prepared for the profession?'

'Yes, I do.' His weathered face, fissured like parched ground, looked puzzled.

'Do you think the orchestra must prove its relevance?' Beat drummed the table. *Ta dum.*

'Of course,' he said.

'Should high art concerts appeal to the young?' She clapped. *Ta dum.*

'Without a doubt.' He unwrapped a toffee.

'Then I need financial backing for a daring, youth-targeted spectacular.' *Ta dum ta dum.*

'I see.' He edged the bowl of caramel toffees her way. She grinned. Pushed it back.

'There's a lamentable attitude…' Beat continued.

'About what, especially?'

'That the classical stream is more important than the rock.'

'Always has been the case.' Christopher looked bemused as she laid out her plans for the fundraiser.

'Which is why I'm combining the rock and classical musos in a special event.'

'And you want?'

'Support. A contribution. A financial…'

'Ah,' he laughed, folding his arms. 'Exactly how will my company benefit?'

'We'll enshrine your company's support on all promotional materials, programs, car stickers, T-shirts, mouse pads, and coffee cups. We'd foot the bill for an interval reception for your…'

Christopher sat back, arms folded. 'Beatrice, frothy items don't interest me in the least and if I'm to support this, I'd want provisos.'

'Try me?'

'I want Connor to direct this spree.' Christopher looked determined, his voice no longer warm but flinty. Beat groaned inwardly.

'Why?'

'He's good with youth orchestras. Literate when it comes to popular music.'

'And your next condition?' Beat asked, suppressing her irritation at another plea for Connor.

'The billing must read, "Sounds Best and Turalong Music School" presents…'

'I can't approve that.'

'Why?'

'There's a chain of command. If Marilyn Thorne, my superior agrees to it, she has to get the go ahead from the University's Vice-Chancellor.'

'How insufferably hierarchical.'

'Maybe.'

'Beatrice, don't faff around. Meet these conditions and I'm prepared to contribute $75,000.' He gazed hard into her eyes.

'I can't guarantee...' her mind in a spin, Beat heard the thump of her heart.

'But you'll try?'

She opened her mouth to speak but with a supercilious smile, he bowed his head and indicated to the open door.

14
MYSTERIOSO

COMMUTERS swarmed towards the bus stop on the main road. Polly had already exited for the day, and it was high time Beat left too. She picked up her holdall, stuffed it with paperwork and turned around, ready to leave, but a trembling Elvira stood in the open doorway.

'What's up, Elvira? You're deathly pale.'

'Come with me.' She grabbed Beat's hand.

Elvira fumbled for the key in her tapestry bag and opened her studio door. Beat sat on the yellow leather sofa studded with Moroccan cushions.

'Tell me what happened?' Beat said gently.

'I was playing the second page of Beethoven's *Pathetique Sonata* where the left hand has that octave tremolo on C.' She demonstrated the fluttering movement on the piano's closed lid. 'I had a pounding headache, because Beethoven's spicy seventh chords has that effect on me.'

'Interesting. Do you see colours?'

'No,' Elvira said.

'I see red and pink when I hear them.'

'Please. Just listen.' Elvira took a deep breath.

'I am.'

'I heard a man's gruff voice. He spoke in German,' she said. "A lot of notes, Madam. Noise." I'm translating but that's the gist of it.'

Beat tried not to look sceptical or, heaven forbid, amused.

'I thought I'd left a radio on or overheard a conversation in the corridor. I kept on playing.'

Beat's eyes scanned the space. If this was hashtag supernatural, the stuff of wraiths and poltergeists, there wasn't a chance she'd get away soon. She might as well make herself comfortable. She liked the studio's energy and how every available surface was swathed in colourful silks and velvet cloths. Tea lights flickered in glass jars, tormenting the fire detectors. Chairs fanned around a smart TV. Elvira adored ambient lighting and she had a medley of assorted lamps. A purple bookcase brimmed with sheet music, a red rug graced the floor, and an iPad streamed images of herself posing at the piano – her students, one of Daisy, her cocker spaniel, and her garden.

No wonder she inspired loyalty in her students with such a comfy, extravagant, bright, and textured studio. An Aladdin's cave, a bowerbird's vibrant hideaway in the grey heart of fusty academe.

'Did you hear the voice again?'

'I did. Yes.'

'What did it say?'

'"Stop woman. My ears are hurting."'

Beat clapped her hand over her mouth to suppress a grin.

'It was freezing in here. When I touched the keys, it was as if I'd pressed my fingers onto ice.'

Beat was engrossed, her journey home forgotten. She was pleased Elvira trusted her enough to share her bizarre encounter. Beat was fond of the piano convenor and yet perplexed more often than not by her sensitivities. Elvira could feel slighted by a real or imagined insult. But auditory hallucinations with a belligerent spirit claiming to be Beethoven, well, that was a first. She had read somewhere that if you hallucinate in sound, you're likely to have a mental illness, if your hallucinations are visual, it could be a symptom of a neurological disease. Beat was entertained by the pianist's story, but sceptical. Elvira obviously believed Beethoven had spoken to her, and she would soon ask the inevitable, 'Do you believe me?' Elvira's alleged visitation reminded her of another phenomenon, but what that had been she couldn't recall.

'I was shivering. So chilled I put that on.' Elvira pointed to a woollen duffle coat slung over a chair. 'I was about to leave but the voice said, "If you want this school to prosper, stage a Beethoven and rock festival."'

'Rock, just imagine, wouldn't that go down a treat?' Beat was taken aback by Elvira's uncanny allusion to rock.

'The voice became demanding. "Feature my *Seventh Symphony,* but on your fire-ravaged, flood prone island, Richard Tognetti is the only one who can conduct it."'

'Really? He mentioned Tognetti?'

Elvira nodded, eyebrows raised.

'You're killing me. What else did it say?'

'Not an *it,* Beat. Please. Show some respect.'

'Go on.'

'"Those dead-eared, ham-fisted trolls you teach devour your energy. Present my masterpieces and celebrate the popular music of the masses."'

Elvira was adamant she'd had a run-in with the irascible nineteenth century compositional giant. Beat's role had some professional perks. In what other occupation would she be having a chat to a colleague about a famous dead person dropping in for a chat? She hadn't had such fun in months.

'Did he say anything else?'

The pianist lowered her voice. '"Assemble an army of true-hearted pianists to perform my sonatas. Not the bash, thump, and rush brigade. I admire Piers Lane, he's performed all of them on a Stewart, an ingenious instrument. How I'd have loved to compose pieces on a magical concert grand with fourteen extra keys. I was glued to the spot. Astonished."'

Beat zipped up her jacket.

'The light intensified, a crescendo of brightness,' Elvira said, 'as if someone was winding a dimmer switch forward.'

Could Elvira have been drinking, over-working, using cocaine, or on some kind of medication? And how could she possibly ask such a thing without causing deep offence? Then, she remembered.

'Elvira, have you heard of Rosemary Brown?'

'No.'

'She was an ordinary woman from the last century. In the mid-sixties, she claimed Liszt, Chopin, and Schubert all channelled new compositions through her.'

'Wow!'

'Yes, she captured a thousand works by dead composers on paper which were all played and recorded.'

'Was she taken seriously?'

'She had believers – Peter Katin, the pianist for one. He recorded all of the 'new' Chopin pieces. The British composer Richard Rodney Bennett was convinced Brown was genuine because she had minimal piano skills and couldn't read music.'

'Far out!' Elvira exclaimed.

'Bennett got stuck with a composition he was working on. Next day, Rosemary Brown knocks on his door. She tells him Debussy had explained to her how he could progress his new work. When Katin tried Debussy's solution it worked.'

'You don't think I'm crazy then?'

Beat shook her head, avoided Elvira's eyes. Flicked through a *Piano Legends* magazine.

'I can see it in your eyes,' Elvira scowled, 'you don't believe me?'

'There are phenomena we don't understand.'

'Whatever.'

'You've had a bad fright,' Beat said.

Elvira closed her volume of Beethoven sonatas. 'Yes, I'm scared. I need a new room.'

Beat looked around, tapped the sofa. 'But there isn't another space where we can fit two grand pianos and all your colourful furnishings.'

'What d'you suggest I do?' Elvira asked.

'Bring in seedpods and lavender and rosemary oil to cleanse the room, just like you did in the recital hall the day before that concert when you performed Carl Vine's *Piano Sonata no. 1.*

'Cleansing is good normally, but I couldn't knowingly spirit Beethoven away. How disrespectful.'

'And if you're keen on curating a festival as... well... yes along the lines Beethoven prescribed you can sell the idea in Monday's meeting.'

Elvira dropped her phone, a worn volume of Chopin preludes, a bottle of peach Kombucha, and three red apples into her cavernous shoulder bag.

'Your odd experience intrigues me. A funny serendipity I suppose because...'

'What?'

'I'm about to ask Sian if she would be the headlining act in a flashy rock-cum-classical fundraiser.'

'How weird,' countered Elvira.

'I'm sure the others will like your concept of pairing rock with Beethoven's *Seventh Symphony*. His *Triple Concerto* would be a showy vehicle for Theo, Melody, and Georgy as the soloists. Providing you agree of course.' Beat shuffled the piano magazines into a neat pile.

'You don't get it Beatrice. This was *not* my idea.'

Elvira pulled on her elegant black suede gloves, pinned her hair back and shook the creases out of her long black skirt. Handing Beat the keys, Elvira said, 'Lock up when you leave,' and she flounced out, head held high, like a prideful heroine in a Henry James novel.

15

FILL

SHE heard Winton's muted, plaintive trumpet in the modal masterpiece *Blue in Green* underscored by a pianist playing an upright piano with a honky tonk voice. She remembered that this had originally been claimed as a Miles Davis original but was actually composed by the jazz pianist, Bill Evans. He would have approved of the young pianist who nuanced the harmonies beautifully in spite of the old instrument's limitations. Seeing her there, Winton stopped playing, opened his office door and the student obligingly closed the piano lid, picked up his things and left. Glue traps for mice and rat traps were everywhere Beat looked.

Polly had often asked Winton if she could borrow the tall kentia palms, which stood sentry outside his door, to dress the recital hall's stage. So far, he'd always refused, not wanting his plants' well-being jeopardised by nervy, classical geeks with sweaty palms.

The rock building was substandard, deplorably run down. Winton complained about it constantly and he couldn't be faulted for that – it was the manner in which he whined about it; his words bloated with belligerent sarcasm. She knew the Music School could never be counted as the place to study rock if it continued to be housed in such dilapidated quarters.

When Winton saw her, he showed her into his office. He laid his trumpet on his desk. She filled him in on the proposed fundraiser.

'Rock and classical?' Winton threw his head back and guffawed. 'Rock is light years away from turntablism, hardcore, plunderphonics, and video game music the kids are into.'

'Sian's cool. And based in London.'

'The woman is operatically trained. She's hardly a rock singer. That's cheered me right up.' Winton slapped a hand on his leg.

'I want to unite the classical and rock streams on stage.'

'What are you fundraising for?'

'State-of-the-art rock facilities. But Sian requires 3% of our profits to go to a wildlife fund to purchase forest for a koala breeding program,' Beat explained.

'You're having me on?'

'No, the idea is to generate enough cash to initiate a rock building project.'

'I appreciate the thought.'

Beat looked around Winton's cramped office and reacquainted herself with the wall of assorted mirrors which created a magical illusion of space. Every nook and cranny hosted a potted plant. A strand of the beaded succulent perched on a tall, pine bookcase dangled almost to the floor. Remarkably, given the plants' confinement, they flourished.

Winton huddled over his desk, sifting through his CD collection. Beat sat down.

'Fuck! Beatrice Snow you're lobbying me.' He grinned, twiddled an earring between his finger and thumb.

'Lobbying? Not at all.'

'Which of your fave dead whites is in the spotlight this time?' Winton asked.

'Beethoven.'

'I won't state the obvious.'

'Which is?'

'Rock doesn't mix with deaf nineteenth century creatives.'

'Except, isn't Greig's *Hall of the Mountain King* meant to be the first heavy metal song?'

'Really?' Winton scratched his head.

'Everybody – well maybe not Matthew – agrees our concert content should be broader. Revamped.'

'Really?'

'Absolutely,' Beat confirmed.

'Yet Beethoven's the star turn.'

'A star turn. You and yours will be in the limelight in the festival's finale.'

Wearily, Winton swivelled around to face her. Beat reeled from his rank breath of cigarettes and booze.

'I'm also organising a staff getaway,' Beat admitted.

'Blimey! What for?'

'To talk. Shake the place up. Kickstart change. Broker meaningful communication.'

'Will you be handing out boxing gloves?'

~

Beat ran up the stairs to the second floor. She walked past a trumpeter rehearsing Copland's *Fanfare for The Common Man*. If she hadn't been in a hurry, she would have stopped to listen, either to the trumpeter or a percussive Latin American ensemble improvising call and response patterns on congas, bongos, claves, and cabara. There was something irresistible about hearing snatches of music in rehearsal because it was raw, a fearless exploration, the element of risk not yet forfeited. But there wasn't time. She had to find Elvira and persuade her not to tell her colleagues about Beethoven's 'visit'. These sessions with Hermione and Connor and co derailed quickly, and if Elvira played a supernatural card, Matthew would peddle comic relief at her expense. But the piano convenor wasn't in her studio or the staff room.

'Hey,' she asked two cellists on the landing, their shoulders pressed together, just as their instruments lay hip to hip. 'Seen Elvira recently?'

'Try Hermione's office.'

Beat knocked on the clarinettist's door and breezed in, out of breath.

'Well, well, well, what a surprise,' sneered Hermione. 'Why aren't you shackled to your desk?'

Beat didn't take offence; she was increasingly immune to Hermione's taunts. Steven had refused to talk to Hermione for weeks after one of her especially mean jibes.

'Sorry, but I need a word with Elvira.'

Reluctantly, Elvira decanted three volumes of Beethoven's sonatas from her batik-skirted lap onto the floor. Beat ushered her to the landing. Elvira's cotton dress revealed too much of her back, a garment she knew Winton would dismiss as beach attire.

'Your concept of a two-day Beethoven and rock festival appeals,' said Beat.

Elvira placed her gloved hands on the banister and gazed into the stairwell.

'Is that what you came up here to tell me?'

'Yes. I'm also thinking *how* the idea came to you isn't important. I wanted to say that attributing the concept to Beethoven is unnecessary.'

'Why don't you introduce...' Elvira countered.

'No. It's your idea.'

'Let's be clear Beatrice. It's yours and Beethoven's.'

~

Violinists, cellists, and viola players clattered down the stairs and Beat remembered Matthew had a strings workshop in the afternoon. Matthew had a bee in his bonnet about string players rehearsing too much. If Matthew had his way, they wouldn't play in piano trios or string quartets. His concern wasn't altruistic but because he wanted them to channel their energies exclusively into the Lyrebird, the chamber orchestra he'd founded.

Restless, she roamed the corridors, her ears buffeted by the crossfire of sound. Dedicated to woodwind, piano, voice, and classical guitar, the second and third floor practice studios were far removed from brass and percussion's hideout on the ground floor. In the absence of soundproofing, there were always competing musical strains, a crowded acoustic, sonic anarchy which inhibited critical listening. Musicians justifiably complained, but all Beat could do was to add soundproofing to her ever-growing and unattainable wish list.

Who would construct a sports centre without a swimming pool, a gym without equipment, a drama school without a stage? The Utzon-designed Sydney Opera House was an architectural wonder admired across the world, yet its poor acoustic had been ignored for decades until the interior was completely refurbished. When Opera Australia staged a production, it had been difficult for the orchestral players in the pit to hear each other, let alone the soloists on stage. A musician paints in sound, and he or she can filter out background noise if they have to, but the player has to concentrate extra hard to create the high standards they're striving for. Practising would be far more productive if a musician's hearing wasn't blitzed by acoustic chaos.

Beat quickened her pace to the ground floor teaching studio, which doubled as a meeting room. If her phone was correct, she was five minutes late. Connor, Winton and Hermione were seated, but where was Elvira? The atmosphere was genial and Beat prolonged the preliminaries in the hope the piano convenor would turn up. But the patience of those assembled was running low. Winton tapped a Latin American groove on the table and from Connor's pained expression he wanted to be anywhere but there. Finally, Elvira arrived and stacked a bundle of scores onto the grey melamine table.

'Elvira,' Beat said, 'tell us about the two-day fundraising festival.'

'Firstly, the idea wasn't...' Beat coughed loudly. 'I want to include rock players, classical pianists, guitarists, singers, woodwind, brass, percussion, and strings,' Elvira said.

'My giddy aunt!' Winton looked sceptical.

'Yep, good one,' Hermione confirmed. 'And we can seduce the public with Mozart's gorgeous lyricism.'

'I'm guessing the world pines for a reprise of Mozart's *Clarinet Concerto* with you as soloist?' Matthew drawled.

'And why ever not?' Hermione checked her appearance in a pocket-sized make-up mirror.

'I'd support the music of Mary Poppins does Death Metal, Red Velvet, Radiohead, Vampire Weekend, retro Cold Play, and Queen,' Winton said.

Hermione flashed today's silky plum nails and reached for a handful of potato chips. Elvira's mouth opened and closed like a koi fish.

'If there's a band, I hope it's an all-woman special.' Hermione brushed crumbs off her top.

'Are there any?' Winton jibed. 'Yes, I know: The Go Go's, The Bangles, The Ronettes, Pussy Riot, and...'

'Sian will need you to put a band together, Winton. You'll play solos and fills.'

'How tiresome,' sneered Hermione. 'Isn't she merely a revved up imitation of Taylor Swift?'

'Beethoven's in the mix too,' said Beat.

Connor groaned.

'Don't be negative. Beethoven's a topical revolutionary who fronted classical traditions initially and blew them apart later,' Beat said.

'Audiences feel a deep connection to him because of his commitment to the everyday man and woman,' Elvira enthused. 'I want Beethoven's *Seventh Symphony* and the *Triple Concerto*, on day one. Sian, on day two.'

Beat heard a collective groan. She couldn't tell if it was directed at her, Elvira, Sian, or Beethoven.

'And yet again we dilly and we dally with composers whose names begin with B.' Connor leafed through an *American Conducting* magazine. 'Why?' he yawned.

'He's embedded in our culture,' Elvira said. 'The Beatles *rolled* over him. Walter Murphy and the Big Apple Band shredded snippets from his *Fifth Symphony* into a funky groove.'

'It's great music,' Beat added.

'The opening motif from his *Fifth Symphony* crops up in *Midsomer Murders* theme music,' Elvira teased.

'Yeah! That's a great series,' Winton acknowledged.

Hermione shook her head.

'Elvira, will you be tripping along to the beach?' Matthew caught Winton's eyes and smirked.

The conversation proceeded like a Wimbledon tennis match, smash, return, smash, return, smash, smash, smash... until Beat tapped a spoon on a glass of water. Code for silence.

'Elvira, anything else you want to add?'

'Yes. Beethoven is channelling a new sonata, through me, which I'll premiere.'

16

FURIOSO

BEAT'S fingers sounded the opening melody of Brahms' *Viola and Piano Sonata in F minor*. Her Juilliard professor had steered her away from Brahms because, she was told, his muscular music was only suitable for men. Hubris or not, she reckoned she could deliver the male elements in Brahms' music just as authentically as a man could communicate the female. Wasn't everybody a unique mix of masculine and feminine?

She knew Connor had pestered Polly for a rehearsal time. It hadn't been easy to get her fingers back into shape because of Dan complaining about the 'noise', and whenever she'd found a vacant practice room in the school, there was often an incident which required her immediate attention. She'd played these sonatas with several clarinettists in the past, but never with a viola player and certainly not someone as picky as Connor, who made her feel awkward.

Condescending and an exasperating Luddite, Connor had a head-masterly, almost priest-like presence. Every time he spoke to her, she feared he would call her out on something, or ply her with advice.

But, in this scenario, she wouldn't be pushed into interpretative decisions, and she'd stop if Connor patronised her. Twenty minutes late he had already squandered some of the rehearsal time and she couldn't linger because she had to attend an important, if dull, health and safety committee meeting next. Health and safety issues were crucial when it came to hearing. Orchestral and rock musicians were at risk of hearing loss even at exposures to sound which are less than the limited values for occupational noise.

Ear protection is problematic in an orchestra or band, because if the players use a variety of ear protection methods or not at all, they will likely hear different versions of tone quality. Winton urged his students to wear ear plugs. If he found anyone playing in a confined space without them, he excluded them from his popular performance class, or worse, replaced them in a paid gig. Beat admired him for that.

~

When Connor eventually showed up there was no apology. He removed his retro green tweed jacket and the smell of Imperial Leather soap dominated the space. Trust him to use the same soap as her grandfather. With its higher register of lavender and lemon fragrances, middle notes of patchouli and geranium, and bass of musk and vanilla, it was like a three-part harmony. Swiftly he took his viola out of its case and applied rosin to the bow. Unimpressed, Beat waited, hands tucked under her arms to keep them warm and pliable. She hadn't greeted him because she was too cross – musicians are punctual, the profession requires it, and yet he seemed incapable of efficient time keeping. She had looked forward to the session but his tardy arrival suggested the rehearsal was nothing but another professional chore.

'I'll pick up the pace from you,' he said. 'Play me an A please.'

Beat's finger shook as she depressed the key. She'd known these sonatas inside and out but that was ten years ago and the fluttery sensation in her belly and a weakness in her legs was disturbing.

Yet, when they began, their musical selves were surprisingly compatible and she eased into the music. Intuitively, she matched Connor's phrase-shaping and sensed when he held the tempo back or pushed it forward. Interpretatively, they had similar ideas. Encouraged by their rapport, she found she could switch seamlessly between taking the lead or a back seat in support of Connor. To find a workable duo partner was pure gold.

After the first run through, Connor marked passages on her score where the piano could sing more robustly. He liked the tempo she'd set, and the mellow warmth of his tone was exceptional. After travelling through the first, second, and third movements, time ran out. Neither had exchanged pleasantries but they'd had much to say musically. Her fingers had regained some strength. The hours at the keyboard had paid off. She was pleased.

Connor had plenty to say about her performance as Dean – she waited eagerly, keen to hear a critique of her playing. Brahm's lyricism played on in her mind while she waited.

'Polish up Cesar Franck's *Violin Sonata*. I'm assuming you know it?' Connor asked.

'Let me guess, you want me to perform with Matthew to forge a connection which will metamorphose into a positive alliance.'

'He's particular.'

'And some.'

'The Franck could be beneficial.'

Irritated, she put the piano lid down.

'For who?'

'You, me, all of us,' Connor said.

'Is that what this was about? Because Brahms doesn't strike me as one of your favourites?'

She felt used. Duped. For her, this musical exchange hadn't just been a tactic to improve workplace relations. Rebooting her pianism had released the musical self she'd hidden away and was something to celebrate. But for Connor it was merely a strategy for her to win over resistant colleagues.

'As these sonatas were also written for the clarinet, Hermione can perform them with you,' Connor said.

Disappointed, she lingered at the keys unable to take her eyes off him wrapping the viola in a silk yellow scarf, and how tenderly he lay it in its case as if it were a newborn baby. She'd have to keep her wits about her in future. She should have been wary when Connor asked her to rehearse with him.

'Did Marilyn suggest you play with me?' Beat gathered her music together.

'She did, but if it hadn't been a winning idea, I wouldn't have pursued it.'

'I see.'

Discovering their musical connection had been a joy, but Connor's collusion with Marilyn had sullied the experience. From the thrilling high she'd experienced only minutes before, her mood plummeted. It was like having great sex only to be told it had been a social experiment.

'Shall I liaise with Polly for another time?'

17

LACRIMOSO

SHE yawned, tapped the steering wheel, changed stations. Cars choked the freeway and had slowed to a halt. On the drive home, the last music she wanted to hear was classical or rock, which reminded her of work. It hadn't been a good day. She'd tuned into a jazz program, but the sultry tone and elastic groove pulled here and there by the saxophonist compounded her gloomy mood. She wanted to tell Dan about the Brahms run through because he had suggested she chum up with Connor. She speed-dialled him but he didn't pick up. Since the day she'd taken Polly for a ride, communication had soured. If Dan had switched his phone off, she only had herself to blame. Hadn't she dodged his calls for weeks?

She rang Elvira, 'I've had the craziest day.'

'How come?'

'Dame Ruth, the visiting soprano from Victoria, fainted at a three-metre python stretched out on the floor in the woman's toilet.'

'Was it Jack? The one which dangles over the back door?' Elvira giggled.

'Yes.'

'That would have been a riot.'

'Then Winton yelled because I'd appointed a replacement trumpet teacher without his input while he was in Sydney. But that can keep. I want to ask you something.'

'Go on then...'

'When Georgy tried out to be the soloist, you told me she could be problematic. What did you mean?' Beat said.

'That's complicated.'

'Right, except there's something you're not telling me.'

'Because I can't give you a quick response.' Elvira sounded defensive. 'Not on the phone.'

'We could make a start,' Beat said.

'She isn't experienced.'

'Agreed. But "problematic"?'

'She's skittish. Nervy,' Elvira said.

'Except pre-performance jitters are a given?'

'But most musicians learn how to channel nerves into a performance.'

'Elvira sorry. A call's coming in.'

But it wasn't Dan. A shame she'd ended the call just as Elvira had begun to open up. Her spirits sank. Panicky, she rang him again but to no avail. She changed the station and turned the sound up on West Side Story's *America* with its quasi-habanera rhythm as if the hammered attack could banish her growing unease. She searched again.

'Stay safe,' chimed Drivetime's Tim Newton. 'This will put pep in your step.'

She smiled at the synth's hum and the snappy six beat intro before Pharrell sang *Happy*.

Exhausting one day, a breeze the next, every day at the school was different and anything but predictable. Routine bored her although she knew it was a lifesaver for others. The job fulfilled her need for novelty. Had Dan got it right? Perhaps she was addicted to the melodramas, the super giftedness, the people scuffles? Distracted and obsessing about work, she'd stopped paying attention to the road. Someone hooted. There was a long stretch between her and the car ahead. Traffic was moving again and she picked up speed.

Tonight, Dan and only Dan would be her focus. She couldn't remember when they'd last eaten out or walked the dogs together.

Hours, days, weeks had blurred and she'd become single-minded and remote. Tonight, she'd cook something special. Apologise. Make amends. The morning after Georgy's triumph, the attempted sex had been a disaster. The memory sickened her. Tonight, she'd rekindle their connection but gently, organically.

As the car rolled on and there were fewer vehicles on the road the greener view brightened her mood. She loved the pastures dotted with cows, white corellas fluttering like confetti onto newly ploughed earth. If she got really lucky, she'd see hawks wheeling under a blushing sky. Daylight faded as she pulled into the driveway. Bolt and Storm were cantering up and down the fence, their hooves churning grass into dust. Surely, Dan or Sally would have fed them by now.

There were no lights on. Dan would likely be having a nap. He could sleep anywhere: in the dentist's chair, watching a film, in a shop. She turned the key in the lock, but the front door wouldn't open. He always complained she jinxed it because she was impatient and made too many attempts in a hurry. She slowed her breathing, filtered out the dogs' frantic scuffling on the hall's wooden floor, the kookaburra's cackled mockery.

Despite the late afternoon's sea breezes, the rafters didn't creak, the joists didn't crack – the Queenslander wasn't talking. The silence made her skin crawl. When at last the door opened, the acrid smell of pee made her cover her nose, she let the dogs out and they shot across the grass and zoomed. Beside the sink, the customary dirty cups and plates had been washed and put away, the stainless steel gleamed. The kitchen table's book burden gone.

Hadn't she always yearned for an ordered home? But the pristine kitchen jarred her senses. She lowered her shoulder bag to the floor, took off her jacket and flung it on the back of the sofa. Dan had waged war on the habitual clutter, the sprawl of bills, junk mail, and the dead lilies slumped over the lip of the vase on the kitchen dresser had been disposed of.

And then she saw it. An unopened letter stuck to the fridge door by the dolphin magnet Dan had gifted her. She took the unopened letter and looked under the house. Dan's bike wasn't there. The Ducati's absence said it all. He'd left. Not out of pique as he had done before but for real. If she'd only left work earlier. Been more affectionate. Listened. Hadn't obsessed about work. Shown interest in his research. Ridden pillion on the bike. Dan had abandoned her, but she was wracked by guilt. Furious with herself. Despite his betrayal self-blame swallowed her whole.

Lightheaded, her legs turned to jelly. She dropped into a chair repelled by the taint of cleaning fluid. The kitchen floor was spotless. The faun greyhound fussed, nosed her hand, buried its head in her lap. Flashbacks plagued her: Dan's withering looks, the diffident sex, the petty complaints. His impatience with her appearance. Ignoring the painful lump in her throat she ripped the letter open.

> *Beat, it's over. Neither of us have wanted to admit it. I'm in love with Georgy. You have the school and the horses. Be happy for me, let's not stain our happier times with blame and recrimination. You have a generous heart. Dan x*

~

Beat sat at her grand. She imagined Georgy firing Tchaikovsky's treacherous leaps towards the end of the cadenza solo. Anyone listening to her that night would have marvelled at her phenomenal skill quite apart from Dan. She turned to her shelves, searching for Tchaikovsky's *Piano Concerto no.1*. In her haste, volumes of music fell, several open-spined. She lifted the piano's lid.

The horses hadn't been the only reason she'd wanted acreage, she'd longed to play the piano all night or before dawn. The house was far enough away not to offend her neighbours, but she hadn't factored in Dan's dogged insistence on silence when he studied, which was most of the time.

Except Wongara's soundscape of frog calls, cicadas, and screeching parrots was insistent and loud and it altered in tandem with the weather. Droning cicadas kept them awake on hot, rainy nights and carolling magpies woke them at dawn. Silence was raw, whipped along by nature and the cacophonic brush-cutters, chainsaws, and ride-on mowers her neighbours used to control it. Dan's preferred silence meant no piano playing, while the natural world's chorus and broadcasted cricket matches caused no offence. Life had been less complicated in Melbourne living in an apartment, Dan had preferred it.

But now she could surf the keyboard's roughest seas, gallop through dissonance, trumpeting rage, wallowing in sentiment and spinning lyricism to her heart's content. Dan had married a pianist and curiously, a life with Georgy would be more, much more of the same. Her confusion of messy, torn emotion tugged and pulled and pinched and scratched. She had to stop it. Get away. Flee. Snatching the second volume of Beethoven sonatas spreadeagled on the floor, she skimmed the pages searching for the *Tempest*. When she found it, she sounded the first sustained chord and let its resonance linger before she began the rapid descent of breathless slurs like sighs.

Transported to a realm, where her fingers rallied despite agonising regret, the passagework sparkled with a finesse her under-rehearsed fingers no longer deserved. She sprinted through Schubert *Impromptus*, Faure *Nocturnes*, and Bartok's folksy *Romanian Dances* until a soupy fog dimmed her brain. She must have played for hours, if her protesting shoulders were anything to go by.

Mechanically, she placed the Tchaikovsky on the stand. She made a brutal attack on the first chord and the orchestra rang in her head. But her clammy hands trembled and her body shook. Disappointed by the jangle of misfired notes, she closed the lid. The virtuosity stored in her body had been reactivated but had just as quickly vanished. Unable to control her chattering teeth, she wrapped a warm throw around her and fell asleep, head propped on her arms on the closed piano lid, the greyhounds at her feet.

18

SPINTO

SUNLIGHT streamed through the curtains, the glare needling Beat's swollen eyes, her vision blurred. It was much later than six, the time she usually got up. A heaviness weighed her down, her temples throbbed. Hauling herself into a sitting position, the gnawing ache sharpened into stabbing loss. Something terrible, something bad was the cause.

Dan had gone. She lay back, pulling the cover up to her chin. But then she remembered a commitment. Hadn't she promised to give Melody feedback on how she proposed to gender-proof the school? She had no hope of getting there in time for a meeting at nine. Her no show would shatter Melody's trust and yet her conscience was numb. Like sticking her bare toe in a fire, but instead of an agonising pain, she felt nothing.

Her phone trilled, her fingers scrambled to silence the Bob Marley ringtone *Get Up, Stand Up.*

'Are you on your way?' Polly sounded stressed. 'Fifteen woodwind, brass, guitar, and rock students have turned up. Eight of them guys. They're saying...'

'What?'

'That you don't care.'

'I see,' Beat managed.

'Melody has threatened to take student grievances to Thorne.'

'She should do it then.'

'Don't be like that. Melody looks up to you.'

The pointy rasp of her assistant's normally appeasing tone prompted tears.

'Beat? Can you hear me?'

'Yes,' and with her head angled and the phone pressed between her ear and her shoulder, she pulled on her jeans.

'Are you driving?'

'No.'

'What's wrong?'

'It's Dan.'

'Has he been in an accident?'

'Not that.'

'Then?'

'He's left me for...'

'Who?' Polly whispered.

Beat swallowed. Paused. 'Georgy.'

'Shit!'

'Yep.'

'You must be in shock.'

Storm clanged a hoof against the steel gate. If she didn't feed him soon, he'd break his hoof or the gate. Both were expensive to fix.

'I can't think straight,' Beat said.

'Shall I say you've got flu?'

'Yes.'

Beat had neglected Dan because of her drive to fix the school. He hadn't been the easiest, but he'd been hers.

'You shouldn't be alone.'

'I'm fine.'

'If you change your mind?'

'I won't.'

'What about tomorrow?'

The plea in Polly's tone was pitiful but the prospect of a tomorrow of any kind, let alone a working one, wasn't possible. Brushing her teeth, seemed an insurmountable chore, let alone driving. Abruptly, she stood up, but her feet sank into a spongy, yielding depth, the room rocked, tilted, began to spin. She lay down but the dizziness worsened. She propped herself up on a bunch of pillows. When she recovered, she raided her dirty washing for a sweatshirt. Gingerly, with one hand on the banister, she trod downstairs. Bolt's whinnying ceased. Venturing outside, she saw Sally, throwing hay into the yard. Beat waved, blew her a kiss.

'When you arrived yesterday afternoon, I presumed you'd come out again to put the 4WD under the house. It's not like you to leave your beloved chariot outside abandoned to the elements. When you didn't come out again, I gave those boys a bucket mix.'

'Thanks, Sally. Much appreciated.'

'Is anything wrong? Your face is all crumpled as if it needs an iron.'

~

In the kitchen, Beat stared out of the window. Aged manure flecked the pasture. Signal grass, which caused colic and cranial swelling in horses, speared the stone path's cracks. The phone trilled all day, but she'd let the calls ring out. Flashes of Dan and Georgy made her head spin. Hours passed. Daylight faded. Beat had spent the day cocooned in grief, she had pins and needles in her leg, she hadn't got up for hours.

Agitated, the greyhounds flew to the front door. Someone must be outside, but who? There was a curt, sharp knock again and again. She nursed a fleeting hope it was Dan. Barefoot, wearing the same sweatshirt and jeans, she gingerly held the door ajar dumbfounded at the sight of Hermione laden with groceries.

'Couldn't you hear me? I've been knocking for days.'

Firmly, she pushed Beat aside. Stomped into the kitchen.

'Looks like you need a glass or three.'

Of all the people to check on her, it was this haughty clarinettist who argued against any idea she aired. And yet, Beat felt only gratitude for her surprise visit.

'Don't look at me like that,' Hermione said.

'Like...'

'I'm a pushy bitch. We have opposite views, but having a train wreck for a sparring partner isn't acceptable. Where's the fun in that?'

'But, why?'

'Call it a truce, an amnesty. Do freshen up. Looks like you slept in those clothes.'

Hermione peeled off her gold rain-proof jacket and plonked a Woolworth's cooler bag on the kitchen table, parsley peeking through the top. She rolled her eyes at the empty fridge and filled it with spinach leaves, eggplant, capsicum, yoghurt, sparkling mineral water, a bottle of white wine, and a slab of tofu.

'Where's the bathroom?'

Beat pointed. 'Down the hallway.'

'Horses make me sneeze, but I'll feed them for you. But with what?'

'Give each one some hay.'

'First, I'll run you a hot bath. You're lucky to have one. It's what I love about these old farmhouses. So quaint, so, so yesteryear.'

The clarinettist put her head to the side and grinned. Beat disliked Hermione's patronising tone, but she'd just have to tough it out.

'There's also a shower.'

'Yep, yep, yep, I'm not being judgy. A ceasefire, remember?' Hermione held out her hands and admired her hot pink nails.

Touched by her colleague's unexpected generosity, Beat keeled over with grief. Not a dainty, dab-at-a-moistened eye variety, but a seismic bone-shaker. Awkwardly, Hermione patted Beat's arm until her composure returned.

'I will have to practise before dinner.' Hermione checked her silhouette in the mirror, pulled in her tummy and sighed.

~

Beat trailed her fingers in lavender scented water as she listened to Hermione's exquisite phrasing in Mozart's *Clarinet Concerto* but she must have dozed off because the bathwater had cooled. Hermione was on the phone, her voice shrill.

'As inconvenient as it is, Polly, Beat's doctor will advise her to take one if not two weeks off. I'd say it's exhaustion compounded by shock.'

Then Hermione's voice dropped to a conspiratorial whisper.

'Perhaps we should...' Beat strained her ears, but she couldn't catch what came after *should*. For the moment, it didn't matter. She dressed in clean jeans and a green linen shirt. When Hermione carried baked potatoes, a tofu stir-fry, and a tomato and onion salad to the spotless kitchen table she smiled. For an insatiable carnivore like Hermione, it was a touching gesture.

'I couldn't believe it when Dan didn't sit beside you that night.' Hermione laid her knife and fork down.

'We've always been independent.'

'Let's just say he's found another victim.'

Panic gripped Beat. She had to stop Hermione talking about Dan or she'd be on the fast track to another sobbing session, this time unstoppable.

'Hermione, please. Don't...'

'How will he cope?'

'In what way?'

'Financially?' Hermione handed Beat another glass of wine filled to the brim.

'I can't do this.'

'He's reprehensible. Such a fool.'

Beat combed her hair behind her ears, fixed her eyes on Hermione as if she might dissolve if she wanted it badly enough. But the hectoring clarinettist continued to disparage Dan. She had the right to do that, but Hermione did not, and the brightness of her colleague's pink kaftan made her eyes dance.

'That night, we were all disgusted, even Matthew, at how Dan constantly topped up Georgy's champagne glass until she could scarcely stand.'

'That was days ago.' Her colleagues had known all about Dan and Georgy before she did. Abruptly, she pushed her chair back, got up and scraped her half-eaten dinner into the bin. Rinsed her empty plate in the sink.

Hermione's tirade was a runaway train.

'I saw Dan drooling in a practice room while Georgy zipped through her scales. She belongs to that rare musical species that plays technical work expressively.'

Beat moved to the kitchen's picture window, cupped her hands to block out the light and waited for her eyes to adjust to the moonlit, silvery world. What had looked like arbitrary shadows was a scatter of grazing wallabies. Much to her surprise, the largest marsupial lifted its head and twisted its upper body towards the house, as if it looked directly into her eyes, and an inexplicable surge of hope coursed through Beat's veins.

'Hermione.'

'Yes?'

'Here's your golden opportunity to tell me about the changes you believe are crucial to make the school great again and, after you've done that tell me about the sinister goings on you hinted at the other day.'

19
FARSA

BEAT'S green 4WD was rickety, its complexion blighted by rust. The suspension juddered as she steered into the school's parking facility and pulled up in front of a crumbling, chalky wall. Getting out of her vehicle was chancy. Someone nearly always wanted to catch up, complain, or confide in her. She'd been away for five days, but it seemed like a month. Her early arrival should give her to time to acclimatise. She hoped there'd be no people conflicts today. Since Dan's departure, her protective skin had sloughed off. She was raw. She'd changed but in a way she couldn't articulate as yet. Arriving at 7am had been an effort, but grappling with emails before Polly arrived would help her gauge the political temperature.

Hopefully she could distract herself by finetuning the details of the retreat. She looked around but saw no-one. Heartened, she picked up her stride. She'd almost reached the canteen when she heard, 'Beatrice, wait,' and she stopped in her tracks.

She was surprised to see Connor. He wasn't a morning person.

'Want a coffee?' he said cheerfully.

'Thank you. A long black.'

'Are you rested?'

'Yes. Thanks for asking.'

Connor engaging in small talk was disturbing. Cynically, she decided he must want something.

'How's the Brahms?'

'Still peddling opulent tunes and metric ambiguity.'

Connor forced a smile. That whole make-music-with-the-staff project was achievable now Dan had moved out. That in itself was a silver lining. Maybe she should list all of the advantages of being single. She was about to top up Connor's glass with water but remembered her resolve not to waitress male colleagues.

'What's on your mind?' A peaceful re-entry to the school had not been realistic. Connor flicked through a student magazine. She waited.

'Winton's in strife.'

'How come?'

'Normally, I'd not get involved.' Connor looked sheepish.

'I know.'

'A friend, an ally, one of Thorne's administrative crew saw a memo on her desk about terminating Winton's contract when it's up for renewal.'

'That's not until September,' Beat noted.

'True. But she wants to give him ample warning and be viewed by the academic union as a caring boss. She's giving Winton notice at 4pm today.'

'What did he do?'

'There's a rat plague in the rock facilities. Winton's endured the asbestos, the rising damp, the white ants, and black mould but the rat attack is a bridge too far. He's phobic about rodents. He's jumpy and tired.'

'What do you mean, Connor?'

'He's been burning the candle at both ends.'

'Doing trumpet gigs all night?'

'No, not at all. He's an uber driver most weeknights.'

'Why? He's on an ample salary surely?'

'The extra isn't for him.' Connor rubbed his temples.

'Meaning?'

'He uses the money for the rock program. To hire venues, tweak the building here and there, commission instrument repair. He's lobbying anyone and everyone about rock's third-world quarters.'

'That's unwise. But, I'd be livid too.' Beat scooped a struggling fly out of her tepid coffee.

Winton's lament about the building was like a Steve Reich refrain on a looping cycle. Reich had got it wrong, repetition wasn't always meditative and beautiful. When she recalled Winton's mouthy put-downs, his contempt, the gender bias, the never-ending reference to London as a musical Shangri-La, his permanent absence would be a blessed relief. And yet he was a magnet for aspiring trumpeters with a track record of producing top players. Recently, a former protégé had been appointed Principal Trumpet of the State Orchestra.

'Connor, why are you agitating for him?'

'I asked him to replace me at a finance meeting. I didn't know there was a proposal tabled to increase the rock school's rent.'

'You hadn't read the papers?'

'No. A few days earlier, Winton had opened an air-conditioning vent and disturbed a rat's nest despite his arsenal of grisly baits.'

'Building a sound-proofed, bespoke rock school is one of my goals.'

'Worthy, but not achievable,' Connor snapped.

Irritated, Beat ignored his negativity. 'What did Winton say at the meeting?'

'He accused the Committee of wilful negligence.'

'Go Winton,' Beat muttered.

'There's more.'

'Oh no.'

'He told the committee to "get off their fucking lazy butts" and check out the facilities because in the event of illness or an accident the Turalong Council would be accountable.'

'I'd call that professional suicide.' Beat leaned back in her chair.

'Thorne did her Queen of Hearts routine. Stood up, pointed at him and ordered him to leave.'

Beat chewed her hair. She knew from experience how Winton abused authority figures.

'He kicked a chair over on his way out.'

'That bad?'

'Yes. Then he told Council members they faced prosecution because rock's facilities were in breach of the *Work Health and Safety Act.*'

Beat scratched the back of her head.

'Can you intervene?'

'Why would I? Winton's rude.' Beat folded her arms.

'But brilliant.'

'I know, but shaming Thorne publicly brings out her worst. I can't promise anything.' Beat sculled her cold coffee.

~

Time had slipped away. When Beat reached the school it was 8am and yet a big crowd occupied the foyer. She wasn't ready to face her colleagues yet. But her hesitation was unnecessary because staff and students were in the thrall of sixteen re-purposed ceramic toilet bowls set out in two rows of eight. Each one represented a note in a scale. The players tapped the rim of the electronically wired bowls with a xylophone beater, a carillon of toilet receptacles. Eight players performed a lumbering take on Cyndi Lauper's *Time After Time*. The ceramic chorus was mesmerising.

Winton gave her a diffident wave, a few mimed, 'good to see you back' and the students' head-to-the-side 'sorries' were hard to decipher. Beat smiled at well-wishers, mouthed 'thank you' before she scuttled down the corridor to her office, only to find it locked. Polly generally opened it when she arrived, but her assistant was running late.

Her airless office smelled musty. Algae covered the aquarium's glass. Not that it worried the goldfish, who dined on a curtain of green. Sunflowers stood in a vase on the right of her desk, gifted by Polly. On the left, an intimidating cairn of paper begged for attention.

Tactfully, Polly hadn't made any appointments for today and Beat was grateful. When she heard a knock on the door, she jumped up and opened it wide. It wasn't Polly, but Theo the violinist from 1 2 3. Head bowed, hands in his pockets, he shuffled scuffed cowboy boots on the carpet.

Matthew had offered Theo the coveted position of concertmaster but much to Matthew's disappointment and to the amazement of Theo's peers, he'd turned the offer down. Despite his giftedness, glum was Theo's default expression.

'Come in.' Beat swept her hand in the direction of her office. Theo shuffled in. Once seated, he tugged in vain at the cuffs of his green and brown plaid shirt, just like he had when he wore the black jacket, at least a size too small, at the Byron Competition. Theo was from Mungindi, west of Goondiwindi. He dressed six parts country and four parts metro sexual. Mousey hair twisted into a man bun.

'I've come to tell you I'm leaving.'

'Why?' Beat avoided meeting Theo's sad eyes.

'I can't go on. I'm behind on everything.'

'Why?'

'Because I'm a shitty fraud.' Theo sniffed and shifted position.

'How come?'

He leaned forward, his lips formed to speak, but no sound came out. She handed him a box of tissues.

'I can't read music. The Suzuki teacher from School of the Air taught me by rote. She demonstrated. I copied.'

'Then you must have an exceptional ear and a remarkable memory. How do you manage in orchestra or in the trio?'

Theo's checked sleeves inched up his arms.

'I memorise. Everything.' He leaned back and stretched out his skinny legs. The Cuban heels of his shabby cowboy boots dug into the carpet.

'When you played the Shostakovich and the Brahms from memory in Byron Bay, it wasn't a big deal for you.'

'That's true.'

'But it must take so much time.'

'That's why music's not for me.'

Theo took a wad of tissues and pressed them to his eyes.

'All you need is a coach. You've been an asset to the orchestra. You deserve every chance to learn to read.'

Hope flared in Theo's eyes.

'Really?'

'Yes. I won't tell anyone. If Melody's willing, we'll pay her to teach you.'

'Awesome. I'm stoked.'

Theo left with a buoyant step.

Beat sighed. How could she tackle the challenges ahead if her time was constantly devoured by emergencies. Polly stuck her head round the door.

'Welcome back. Sorry I wasn't here. I've been typing the agenda for the union meeting at lunchtime. We're voting in a new president.'

'Thanks you've given me a great idea.'

Polly looked puzzled. 'Talk later?'

'Yes. Best get back to it.' Beat searched for Winton in the staff directory. She'd memorised most extensions, but not his since she never used it. When she rang, he picked up.

'Hey, can you come over now? We have to talk.'

'Are you changing the room bookings, because some classical dude had a meltdown?'

'No.' Beat doodled on a torn envelope.

'Come and check out our facilities,' Winton said.

'Can't today. There's an emergency,'

'All righty. Keep your hair on.'

When Winton arrived, he sank into a chair and rested his crossed ankles on the coffee table.

'Okay, shoot.'

'Are you meeting Thorne at four?'

'How d'you know about that?'

She shook her head impatiently. 'Thorne will be advising you your contract will not be extended.'

'You're messing with me?' Planting his feet on the floor he sat tall.

'If only.'

Winton's face blanched. 'That damn budget meeting. So, what can you, or I, or anyone do about it?'

Beat wondered at Winton's dress sense, although she was a fine one to talk. But in today's fire-engine red suit, maroon shirt, and black and white music-note socks, he looked like an over ripe tomato.

'I've got an idea.'

'You do?' Winton leaned forward.

'Attend the union meeting at 1pm.'

'What for?' He popped his phone into his breast pocket.

'You could be the next staff union president.'

'That won't happen.'

'You're a member?'

'More's the pity.' Winton undid his jacket. His face had a sweaty lustre.

'Let it help you.'

'No! Its members are woke, gutless chest beaters. Tossers. Political...'

'I heard you're driving an uber. Finances must be tight.'

'None of your beeswax.' He struck the chair's arms with balled fists. 'Way below the belt. Manipulative.'

'Or, a reality check.'

'What would people want from me?'

'That you accept the nomination. Thorne will think twice about not renewing your contract if you're the union president.'

'But that's bonkers?'

'Do you have an alternative suggestion? We both know you'd be the worst,' Beat said. 'But you'd resign when Thorne gets off your case.'

'Right.' The trumpeter sneered but looked thoughtful. Beat wondered how aggravating people like Winton ever get a job in the first place.

'Make a decision,' Beat said.

'I say no. It's a dud solution.'

'Winton the clock's ticking.'

He thumbed his phone but soon tossed it aside.

'Okay.'

'I've still got to persuade the current president...'

Winton sucked his teeth. 'I thought this was in the bag.'

'I can't act without your consent.'

'I shouldn't be in this predicament.'

'But you are.' She held an imaginary gun to her head.

He took a nebuliser from his pocket, turned away to inhale.

'What d'you want in return?' Winton shook the nebuliser like a maraca for another use.

'Nothing,' she shrugged.

'Well?'

'Stop being a disagreeable prick.'

'Never thought you'd support me.'

'Neither did I.' Winton walked to the door. Rested his fingers on the handle, looked over his shoulder and grinned. 'Those fish are hungry.'

~

Beat strolled towards the Botanical Gardens. On such a sunny day it could clear her head after the tense morning. Sally often asked her to describe what an average working day was like. Next time, she'd use today's shenanigans as a prime example. Even she'd not foreseen there would be two tricky problems for her to solve on her first day back. She sometimes longed for occasional periods when all she had to do was drive her desk.

No one saw her leave but, as always, she was energised by the mash of sound: booming trombone and laughter, singers zipping up and down vocal exercises, and the delicate finger work of classical guitarists. By the staircase, Beat waved at Hermione. Burdened by a massive tote bag, the clarinettist mouthed, 'You look great,' as her backless gold heels clattered upstairs.

A cautious optimism settled on Beat. It was a ten-minute stroll to her favourite spot by the grand lake and, as she wasn't in a hurry, she'd take it at a leisurely pace. But she heard her name and froze. When she turned in the direction of the voice, she was appalled to see Georgy running towards her.

'Beat, can we go to the café?'

'What for?'

Crows swaggered across the grass, like gun-toting outlaws in an old-school western. She heard a sobbing baby, human chatter, shrieks of laughter, the rumble of traffic. She stared at the ibis in the café's courtyard, the backs of the 'bin chickens' heads like black socks darned with white thread.

'To talk things through.'

'I can't see the point.'

Georgy's spindly fingers tightened around her forearm. Beat flinched.

'Five minutes?'

It was too, too much. Dan's betrayal was bad enough, but in partnering a young pianist Beat had a professional responsibility for he had magnified, compounded the hurt.

'Okay, but here.' Beat sat on the seat's edge poised for a quick getaway. Dread and rage swirled in her chest and coursed down her arms at the thought of Dan confiding in this naïve woman's ear. Beat's hands shook and she pushed them deep into her pockets.

'Beat, I'd never have taken up with Dan if you and he were still, well... um, you know... together.'

'Meaning?'

'When Dan started to hit on me, I ignored him at first.'

Beat fixed her attention on a little girl throwing bits of cake for a gang of scavenging ibis.

'Good for you.'

'Dan hung on, not wanting to let you down, but he had to leave for the sake of his nerves,' Georgy gushed.

'Is that so?'

'We totally get each other,' Georgy beamed at the thought. 'We want the same things. He doesn't begrudge my piano routines.'

'Not yet,' Beat muttered under her breath.

'Don't do that.'

'You have your end-of-year recital in November. You'll do really well if you focus. Dan spins a good line. He'll distract you.'

'Sour grapes.' Georgy shifted away from Beat. 'He told me you'd be clingy, because he's been your unpaid lackey.'

Beat wouldn't reveal her side of the story to this suckered, love-struck pianist because Georgy wouldn't believe a word of it.

'Play the piano, Georgy. Don't get played.'

'Dan told me the school always, always, comes first.' Georgy leaned back and squinted at Beat as if she were looking through the sights of a rifle.

'It's my job.'

'Dan detests your horses.'

'You ungrateful...'

'No.' Georgy clenched her fists. 'I did you a big favour stepping up for that concert. I got you out of a hole. People say you're power mad. Out of your depth.'

Beat walked briskly propelled by anger and shame. Tears rolled. Georgy's taunts looped in her brain. She bumped into people, tripped on a child's tricycle in her haste. Striding through Polly's office to reach her own, her bright-eyed assistant was cheerfully gossiping on the phone. Grinning at Beat, she gave her a thumbs up sign and held up a sheet of scrap paper on which she'd scrawled, 'WE WON.'

~

Inside her office, Beat grabbed the file on the staff retreat and knocked a box of paper clips off her desk. She'd pick them up after she edited the staff retreat's program one last time. But she couldn't concentrate. Her pulse raced. A gloating Georgy haunted her, she recalled her voice, the smug sexual supremacy in the young woman's eye.

Polly interrupted.

'A group of us are off to the pub to celebrate our new Union President. Winton's buying the first round. Come along. Have some fun.'

'I should really...'

'What?'

'Go home.'

'Come on,' Polly puffed out her chest, hands on hips. 'You're the one who sorted this.'

'I was going to...'

'Beatrice Snow, it will keep.'

20

KEY CHANGE

POLLY edged into the office.

'Sorry to interrupt.'

'It's Dan. I tried to fob him off but he insists he has to see you urgently.'

'Do I have time?'

'Yes, the morning's free.'

'Give me a minute, I want to tidy up.'

Polly looked approving, no doubt thinking she meant the mess on her chaotic desk. No. She wanted to smarten up herself. A mirror hung on the back of the cupboard door. Her reflection showed an unhealthy pallor, shadows under her eyes. She flicked through the clothes she kept for unexpected occasions. But neither the smart black dress for concerts nor the smart blue jacket she wore to council meetings were suitable. She ought to put more clothes in there to reflect a range of situations. But come to think of it what would be the ideal outfit to meet an ex?

'Come in.' Beat's voice was monotonal, her face blank.

Polly's phone rang, 'Matthew, she can see you after lunch.'

A pity he hadn't rung a minute earlier. But avoiding Dan wasn't going to help. Once they'd settled the finances, there would be no reason for her to talk to him ever again.

'About bloody time.' Dan pushed past her. He grimaced at her desk. 'Whoa... you've got some catching up to do.'

There was a lawyer's card stuck on her computer. It had been there for weeks. If only she'd used it. Beat grabbed her notebook and a pen.

'D'you really have to...'

'What?'

'Take notes?' Dan said.

'Yes. What's up?'

Dan leafed through a concert brochure, undid the buckle of a tan shoulder bag and popped the publication inside, for Georgy she supposed. He'd always told her he disliked man bags.

'There are matters,' Dan said.

'Matters?'

'You've paid all the bills for five years.'

'Don't I know it.'

If she lost her temper, Dan would get the upper hand.

'I don't have a job. I'm still your dependant. We've separated, but I have to eat.'

Dan put his hands on the chair's arms and leaned forward. Close enough for her to smell the tang of an unfamiliar sandalwood aftershave.

'We've got joint assets, including equity in the property. I need access to that.'

'Is that so?'

'We don't need the expense of lawyers,' Dan buckled up his bag. 'We could sort everything ourselves.'

He had the latest model of iPhone and the leather bag would have cost a bit. Dan looked smarter, different. She didn't recognise the clothes he wore except for his red socks. When he was with her, he'd never have worn a tight jacket, fastened with one button, the cloth pleated like rays of the sun. In only a matter of weeks, her intimate partner had become a stranger.

'When were you hoping to finalise arrangements?' Beat asked.

'Soon. Debts are ramping up.'

'Until I get legal advice...' she began.

'You mean you haven't?'

'No.'

'Typical.' Dan sounded furious. But then in a warmer, lighter tone he said, 'I'll settle for a weekly sum to tide us over. It could be paid back to you after settlement.'

'No. Your lawyer needs to consult mine.' She stood up, the universal signal for the meeting's over.

Dan paused. 'Are you coping? You look all used up.'

He'd found his stride. Dan always gained the upper hand.

'Go now or I'll...'

'Cry?'

She took off her boot and threw it at the closing door.

~

'Cherry kombucha's a pick-me-up. Good for the digestion,' Elvira quickly cleared a space on Beat's desk to place the drink on her desk.

'How thoughtful.' What a pity its healthy ingredients compromised the taste.

'A snazzy outfit or two would hit the refresh button, a welcome transition into a brighter key,' Elvira said.

'Are you listening?' Polly gently prodded Beat's shoulder.

'Why wouldn't I be?'

Her assistant frowned.

'I'll get around to it. I admit I need to update my look.'

'We all know you won't make time to do it,' said Elvira.

'Let's make a date.' Beat took another swig of kombucha and liked it better.

'You're a looker, Beatrice Snow, with that figure and those long legs,' her assistant sighed. 'However much you hide in dowdy outfits.'

'You're embarrassing me now,' Beat protested.

'We've chosen a selection of items from an online site. Whatever takes your fancy, we'll order for you.'

'Now?'

'You bet.' Polly and Elvira said in unison.

Beat exchanged places with Polly who sat down and typed in the browser bar.

Beat supposed they'd favour a beige jacket, a gold violin brooch, a box-pleated skirt, white linen shirt, and cream court shoes. She crumbled a flake of food into the fish tank.

'Take a look.' Polly angled the laptop towards Beat.

Much to her surprise, it was a vivid green jumpsuit and matching bolero jacket, paired with snazzy green boots.

'Size?' Polly asked.

'Ten,' Beat mumbled.

'You'd wear this at functions, concerts, and whenever Dan shows his face around here. By the way, it's made from biodegradable bamboo,' Polly said.

'I'll buy that then.'

'Take a look at this,' Elvira said.

A red shift dress popped up on the screen. 'You glowed in that red jacket,' Polly prompted.

'I'd no idea it was radioactive.'

Elvira rolled her eyes. Polly tapped the screen.

'You've got really toned legs,' said Elvira.

'Because of the horse riding,' Beat said.

'How about these black jodhpurs?' Elvira asked. 'But do not get them covered in dog hair.'

'Yes, but what would I...'

'We chose these.'

Polly pointed at a couple of frumpy, floral tops. One with ruffled sleeves in baby blue and lemon pastels and the other a chintzy number with oranges floating on a black background.

'Not. For. Me.' Beat shuddered.

'Just teasing. But this silky black top, with a V-neckline would look great with your jeans,' Elvira prompted.

She was cornered. Trapped.

'Here's the deal.' Elvira put her arm around Beat's shoulder. 'You buy two outfits. I'll lose the batik.'

Beat glanced at Polly, who stared at the carpet.

'I know you disapprove,' Elvira said. 'Feelings have nowhere to hide on your face.'

'Elvira, it's not that...' Beat protested.

'Winton's jokes about my on-the-beach dresses are getting old.' Elvira added.

'Don't do it because of him?' Beat turned back to the screen.

'Never.' Elvira smiled.

'I'll retire the pink hoodie,' Polly promised.

'Not the one with your sweet moggie?' Beat rubbed at her eyes.

'The very same.'

'But Pol it's your go to comfort top,' Beat said.

'The school's changing. We should all celebrate with a new look.'

'Hermione's the fashion plate, how come you didn't involve her?'

'Impossible.' Elvira shrugged. 'You'd end up with...'

High heels. Animal prints. Plunging necklines?' Beat joked.

'A draw full of crimson lippy and a theatrical trench coat sweeping the ground,' Polly grinned.

'Decision time. What's it to be?' Elvira prompted.

'The green jumpsuit.'

'And?' Polly queried.

'The red dress and the black top.'

'You won't regret it.' Elvira dashed into the dean's studio, sat at the piano and Chopin's *Revolutionary Etude* peeled in triumph.

21
UNISON

'BEATRICE, the University will never agree to Sounds Best securing naming rights for your fundraiser,' Thorne said.

'And I don't want to lose the sponsorship.'

'Naturally, but you're losing a percentage anyway because you won't engage Connor.'

'Maybe.'

'According to Matthew, who bent my ear about it, your inner circle rates Connor highly. He's not as drab as he looks. Don't judge a book by its...' Marilyn cupped her hair, used her fingers to comb it behind her ears.

Beat wanted to scream. When would the staff talk to her first about the school's business?

'But no one factors in Connor's reluctance to conduct.'

'You're people smart but wrong-headed about him.' Thorne struggled with the clasp of her gold-hooped earring; its bold size flattered her sleek cropped hair. A loose thread dangled from her skimpy fitted jacket, she reached for a pair of scissors and snipped it off.

'So, who will bring in the numbers?'

'Sian.'

'Has she won awards?' Thorne scissored the offending thread.

'Billboard awards for Top Artist, Top Selling Album, and Top Touring Artist.'

'Sounds impressive.' Thorne was in a happy-go-lucky, friendly frame of mind.

'Agreed.'

'Negotiate alternative benefits with Sounds Best.'

Beat touched the groove on her bare ring finger and not for the first time wondered if it would ever go away.

'You've drifted, Beatrice.'

'How about Sounds Best is credited as Sian's sponsor?'

'Now, that has legs. Go with that. And the staff retreat? How's it shaping up?'

'See what you think. Could you read the program?' Beat picked it up and handed it to her. But Thorne waved it away. 'Marilyn it's important you—'

'Agreed. But I've a lunch date.'

'I need to explain something—'

Thorne's attention shifted to the tall man on the other side of her frosted glass door. On her way out, Beat was surprised to see the vice-chancellor.

22

GROOVE

'LAST night was fun. Never thought I'd enjoy socialising with colleagues. Dinner wasn't bad either. The plant-based meat lasagne was surprisingly tasty,' Elvira said.

'Thanks for the feedback.' Beat knew Elvira was angling for something.

'Fancy bringing horses to a professional do. Now that's a first.'

'Equine Assisted Learning otherwise known as EAL is used quite often to better communication between working groups and especially in America. It's catching on here too.'

In casual clothes, her work mates looked like friendlier versions of themselves, versions she could more easily relate to. Elvira wore jeans, a green tee, and silver sandshoes. She had her hair in a plait, draped over one shoulder. She carried an umbrella because, "with her delicate complexion," she risked sunburn. At work, Connor's tweed jackets matched his aloof behaviour but today's denim shirt and Panama hat had neutralised this distance. She'd seen him smile at Matthew. Maybe he'd be open to new ideas? No. That was unlikely.

Winton had gone cowboy. His hat had an upturned brim, and he resembled a Texan oil magnate. Cowboy boots and a silver-buttoned flowery shirt completed the look. Hermione wore a charcoal grey polo shirt and shorts without costume jewellery cluttering her neckline. Despite everyone's relaxed appearance, Beat had to remember, their casual optics didn't mean their outlook would be any different.

'That green jumpsuit looks great,' Elvira said. 'Be prepared. Compliments will fly today.'

'I've friends with good fashion sense.' And the irony of her dressing up while the staff had dressed down hadn't escaped her.

'Can I?' Elvira pleaded.

'Can you what?'

'Skip the session?'

'Because?'

'I'm allergic to horses.' Elvira flicked her plait off her shoulder. Grey-winged galahs screeched in the blue sky.

'Antihistamine will stop that. I've got plenty.'

Elvira bunched her lips, pouted. 'There's a Yamaha grand in the manager's cottage.' Elvira rubbed her blue fingerless gloves together. 'She's happy for me to practise there all day. The garden is amazing full of ginger plants, purple bougainvillea, and red bottlebrush. I saw honeyeaters feeding off the golden grevillea which frames the fence line.' She pressed the sheet music for Grieg's *Piano Concerto* to her chest.

That Elvira had found anywhere of appeal in this determinedly dreary centre impressed Beat. Three identical meeting rooms and computer stations lined the perimeters of a closely cropped circular lawn. Each had the same blue carpet with cream swirls in the weave. Everywhere Beat looked trite captions *Make It Matter* and *Gender-proofing Futures,* made her cringe.

Elvira's eyes glistened. Any moment the tears would flow.

'Thing is,' Beat spoke in a kindly tone because she knew Elvira was the soloist with Orchestra Queensland next month and needed to practise to keep her anxiety at bay, 'the purpose of EAL is to foster better relationships.'

'If you say so.' Elvira rolled her eyes.

'Can you practise after dinner?'

'No. I'll be a cactus.'

'Could you eat earlier?'

Elvira turned her back on Beat just like Bolt when he didn't get his own way.

'Who knows, you might even *enjoy* yourself?' Beat regretted her sarcastic emphasis on enjoy. Why did that narky tone surface with one of her few professional allies? Now she'd made Elvira sulk.

Beat swiped at a fly. She loathed being the gatekeeper, the ogre who had to say no. In other circumstances, she'd have gladly let Elvira freewheel on the keys. She hadn't expected anyone to give up on practice routines, because practising for a musician was as essential as breathing. She remembered how stressed she had felt when a concert loomed on the horizon. Begrudgingly, the manager of the conference centre had allowed Beat to arrange, at the school's expense, a renovated shipping container for use as a practice facility. Hermione had been in there since 5:30am wrestling with Copland's jazzy *Clarinet Concerto.*

In six weeks, Matthew was a soloist with the Sydney Symphony Orchestra. Whenever anyone spoke to him, he looked preoccupied, his eyes glazed as if he was performing Bruch's *Violin Concerto* in his head. His interpersonal skills were wanting, but when he sang through the violin, he could melt the hardest of hearts. His sublime tone and interpretative flair were harnessed to a phenomenal technique. She had learned the hard way that any generosity of spirit Matthew possessed was channelled through his Guarneri.

Increasingly canny at seeing around corners, she hadn't anticipated there would be requests to rehearse during scheduled activities. The others would be just as keen as Elvira to dodge the EAL session and if she excused her, Matthew and Hermione would demand exemption too.

At least the conference centre's accommodation was comfortable enough and in this environment it was the mundane, not the musical, that copped criticism. The air-conditioning was too cold, the TV controls were sluggish, gluten-free bread wasn't on the menu. Beat promptly fielded these complaints to Polly.

Matthew and Winton had chummed up and, even if the alliance was temporary, it was a breakthrough. Winton had contributed to discussions, even though his arcane world view had alienated his peers. He was unpredictable. When Beat had told Winton she'd brought her horses, he'd readily volunteered to assemble the round yard.

Elvira turned to look out across the scorched russet lawns. But Beat was distracted by a brown paper bag somersaulting across the grass in a gust of wind. She had to catch it because if her horses spooked everyone would get a fright.

Courtney, who was taking the equestrian session, stood in the round yard and gestured for everyone to come nearer. Elvira's sullen demeanour annoyed Beat but, in this session, it was Courtney's responsibility to handle it.

'Hey, Elvira,' Courtney opened her arms in a welcoming gesture. 'Good to meet you. I've bought a ticket for the Grieg.'

The pianist shrugged. Moved closer towards Matthew.

Ready? Beat texted Courtney.

Yes. But stay out of it.

Totally, Beat thumbed back.

What bliss to be just another face in the crowd, not searching for solutions, mediating, justifying. Courtney opened the yard's gate. She had authority, exemplary posture, her sleek black hair tucked into an Akubra hat. Years as principal clarinet with the Melbourne Orchestra had given her a commanding presence.

'Who would like to go first?'

Winton's hand shot up. Hermione nudged Beat, amused by the trumpeter's eagerness.

'He's smitten with Courtney and her sprayed-on jeans.'

Beat laughed. Polly loped off and stood by Connor.

'I'll model it, Winton.' Courtney looped the excess rope in her left hand and swung the other in a circle from her right fist. 'Watch closely.' Storm faced Courtney. 'I swing the rope at his neck, he moves on. I stare at his hip, he turns into me.'

Storm travelled at an easeful trot, ears to the side, attentive.

'Now you Winton.'

Intrigued, his peers moved to the rail for a better view. But the trumpeter swung the rope with major force and Storm bucked, cantered, stopped parallel to the rail and pawed the ground.

'All that's needed is a clear signal, nothing Shakespearean.'

Elvira hit herself in the leg when she twirled the rope. The men laughed, yet the horse came to her and delicately sniffed her head.

'Storm's bonding,' Courtney said.

Matthew grappled with the steel chain on the gate. He was unaware the noisy *chinkety chink* scared Storm, who leapt sideways. Beat knew Storm's every move, every muscle, every ripple of his skin. She could play her horse superbly, just as Matthew commanded the violin.

'Wake up, Matthew,' Courtney yelled, and he crash landed in reality. But in swinging the rope he clipped the horse's hip whose hind quarters powered up and tucking his legs beneath him he cleared the rail. Onlookers gasped. Storm pulled up to graze. Beat placed a reassuring hand on his mane and led him back into the round yard.

'Matthew's cues were too strong. But it takes time to learn how firmly or how softly to ask the question, just as it does on a musical instrument if you want to play in a hushed or a robust tone.'

'Explain the relevance of this Courtney,' Hermione demanded.

'Horses mirror our emotions, our energy, and read our faces. A British researcher proved that horses exhibit calm behaviours when classical or country music is played.'

Winton winced playfully at "country."

'Rock can incite windsucking which is when a horse arches his neck, opens its mouth and swallows air.'

'In me too,' Matthew quipped.

'Courtney, that doesn't answer my question.'

'Beat addressed the relevance last night. Let's chat privately.'

~

Connor's blank expression made Beat anxious. She feared he'd leave, but why was his involvement more important than any of the others? Somehow his presence validated her.

'Rhythm and pace are crucial. The horse should keep a consistent pulse. I've seen riders use Taylor Swift's *Cruel Summer* or Bach, but today's choice is Ed Sheeran's *Perfect*.'

The trumpeter feigned a yawn, but Courtney looked away.

'Press play, Winton.'

When Sheeran crooned, 'I've found a love,' Storm's stride meshed with the pop anthem's pulse. His hooves drummed the sand, in synergy with the flute, piano, and thrum of acoustic guitar. He was grace itself.

Matthew gawped at the animal's steady rhythm.

Winton unscrewed a bottle of water. 'If that animal wants to study rock, he'll pass the audition with flying colours.'

'If only it were that easy for women applicants,' quipped Polly.

Everyone laughed except Courtney, who cued Storm to stop.

'Polly, how do you deal with complaints?'

'I don't engage with a person's emotions but try to help.' Polly smiled, her face open yet calm.

Winton and Matthew exchanged meaningful glances. Both had been inexcusably rude to Polly.

'Okay. Demonstrate that,' Courtney said.

Polly gestured to Storm and he trotted off, transitioned into a canter, back to a walk and turned in to face her.

'You're a natural.' Courtney looked pleased.

When everyone clapped. Polly glowed. Storm stole the moment to roll in the sand. Courtney waited for silence.

'Beat doesn't know about this but before lunch we're going to watch a demo.'

When Connor shepherded Bolt into the yard to join Storm, Beat was shocked.

'Well, I'll be...' Hermione's arms dangled over the yard's top rail. Beat noticed her unpainted fingernails. Miffed Courtney hadn't told her about a demonstration, she decided it was karma. When Elvira complained she hadn't been consulted about Georgy being the Tchaik soloist she hadn't really been sympathetic. Connor had a special rapport with her horses and at his direction the horses executed each change in gait or turn or stop, echoing each other precisely. The sight of her colleagues' animated faces pleased her.

'Connor studied natural horsemanship with American guru Pat Parelli, long before he became a conductor. Let's give him our support,' Courtney's words triggered a torrent of whoops and whistles.

Beat was pleased she'd programmed the EAL class until she felt a sharp pain in the ribs.

'That really hurt Hermione. Don't elbow me.'

'But we have to talk.'

Beat wondered at the clarinettist's agitation, the rare dishevelment, her unruly gingery hair which fired red in the sunlight, the grass-stained shorts.

'About?'

'Come on, you feel it too,' Hermione tapped her foot.

'What are you on about?'

'Watch your back.'

23
FUOCO

A cloudless sky, too much alcohol the night before, and a cloying humidity had curbed breakfast appetites. Organic delicacies supposedly procured from the property looked tempting enough – croissants, toast, bacon, eggs, mushrooms, spinach, tomatoes – but had largely been ignored. Wherever Beat looked, she saw parched dried-to-a-crisp pasture. How could any homegrown produce have been harvested on such sun-bleached, exhausted land?

'Can I join you?' Hermione lay her orange cap on the floral tablecloth.

'Sure.'

'How's it going with Dan?'

'Oh, he's sabre-rattling. Finances mainly.'

'The hide of him.' Hermione reached for a generous teaspoon of sugar and sprinkled it over a meagre helping of muesli.

'I'm not completely free. There's a legal process to go through first.'

'How about Connor's exhibitionism?' asked Hermione.

'I'd no idea he was good with horses.'

'And?'

'Stunning. His rapport amazed me.' Beat said.

'Great timing. I'll give him that.'

'Hermione, I'm tired. What are you *not* telling me?'

'Matthew's a pain. But it's not him you should be wary of.'

'It's too early in the day for riddles Hermione. Besides, I'm not up to it.'

Beat nursed a coffee, Elvira's loose hair tumbled onto her shoulders. She clutched a mug of herbal tea and hid behind sunglasses. Winton's eyes were closed, his breakfast untouched.

'Hermione, look at Matthew,' said Beat.

'I am.'

'He's in violin land.'

Matthew stared, eyebrows knitted in concentration as he nibbled absently on buttered toast.

'Ah! He's reached his big solo.' Hermione said. 'Now look at Connor.'

He had his nose in a book. His showmanship yesterday had prompted wild celebration. Yet, while others drained cartons of beer and bottles of wine, he retired early.

'What for?' Beat asked.

'Why did he do it?'

'Ask him. I put it down to unfathomable Connor being unfathomable.'

'His display meant we ran out of time before you gave us a demonstration. After all, they're your animals.'

'Hardly a problem.'

'Connor should have cleared it with you first.'

'Never mind. I enjoyed his showmanship.'

'Exactly.'

'Hermione why did Steven leave so suddenly?'

'He had a gambling problem.' Abandoning her muesli, the clarinettist flounced off.

Connor was pedantic and annoyingly late for meetings but it hardly put him in the enemy camp. He didn't look like he was about to stage a coup. Tucking into avocado, fetta, and toast, nose deep in *Nationwide News,* he looked incapable of deceit despite his industrial-strength arrogance. She poured a glass of water, grabbed a lemon and ginger muffin and joined Winton, even though today's neon lime green cowboy shirt hurt her eyes.

'Mind if I sit here?' Beat said.

'Well, aren't you are a bloomin' marvel? Not a bad dean for a horse wrangler.'

His taunt was a slap on the face. If she could only throw a pearler back. But in the heat of the moment her mind went blank. Not that it mattered, because Winton wisely changed tack.

'What time does the bus leave?'

Beat looked at her phone. 'Whoops. In five minutes. Hey, we have to board.'

'Don't fret. Do what you have to do. I'll muster the stragglers.'

'Good luck with that.' Beat said.

On board, the mood flatlined. She'd hoped the hour's trip to the farm of North Coast composer Lex Canon might raise her colleagues' spirits, as the bus drove through stunning green hills embroidered by a winding creek. Yesterday's chatty vibe, which had explored comical mishaps on stage, the rock world, the antics of despot conductors, and follies of a big band, had been fun. She'd felt included and had enjoyed it because, against her better judgement, she wanted to befriend her workmates.

'How long to Cobbler's Reach?' Connor squinted at his Rolex. 'I'd hate to miss Lex's performance.'

'An hour,' said Beat. 'He won't start without us. The scenery's spectacular. We'll see Blue Nob, the volcanic plug, breathtaking valleys, and then there's Nimbin with its giant mural of a spliff. Nostalgic posters of Bob Marley all over town.'

'Must you prattle on like a tour guide. This isn't a frivolous jaunt. Nimbin I could well do without,' mumbled Connor. 'Marley was more distinguished than most, but reggae's repetition numbs the mind.'

'Yet you're a fan of minimalist music,' Beat challenged. 'Lex's property is open to the public several times a year because of his gigantic bronze sculptures.'

'Is that so?'

'Yes, a giant ant rears in a lily pond. A massive kookaburra crowns an old dunny.'

'I've come for Canon's performance. Landscaping in questionable taste is of no interest.'

Crushed and irritated, Beat snapped back. 'Music isn't everything. A pity you can't engage in anything else.'

~

The party's curiosity as they approached Canon's property heartened Beat. The grass was lush, there were no brown patches of grub-infected grass like those spotting her own lawn. A weathered, upright piano, lid open and soundboard removed, sat in front of a horseshoe of camping chairs. Positioned on a grassy expanse, clearly it was a vital element in the performance. Microphones taped to the strings and another on the keyboard were crudely attached with industrial tape.
Elvira tapped Beat's shoulder.

'What's with the piano?'

'Ask Lex.'

That wasn't her best idea, because Lex plunged into a detailed account of how the piano would be burned to a cinder in the performance.

Elvira drew a swathe of paper hankies from her shoulder bag. 'But pianos are soulful. How can you sacrifice them?'

'I'd agree,' said Lex, 'But this,' and he slapped the piano which shone in the sun on the cropped lawn, 'is no longer a sound maker. The hammers are threadbare, the pedals rusted. It's a theme park for white ants.'

'You could always spray them,' Elvira blew her nose.

'Except the tuning's beyond repair, it's given up the ghost.'

Lex pulled at his finger joints until each one had clicked.

Elvira stared mournfully at the old Beale upright piano. With its soundboard exposed and microphones stuck on the strings with gaffer tape its vulnerability was provocative.

'Can I have a play?' blurted Elvira.

'Be my guest.' Lex's fingers combed his curls as Elvira began Chopin's *Waltz* in *C# minor*, her go-to encore for recitals. But with crucial keys jammed, the effervescent waltz hobbled rather than danced. Forlorn, she went back to her seat.

Then Winton pointed to the mics wedged between the strings.

'I can't stand to see decent equipment junked. Must you?'

Beat stared at the grass, sensing Lex wanted her support. But she would have to weather testy exchanges during the afternoon's gender equality session, and she'd need all her wits about her then.

Lex's gnarly hands perched on his stomach. 'Welcome to Cobblers Reach and thanks for coming to today's *Burning Questions*. Burning is a sonic union between breaking strings and audience reaction. A piano on fire provokes emotional responses. As it's consumed by flames a human soundtrack of moans and coughs and muffled protest emerges. I record the event with the mics placed inside and outside the piano.'

'More's the pity,' chimed Winton.

Beat flashed him a shut-up-and-listen look.

'You'll hear me play the first movement of Beethoven's *Moonlight Sonata* until the scorching keys toast my digits.' He grinned and wiggled fingers in the air. 'The degeneration of Hi-Fi into Lo-Fi sound caused by mic meltdown underpins the work.' He paused.

'I see alarmed faces but no way I'd destroy this instrument if it wasn't a throwaway.'

He sat down at the keys.

Turning to his audience he added, 'By the way, don't fret about safety issues. My wife and her brother are standing by with fire extinguishers.'

Lex held a match to a scrunched-up page of the 'Moonlight' threaded between the strings, when it caught fire he rolled up his sleeves, brushed a lock of hair away from his eye and began.

The music was choppy, riddled with gaps. Beat found herself singing the missing notes of the melody in her head. When he reached page three, the composer blinked as the fire devoured the sheet music and the piano's husk spewed smoke. His face reddened as he stood up and the piano stool toppled and he clamped a handkerchief to his nose. Purple, red, and yellow flames licked the varnished wood. The flames soared skyward through the upright's open lid. The stench of burnt lacquer made Beat cough.

Pianos had once been as coveted as iPhones or expensive cars and were a prized status symbol of respectable society in colonial days. Now they were giveaways posted on Facebook forums, abandoned on kerbsides or marooned in junk shops, with yellowed keys like rotting teeth. Tortured strings and chargrilled wood melded with Elvira's plaintive, 'How sad, sad, sad.'

Eyes closed, Beat tuned in to the instrument's heart. She breathed in arpeggios, scales, and ornamental trills. Inhaling Chopin's lyricism, Rachmaninov's grandeur, Lizst's virtuosic reaches, she sat tall to Scott Joplin's bounce and verve, Tim Minchin's satire, and Norah Jones' silvery licks.

Soon, the Beale and its ghostly strains spun by fingers past, was charcoaled and misshapen. The white-hot blaze had mottled Beat's cheeks, needled her eyes. She had inhabited the aroma of hope, the scent of ash. Polly, Elvira, Matthew, and Beat remained in their seats, silenced by the ghostly thrum of choruses, tunes, and skeletal chords.

Hermione and Winton went in search of wine. Nobody clapped.

'Wasn't that a cremation?' Beat said to no one in particular.

'Let's go to the massive iron bark over there,' Lex pointed. When everyone was seated in the shade of the tree, he called for questions.

'Were you influenced by auto-destructive art?' Connor asked.

'Probably,' said Lex. 'I watched The Who and especially The Yardbirds' segment in the film *Blow Up*, but issues with this music have been explored endlessly. Let's not go there.'

'That wasn't music,' said Winton pointing at the fire-ravaged instrument. He looked coy when his audience tut-tut-tutted sympathetically.

'From your perspective,' broached Lex with mean eyes.

Connor raised a hand. 'Do you admire Hanatarash, the Japanese art band?'

'No. Aren't they the ones who destroy the set with power tools? And it's a questionable enterprise because the noise is so amped up it can damage the eardrum,' Lex responded.

'The symbolic examples are mind-boggling. Take Nam June Paik's *Danger Music For Dick Higgins* that instructs the performer to "creep into the vagina of a living whale."'

The debate raged on. Beat was distracted by black, yellow-tailed cockatoos combing the lawn for grubs. She half-heartedly tracked the discussion until Connor hauled the debate into complaint.

'Thanks for such an unusual performance. Open debate is stifled at the school. We eternally recycle 'B' word composers – Boccherini, Bach, Brahms, and Bartok. Beethoven stalks our concerts – when as an educational school we ought to embrace today's music,' he said.

Hermione was too busy fussing over a slobbering golden retriever to care. A shame, because needling Connor was one of Hermione's favourite pastimes.

'If that's so,' said Beat, rankled by Connor's public criticism, 'perhaps we could run an annual festival to champion new works by Aussie composers and songwriters?'

'Yes,' agreed Elvira sweeping her loose black locks off her face. 'I nominate Connor to be artistic director.'

24

FERMATA

BEAT hesitated. If only she'd cancelled the discussion and given everyone free time to practise or sleep. Besides, listening to Winton strumming, *While My Guitar Gently Weeps* on an old acoustic guitar he'd discovered in a cupboard was entertaining. She hadn't known he could play that too. He wasn't Prince or George Harrison by any stretch of the imagination, but he sounded credible. She wondered what else she didn't know about Hermione or Elvira or any of them. It could have been just as valuable to sit around and chat agenda free. There wasn't much to see outside except a balding, dun-coloured landscape spiked by spinifex, but soon Courtney in her Akubra hat, riding Bolt and leading Storm, brightened the view. She opened her mouth to begin the meeting but Connor gazumped her.

'Where did this occur?'

'In a rock class,' Elvira replied.

Beat dared not look at Winton. In the glary light, the carpet's swirls were floating, merging, changing shape.

'To summarise,' Connor stated, 'two hoof-shaped fermatas, pause signs, were drawn on a whiteboard upside down intended to resemble a woman's—'

'Breasts? Cut to the chase,' said an exasperated Hermione. 'Boobs, bubbies, bristols, whatever. Milk duds! Ha!'

'Yikes! This is drivel. Preposterous.' Winton propped the guitar against the table.

Beat snatched an agenda and ripped it up. Shock value was a useful distraction. This particular topic could lead to legal repercussions.

'We're *not here* to discuss alleged sexist incidents.' Beat's stern tone swashbuckled through her colleagues' huffs and puffs and mutterings. 'Every enrolled student, regardless of gender has the right to—'

'Dob in the teachers?' Matthew scowled at Beat.

'Learn,' she said firmly.

'Tell these friggin' bleaters to pull their heads in,' Winton said, 'Complaints like that would be ignored in—'

'London.' All of them chanted in precise unison. Elvira chuckled.

Winton pounded his palms on the table.

'Nonsense, Winton,' Beat hesitated. 'Guidelines regarding sexual discrimination, racism, and ageism have been enshrined in policy for decades,' said Beat.

'How very true. We've done this before ad nauseum,' Connor moaned.

'A pity then nothing's changed because discrimination is still alive and kicking.' Beat struggled to slow her breathing. Indignation burned deep inside, down her legs and into her feet. She flexed her toes and lowered her heels comforted by the feel of her boots on the carpeted floor.

'This is new. Never thought you'd go all bloomin' woke on us.' Winton stared at each of his coworkers to enlist support.

'Thanks, I think.' Beat skimmed her notes.

Pursuing this pointy topic after Lex's hospitality was foolhardy. The bonhomie soured the moment Connor had opened his mouth. Polly had predicted antagonism, but she'd stubbornly underestimated the degree of resentment. Clearly, any mention of gender proofing irritated the men.

'The only issue we're considering today is the imperative for the school to offer women the same opportunities as we do the men; to solo, improvise, enter a competition, conduct, or compose,' she said.

'How's this relevant exactly?' Matthew growled.

'All students are entitled to optimal learning conditions. That's the crux of it,' Hermione reasoned.

Beat noticed Connor cradling his head in cupped hands.

'Say something Connor,' Elvira chipped in.

When he didn't reply, the pianist playfully knuckled his shoulder. When there was still no response, she shook his arm and he jolted awake to hoots of laughter. Connor quickly picked up his papers, stood up, pushed his chair under the table, flashed a look of fury at Beat and handed Polly a sealed envelope marked 'confidential'.

Matthew winked at Hermione as Connor marched out.

25

JAM

BEAT looked around the Conference Centre's reception area, hoping to see Connor. It was forty-five minutes until the cabaret, as the bar attendant called it, was to begin. Where could he be? They should at least warm up beforehand. She'd borrowed one of Hermione's tops, a black sequinned number but, to the fashion-conscious clarinettist's dismay, Beat had paired it with jeans. From her perspective she felt overdressed and self-conscious, but a far worse problem was the chill in her clammy hands. Her legs had turned to jelly. Elvira had offered a betablocker for her nerves but she'd refused, thinking it would be cheating, but she'd underestimated just how shaky she'd feel, and how unaccustomed she was to playing in front of an audience. Madison, the Canadian pianist, hadn't played in public for three years, in her case it was five at least. In her own way she was just as arrogant as Connor but she pushed the thought away. She fretted about Connor. Surely, he wouldn't be late for a performance. There was an audience gathering in the lounge area.

'He's gone. The room's empty,' Polly caught her breath. 'I asked reception if he'd checked out. They handed me the sheet music for Cesar Franck's *Violin and Piano Sonata*. A note's attached.'

'What does it say?' Beat said.

Regrettably, I can't play in the concert and Hermione refuses to stand in for me. Suggest you ask Matthew to perform the Cesar Franck. I've marked up Matthew's preferred speeds in the sheet music. Connor

Beat's face flamed. It had been Connor's idea. They'd rehearsed. He'd pushed for the performance only to make a fool of her.

'Hermione, why won't you...' Beat began.

'I'm not up to scratch with the Brahms sonatas. It's heresy, because they're well-crafted but I've never liked them. Connor should have remembered.'

'No way I'll perform with Matthew,' Beat said.

'Why not?' Hermione asked.

'We're incompatible.'

'It's impossible to second guess if there's a musical kinship with someone or not. Even if you perform with a lover, it doesn't necessarily mean there's a musical bond.'

Elvira chewed on her lip. 'I'll do it.'

'Except I wanted to prove that I'm more than a bureaucratic desk jockey.'

'How well d'you know the Franck?' Elvira said.

'Thoroughly.'

'That second movement is treacherous, with its turns and twists and swirling semiquavers sweeping through a range of keys. It's too fast to sightread.' Elvira cautioned.

'I've played it many times.'

'But not recently?'

'Come on Elvira. Out with it,' Hermione cajoled.

'Matthew's a game player.' Elvira cleared her throat, coughed into her hand.

'In a concert?' Beat asked.

Elvira bowed her head, 'I've said enough.'

When Matthew walked in, he picked up on the tension. 'What's all this?'

'Would you play Cesar Franck's *Violin Sonata* with me for the cabaret which begins in forty minutes? There's already a crowd out there waiting.' Beat accented each syllable like nails hammered into wood. 'Connor has pulled out of the Brahms.'

'Smart bugger,' Matthew muttered.

'Will you?' Beat was just as surprised at her change of heart as Elvira and Hermione were.

'Too easy, but then,' Matthew tapped his black patent shoe. 'Can you deliver? You know the music's virtuosic, a piano concerto in all but name,' he said. 'My Franck's fast and furious.'

'Talk is cheap,' quipped Winton.

Elvira studied her phone.

'Not to flaunt your velvet jacket and silver bow tie out there is almost a crime,' Beat teased. 'So, is it a yes?'

'I wouldn't pass up an opportunity like this for the world.'

~

During the run-through, Matthew had been civil and they'd rapidly agreed on the basics and Beat was relieved the tempo they'd settled on for the second movement's spinning finger work was manageable.

Cesar Franck had written the Sonata as a wedding present for the violinist, Eugène Ysaÿe, and the pair of them had performed the work at the reception after the briefest rehearsal. The thought encouraged her, because the run-through with Matthew had been less than ten minutes.

After Hermione's upbeat introduction, expectation ricocheted around the conference centre's guests who lounged in armchairs, leant against walls or sat at the bar. Matthew nodded for Beat to begin, and her sensitive introduction foreshadowed the effervescent figuration she loved to play. They scaled the drama in the big-boned first movement, but at its end, premature applause interrupted the progression to the second. Beat turned her head to acknowledge the crowd's appreciation, but Matthew dived into the second movement before the clapping had petered out.

Somehow, she launched her part and dovetailed with the violin. To explore the searching romanticism, they'd committed to a brisk, yet manageable pace. After Beat fired her solo in anticipation of the big emotions ahead, she understood Elvira's misgivings. Matthew whipped the tempo into a punishing pace, making it a struggle for her to execute her part. She hung on in the purling drifts, missed out too many notes just to keep up. Sweat soaked the keys. She'd read about an Elton John concert in Melbourne where hoards of bogong moths swarmed the stage. Many landed on the keyboard and were crushed by John's fingers. "The keyboard was too slippery to continue," he'd explained as he stomped off stage.

When Elvira delayed the page turn by a blink, Beat's fingers misfired and she stopped. Elvira buried her face in her hands.

The audience was confused as Matthew skittered on, a driver without a car. Seething, Beat rebelled against the classical world's precious rules and perfectionism. Lifting her arms for maximum impact, she slammed them onto the keys with the force of a felled tree. She pinned the sustaining pedal down, and the beefy resonance of random tones drowned out the violin. Shock shadowed Matthew's face when Beat's fingers channelled *Down Under* and the fickle crowd happily belted Men at Work's tongue-in-cheek anthem. Her intervention had been empowering but she was marooned in the limelight with the only rock song she knew by heart rolling to an end. The guests clapped a steady pulse which alarmed her until she realised it was for Winton who was making his way towards the piano, lithely turning his hips between tables and chairs, trumpet aloft.

'Now the fun begins!' he shouted at the crowd as he placed a volume of jazz standards on the piano's music stand. Ever the showman, Winton lifted his arms and roared as if he'd scored a goal. Then before the laughter subsided, he cued Beat in.

In *Take Five*, she swung Dave Brubeck's five-beat-in-a-bar toe tapper and Winton's persuasive playing turned the crowd into a jiving tide. He mouthed 'Summertime' to Beat, and Gershwin's classic sailed as she powered a chunky bass for the trumpet's melody. Relief washed over Winton's face as Beat channelled a few more jazzy classics convincingly. Finally, Beat and Winton, hand in hand, took a bow.

26

MARZIALE

'WHAT a traitor!'

'Hey, Beat, don't let the entire canteen hear you,' scolded Polly.

'He never told me his views at the time,' Beat reeled after reading a letter of complaint from Connor.

'He attended everything, well except for the concert. And I don't recall him being late, not even once.' Polly's advocacy only amplified Beat's frustration. She fisted the table.

'Do you know what I heard Connor say to Matthew?'

'No. What?' Polly warmed her hands around her coffee. It was a brisk morning, the sky a palette of greys and dirty white.

'Oh, never mind.' Beat shook her head, 'Listen.'

I'd hoped we'd debate music history and its relevance to performance, review our courses and revamp the concert program. Instead, the schedule involved an equine assisted learning workshop, gender discrimination, and a lengthy coach trip to attend a brief outdoor performance.

'Keep it down.' Polly put her hand in the air and lowered it step by step. She'd obviously been a close observer of Garrett's conducting.

'He was majorly involved in the EAL. Keen on Canon's music.'

'I'm guessing he went along with those things but it doesn't mean he approved of them,' Polly argued.

'He hijacked Canon's post-performance discussion to moan about our insufficient focus on contemporary composers.'

Polly put her coffee down. 'I can see why you're concerned about his er... strong views.'

'How about this?' Beat spoke in a hushed tone.

This misguided event was financially wasteful without identifiable outcomes.

'Okay,' Polly said, 'I get it.' Her assistant shrank back, hugged her arms to her chest. 'No wonder you're upset.'

'He's a backstabber.' Beat's voice turned shrill. 'How about his no show for the performance he initiated?'

'Now that seriously wasn't good,' Polly said.

'Pedantic twittery.' Heads turned towards Beat's table as she waggled the letter in the air.

'Ssssh, lower your voice.'

Beat cast an eye around the canteen.

'Did he find the retreat confronting?' Polly asked.

'Meaning?'

'Has he ever attended a stay away conference?'

Beat rolled her eyes. 'He hijacked Courtney's session. Showed off with *my* horses.'

'But you liked that.'

'I did?'

'You thought he set a good example, remember?'

'Swanning around in deluxe casuals, like a smug escapee from an R.M. Williams catalogue. What was that about?'

'For what it's worth, I thought he showed willing,' said Polly. 'Everyone knows he has a thing for brands, he wears Barbour jackets like an English nob.'

'Oh, Pol. Everyone drank too much because of him, including me, and we all nursed hangovers all the way to Coffee Camp. Now this.' Beat screwed the letter into a tight ball and lobbed it along the floor like a pebble skimming a creek's skin.

Beat didn't hear the *clackety clack* of Hermione's approaching high heels.

'You dropped something,' she said, handing Beat the scrunched-up letter. 'Enjoyed the time away. It was refreshing.'

'Refreshing?' Beat queried.

'To talk about stuff besides music.'

Beat ignored Hermione's sarcasm.

'Not everybody agrees, mind you.' She placed a hand on Beat's shoulder. 'And airing your wounds in public isn't a great idea.'

Despondent, Beat turned to Polly. 'I thought our time away had opened up communication?'

'It has. That letter's addressed to you. No one's been copied in, which means Connor's views are contained.'

'I suppose.'

'Please don't shoot the messenger.'

'Now what?'

'An official letter has arrived from Thorne. You'd better read it in private.'

'Oh great. What now?'

'No idea. Sorry.'

Beat nodded, grabbed her stuff and left. A string quartet had set up on the lawn to rehearse. She loved the lament in the slow movement of Schubert's *Death and the Maiden Quartet*, even if its European origins were alien under an Australian sky. She slowed down to listen.

'Beat, I need to see you.' She turned recognising Theo's voice. He looked dejected despite his smart clothes and revamped image. Now, he could read music, he was getting masses of freelance work around town.

'How's it going?'

'Better, thanks.' Theo kicked at a stone.

Beat caught a glimpse of Connor ahead. He'd seen her but pretended he hadn't.

'Walk with me, Theo.'

He fell in step, violin hooked over his shoulder. Rock students strolled past. A guitarist's hair stood to attention like a cockie's comb, shaved at the back and sides. White-soled trainers, black tees, and jeans were today's look. Theo's pale blue shirt and camel pants anchored him on the classical side of the tracks, his cowboy boots cast aside for brown lace-ups, hair razored short. A large frill-necked lizard soaked up the sun on the concrete steps leading to the Dean's studio, diving into a clump of long grass as they approached.

Once inside, Beat tried not to catch Theo's troubled eyes lest she intimidate him. A sizeable cockroach sashayed along the lip of the skirting board. What with the occasional mouse, a huntsman spider's leg slung over the air conditioner on hot days, and ant trains following rainfall, the studio was becoming a wildlife reserve.

'I can't learn from Matthew anymore,' Theo said.

Requests for a different teacher were common, because the dynamic in a one-plus-one lesson – good or bad – was intense. If there was a clash of wills, a touch of the bully, a sexual frisson, the relationship soured. Sometimes, a student got a crush on the teacher or the other way around. Despite the shortcomings, the old-school, master-apprentice teaching model was held sacred by those training professional musicians.

'Why? Matthew thinks highly of you.'

Polly's *rat-a-tat-tat* on the door was a superfluous reminder about Thorne's letter. Were all personal assistants this intrusive? 'Keep going Theo.'

'Matthew's always late. I go in, set everything up and tune and then the phone rings. They're business calls. I've already lost, say, ten minutes waiting outside his door, but he never says, "I'll call you back I'm teaching." Instead, he chats for fifteen, sometimes twenty minutes.'

'How's his teaching otherwise?'

'Great. He's supercritical yet constructive. He has cool ideas about how to play a piece.'

'Theo, I'll remind staff not to accept calls during a lesson. And I'll find you another teacher if things don't improve. How's that?'

No sooner had Theo left when Polly walked in and pointedly placed the letter on her keyboard.

'Forewarned is forearmed. Go somewhere you can be alone to read it.'

~

Beat unlocked the door of the recital hall. With the blinds drawn, it was dark, the air stale. She sat in the very back row. Between concerts, performance classes, and rehearsals, the hall was people-free. It was her refuge, where she could take stock and revisit treasured performances. Here, she'd heard rock, jazz, classical, and experimental groups and some of the world's great musical stars: Ann Louise Cole singing *Brunnhilde* from Wagner's *Ring Cycle*, violinists Ray Chen and Hilary Hahn, First Nations rapper Kid Laroi, Katie Noonan, Diana Krall, Crowded House's Neil Finn, William Barton the internationally feted didgeridoo player, and Tom Thum, Queensland's genius beat boxer. The Australian String Quartet's cinematic spin on Shostakovich's post-Second World War *String Quartet no. 8* with the KGB's *rap-rap-rap* on a victim's door, portrayed in the music, had chilled her to the bone. Elvira's barnstorming spin on Beethoven's *Waldstein Sonata* with daring extra-stretched silences had been stunning. If only she could sit here and relive performances all day, but she was procrastinating. Her heart pumping too fast, her mouth dry. She forced herself to read.

> *Dear Beatrice*
>
> *It has been brought to my attention that the recent staff retreat was financially wasteful without identifiable outcomes. I summons you to a formal meeting. Please note the University's Vice-Chancellor will be in attendance. Date and time to be confirmed.*
>
> *Yours sincerely,*
> *Marilyn Thorne.*

She was incensed. All she'd done was organise a professional development getaway as the Turalong Council had recommended. The wording bothered her and then she realised they were from Connor's letter. It was unfair of Thorne to criticise the retreat, especially since she'd obviously not read the draft program. Connor would no doubt say authority figures didn't like surprises and, if she were honest, she wasn't keen on them either. Why hadn't she rung Thorne and asked her what she thought of the itinerary. Had she been afraid Thorne wouldn't approve of her ideas?

She parked her feet on the plum-coloured seat in front. She constantly upset people and muddled protocols. If she didn't lose her job, she'd stop initiating anything risky, challenging, overly stimulating, innovative, or brilliant. Oddly, especially exciting projects seemed to get the authorities and Thorne offside. She'd imagined she would be praised for chasing excellence. Bitterly, she concluded, the fallout wasn't worth it in a higher education environment.

27

INTERLUDE

'HOW are things?' Sally's tone was caring. She looked immaculate in a white top, long camel skirt, her fingernails shellacked white. Everything was white as far as Beat could see, from the soft furnishings and sofa to the carpet and walls and even the cat. She wondered if it would be rude to keep her sunglasses on. Beat regretted her faded shirt and jeans but she couldn't compete with Sally. Her friend cooked, gardened and did the messiest of chores in pastel maxi dresses which remained crisp and clean. She had neglected Sally since her promotion and she'd forgotten her knowing eyes could be so intimidating. She felt stripped, not to the buff but to her very soul. She lay on the floor, unable to resist the comfort of her friend's soft rug and her white cat purring on her chest. She hadn't intended to talk about workplace politics but concealing anything from Sally, who was the most intuitive person she'd ever met, was impossible.

'Seriously, how are you?'

'Scarcely sleeping,' Beat confessed much to her own surprise.

'Dan?'

'Not really. It's nothing.'

'Not if it bugs you?'

'Look, who am I to think I could heal the rift between the classical mob and rock.'

'That's why you took your team away.'

'Team? Dream on.' Beat reached for a homemade biscuit, the icing also white.

'Dysfunctional perhaps but a team nevertheless.'

Beat rose and went to the picture window. 'Look at the blue sky. Not a cloud in sight.' The profusions of orange and red nasturtiums spilling from the repurposed whisky barrel looked inviting. 'Sally, can we sit outside on the patio? I spend too much time indoors.'

'Sure. Take the Adirondack. I sit on it when I take a break and watch the horses.'

'Really?'

'Yes, especially when Bolt lunges at Storm's neck and plants a bite.'

'Sadist. I like it when Bolt's all frisk and buck and his agitation mirrors mine.'

Blue-flowered ageratum weed blanketed a vast corner of Sally's yard. Soon, it would spread across the entire paddock. The property was on vegetated protected land like her own and if the Council came for a weed inspection, Sally could be fined. She'd have to clear it for her friend's sake and the horses since it was harmful if they ate too much of it. A pity, since she loved the deep blue blossom, and it was a delicacy for bees.

'Beat, were you happy with the staff sleepover?'

'It kick-started better communication.'

'Not to be sneezed at.'

'True.'

'Why aren't you over the moon about it?'

'Hey look.' Beat pointed at Bolt, 'He's got passengers.'

'Those orange-beaked egrets stick close.' Sally smiled.

'Never seen two on his back. He's mellowing. Couldn't we yarn about fun things on such a lovely day?'

'Not until you cough up what's gnawing at you. I can feel it.' Sally put a hand on her heart.

'Marilyn Thorne thinks the retreat was misguided and she quoted a sentence from a critical letter I received from Connor.'

'She's the big kahuna?'

'The very same. How, I've no idea, but she knew the content of Connor's critical letter.'

'Is it the treason or the criticism?'

'Meaning?'

'What bugs you the most?'

'Mmm... the betrayal.' A quivering unease stirred in Beat's gut.

'Because of Danny boy?' Sally's mouth was full of biscuit.

'Don't! This isn't about him.'

'Here's to progress,' Sally took another bite. 'Who then? Hey, look at Storm. Should he be lying down?'

'He's snoozing.'

'D'you suspect anyone?'

'Connor.'

'Because?' Sally rolled up her sleeves.

Indian Mynas chased a crow across the sky.

'Of his private letter which somehow Thorne must have read.'

Sally pulled a face. 'Surely the man's entitled to an opinion?'

Beat flinched when the birds savaged the crow mid-flight.

Sally ruffled her blond hair. 'Was it lavish?'

'I economised in every way I could.'

A helicopter flew low. The brutal *thump, thump, thump,* of the rotors hurt Beat's ears. No wonder Stockhausen's quartet for airborne choppers had made such an impact. Startled, the horses reared, running in fits and starts.

When the bruising chopper sound waned, the horses dropped their heads to graze.

'Connor's negativity can't invalidate anything unless you let it.' Sally picked a crumb off her shirt.

A magpie trilled. A breeze picked up.

'It already has,' Beat admitted.

'Do you have feelings for him?'

28
ARDENTE

TODAY'S committee had the mentality of a hunting pack out to catch a fox. Beat gasped when Connor arrived. Spluttering an apology for being late – if only he afforded her the same courtesy – he grinned at the Vice-Chancellor and sat beside him. Connor's tailored jacket had a charcoal sheen. He may as well have been on the University's payroll. He looked over-dressed. Prideful. Just another suit.

'Beatrice, we're looking into the recent staff retreat, and the expenditure on a horsey encounter group.'

Connor whispered in the VC's ear.

'Sorry, I meant, Equine Assisted Learning. Beatrice, do you wish to table any documents?'

'Yes,' said Beat, louder and more emphatically than she'd intended. She mustn't let Connor's presence muddle her thinking; she had to filter him out, like an unwanted sonic strand in a recording.

'This is a paper charting the use of horse workshops in America and Britain to aid workplace communication.' She hesitated, swallowed, curled a strand of hair around her ear. Beyond the window, the rhythmic *whoosh whoosh* of passing cars compounded her apprehension.

'I've also a petition lodged by a second-year cellist accusing the school of gender bias. A charge which implicates Turalong Arts.'

Thorne tensed, infuriated. If looks could harm, Beat was pretty sure she would be on her way to hospital.

She reached for a tissue. Her supervisor's Dolce and Gabbana scent tickled her nose. Perched on Thorne's bookcase was a spherical shape suspended in a jar of murky water. Its resemblance to a frog sickened her, no doubt a concoction prescribed by an alternative medical practitioner.

'Marilyn, please share your concerns,' said the VC.

Thorne's kohl-rimmed eyes narrowed.

'The equestrian malarkey was a blatant misuse of funds.'

'You mean EAL,' the VC corrected.

An ambulance screamed down the main road.

'You can't say that, Marilyn.' Beat insisted, speaking too fast. 'You didn't attend although you were invited. I gave you the draft program to consider. If you didn't like the idea, why didn't you say so? Connor played a major role in the horse activity. He and I are the only ones who can judge its effectiveness. We were there.'

Beat recognised the heavyset, carved Indonesian table moved into Thorne's office. It was the one used in her interview to be director. Her hands had trembled then. Today, they shook so much she had to thread her fingers together to still them as they lay on her lap.

'I don't like your...' Thorne began, but the VC silenced her with a steadying hand on the small of her back. Outside, a grumbling motor bike meandered through the traffic.

Propped against the bookcase was her supervisor's antique walking cane. To Beat's disgust, the handle appeared to be real tortoiseshell. Thorne used it when she walked from the car park to her office. Turalong staff debated its purpose, some said it was an emotional prop, others argued she'd damaged her knee when she fell off a bicycle on a cycling trip in New Zealand. Beat thought about snapping it in two.

The VC looked around the table. 'Connor, our staff representative, has a question.'

'Beatrice, why did you organise a retreat?'

'I responded to a directive. I've copies of the relevant extract from the minutes of the Council's December 10th meeting last year.'

Thorne's assistant circulated photocopies.

Beat ran her fingers through her hair.

'A motion was carried that the dance, art, and music schools should organise professional development activities to explore issues of general and specialist concern.'

'I see.' The VC nodded.

'Gender bias was our general topic.' Beat met Connor's eyes, but his stony expression was impossible to decipher.

'Why pay for a conference centre?' Connor said.

'Steven Hadley made several efforts to draw the staff together; in meetings, on picnics, and even a forest bathing excursion, but his efforts failed. If insanity is trying to get a different outcome by repeating the same means to attain it, well, I'm guilty of attempting something new. I took everyone out of their comfort zone.'

Her heart raced; she dug her fingernails into her leg. The deafening silence was intimidating not only for her but for anyone dragged into its centre.

The VC flicked his pen onto the table. 'Do you regret the gender deafness session?'

'Absolutely not,' Beat shook her head. 'But it's a touchy issue.'

Beat eyeballed Connor, but he looked away. What a pitiful grub. Dan was wrong about him. She traced a pattern on the floor with the toe of her boot and she was cantering on Bolt, his black mane streaming in the wind as he splashed along the Nudgee Beach shoreline.

'Women are being disadvantaged. If I hadn't taken action, the student lobby group could have gone to the press,' Beat said.

Closing her eyes, Thorne groaned and sank deeper into her chair.

'I see.' The VC's red and yellow African waistcoat strained against its buttons, begging for release. 'According to Connor there was little music-related discussion. Is this true?'

'Not at all. He may not have *liked* the particular musical content, but that doesn't mean there wasn't any. I shared my goals. We agreed to broaden our specialisms to include the didgeridoo, the guzheng, a Chinese zither, sitar, theremin, and accordion. Debated an ambitious fundraiser.'

'What would you spend a surplus on?' asked the VC, tapping his gold Mont-Blanc pen on the table.

'Two awards for women, one for composing and another for conducting.'

'Reasonable objectives.' The VC scribbled in his diary.

'Yes.' Beat slipped her trembling hands under her thighs. Thorne reached for a handful of smoked almonds but her elbow jogged the VC's arm and his coffee spilled. Beat teetered into her own world, sitting forward in the saddle. Bolt quickened his gait, tucked his front legs under and cleared the massive trunk of a felled tree.

'Beatrice, your recruitment of an,' he ran a finger down his notes, 'equine therapist is puzzling. Please explain,' the Vice-Chancellor said.

'The school's divide between genres is untenable.' Beat drank some water, wiped her mouth with the back of her hand.

'Go on.'

'EAL best suited our needs. To economise, I used my horses. The course leader was formerly a professional musician.'

'An insignificant saving.' Thorne exchanged a meaningful look with the VC.

'We'll adjourn now.' His words prompted grateful nods and Connor and Thorne's assistant got up and headed for the door.

'Wait,' Beat cried out. Everyone froze. Connor frowned. About to push his chair under the table the VC stalled. She heard the keening bassoon heralding Stravinsky's *Rite of Spring*. 'What are the likely outcomes of this review process?'

29

GEMONDO

ROUND in the face, with thick-rimmed glasses, the intensity of the lawyer's piercing blue eyes, the colour of a Caribbean Sea, made her uncomfortable. Much to her relief, he took off his glasses, blew on the lenses and polished them vigorously with a cloth whipped from his desk draw. In the background, Mendelssohn's *Fingals Cave Overture* distracted her as the foaming orchestral waves lapped at the Scottish cave's rugged lip.

'Times have changed, Ms Snow.' Cholmley stole a glance at his paperwork. 'It's an unpalatable reality, but you may be obliged to continue to support your husband until your joint assets are legally split. Dan's doing a PhD?'

'Yes. But it's not fair.'

A musty odour mingled with beeswax polish repelled her.

Repositioning his glasses on his nose, he asked, 'Was there some kind of monetary agreement between you and Dan?'

'Yes. I paid the bills. In exchange, Dan took care of the household and the property's two-and-a-half acres.'

'Was this documented? Signed? Dated? Witnessed?'

'No.'

'Ah.' Cholmley clamped his lips together, shook his head. 'Women pioneered the argument that homebodies contribute, not a salary as such, but an *in-kind* contribution to a shared economy.'

'He never did it well or graciously.' The ebb and flow of Mendelssohn's surging swells heightened, the spume of salty foam reaching for the sky.

'Alas, Ms Snow how *well* Dan fulfilled these duties is irrelevant. The point is he assumed a mutually beneficial role.'

'Well paid, are you?' Cholmley scanned her outfit, her neck and wrist for jewellery. Self-conscious, she knew her R.M. Williams boots were her most expensive item but he was hardly going to look under the table.

'The job's demanding.'

'No need to be defensive. Your Tchaikovsky concert with the barefoot lass was a feather in your cap. Won't be forgetting that anytime soon. Now...'

Cholmley peered at his notes, knitted his brows. 'Let me see, where was I?'

The antique mahogany furniture crammed into a small office ensured an air of solemnity. Grey paintwork did nothing to ease the gloom. She was grateful for the sliver of sunlight beaming through a wooden blind's open slats which patterned Cholmley's desk. Dusty hard back books claimed all surfaces, his desk and even a plant stand. Twin towers of paperbacks balanced on the floor. She decided he needed urgent assistance from a de-clutterer or Feng Shui specialist.

'If Dan used a ride-on mower to cut the grass, for instance, that saved you from paying a professional around $350 per fortnight in summer.'

Beat frowned at this man who seemed to argue in Dan's favour. She wished she'd tracked down her own lawyer and hadn't so quickly settled on Hermione's recommendation.

As if reading her mind, Cholmley sighed.

'You think I'm batting for your husband's team?'

'Well...' Mendelssohn's pleading intensified, a flute sang like a shaft of light on a gnarly treacle sea.

'I'm not, but, if I'm to represent you in the Family Court, I have to make you aware of alternative perspectives and feasible outcomes. You need to know what you're up against.'

'Fair enough. Dan's been harassing me for money.' Beat unwrapped a mint and popped it in her mouth.

'I imagine you're reluctant to give Dan any in light of his infidelity.'

'Correct.'

'Nowadays, my dear, divorce has a 'no blame' ethos. It's no longer the squabbling circus of who-did-what-to-whom.'

Absorbed by a violent tussle between woodwind and strings she didn't respond.

'The Court's brief is to ensure both parties have a fair and equitable distribution of assets. Now let's get down to brass tacks.' Cholmley tucked his chin into his chest and peered over his glasses.

'The cave music? Shall I turn it off?'

'Please.'

'Does Dan have assets? Stocks? Shares? Does he own luxury items? A sports car, Patek Philippe watch, a holiday house? Does he have capital squirreled away?'

'His Ducati is probably more of a liability than an asset. He has no capital or anything of value.'

'I see. Do you happen to know whether the Ducati was second-hand, new, or a classic?' Cholmley underlined something in his notes and swept his hand high in the air, like a violinist's elevated bow at the end of a performance. Only yesterday, she'd witnessed a string quartet make the same theatrical flourish after sounding the final chord.

'He told me it was second-hand but in good condition.'

'How about you?'

'I own a Stewart piano, worth $100,000.'

'Anything else?'

'No, except for Wongara, the farm and contents, but that's a joint asset.'

The lawyer cleared his throat. 'The settlement may involve the sale of the farm.'

'Oh no but...'

'Think about your situation. As an academic in a dean's position, you will be accruing superannuation, you probably have private health cover. Think about what you'd be prepared to sacrifice.'

Beat shrugged, her legs heavy, weighted to the floor.

'You own *two* horses?' Cholmley continued.

'Yes.'

'Are they stabled?'

'In poor weather.'

'You've a hay shed?'

'A modest one.' Beat looked at her hands. She'd bitten her nails to the quick.

'Could you rehome these steeds?'

'Never.' Beat had to leave. The office was airless and the walls pressed in. Her forehead prickled with sweat. Hastily removing her jacket and not wanting to meet Cholmley's eyes, she bowed her head.

'Not even one?'

'No,' a tear rolled down her cheek. 'They're family. I won't separate...' She gulped, her face washed with colour. 'Horses have close relationships, just as humans do.'

'Then we've established the line in the sand, your non-negotiable asset.'

She gathered from the framed cricket bat signed by Allan Border, and the photographs of Cholmley dressed in white about to bowl, that cricket was the lawyer's non-negotiable.

'Would you consider giving Dan a third of your super and continue to pay his private health cover in exchange for reducing his share in the property?'

'It's so unfair.'

'When has life ever been fair Ms Snow?'

30
SOTTO VOCE

AS the practice room door opened, Beat froze at Connor's imperious tone. 'A word, please. It's important.'

She'd reached the third movement of Beethoven's *Appassionata Sonata*. Her fingers pliable and fired but she lost her focus. What a nerve. She was in deep water because of him, and this was her never-to-be-interrupted-time. Her managerial self in lockdown, her mind immersed in music. For ninety minutes each week, she played the piano. Thorne had urged her to as a stress buster. Not once had anyone bothered Beat during this time, not even Matthew or Hermione. If she had to be interrupted, she would have preferred Winton or even Dan to do it.

Well, not Dan, she really had to curb her tendency to exaggerate.

'I'm unavailable.' For him anyway, after his accusatory letter and attendance at that dreadful meeting.

'Yes, that's true for now, but I checked your diary. Polly's so helpful,' Connor said cheerily. 'You finish in an hour. Let's meet at *Poco Mosso* in the Arts Centre around midday.' She didn't make eye contact but stared at the music.

At a management course, the course leader had stressed how important it was to keep the "lines of communication open" but she doubted that she'd ever encountered an insufferable, know-it-all like Connor. She remembered his arrival at the disciplinary session and how he smiled at the VC as if they were buddies, and a dull ache took up residence behind her left eye. Connor was a health risk.

'I'll come if I can, but something could crop up.'

'It already has – lunch. Polly crossed out two hours in the diary. I'll wait.'

She flexed her toes, gritted her teeth. How could Polly have arranged a two-hour lunch without talking to her about it first especially since she knows how she feels about Connor.

'That's up to you.' Beat's mood darkened. After all the trouble he'd caused, the last thing she wanted was a cosy, tête-à-tête. Positioning her fingers on the keys, she began to play, but couldn't rekindle her former engagement. Her concentration was shot. Fielding Beethoven's extreme tonal contrasts was no longer pleasurable. Five minutes alone with Connor was awkward, two hours, interminable. Maybe Hermione's instincts about him were accurate.

~

Connor ordered tea, Beat an Americano. She disliked the café's memorabilia. She'd never been a fan of music-inspired décor. All those dreary dust gatherers, the Bach, Mozart, and Beethoven busts colonising bookshelves, wallpaper freckled by quavers, and decorative piano music boxes. Staff wore black tees with *Belissimo* italicised across their chests. If anyone had failed to notice the café's cultural aspirations, famous operatic arias were piped into the dining area, but castrated by a hushed volume. Today's aria featured Maria Callas' impassioned *One Fine Day* from Puccini's *Madame Butterfly*. Arias of doom like this one were tear chasers. Puccini, if somehow spirited to life, would shake his fists at how strangled, how compromised his heartrending aria sounded when reduced to a whisper. Connor, she noticed, seemed at ease among the crass pretension.

After spooning not one but two heaped sugars into his tea, Connor stirred the saccharine brew for many more circuits than necessary, and he spooned *chinkety-clink chinkety clink* on the rim of his ceramic cup, irritating the elderly woman on a nearby table. An obsessive-compulsive disorder, she assumed. It was all she could do to sit opposite him. She'd have words with Polly when she got back because this unwanted get together could never happen again.

'What's the afternoon have in store?' asked Connor.

'Paperwork.'

'There's no way I can put what I have to say delicately,' Connor began.

Beat waited, but he said nothing. Instead, Madame Butterfly's high G speared the lemon painted ceiling. She studied the collage of composers pinned under the round table's glass cover. All the usual suspects, but she was heartened to find Hildegard of Bingen's portrait, one of the first women composers in Western music's history.

'I should apologise,' said Connor.

'For?'

'The... um... letter,' spluttered Connor. 'I was out of line.'

'You think?' Beat picked up the menu conveniently large enough to hide her flushed face. Lowering it she said, 'Not to mention your no show for our performance.'

A young waitress parroted the specials, 'Slow cooked lamb on a bed of roasted tomatoes. A Thai prawn curry. Seafood risotto with endive and orange garnish.'

'Anything vegetarian?' Beat enquired.

'Eggplant and lentil moussaka,' the waitress said.

'I'd like that.'

'Me too,' said Connor.

The waitress tripped away. Connor studied the table in silence.

'Don't keep me in suspense.'

'Very well. At State Orchestra's concert last week, the one with Philip Glass' *11th Symphony*, Ralph, the VC and I got chatting.'

'Ralph?' Beat sounded sarcastic.

'We went to school together. And he copped an earful.'

'I bet he did. Do you want to completely ruin my day?' Beat looked around. Nearly all the tables were taken. She hoped the service would be prompt and this testy exchange could end. Connor rubbed at his neck compulsively and his sun-savaged skin reddened. It reminded her of Bolt, who scratched his neck repetitively against a fence post. Now she was really losing it, comparing people to horses.

'Thing is, Ralph liked the retreat program's balance between music and its general focus on equal opportunity,' Connor said. 'He told me, in his high-handed fashion, well, lectured more to the point, that unless specialist staff enshrined non-discriminatory principles in all of our activities, regardless of how many brilliant performances we chalk up, the school's credibility was at risk.'

'Why?' asked Beat.

'Our concerts and course offerings must reflect equality and offer opportunities to all students regardless of gender, race, age, or sexual orientation.'

'Everything I raised at the retreat, basically.' Beat clenched her jaw at his mansplaining and fanned herself with the laminated menu. Anything to deflect her anger, because she longed to shriek at him until his eardrums burst.

'Yes, but there's more.'

The waitress arrived with the moussaka, Beat ignored the steaming dish.

'Back up a minute. Why did you send a copy of your letter to Thorne?'

'What on earth makes you think I did?' Connor raised his voice.

'Why else did she say the retreat was extravagant. You're chummy with Thorne and her chorus of suits.'

'No. How wrong you are. Had I wanted Marilyn to read it, I'd have copied her in. What else are you het up about?'

'Since you strongly disapproved of Courtney's equine session, why did you have a major role in it?'

'I was persuaded it would raise morale.'

Beat shook her head. 'Rather hypocritical.'

'I was flattered. My ego got in the way.'

'And you still owe me an apology for leaving me high and dry before the Cabaret at the Conference Centre.'

'Can we discuss that another time. I have to tell you something. It's important.'

'Go on then.'

'Now this next bit is difficult. Really difficult.'

'I'm all ears.'

Beat sighed, trilled her third finger and thumb on the table, pleased by their dexterity since she'd begun practising again. But she was exasperated by Connor's stops and starts and how, for no apparent reason, his voice tailed off and he'd stop talking. She tapped his arm for him to continue.

'You're in strife with the university, the school council, and Thorne.'

'I know.' Her mouth was dry, she drank some water.

'But you'll never guess why.'

'Surprise me.' She tried to catch the eye of a friendly State Orchestra player. Recognition from just about anyone else right now would be welcome.

'But don't...'

'What?' Beat said.

'Take it out on me.'

'That I can't promise.'

'The powers have come down on you like the sword of Damocles.' Connor paused. 'Not because you're doing a bad job.' He inhaled deeply, fingers pressed into his temples. Beat scanned *Poco Mosso's* black marble counter which harboured the faux gold busts of Verdi and Wagner, offset by vases of white peace lilies. The interior designer evidently had no idea that Verdi and Wagner were staunch rivals, poles apart creatively. Adversaries who shunned each other's operas.

'Don't stop now, Connor,' Beat warned.

'You're in trouble because you're doing a *great* job.'

Her heart skipped a beat. She replayed his words in her head.

'That's crazy. What are you talking about?'

'You got the position of dean because the selection panel thought you'd be inept, out of your depth and the school's reputation would plummet.'

'Oh, great.' She looked at her now cold and unappetising dish. Connor had somehow eaten all of his even though he'd been doing most of the talking.

'And now our stocks are running high,' he said.

'"Running high" is a bit strong. Our reputation has improved. Are you absolutely certain about this. It doesn't seem plausible.'

Connor shrugged, stared at her with earnest eyes. 'Our public profile soared after Georgy upstaged the university's Luna Medina bash. Brace yourself.'

'Why?' Beat stabbed the neglected lasagne with a fork. 'What could be worse than I was appointed because I'd make a mess of it?'

'You've gone pale. Are you okay?'

'No. And nor would you be if your job was on the line. I'm my family's sole breadwinner. I've a hefty mortgage on my farm and it looks like I'll have to sell up.'

She ate a mouthful of her tepid lunch. Forced herself to concentrate on Connor's bizarre revelations.

'Why would Thorne or the University want us to fail?'

'The University's grand plan is to amalgamate our school with its own music faculty. When the time comes, the Uni will nominate someone, I'm guessing a tame, biddable individual they can trust. Probably someone without a music background.'

'Ludicrous,' said Beat.

'Musicians are branded as troublemakers and you,' he pointed at her accusingly, 'fit the stereotype. Passionate, driven, and willing to do anything to protect or better the school.'

'And those aren't virtues?'

'In a university? Definitely not. No. It means you care for the discipline, and you'll fight for it. They'll transfer you. Give you a reasonable golden handshake or a mundane role somewhere where you'll have no influence because of your sex.'

Beat winced when she remembered the naïve, ambitions plans she'd proclaimed in her interview.

I want to make the school reach for the stars.

The panel had responded with sparkling eyes and fulsome smiles. Optimism had surged through her veins. She had felt proud. Excited. But they'd chosen her to tank the place, to ensure its demise? Gloom weighed her down. She'd lost Dan because her professional mission had become more important to her than him and she'd neglected her horses and dogs. Constantly on alert, tackling one crisis after another, like the Beatles' song she'd been pulled here, there, and everywhere. Despite all her efforts, Thorne's support had dwindled. And now this upstart fuddy-duddy with friends in high places confides in her. Why? She'd noticed how Thorne gave him approving looks. Quite clearly, she favoured him.

'Why the silence?' Connor placed his knife and fork together on his clean plate.

'I'm trying to digest what you've told me and this,' she said, tapping the congealed cheesy topping with her knife. 'I'm not sure which is worse.'

Outside, the world glistened, slick with rain. Water sluiced down the kerbside. Raindrops bounced off the pedestrian's umbrellas.

'Look, I have to go, I've a meeting with Opera Underground,' said Beat.

'Cancel it. We're talking mine and yours and everyone's future.'

'After the mayhem you've caused... and exactly how long have you known why I was selected to be dean?'

'I can fill you in about that. But listen, the school's future is at stake,' he said.

'Really. Or is yours?' Beat was taken aback to see Johnny Wood a few tables away spearing crispy calamari coils as he hung off Matthew's every word. The violinist would be lobbying Johnny for his own ends, and no doubt at her expense. But far worse was seeing Thorne and the VC in the restaurant's far corner. When she spotted them, they looked away. She leaned forward and whispered, 'Thorne and the VC are here.'

'I'll go,' said Connor. 'Take this to pay the bill.' Placing a hundred-dollar bill on the table he waved her protest away.

'We have to talk again.'

'I don't think so.'

'There's more you need to know.'

Could he rattle her any more than he'd already done?

'Then just once.' She sliced her hands through the air as if she was directing a choir to round off a final sustained chord.

31

A PIACERE

RAPPITTY-rap.

Who could it be? The clock read 8:15. She looked around for the incriminating empty wine bottle which had rolled onto the carpet, but craning her neck made her queasy. She clutched the back of her desk chair to steady herself and reached the door.

Rappity-rap Rappity-rap.

If it were security, they'd use their key. It had to be Matthew. He often worked late. She flung the door open expecting to see her violin-toting nemesis but instead her rheumy eyes met Connor's who stared in alarm. Was he shocked? Was it her unruly hair or because she was stonkered? Stifling a hiccup, she clamped her hands over her mouth and ignored a curious impulse to rest her head on his chest. Where did that come from? A sexual harassment complaint on top of the other misdemeanours she'd been accused of would be too much. She ushered him in but clung to the door handle.

'What d'you want?'

'Your light's on,' he explained. 'People strolling past your office at night get a clear view inside.'

'So what?' But she had, only moments before, been dancing to David Bowie's *Let's Dance* with flailing rubbery arms, like an intoxicated octopus. The cool groove, Stevie Ray Vaughan's bluesy edge, Bowie's deadpan delivery and humanitarian plug for the plight of Indigenous Australians made her kick off her shoes and spring to her feet. She'd swung her hips, fluffed up her hair and a bag of cashews in her hand had scattered everywhere. One had landed on the glass top of the aquarium.

Having knocked back a bottle of pinot grigio, which she'd found in the bar fridge, her scratchy thoughts about Thorne, Dan and Georgy, and Connor's disturbing news had retreated. The irony! All she had to do to be appreciated was fail and the more spectacularly the better. She glanced at her overcrowded desk but the urgency to organise it had gone.

'I thought we could talk.' Connor's keen eye registered the scatter of nuts, the discarded bottle. 'Clearly, this isn't a good time.'

'Sit.' Beat pointed at a chair. 'I'll get you some wine.'

She fetched a bottle of Reisling from the fridge. She swigged on it but its sweetness offended her tongue and yet she offered him some anyway.

'No,' Connor blinked, held up a hand. 'I have to drive.'

Well of course he did, he was a tiresome, rule abider. Why be spontaneous? Why take a risk? She bet he left nothing to chance when he conducted. His beige performances would be scrubbed, pressed, pleated, and suffocated. He was the kind who fostered dull music making.

'Yes. Me too.' She belched. A sickening cashew-smell choked the air. Beat jabbed her forefinger onto Connor's chest and hiccupped. He frowned.

'Why're you here?'

'It'll keep. You've been through a lot,' Connor said.

'Like?'

'Dan and...' Connor looked away, embarrassed.

'That's not... Dan's not your...'

'Hey, you're looking seedy. Would you like some water?'

She remembered her outburst. He'd offered her water then too. What made her behave badly around him?

Connor put a hand on her shoulder, but a sympathetic gesture was the last straw after weeks of rejection, critical flak, treachery, and now a conspiratorial twist.

'Are you okay?' he asked gently.

When his hand squeezed her shoulder again, she sobbed. How dare he be kind? The walls began to rotate, slowly at first, but then it was if she was inside a spinning, washing machine. Her stomach heaved. Something bubbled up. Singeing her throat. Connor snatched the wastepaper bin. Positioning it for her, he awkwardly pulled her hair back while she retched and retched and retched. Embarrassment would mortify her soon, but not now.

'Here,' Connor handed her the box of tissues she reserved for other people's crises.

'Driving's not an option.'

'I'll sleep in there.' Beat gestured at the dean's studio. 'I'm due for another auto-da-fe inquisition tomorrow morning.'

'Must you?' Connor said.

'What?'

'Catastrophise.'

She moaned, put her head between her knees. Not knowing whether she was too hot or cold, shivery yet burning up.

'Wait here,' Connor ordered. 'I'll fetch my bag and drive you home, I'm heading your way in any case. I don't live far from you.'

~

She'd alternately sang and slept the entire way, but when Connor pulled into her driveway, the headlights cast a radiant glow. She woke up and knew she should thank him but couldn't voice the words just as she wanted to open the door to get out but sat there immobilised. He turned the engine off. A distant owl hooted in the darkness.

'Beat, give me the key.'

She watched as he too struggled with the lock. Inside, he offered his arm and with one hand on the banister rail and the other threaded through Connor's she climbed the stairs, the greyhounds following close behind. In her bedroom, she dropped her jacket, kicked off her boots, climbed into bed. He stood there looking on. How comforting it would be if he lay beside her.

'I'm going to bring you two glasses of water. Your head won't hurt quite as much in the morning if you drink both.'

When Connor placed the water on her bedside table, she was drowsy and on the cusp of sleep.

'I'm going to stay the night,' he announced.

He didn't resist when she squeezed his hand but when she pulled him towards her, he stepped back in a flash.

'Downstairs on the dog haired sofa. I'll take you to the meeting. Tomorrow, the questioning will be directed at me.'

32

PESANTE

'WHY have you changed your mind?' the VC asked. Connor's tendency to stall when asked a direct question irritated Beat. Now, it amused her to witness the committee's impatience as they waited for Connor's response. Thorne sighed. Time stalled. Outside, crows, the heavy metal crooners of the avian world, provided a rowdy distraction. Beat watched as seven dancers circled on the lawn in red chiffon costumes. They linked hands, shoulders in and shoulders out, looking like they'd slipped out of a Matisse painting.

'Shall I repeat the question?'

'Steven rarely held staff meetings. I'm old-school. A cynic. Like Oscar Wilde said, I was "the man who knew the price of everything and the value of nothing". All I cared about was the inconvenience, the price tag. Beat's crusading zeal is refreshing but that didn't make me want real change.'

The VC nodded.

After Connor's explanation, Thorne's assistant put her pen down. The moment was charged, like a minor key's sudden shift into a major tonality, a realm of renewal and positivity.

'Is there more you want to say?' Thorne asked.

'I've been comfortable with the status quo. I have to admit our courses need updating.'

'In what way?' the VC asked.

'Our mission is to cultivate performers and what we teach has to reflect that. We need more practical classes during which students play or sing.'

Thorne scowled. A fly buzzed around her but either she didn't care or hadn't noticed. When it skated on the VC's sleeve, he flicked it off. Reaching for the agenda, he asked, 'Is there anything else?'

'I believe classical music is superior to rock,' Connor admitted. The fly landed on his papers. Beat stood up and opened the window, perhaps it would sense the fresh air, find its way out and not suffer a protracted death in this cloying room.

'That's old-fashioned and a divisive notion. Academic quicksand,' the VC scoffed. He took off his glasses, chucked them on the table and leaned back, his waistcoat buttons mercilessly stretched.

'Beatrice, it takes courage to tackle gritty issues.'

'Thank you.' Dehydrated and queasy, she wasn't bothered whether she lost her job or not, she longed to sleep.

'Maybe there are better ways to address problematic issues than equine therapy,' said the VC. 'But, have you found it has brokered better communication, Ms Snow?'

Thorne whispered into the VC's ear.

'That's not happening Marilyn,' he cautioned in a hushed tone.

Thorne's brows pinched in frustration.

Beat saw Elvira in a white sequinned dress seated at the grand piano in the Queensland Performing Arts Centre, the stage lights angled on the keys, the orchestra fanned out behind her. A drum roll prompted the piano's quicksilver introduction, from the top register to the bottom, *Dum, da da Dum, da da Dum, da da Dum, da da Dum, da da Dum, da da Dum,* in Grieg's *Piano Concerto*.

'Beatrice, quit,' Thorne urged. 'Resign.'

Horrified, the VC dragged his hand down his face, closed his eyes, hands locked together on the rise of his waistcoated belly. Beat's heart hammered in her ears. There was a space, a momentary breath.

'No. Never,' Beat erupted in anger. 'File disciplinary proceedings, Professor Thorne,' the stabbing pain in Beat's brain stopped. 'But, if I'm asked to attend this, this... grubby charade again, I'll bring a union representative and,' Beat planted her RM Williams boots on the floor, brandished her mustard yellow iPhone at Thorne, 'the sharpest industrial lawyer money can buy.'

33
SFORZANDO

'IT can't be true,' trilled Elvira.

The commotion in Polly's office escalated.

'Read today's *Queensland News* if you don't believe me.' Winton handed the newspaper to Elvira who huffed and puffed as she skimmed the story.

'It's nothing but stupid, stupid clickbait,' and she tossed the paper into Polly's wastepaper bin and pressed it down with her foot.

Intrigued, Beat opened her door to find out what all the fuss was about. When she appeared, the noise shrank from fortissimo to pianissimo in a flash.

'What's going on?'

Polly looked sheepish. Matthew tweaked his green bow tie. Winton's chin angled north. Hermione nervously tapped a rolled-up newspaper against her leg.

No one except Elvira would meet her eyes. She'd hardly slept the night before and today she had zero tolerance for theatrics.

'Hermione, come in please.' Beat made a sweeping gesture towards her office. 'I'll talk to the rest of you later.' The door clicked behind her.

'Beat haven't you seen the story in today's paper?' A tight suede headband curtailed Hermione's wild hair. Beat watched as the clarinettist smoothed out the creases of the Queensland News before giving it to her.

Horse Whisperer Dean Spelled

Beatrice Snow, whose appointment earlier in the year as Turalong Arts' dean of music was considered to be inspired, has allegedly been suspended by the university. Recently, Snow ran a controversial staff retreat to discuss gender discrimination and new directions for the school's programs and concerts. Snow is said to have spent a significant sum on a motivational equestrian workshop to improve workplace communication.

'But this can't be true. I haven't been told about this,' Beat said.

'Let's grab a bite before the place buzzes with speculation,' Hermione suggested.

'I can't go out there.'

'Look as if you haven't a care in the world.'

Beat grabbed a hat.

'We'll use the back stairs.' Hermione opened the door.

Beat felt numb and hoped she'd stay that way.

'We'll go to Poco Mosso,' Hermione said.

'Thorne and Matthew hang out there,' Beat protested.

'At 9:30? No chance.'

'I hope you're right.'

Hermione bent over to wedge a folded business card under one of the table legs to stop it wobbling.

'I'm still reeling from the headline,' said Beat.

'If your leadership's compromised...'

Beat chuckled, there was nothing funny about the situation but she giggled, hooted, snorted and hugged her chest but couldn't stop. The last time she'd laughed this much was about Madison's request for ghost-busting garlic bulbs.

'Hey, sip on some water. The blond waitress over there is giving you a death glare.'

Beat breathed in for four counts and out slowly.

'What I said wasn't funny,' Hermione said.

'Who cares? I'm feeling better.'

Puccini's *One Fine Day* from *Madame Butterfly* began and Beat's anxiety flared into life. She took off her sunnies and buried her nose in the menu.

'Maria Callas singing that makes my skin tingle.' Hermione put the menu down.

'Although why play such downers? Way too tragic for breakfast.'

Beat's mobile rang. She looked at the screen and screwed up her face.

'Dan, what's up?' She clenched her jaw but continued to listen. 'Yes. I've consulted a lawyer.'

'What did that mongrel want?'

'Money, money, money,' Beat sang.

'Don't start again, my nerves won't stand it. Polly wouldn't tell anyone where you were yesterday. Why was that?'

'It's complex. Thorne is critical of the retreat and what she's saying echoes Connor's feelings about it.'

'Really?'

Beat changed the subject. 'Hermione do you know why Steven resigned so suddenly? It was so unlike him. I can't help thinking his departure is somehow linked to Thorne's negativity towards the school.'

'Steven was comfortable in the role. He was good at chasing sponsorship which pleased Thorne but...'

'I've tried ringing him but I get a recorded message saying he is no longer available on the number.'

'There have been rumours,' Hermione said.

'About what?'

'Shady dealings. He and Matthew were thick as thieves.'

'Tell me something I don't know,' Beat said.

'About the letter...'

'What?'

'Yep, yep, yep I warned you about him.' Hermione popped the menus on an empty table behind her.

'Matthew?'

'No, Connor.'

'Not again Hermione.'

'Darl, you're a gem. But you know diddly squat about the human condition. Connor's in Thorne's pocket.'

'You don't stop, do you?' Beat fumed. She hadn't come out with Hermione to be harangued with conspiracy theories. She was about to leave, but the waitress arrived with two plates of croissants and jam.

'If not Connor, then...?' Hermione pressed.

'If I only had Thorne's support. I can't get my head around her change of heart.'

'Marilyn waxes and wanes with the cycles of the moon.' Hermione mused. 'She's mercurial.'

'Malevolent more like. A walking, talking horror show.'

'Wow!'

'Look, I'm grateful for your kindness post Dan and now with all this cloak and dagger nonsense but—' Beat's mobile rang. Confronted by the university number, she breathed deeply before accepting the call. Hermione laid her knife and fork down. Shimmering strings heralded Luciano Pavarotti singing Puccini's ever popular *Nessun Dorma*.

'Am I suspended?'

34

AD LIBITUM

SNATCHES of the day's events paraded through Beat's head. She strode up Sally's uneven stone path. Her grass thrashing neighbour was burning a massive pile of branches. Woodsmoke thickened the air and she spluttered and coughed. Any reluctance she'd once had to confide in her friend had long gone. She rang the bell twice. She couldn't wait to unleash the tangled thoughts in her head. When the door opened, Sally rushed out to give her a hug, but soon pulled back, her eyes full of questions. She placed her hands on Beat's shoulders.

'Has something happened?' Sally's cat rubbed its head against Beat's leg. 'I'll chuck the cat out the moment she bothers you.'

'She won't,' Beat said.

'New developments?'

Beat rolled her eyes. 'If only I knew where to start.'

'Anywhere.'

When Swift leapt onto Sally's lap, she gentled her to the floor.

'Let's go with the divorce?'

'According to Cholmley, my lawyer, Dan's been my dependent for five years and is entitled to interim financial support until we split our assets fifty-fifty.'

'How annoying, but your lawyer's probably right.'

'What a mess.' Beat pressed her palms to her face.

'But without sorting the financials you're forever tied to him.'

'Dan's betrayal gutted me. Now, I can't trust anyone, especially those I work with.'

'Not even goody-goody two shoes Polly?'

'Okay, not her, but someone's creating havoc.'

'Have you talked to Thorne about it?'

'She's not on side,' Beat said. 'Nowadays, there's an antagonism which I don't understand.'

'Could the politics have changed? Is she under pressure?'

'No idea,' said Beat.

'Did you know the job would be political?'

Beat rubbed her eyes. 'I was one of six shortlisted for the position. This is where it gets crazy.'

'Oh, I like crazy. Surprise me.'

'The University wants to amalgamate the school with their music faculty. I was chosen because the panel thought I'd stuff up and do a bad job.'

'And do you?'

'What?'

'Do a bad job?' Sally said.

'No.' Beat's voice cracked.

'Why are you fixated on Thorne's approval?'

'She's my boss.'

'Big deal. I never thought you were a simpering toady?'

Beat threw a cushion at Sally.

'Fight. Rock the boat. Get a megaphone and bellow "I'm the dean" from the rooftop.'

'Sally you're mad as a cut snake.'

'It's why you like me.'

'Right, I forgot.'

'Ah, but maybe you like playing victim?' Sally asked.

'No. Absolutely not.'

Swift kneaded her paws on the arm of Beat's chair.

'Come on. Out with it. What was that niggle in your eyes just then?'

'Don't know what you're on about,' she said.

'Ha! I know you better than you think.'

'Connor,' mumbled Beat.

'You were spitting chips about him last time we spoke.'

'I thought he'd rat-fucked me.'

'Yikes! A vile expression.'

'But now...' Beat began, 'I like, I mean, I really like him.' Swift curled up to sleep.

'No surprises there.'

'He's been supportive,' Beat said.

'Does your contract have a celibacy clause?' Sally's eyes twinkled, a grin danced on her lips.

'No,' said Beat.

'So?'

'It's unprofessional.'

'Not ideal,' Sally pulled a face. 'But orchestras, universities, hospitals, schools, newsrooms are rife with sexual longing, unrequited love, and shattered dreams.'

'I've been ordered to take a week's leave from next Monday.'

'Does that bother you?'

'I could be fired.'

'Nah, you're not that lucky. Celebrate. Do fun stuff.' She rubbed her hands together vigorously. Wagged a finger, 'Use the time.'

'To get a divorce.'

'Go girl!'

35
DUO

SHE thought it strange that Connor had never told her about his interest in horses. Perhaps he was as private as she was, and how could she blame him for that? Her latest Miley Cyrus ringtone from *Flowers* interrupted her thoughts.

'How are you Beat?' Polly spoke brightly.

'Enjoying myself.'

'Doing?'

'Fence mending, cutting up a fallen tree with a chainsaw, and most important, not fretting about work.'

'Missing us.'

Beat hated to be locked into one definition of herself. 'Don't take this the wrong way Pol, you know me as dean, but I'm a friend, a reader, a loner, gardener, cook, adventurer, horse owner, homemaker, pianist, landowner, and...'

'A soon-to-be-single-woman.'

'Must you?'

'Well...'

'Yeah... I know that tone.' Wild ducks landed on the lawn. Beat counted nineteen. A leggy, grey waterbird with a long, slender neck, an elegant avian giraffe, stepped out among them.

'There's another letter. Just so you know.'

'Another?'

'Signed by the staff.'

'About?'

'Appointing an acting dean.'

'Pol, I'm back next Monday. After today, that's four working days.'

'Yes, I know, but when Steven was on tour, decisions were delayed.'

'Pol...' She breathed deeply. A familiar vice squeezed her shoulders.

'Yes.'

'Steven was absent for three or four months at a time.'

'True. But you were absent after Dan...'

'On. Sick. Leave.' She'd have to calm down, slow her words. Annoyed, she felt edgy about the injustice of it.

'I'm merely passing on...'

'I know. But it's infuriating.'

'Matthew's keen to plan next year's concerts.' Polly offered by way of an explanation.

'Even though it's only—'

'Conductors are booked years ahead. If you want to enlist fancy international conductors and not Connor, which everyone would prefer, even Winton, then it's...' Beat ended the call. It was too much. As if she didn't know world class conductors were engaged years ahead. She'd been patient but Polly's tactless advocacy and how she parroted Connor this and Connor that... She took a deep breath and exhaled for three counts. Soon she felt better and rang back. 'Sorry the reception isn't the best. How about Connor chairs the meeting then?'

'Mmm...'

'What?' Beat cleared her throat.

'No. It has to be an orchestral player. He's a conductor. Matthew's batting for Hermione,' Polly said.

'Okay.' Beat thought that was bullshit but didn't want to argue. She scratched at the tailings of her porridge. 'Hermione it is. Providing she and I meet next Monday. Don't want anything locked in. I've still to cement the rock project.'

'That's about it except...'

'What?' Beat became aware of the shrill tick of the green clock above the fridge. She longed to be outside, the sky had darkened. Rainfall was imminent.

'Hermione, Matthew, and Connor asked...'

A kookaburra's stuttered call eclipsed Polly's words. It sat on the veranda rail. She hoped the bird wouldn't hurl itself at the window again.

'Polly, I didn't catch that.'

'Hermione, Matthew, and Connor want to visit you,' said Polly.

'Here? Not a chance.' Beat shuddered at the thought of Matthew's snide dismissal of her property, her sanctuary. A wind picked up. Something was making her sneeze. She pulled a packet of paper tissues out of her pocket and blew her nose.

'I don't mean all at the same time.'

'Regardless, I'm on...'

'Connor insists it's urgent.'

A ghastly flashback to her humiliating drunkenness made her belly flip. Quite apart from throwing up in front of Connor, she remembered how he'd covered his ear whenever she'd screeched another ghoulish round of *Dance Monkey* by Tones and I on the drive home.

'Except for you or Elvira, the others aren't welcome.'

'Connor's adamant.'

'Can he come tomorrow?' Polly's bias towards Connor was tiresome. She was like a cheerleader. She could talk to Polly about it but she might get her offside and make herself seem petty.

'No. He's all...'

'Shook up like the Presley song. Tell Connor to come this afternoon.'

Beat ended the call knowing she'd have to change out of her moth-eaten black tee. She'd better look presentable to salvage some dignity after her excruciating carry-on the other night. Besides, Dan's accusation of 'frumpy' preyed on her mind.

Upstairs, she changed into an inky-blue polo shirt and jodhpurs to match, tied her hair in a ponytail, and gave her boots a cursory brush. She wasn't wearing a bra and she noticed that her nipples were visible.

Too bad. Despite her frazzled mood she looked in the mirror and was pleased with the outcome. She'd send a selfie to Sally to prove she could scrub up occasionally. Now she wished she'd made a specific time. Afternoon could mean anything and as half the day had already flown by, she'd start working the horses rather than lose time waiting. She scribbled, 'I'm round the back' on a yellow post-it note and stuck it on the front door.

The horses were skittish, a gusty breeze ruffled their manes and yet they followed her cues. But, getting them to move in unison as Connor had done was beyond her. She rewarded them with an encouraging tone, scratches on the wither and carrot pieces whenever they did something right, however minor, but she'd have to lower her expectations because the wind was too distracting.

She turned the radio on, Vaughan Williams' *Oboe Concerto* was in flight, a narrative sprung from Britain's greener terrain. A sharp contrast to Queensland's muted, modest plains. Yet the mellow oboe wheeling above searching strings restored her equilibrium. She closed her eyes. Breathed in the pungent sweetness of cherry tomato plants that flourished in her, neglected of late, round yard. Enjoyed the sun's occasional warmth.

'Storm's favouring his right fore. He could have an abscess.'

Beat was startled and wondered how long Connor had been watching. She was irritated by his observation because she should have noticed it herself. She'd examine Storm's hoof but only after he left.

'How did you get the horses to do those unison routines?'

'Mmm...' Connor stroked his chin. 'That depends on whether you ask your piano students to practise the right hand first and then the left, or whether you work on small elements, both hands together, joining each new segment to the episodes already mastered.'

'I'd use both approaches.'

'Do you reward the horses after any win, however minor?' he asked.

'I do. But tell me, when did you find the time to train them?'

'Neither Courtney nor I socialised on the first night. We showed our faces at dinner but soon slipped out. We had a final session at dawn which wasn't fun.'

'But the routine was impressively synchronised.'

'Mostly Courtney's doing.'

'Why didn't you give me the heads up about it?' Beat said.

'Courtney reckoned if I put on an unexpected display it would lift morale.'

Drops of rain splashed on her skin. Dark clouds streamed across the sky, thunder rumbled in the distance. A strengthening wind whipped the trees. Connor looked concerned.

'Come on, we'd better release them,' he said. 'Presumably they go in their shelter when it pelts down?'

She handed Storm's lead rope to Connor, but in doing so, brushed his fingers with her own. Her face glowed the colour of a galah's rosy chest. She was thirty-two, not a teenager, but when she had flashbacks of her drunken behaviour the other night shame overwhelmed her. She'd given Connor a guided tour of her vulnerabilities. But her immediate task was to remove Bolt's halter and he tugged and side stepped and it kept her outside in the worsening weather. When at last both thoroughbreds were free, they dashed off, tails up, mud flying. It was in conditions like these they had accidents, crashed into fences, or became entangled in loose wire hurled around in the wind. She hoped they'd settle soon and seek shelter, their bravado a show of rebellion. Beat stared at the darkening sky and, like the outside world, she held her breath. Marshalled by strong wind, the towering eucalypts lunged right, left, forward, back. Heavy rain thrashed the roof, bullied the balding lawn. Connor swept his dripping hair off his face, bracing against the squall on the way to her house.

'Be quick. Inside.'

'Do you get nervous at night now Dan's gone?'

'No, but the curlew's cries have always made my blood run cold.' Beat gestured he should sit on the sofa but cringed when she noticed skeins of dog hair which Dan had, on reflection, been justified to complain about. She handed Connor a towel and hoped he wouldn't notice it. Half-heartedly he dried his hair and sat down.

'Some land feels mean, uneasy, but there's a benevolence, a serenity here, despite the storm.'

'Tell me about your horses,' Beat said.

'There's only one, Springer, a bay ex-racehorse.'

Was that what Polly had wanted to tell her on that ride?

'What do you do with her?' Beat closed the kitchen windows against the splashing rain.

'Trail riding, sometimes on Nudgee beach. When the tide's out and there's no one around, I gallop her along the shoreline. I get ideas.'

'About?'

'Mainly my research.'

'What are you working on?'

'Exploring whether music can be referential. You know the old chestnut about whether music can portray extra-musical influences like landscapes, ships, animals, people, and objects?'

'As in Debussy's *La Mer*?' Beat suggested.

'Yes. But if someone listens to that, without knowing its title, or knowing who wrote it, would they have any idea it portrays the sea?'

'The focus is classical then?' Beat asked.

'Yes.'

Heavy rain thrashed the galvanised iron roof, a bedraggled pigeon sheltered underneath. Propelled by a gusty squall, a pot of red geraniums rolled across the deck, spewing soil and petals. She sat beside him. 'There's overlap between your topic and Dan's.'

'I know Dan is examining Mussorgsky's *Pictures at an Exhibition* and how the composer illustrated his friend Victor Hartmann's paintings through music, and it relates to my own work.'

'Out with it. Enough beating around the bush. We've done horses, birds, music, and the weather. What do you really want to discuss?'

Connor toyed with the black and white greyhound's ears and the dog gazed at him appreciatively with the fond expression he once reserved for Dan. Outside fallen branches and nature's debris carpeted the pooling ground.

'Why did you give up conducting?' Beat's question popped out surprising herself as much as Connor.

'That's not up for discussion.'

~

'Thorne's bite will be sharper on your return. We need tactics.' Worry stalked Connor's face.

'I know,' said Beat.

'Somebody is mischief making.'

'Matthew from day one,' she said.

How had this maddening man, who had stirred such trouble, become a person she relied on? Someone she enjoyed talking to. He didn't look too bad in his black T-shirt and jeans either.

'What can I do about it?' Beat asked.

'Plenty. Breathe fire,' said Connor.

'Like a dragon?'

'Beatrice, please. Manage the bureaucrats like you do those.' He pointed beyond the window at the dozing geldings, side by side, in the shelter. 'Your communication is clear with them.'

'Hardly the same though.'

'Priceless.' Eyebrows raised and smiling Connor scratched the back of his head.

'What?' Beat angled her head.

'You have the gall to say that after inflicting Courtney on us?'

Beat smirked. 'Am I "a shiver in search of a spine" like Paul Keating said?' Beat pulled her damp hair into a ponytail.

'No.' Connor looked thoughtful. 'But you're in a tight spot and under pressure and oddly, you think it's time to bail.'

'Isn't it?'

'No. Mandate your vision. Fight. Let your inner mongrel do its worst.'

The massive branch of a ghost gum slammed into the ground.

Connor rested his hand on hers. Pity? Affection? Beat wondered.

'You've been doing it tough,' Connor looked her square in the eyes. 'Stranded between a toxic workplace and an ailing marriage.'

'I hate the judgement. The lack of faith in me,' Beat explained.

'Fight back. It's in your job spec. Remember, you said much the same to me.' Connor held her gaze.

Sally had said the same. She wanted to thread her arm through his. A nerd he may be, but Connor talked sense. She turned to face him but he withdrew his hand and the moment of connection passed.

'You were terrifying in your refusal-to-resign-speech!'

Connor brushed the hairs off his clothes, frowned and shifted to the new bright pink bucket chair which Beat had bought to celebrate her singledom. He leaned forward, 'Thorne's going to fabricate another catastrophe. Something which is likely to be a hanging offence in the kingdom of academe.'

'Why are you helping me?'

'I'm moved by your crazy, burning mission to make our humble school one of the best music institutions in the world. For the wannabes, lurking in the shadows, it's all about them.'

'You were appalled by my appointment,' Beat said.

'Your use of hyperbole is...'

'Endearing?'

'Annoying. Was I appalled? No. Surprised? Yes. I'd never noticed you. Now, I find you... er, capable, worthy.'

'Even though I regard you as arrogant, curmudgeonly and an insufferable know-it-all?'

Beat locked her eyes onto his until Connor's taut expression gave way to laughter.

36
BARBARO

BEDLAM reigned at Poco Mosso. Harried waiters dashed back and forth. Eager to pay, fuming patrons waved credit cards. An enormous crash stopped the conversational hum. A waitress had dropped a tray of cream-topped desserts and she crouched down to clean up the mess. Impatient lunchers fizzed and furied. Unperturbed, Thorne's face was grim, her hand on the table cupped on its side like the head of an eastern brown. Her boss had something unpalatable to say and Beat gritted her teeth as she waited in suspense, beads of sweat prickling her forehead.

'Music is a parasitic drain. The Government's going to cut higher education funding and the impact on the school will be...'

'Devastating.' Beat peered at the menu.

'Correct.'

'Music must—' Thorne said.

'Economise,' Beat said.

'Luckily, you can trim the—'

'Fat,' Beat said.

'Stop finishing my-'

'Sentences.' A false eyelash had parted company with Thorne's eyelid. Beat weighed up whether to tell her but decided against it.

'Steven refused to curb spending on your old-school, one-to-one teaching model.'

'Naturally,' Beat sighed.

'One student taught by one teacher is an impossible luxury in these economically stretched times.'

Beat's panic was like a ball spinning down a steep slope, picking up speed, bouncing off dangerous rocks. Her adversary was momentarily distracted by the arrival of a blueberry pavlova slice, surrounded by whipped cream topped with pink delicate flowers. Beat recoiled as her boss immediately picked up a spoon and smashed the saccharine flora.

'One of our rock groups is a major drawcard at next year's Byron Bay Blues Festival.'

'Don't bamboozle me with graduates who have become superstars.' Thorne slapped the table, rattling her gold bracelet's guitar, violin, and trumpet charms.

'I could recite the arguments in favour of the anachronistic one-to-one in my sleep.' Thorne dabbed at the corner of her mouth.

'It's my job to—'

'Support me.' Thorne said.

Beat popped a big piece of meringue into her mouth. The café's sound system channelled Lucia's aria from the mad scene in Donizetti's opera *Lucia di Lammermoor*. The outrage in Beat's head which began as a whisper soon reached ear-splitting level as a scream. For once, Poco Mosso's background music echoed reality.

'That you'd object to trialling online group learning is of no surprise.'

'We already do that Marilyn.'

'Regardless, if you won't teach instruments in reasonably sized groups, then my only choice is to stop specialist instrumental and vocal teaching altogether.'

'No, no. You can't...'

'Except, I can.'

Thorne mashed the berries with the meringue. Murderous thoughts crossed Beat's mind as her superior wiped her mouth and her mauve lipstick bled into the cream. She saw herself smash pavlova onto Thorne's immaculate hair. But Beat's vengeful thinking ceased when she spied Connor and Hermione engaged in an intense conversation in the corner.

'Well?' Thorne's eyelid twitched.

'This will damage our reputation, just when the school's status is picking up.'

'It's not debatable.' Thorne cast her eyes around the café. 'Inform the staff this afternoon. I'll be there. If I suspect trickery...'

'Then?'

'Find another job.'

Beat hesitated before asking, 'Is our budget in credit?'

Thorne didn't answer.

~

Staff and student representatives were waiting in the lecture theatre. Hermione and Elvira huddled over a score. Winton thumbed his phone. Sessional teachers and Union reps sat together. By three pm everyone, including Thorne, was seated. Beat had no strategy; she'd have to muddle along.

She picked up a handheld mic just as Matthew swept in to take his customary position in the front row, today's purple bowtie tipping left. He crossed his legs and exposed a green sock patterned with bees.

Beat began to speak, but there was a catch at the back of her throat. She coughed into her elbow. Something was wrong with her voice; it sounded higher, clipped, and prompted laughter. Thorne knitted her brows.

'The Federal Government's cuts to higher education are predicted to be savage. Professor Thorne believes savings can be made by replacing one-to-one teaching with group classes.'

'You've gotta be kidding,' Winton dropped his phone. Hermione slammed the score shut. Matthew's hand shot up.

'Now, I'll ask each of you to confirm your support of this,' Beat squeaked. She sipped from a bottle of water Polly handed her but her reedy tone continued.

'Matthew?' Beat squawked.

'Never.'

'Hermione?' Beat's voice cracked.

The clarinettist closed her eyes, tweaked her curls, widening the circumference of her hair.

'No, no, no,' she exclaimed.

'Elvira?'

'Surprised you even bothered to ask.'

'Connor?'

He rose to his feet. 'Professor Thorne and Ms Snow, this economy strikes at the heart of the music profession. It insults all our luminary teachers gleaned from the State Orchestra, State Opera, and the Rock Industry.' His words sparked applause.

~

'Beatrice, you failed,' said Thorne.

'I did my best.'

'To obstruct my decision?'

'No. But our teachers will walk.'

'Hire new ones,' Thorne quipped.

'If only it were that easy. Young players choose to study here because of the crop of high-profile pianists, oboists, drummers, and singers on offer.'

'What's all the fuss about?' Thorne asked.

'Why work for us when students can be taught in an appropriate and preferred format at the University's Music Faculty or in a high school?'

'You owe me your—'

'Loyalty. Yes, I do. But not if a policy change threatens the credibility of the institution you're responsible for.'

~

In reception, vocal warmups, frantic scampering up and down the piano, and a pounding *doof – doof – doof* competed with heated debate among teachers and students. The complaints grew louder and more insistent and culminated in a generic whiny yowl. According to Polly, a journalist had rung three times. Back in her office, Beat watched her goldfish torpedo stones on the aquarium floor and stir a slurry of sediment. It occurred to her she was just as contained as her fish. She couldn't venture outside because she'd be bombarded by angry protestors. When her phone rang, its shrill call set her teeth on edge. It was Thorne.

'About your budget it's—'

'Solvent and some.'

'No, it's absolutely not,' Thorne crowed. 'The VC's livid. He wants the debt cleared quickly. I've done the maths and my solution will balance the books.'

Beat rang the Financial Officer. 'Professor Thorne informed me a few minutes ago our budget is overspent. What is the deficit please?'

'$305,000,' he said.

'How is this possible? What caused this shortfall?'

'Certain items hadn't been factored in.'

~

'Polly, this group teaching approach can't replace the one-to-one. We'll have to lobby Council members before next week's meeting.'

'And?' Polly grimaced.

'How about an online petition?'

'Connor could organise it?' Polly's fingers reached for her locket. 'After all, protest in a printed form is his superpower.'

Polly's jest sailed over Beat's head.

'We'll lobby the State's music organisations,' Beat said.

'Elvira could help Connor.'

'But can he be trusted?' Polly asked.

'You've *always* been quick to tell me so,' Beat said pointedly.

~

Protestors jostled for attention in the foyer. Beat pushed a 'Teach in Threes Reduce our Fees' placard away. She dodged, 'CEO Shoots School Dead.' Melody and Theo's 'Proposed Change is Strange,' bobbed in her face.

Winton elbowed his way through the crowd. 'Clear off. Go about your business,' he shouted. He raised his trumpet case and aimed it at the protestors, a ghastly echo of Simon wielding the fire extinguisher like a gun.

Winton fronted her, 'Are you okay?'

She'd no time to answer because a reporter from *Queensland News* grasped her arm.

'Professor Snow why are you altering the way future performers are taught?'

This matter was of no interest to the media, Beat mused, unless someone had worked hard to persuade them otherwise.

'Contact the CEO Marilyn Thorne if you want more information,' she said.

Polly peeled the journalist's nicotine-stained fingers off Beat's arm and hustled her down the administrative corridor.

~

When she arrived the next morning, Beat was stunned to see paperwork piled on her desk, a chair, the floor and on top of the fish tank.

'What's all this?'

Polly pointed at her desk. 'Connor's change.org petition has attracted twenty thousand signatures. What you're looking at are letters of support from local and national well-wishers in the music industry.'

The office door opened and Polly and Beat ducked as Winton lobbed a bulky hardback at the filing cabinet which bore the dents of previously flung missiles. *Rock History* landed spine open. Polly slipped out.

'Hey!' Beat motioned for Winton to sit down.

'Hey,' He parroted.

She leaned towards him, close enough for her to smell the acrid whiff of sweat. 'How does throwing a book help?'

'We won't survive,' Winton raised his voice.

'Neither will I if you throw things at me.'

'It's a frigging joke.' Winton wiped spittle off his chin.

'And your ugly attitude only makes it worse.'

'Is that so?'

Beat nodded. 'By the way, next time, I'm lodging an assault complaint.'

'Okay.' Winton looked sheepish.

'Besides, you could hurt the goldfish.' Beat was relieved when Winton half smiled.

The door opened. 'Everything good?' Her assistant queried.

'Yes.'

'I'm sorry I...' Winton's foot nudged his instrument case.

'Apology accepted.'

'Winton, how could you help?'

'No idea.'

'You have weaponry,' Beat said.

'I'm not following.'

'Guitars, saxophones, drum kits, trumpets.'

'So?'

'Remember *The Chariot*, the old Cat Empire classic?'

'Vaguely. That's going back a bit.'

'There's this hook. "Our weapons were our instruments made from timber and steel."'

Winton licked his lips and rubbed his hands together. 'Yes, I have an idea.'

'Winton, don't forget the missile.'

'Come again.'

'The reference book,' she said.

Beat rang the VC's office to arrange a meeting. The only way to stop Thorne's destructive plan was to talk to him face to face.

37

ABBANDONAMENTE

SHE glanced at her reflection in a vast, gilded mirror which hung in the entry foyer of the University staff club.

A waiter approached.

'I'm here to meet with the VC.'

'He's at the bar. Enjoyed the Tchaikovsky concert,' the waiter said. 'Shall I say Beatrice Snow is waiting for him?'

'Please.'

Any chance of salvaging the situation depended on how well she presented her case. Those milling around the bar were intrigued, no doubt curious about her presence. Beat greeted the VC with an apology.

'Sorry. I've been waiting in the wrong place.'

'Well, you've lost five minutes, let's not waste the next twenty-five.'

'Agreed.'

'Beatrice, shouldn't you be talking to Professor Thorne about whatever it is you want to tell me?'

'No,' Beat said firmly. 'I'm addressing you in your capacity as the chair of Turalong Council.'

'Let's sit down, shall we?' he said.

Beat followed him into a formal sitting area. Green Chesterton armchairs fanned around mahogany tables. Portraits of famous alumni graced the walls. Her eye lingered on a bright-faced young Connor, baton in hand, looking every bit the conductor.

'I'm all ears,' said the VC, unbuttoning his jacket to reveal a vibrant waistcoat of embroidered flowers, the type a fiddler in a Romanian Folk Band might wear.

'Professor Thorne is going to implement group instrumental teaching.'

The VC nodded at a colleague. Looked askance at a romantically entwined couple seated at the far wall. She knew his patience would soon wear thin.

'This expedient method change without consultation will anger our instrumental and vocal teachers who will then be disinclined to encourage their talented students to study with us.'

'Beatrice, a $305,000 deficit signposts sloppy management.'

'Yes.'

'Then why are you here?'

'Because as of last month there *was* no deficit, and because I know which cost-cutting measure will least compromise the school's mission of *'inspiring performance*."

'There are alternatives?'

'I've identified ten. Here are three. One, cancel the opera production. Two, teach music history in classes twice the size. Three, we won't upgrade the school's computers.'

'Why not negotiate these alternatives with Professor Thorne?'

38

RUBATO

BLUE Note was hipster heaven. Everywhere she looked were bearded men in skinny jeans, sleeveless sweaters, white-soled sneakers, thick-rimmed specs. She couldn't see Connor, but several rock students waved at her. Beat was next in line to talk to a waiter.

'It's an hour's wait,' barked the tall waiter wearing a long black PVC apron, a menu clamped to his chest. Beat approved of the huge poster of Miles Davis behind the counter. In her mind she could hear the trumpeter's smoky lines in *Kind of Blue*.

'I'm joining a friend.'

'What does he...'

'Tall. Wears a herringbone tweed jacket. Carries a backpack.'

'Connor? He brings masses of musos our way. Let me look.' The waiter deftly shuttled between tables. 'He's over there by the window.'

Beat saw Connor glance at his watch. She wondered which one it was today. How many watches did he need, or for that matter, how many backpacks? Today's was crimson.

'You're...' He tapped the watch.

'Late and people in glass houses...'

'Is this overspend bothering you?' he said.

'I can't think of anything else.' She dumped her heavy, recycled supermarket bag stuffed with paperwork beside his backpack.

'This deficit pops up out of nowhere. It's too convenient.' Connor takes a book and his scarf off the empty chair beside him and pulls it out for her.

Chet Baker's drizzled trumpet wrapped around her like a warm scarf. Background music she'd love to lose herself in. She wondered if Winton was a Miles or a Chet fan. Connor offered her a slice of poppyseed cake which she guessed would be gluten free. When she refused, an unmistakeable relief filled his eyes. She reached for the recycled jam jar filled with sprigs of yellow wattle and placed it on the floor. She was already fighting the urge to sneeze. Wattle was a trigger.

'Deficits get managers dismissed,' Connor said.

'But what caused it?'

'Somehow we'll have to find out, because if you're found to be fiscally irresponsible, you'll be replaced quicksmart.'

'I should have been more explicit with the VC about my suspicions?'

'That might have stirred up a hornet's nest.'

'Steven never mentioned a shortfall to me.'

'Thorne probably created it, easing the way for the VC to merge the school with the University's Music Faculty. She could have been promised a big incentive, think the King's Birthday Honours List, if she slides the school into bed with the university.'

'How Machiavellian.'

'It is what it is.' Connor frowned as if shocked by his use of an exhausted cliché.

'Our own *Game of Tones*.' Beat blew her nose. 'What should I do?'

'Sit tight. Investigate the overspend. Dream up the fund raiser. Get a surplus under the belt. Continue with your goals: new facilities for rock, create more performance classes and diversify concerts.'

'Easy to say but...'

Connor looked earnest. 'I'll champion any money-spinner you dream up.'

'How about an orchestral-cum-rock special?'

'Ghastly.' Connor ate the last morsel of cake.

'Sian packs a punch. An ex-student. A superstar.'

'It's belittling, but I'm supporting it.'

'When the hip hop band, The Hill Top Hoods performed with four mainstream Aussie orchestras several years ago, it generated huge box office.' Beat removed her jacket.

'But we're a performance training institution,' Connor said.

'Exactly. Our trainees need exposure to multiple genres.'

'I understand the logic behind it, Beat.' Connor sounded weary.

'We'll lure a younger crowd, showcase a woman, and the rock players will be—'

'Stop!' Connor rubbed at his forehead, exasperated. 'I'm already onside.'

Five guitarists wandered in. She watched each of them hand their guitars into a special cloakroom. There were safe quarters tailored for bulky instruments. No wonder the café was popular. A major airline had lost the custom of many professional musicians because they were not allowed to take their valuable instruments on board. She remembered how United Airlines had broken Dave Carroll's guitar in 2008 and he had written a trio of protest songs about the incident called *United Breaks Guitars* which became a big hit on YouTube and iTunes. Her tension eased when she heard Miles Davis' *So What* on the café's sound system.

'And today's backpack is?' Beat changed the subject.

'A Herschel.'

'Tell me why you like it?'

'Bright colour, good size, lightweight, tear proof, my back doesn't get hot.'

'If I ever want a backpack I'll be taking you along.' Beat picked up the menu. Perhaps she'd have some cake after all.

'The Council meeting could...' Connor began.

'Turn nasty. Where's the Rolex?'

'You're not taking this...'

She put down the menu, elbowed the table. 'Yes, I am,' she sighed. 'Tell me about your ideas for a better school.'

39
GRAVISSIMO

WINTON had marshalled a protest for today's Council meeting, but Beat had no idea what form it would take or when it would happen. She couldn't catch Hermione's eye because she was in an intense discussion with the student union representative. She ignored the coffee, its bitter taste held no appeal, besides her pulse raced as it was without caffeine. Confirmation of the last council meeting's minutes was long winded and tedious. Several members leafed through the paper piles before them, others thumbed their phones, the major had nodded off. Inside her head, Beat moaned when the VC invited Thorne to address Fiscal Management.

'Recently, we've been charmed by the music school,' Thorne crowed, 'especially when Georgy stepped up as replacement soloist for Tchaikovsky's *Piano Concerto.*' There was a trickle of applause. Thorne's cropped, sleek red hair and puritanical, white-collared green dress made her look the epitome of compassionate, yet efficient leadership and she summonsed all her charisma to grind Beat's reputation into the dust.

'Regrettably, this event's price tag was exorbitant.' Thorne raised her eyebrows, shook her head. 'It depleted the school's already strained budget.'

'Consequently,' she caught the eye of all the council members one by one, 'there is a deficit of... $305,000.'

Her accusation unleashed puzzled glances between Council members and an undertow of indignant *oohs* and *ahs*. As Thorne continued her tirade, Beat reminded herself not to become defensive because it would diminish her credibility. Dan used to say let negativities flow over you like water over rock. The VC flashed Beat a hearty don't-you-worry-grin, but with Thorne intent on dismembering her reputation how could she not.

Beat heard it then, a barely audible yet eerie choral mewling. A growly instrumental force joined in, growing and growing into brutish dissonance. Thorne's oratory was silenced by a slashing dissonant chord, an ear jangler Alfred Hitchcock would have paid a fortune for. Rock, brass, and wind students in black eye masks, hugged the sweep of windows. Then a sustained cacophony of excruciating decibel levels forced all present, including Beat and Hermione, to press their fingers into their ears.

Security was called, but the rebellious troubadours refused to be silent until council rejected Thorne's proposed teaching method. Eventually, to everyone's relief, including Beat's, the students fell silent when Thorne's assistant opened a window and spoke into a mic to tell the demonstrators the VC was coming to talk to them. Meanwhile caterers refreshed coffee cups and offered triple tiered sandwiches to Council members.

Cannily, the VC went to the window and praised the students' protective instincts. He told them he regretted that the proposal for a group teaching method had distracted them from practice routines. He invited all fifty protestors into the Council room, standing room only, to listen to the debate. When the meeting resumed, a forest of arms bobbed in the VC's eyeline.

'Overspending will not be tolerated,' he began, 'but I believe the music school should have the right to choose its preferred cost reductions.' Then he referenced the Change.org petition which had 23,000 signatures endorsing the same.

'I couldn't agree more,' chimed the student representative.

The VC then invited everyone to peruse Beatrice Snow's list of proposed economies.

Hermione raised a hand but lowered it when Lady Winsome thrust a sparkling braceleted arm above her head.

With one hand on her liver-spotted decolletage, the rich patron pouted, 'Surely, musicians would be honoured to teach at the school, under any circumstance, simply to glory in the prestige?'

Hermione opened her mouth to speak, when the Major cut in. 'Is this toothless Council going to be bullied by an anarchic rabble? I say we mandate Professor Thorne's proposal.' The major fisted the table. 'That'll show them.'

'And me,' the VC muttered under his breath.

'If we are to remain competitive and credible we have to stick to the accepted teaching mode adopted by music institutions nationally and worldwide,' Beat proclaimed.

'Be warned the VC believes amalgamating the school with the University's music faculty is the most expedient means of solvency,' Thorne said, which prompted a backlash of groans and agitation.

'Beatrice, you're gorgeous... ah hem... if in need of a fashion consultant,' said the Major, 'but since we're talking brass tacks, dearie, I'd say you're unsuited to a position where leadership and rational argument is essential.'

Instantly, the student union representative's hand shot up closely followed by Hermione's. Anticipating the women's objections, the VC said, 'The Major's comments about Ms Snow's leadership are inadmissible and must not, I repeat, *must not* be minuted.'

Multiple arms speared the air.

'Professor Thorne,' the VC adjusted his tie. 'Will you allow Ms Snow to choose the most suitable economies for the discipline?'

'Yes. But the school's financial woes will worsen,' Thorne's face clouded.

'Why?' Lady Winsome's arthritic fingers clawed at her pearl necklace.

'The cause sits at this table,' Thorne griped.

A police car screamed *yee da – yee da – yee da* down the main road. Beat pretended to search for something under the table in a ruse to cool her temper but on hearing Thorne say, 'Music's budget will be a fixed agenda item,' Beat rose up like a whale breaching out of the sea.

'Turalong Council needs to know the school's shortfall existed weeks before Steven Hadley, the previous dean, resigned and well before I took on the role.'

'What are you saying?' the VC asked.

'The deficit should be looked into as a matter of urgency because it has nothing, I repeat nothing whatsoever to do with the Tchaikovsky concert. Box office takings exceeded all expectation.'

Gasps of outrage colluded with the chink of spoons on ceramic. Hermione elevated her arm with the speed of a sword whipped out of a scabbard.

'I call for an urgent investigation into the deficit.'

40
TERRACED DYNAMICS

ELVIRA'S plate of vegetarian fare was piled perilously high, a slice of crumbed eggplant schnitzel balanced on top of a mountain of mushrooms and capsicum risotto. Polly and Winton burst in laughing and, as always, Connor's lateness gnawed at Beat. When the door opened, her expression brightened, but it was Johnny, the State Orchestra's CEO, wearing a shiny grey suit offset by black and white brogues. He hungered for attention and yet no one welcomed him except Beat.

Not long after Johnny's arrival, Hermione pointed at the clock on the wall impatiently. Beat fired up. 'Thanks for being here today. I've chosen this private dining room for our meeting because I wanted to reward your hard work with a decent catered lunch.'

'It's so tasty.' Elvira spoke as she chewed.

'Beat do you have something to say?' Winton said.

'I want us to reflect on how we can make a clear contrast, a radical point of difference between our school and the University's music faculty.'

'I-have-a-dream,' quipped Matthew.

Beat filled her glass with water and waited for the laughter to subside.

'We talk up the classical stream's courses, concerts, and competitions, meanwhile rock's treated like an after-thought, a second fiddle to classical music's royal status. How can the school achieve its true potential when we ignore our own rock stream, which has the biggest cohort of students?'

'Very easily. We've done it for years.' Connor sat down. 'Sorry I'm late.' Winton, clearly annoyed, shuffled his chair away from the conductor.

Beat ignored Connor. 'I want to mount a revenue-raising collaboration involving orchestral professionals,' she gave an appreciative nod to Johnny, 'our orchestra, Sian, and our rock band.'

'But that's kinda old hat now. All the Aussie orchestras have teamed up with pop and rock musicians and celebrities.' Hermione said.

'Well, I'm adding an element that's not been done before and Sian's the drawcard,' said Beat.

'She studied with us, but I've never seen her perform,' Matthew heckled.

'You're about to.' Polly prepared Beat's laptop to show a video clip.

'This is the London Symphony Orchestra in concert with Sian,' Beat said.

Hermione bristled. Connor's face was impassive. Eagerly, Winton closed the curtains to block out the light. The LSO were on London's Barbican stage in black pants and tee shirts, with whatever instrument they played printed on the front. Matthew cast his eye around the room for a dissenting colleague but when the LSO's concertmaster began the tuning ritual, he bent forward, head in his hands, glued to the screen.

Soon a young conductor dressed in a red jumpsuit used her hands, and not a baton, to command the solo trumpet, guitars, strings, keyboard, and drum kit. Assorted electronica and synth sprinkled the sound stage with catchy hooks. Suddenly, the post-lunch haze was shaken by a pounding riff, and the LSO sounded like a punchy backing band with a scorching groove.

When Polly pressed stop, a bewildered silence, taut as the skin of a snare, captured the room. Beat's fingertips clung to the table's edge like a fruit bat in a banana tree. She glanced at her notes before diving into an explanation she imagined would be a battle fraught with haughty disdain and Shakespearean sighs.

'Australia's professional orchestras have already partnered with the rock world's superstars,' Beat began. 'But it's a radical step for us. I want to know how you feel about this.'

'Must we jump on the band wagon of mediocrity?' Matthew asked.

'We need to set new trends and not merely respond to existing ones.' Beat paused. Pushing her plate of plant-based delicacies to the side she asked, 'What d'you think?'

'The University's Music Faculty wouldn't consider such a tacky...'

'Exactly.' Matthew's attitude towards Beat had worsened since their aborted performance at the Conference Centre. Beat mocked him with praise. 'And this alternative happening of one classical and one mixed genre concert could refresh our profile.'

'I'm with you on that,' Hermione concurred. 'But teaming up with Sian is...'

'Low brow.' Matthew scrutinised the spatula shape of his manicured nails.

'Yep, yep, yep, Rachmaninov's *Symphony No. 2* would be a great play for the classical concert.' Hermione's front teeth were lipstick stained yet again.

'Funny how that particular Rach just happens to be flush with clarinet solos,' Matthew sneered.

Elvira's hand went up except Connor butted in. 'Or maybe Stravinsky's *Rite of Spring* which showcases all orchestral sections.'

'Bartok's *Concerto for Orchestra* would also be a winner,' said Matthew. 'Or Rimsky-Korsakov's *Sheherazade,* the latter ideal for Theo because of its lovely violin solos.'

Elvira's arms danced above her head as if she were waving the British flag at the last night of the Proms.

'Beethoven's *Seventh Symphony* is my choice because the composer's world view drives the project. The first concert will present his *Seventh Symphony* and the *Triple Concerto in C Major op. 56* with Theo, Georgy, and Melody as soloists.'

'What on earth do you mean by "Beethoven's world view?"' Matthew removed his blue bowtie, folding it neatly he tucked it into his jacket pocket.

'Beethoven considers rock to be the voice of the people.'

'Get a grip Elvira.' Matthew undid the top button of his charcoal grey shirt. 'Beethoven died from cirrhosis of the liver in 1827. You're talking as if he's still around.'

'Oh really? Is that so? Well, he...' the piano convenor spluttered.

'All your suggestions are worthy,' Beat jumped in, 'but as Elvira is the curator, she has the final say.'

'Will the woodwind be involved? Those saccharine arrangements for rock and orchestral combos overdose on surging strings,' Hermione pouted.

'The LSO's arrangements feature all instruments,' Beat pointed out.

'That's reassuring,' said Hermione.

'Who will do ours?' A stern-faced Connor twiddled a pen between his fingers.

'No one. We're hiring the LSO's.'

'Good, because arranging is time intensive.' Relieved, Connor sat back.

'The concept's moronic,' said Matthew.

And to Beat's delight, he was ignored.

'I applaud the venture,' Johnny spoke through gritted teeth as he applied a toothpick to excise a sliver of spinach wedged between his front incisors. 'Professionals have to walk on the wild side now and again.'

'How do the State Orchestra players feel about it?' Hermione asked Johnny.

'Many are in favour.' Johnny skewered a falafel.

'Why?' Hermione held a tiny mirror and used her finger to apply more lipstick.

'Because our professionals want to support your fledgling players.' Johnny said.

'But the program celebrates the talents of the rock stream,' Hermione persisted.

'We'll lure a younger audience,' Winton nodded.

Piqued by Connor's acceptance of the idea, Matthew closed his eyes and grimaced.

'Beat why are you keen on this?' Elvira said.

'I want to give us an edge, I want...'

'Okay, okay.' Winton smiled. 'Spare us the reprise and yeah, thanks for involving us.'

'We could make a profit,' Elvira reasoned.

'For?' Matthew harrumphed.

'A building fund for rock's new headquarters,' said Beat.

'Does everyone here agree...' Connor began.

'To an unnecessary new building?' Matthew scowled, picked up his things and left.

'Well,' said Winton. 'What's the secret ingredient?'

'Gecko and Sophie, two muralists from the art school will paint a new age rock building on massive banners positioned on either side of the stage during the show. Sian uses aerial acrobatics when she sings.'

'We'll all help out,' Winton nodded.

Beat yielded to the warming glow of an F# major contentment.

41

BRAVURA

ABOUT to begin his lecture-cum-recital, Garrett tapped the handheld mic. To Beat's surprise, around twenty-five string players and a contingent of flautists and clarinettists rushed into the Recital Hall and filled the middle rows. Nearly all the seats were taken. Events like these were all too often under attended and Beat felt heartened by the show of interest. Winton had evidently had a change of heart, his prime kentia palms waved from the left and right side of the stage. With its lid fully open, the ebony concert grand's white keys looked inviting. Beat looked around, waved at Melody and Theo, but couldn't see Georgy which surprised her because the young pianist admired the American and had been chosen to perform in his masterclass.

'A show of hands – don't be shy – if you want to be a concert pianist.' Garrett paced the stage. Picked up by the stage lights, his white trainers glowed.

'How many of you practise four, five, six, or seven hours a day? I see a healthy show of hands, which should delight Ms Snow. After a lengthy practice, how do you feel? One-word descriptors only.' Garrett grinned, held out his arms and cocked his head like a parrot.

'Exhausted,' said a first year.

'Proud,' said the student with a piano tattooed on her arm.

'Defeated,' said another.

'Fulfilled,' Elvira yelled at the stage as she crept up the aisle and slipped into the seat beside Beat.

Now at the stage's edge, Garrett paused, lowered his voice, whispered into the mic.

'I've reached the top. Is that your dream? Is that why you drill your fingers to the bone instead of hanging with friends, having a quickie, surfing, dancing, or writing essays?'

Garrett cupped a hand over his ear to receive the inevitable soupy groan at the essay reference.

Elvira, Hermione, and Matthew resented the time Connor's theoretical tasks stole from rehearsal time. But Connor insisted aspiring performers had to be musically knowledgeable, to make informed decisions about how to translate sheet music into live performance. Garrett was as much a scholar as he was a performer and Connor consequently admired the American's deeply informed interpretations of piano works.

Beat whispered into Elvira's ear. 'Where's Georgy?'

Elvira shrugged. 'I can't reach her.'

'Running late maybe?' Beat pinned her eyes on the stage.

She wondered why Matthew disapproved of Garrett. Hermione wasn't too keen either. Other Australian performance schools hosted guest musicians to foster fresh ideas. Ideally, the school ought to host at least ten international artists a year. It was healthy to encourage a global perspective to supplement a local mindset. Yet, she'd met hostility towards him. She hadn't been told why, but to be fair, she hadn't asked because she feared the negativity she'd encounter which was cowardly. She'd have to build up the courage to do it.

Steven had hired him because he and Garrett were friends, but she could see the American had much to offer. Despite the uneasiness between them weeks back, she valued him. Next year, she'd invite her own selection of male and female stars from the rock and classical worlds. Then realised Winton and the others should nominate who they wanted.

She was glad Theo and Melody had come. She imagined they would enjoy Garrett's direct delivery, droll humour and his denims and sneakers look which defied the classical musician's stuffy stereotype.

Garrett loved conducting and, like Vladimir Ashkenazy, Daniel Barenboim, and the late Leonard Bernstein, he was a wizard on the keys. Garrett performed in extraordinary places. She'd loved his recital on the headland of Stradbroke Island. There, he'd cruised through Rachmaninov *Preludes* in a bright Hawaiian shirt and board shorts against the spectacle of a school of dolphins leaping out of the water. Playful in a foaming sea. Eastern European music delivered in an Aussie context appealed to her.

Elvira had pressed Garrett to give Georgy a lesson. He wanted to choose a gifted pianist eligible for the prestigious Los Angeles Symphony Orchestra's Scholarship. The award covered travel, accommodation, living expenses and tuition fees, and two concerto engagements. But not turning up to Garrett's workshop could spoil Georgy's chances.

'Be careful what you wish for,' Garrett drawled as he tramped up and down, his dancing hands reminding her of a motivational speaker. 'Remember, it's a job, despite the allusion of glamour and travel. The latter, a death knell for intimate partnerships.'

A stooped photographer from *Nationwide* duck-waddled between the front row and the edge of the stage, an arsenal of cameras bumping and jostling across his back. He popped up, snapped a volley of Garrett shots, and headed to the exit.

'Pests like him,' Garrett pointed at the departing cameraman, 'are another disadvantage.'

Elvira stood. Theo rushed over to give her a handheld mic. 'Do you enjoy the travel?'

'Waiting around in airports when there are delays because of treacherous weather isn't fun. Because the hours I've allocated to practice on arrival won't be possible and my anxiety soars. Soon after arrival I'm expected to conduct or give a recital.'

'Sounds like muso abuse,' Theo heckled prompting whistles and rowdy laughter.

'Listen up, a six-hour practising stint is a *romp*.' Garrett rubbed his hands together. 'Try ten with bruised fingertips and a sore neck.'

'Where are you going next?' Melody jumped to her feet, waved away Theo's offer of the microphone and ignored her bemused friends, who giggled at her affrontery.

'London. I'm playing Beethoven's *Emperor Concerto* with the London Symphony Orchestra in two weeks. I haven't performed it for three years.'

Melody popped up again. 'Do you get to choose the concerto?'

'No. The artistic director picks one from my repertoire list. It could be Mozart, Schumann, or Prokofiev.

'Do you think performers should take betablockers?' Theo asked.

Garrett rubbed his hands together. 'Learning how to channel nerves into the music is the best option. Ms Snow wants to initiate classes on the management of performance related anxiety.'

'But what if a player's hands turn to ice, their knees shake or their heart races?' Theo pressed his point. 'Are there circumstances when drugs are warranted?'

'A curly one, Theo,' Garrett spoke softly.

'Do you use them?' Melody said.

Beat craned her neck. Stared at the cellist hoping to deter her from becoming too intrusive.

'Stage fright tortured me years ago,' Garrett said. 'My mind went blank. I threw up.'

'How did you perform like that?' Asked the pianist with the tattoo.

'Some of my best recitals were given in a nervy state, because the fear and flight reflex, which is what performance nerves are, releases energy. Learning how to alchemise this adrenaline-spike productively is the way to go.'

'Orchestral musicians take them,' Melody said.

'But pills take the edge off the potential intensity,' said Garrett. 'The use of betablockers or not is the fine line between a competent professional and a great star.'

'How do you control yours?' Melody persisted.

'Nothing beats regular engagements. But there's meditation, tai chi, yoga, and doing one or all three helps a person achieve 'flow.''

'Meaning?' Theo asked.

'When an artist is totally immersed in a performance, only the music matters, time halts and the ego is silenced.'

'Can this be taught, Garrett?'

'Yes, up to a point.'

'Supposing a student can't conjure *flow*?' Matthew asked and a quorum of violinists and cellists clapped and cheered.

Beat wondered when Matthew had arrived. He must have come from the back of the hall because she'd been keeping an eye on the main entrance.

'Maybe they're suited to an alternative profession?' Garrett snapped. The young crowd groaned on mass.

'That's harsh,' Matthew said. 'Rather than lose a gifted musician, a judicious use of medication could be the go.'

Beat noticed Elvira nodded in agreement. Meanwhile, Melody filmed Garrett on her phone.

'Sports psychology can teach us a great deal,' Garrett said. 'Coaches know by the way a tennis player walks onto court, their body language, expression, attitude, whether they have a chance of winning. A performance mindset begins before a musician walks on stage.'

'And a betablocker can assist with all that.' Matthew got up and took a seat closer to the stage. Several string students nudged each other, whispering and laughing.

'Emerging players should try to control the jitters through a natural means first,' Garrett said.

Heated exchanges passed between the students.

The Californian ignored the kerfuffle, whipped a hip flask out of his pocket, gulped the liquid down, wiping his mouth with the back of his hand like a swashbuckling pirate. *Oooooh* chorused the crowd.

'So that's your natural means?' Matthew stood up and pointed to the stage. Garrett ignored him.

'Now, my fingers will do the talking. Today, I'm performing three Scriabin preludes, which are snapshots of emotions and memories.'

Beat longed to listen but Elvira tapped her arm wanting her to leave. Reluctantly, she wrenched her eyes away and crept out as Garrett sat examining the keys, like a pilot scans an aeroplane's controls before take-off.

~

'Have you had word from—' Beat began.

'Georgy? No,' said Elvira.

'Talk to her, Beat. Theo and Melody say she's a no show at 1 2 3 rehearsals. Can you ask her what's going on?'

'That's... awkward.' Beat looked away.

'Why?'

'I'd rather not—'

'But it's your—' Elvira interrupted.

'Too bad.' Beat folded her arms.

'How unbelievably thoughtless of me.' Elvira hugged Beat tightly. 'Are you all right?'

'No, you're squeezing me so hard I can't breathe,' Beat grinned.

'Does Hermione coach 1 2 3 now?' Elvira said.

'Yes.'

'How about Hermione initiates a chat with Georgy about her dwindling commitment? And you and I are there as back up,' Elvira suggested.

42

ENSEMBLE

BEAT should never have agreed to come. Her irreconcilable emotions of hate, admiration, rage, and pity for Georgy wrestled for supremacy. Counselling a person who has absconded with your partner was beyond anyone's call of duty, even if she'd recently begun to realise Georgy had done her a favour. From the young pianist's lethargy and the way her fingers lay lifeless on her lap, Dan wasn't good for her either. As much as she had loathed Georgy's arrogance when they'd met in the Botanical Gardens, she hated to see anyone broken. Georgy was striking rather than pretty and like a chameleon her features altered with the weather, the light, her mood, and the music she played. Her deep immersion in the music when she performed made her stage presence gold. Now, her bright eyes had dulled.

'What's this about?' Georgy asked.

'You,' said Hermione.

Georgy looked at the clarinettist's accusatory eyes and Hermione looked to Elvira for support. The young woman ignored Beat as if she wasn't there.

'How are things?' Elvira spoke lightly.

'Fine. Why?'

'I was flummoxed by your no-show at Garrett's workshop.'

Georgy stared at her lap.

'You badgered me for the chance to perform a Scriabin *Etude* in one of Garrett's classes,' said Elvira. 'Pestered me for an individual consultation.'

Darkness shadowed Georgy's face. The second year was stubbornly mute. Beat looked outside. The main road's traffic stretched as far as she could see. A bunch of cellists got off the bus for an ensemble class. The dense, multi-layered voice of thirty-five cellos playing Coldplay's *Fix You* or John Williams' *Hedwig's Theme* wasn't to everybody's liking, but Beat was a fan.

She scanned the décor of Hermione's office and was pleased she'd steered clear of the all too prevalent Beethoven, Bach, and Mozart posters. Instead, photos of famous clarinettists including Martin Frost, Stanley Drucker, and Julian Bliss studded the wall. Beat made a mental note to ask Hermione why she hadn't hung women virtuosos too.

In the corner, there was a slim IKEA wardrobe and the hem of an emerald-green evening dress spilled through a half open door. Photos of Hermione's past and present students, and of herself, were on the wall above her desk. The pick of them was a shot of Hermione in which she looked radiant, post-concert with conductor Lenny Battle's arm around her. A can of lilac air freshener sat on her desk, the cloying fragrance better suited to a deluxe bathroom rather than the engine room of a woodwind specialist.

Hermione asked Beat if she'd like to say something. She shook her head. Elvira sniffed Mimulus oil, a natural remedy for just about anything from spiders, dental treatments, and underachieving students.

Elvira raised her voice. 'How can we defend you to Theo and Melody, who are livid you've missed several 1 2 3 rehearsals?'

A singer in the adjoining room sang Katy Perry's snarling, upbeat *Roar* with its catchy tune and infectious backbeat. When Georgy spoke, it was as if the words had been dredged from the depth of her soul.

'I live a long way from the school. I've got a piano, but the neighbours thump on the wall when I play. Dad gave me a generous allowance when I was—'

'Unattached,' interjected Beat.

'He disapproves of—'

'Dan,' Beat chipped in.

Elvira and Hermione glared at her, and she turned to the window again.

Turalong Arts was rife with dalliances, between staff and staff, students and staff. But a student and the dean's spouse had to be a new twist on college couplings. On the outside, Beat mustered neutrality, but inside she fumed. Dan hadn't been an ideal partner, but there had been a comforting familiarity, a history, and despite all his foibles, he'd been hers.

'How are you managing?' asked Beat. 'Do you have a part-time job?'

'Yes.' Georgy glanced at her hands. 'I work in a produce store. I carry animal feed and potting mix to people's cars. After a shift, I'm too tired to play.'

'Oh my, oh my, what must all that lugging, all that hauling be doing to your hands?' Elvira said. 'We want you back on your—'

'Fingertips,' Hermione quipped.

'What makes you think I'm not?' Georgy said defensively.

'Because...' Elvira wagged her finger at her student's hands in disgust. 'Those chipped nails and reddened hands are not a soloist's.'

Hermione laid a steadying hand on Elvira's arm. Like many pianists, she was scrupulously protective of her hands. Elvira's were permanently encased in fingerless gloves, regardless of the weather. She never lifted anything heavy. Sport was out of the question.

'I've a suggestion. Sorry, Beat, I haven't run this past you yet,' Hermione said.

Did anyone ever talk to her first?

'Georgy, we're not going to pry. Clearly, you'd rather not discuss certain things um... in *this* forum.' Hermione tipped her head towards Beat.

'I propose you stay with me for four days,' said Hermione. 'My Yamaha grand is in a sound-proofed room. There's a bed and a fridge in there. You can practise day and night. Aria will keep you company.'

'Aria?'

'My old cat,' Hermione said.

'Georgy, there's still time. Garrett's performance class is in five days,' said Elvira. 'I know you've set your sights on the Los Angeles Symphony Orchestra's Scholarship.'

Hope flared in Georgy's eyes.

'I've nominated you, but Garrett has to hear you play some solo repertoire.'

Georgy hung her head.

'You can whip up a *Scriabin Etude* or two in no time,' Elvira encouraged.

The young soloist sighed. Flexed her toes.

'There are conditions.'

'Thought as much.' Georgy rubbed her eyes.

'Time out. From Dan. Your job. No distractions,' said Hermione.

Georgy frowned, closed her eyes.

'Let Hermione know what you decide later today,' prompted Beat.

Georgy made eye contact with her for the first time in weeks.

'I'll do it.'

43
BERCEUSE

BEAT thought she'd timed it to arrive when it was Georgy's turn to play, but evidently the masterclass was running late. A white-faced Tiffany sat at the piano, her fingers trembling on the keys. When she began Chopin's *Berceuse*, Beat admired her singing tone and the suitable balance between melody and accompaniment. Not bad for a first year, although the student's jiggling right leg drew the eye. She'd barely reached halfway when Garrett stood in front of the Stuart Grand. Tiffany continued.

'No-o-o-o- stop. Stop.' Garrett's hands ploughed his untamed hair. Tiffany hung her head, dropped her hands in her lap, pinning her eyes on them lest they try to escape.

'Your monotonous phrasing,' Garrett tipped his weight forward and back, forward, back, like a boat moored in choppy water, 'is making me seasick.'

Tiffany was crushed. A fat tear plopped on middle C. She wiped it off with her sleeve, picked up her music and returned to her seat. Garrett had no pity for the girl's humiliation or her drummer boyfriend, whose hands were balled into fists, nor was he aware of the tension he'd fired among the audience with his harsh critique. It was old-school teaching or, as Beat called it, "shout and shame, bully and blame" which sooner or later she would phase out.

Garrett sat at the piano, rolled up his denim sleeves. In his hands, the *Berceuse* breathed, his tone radiant and Chopin's poetic lyricism whispered to her.

Georgy was invited to the stage. Beat cast her eyes around and saw peeved faces. She pitied Tyson, another student of Elvira's, who had also prepared the Scriabin *Prelude, no. 20, Opus 11*. Georgy would be a tough act to follow. Students resented Georgy's privileges, for rules were tossed aside to fast-track the exceptional into the competitive realm where soloists were forged.

Georgy's peers were hypercritical. Add a dash of jealousy and they were merciless. Georgy's gaunt face, frayed jeans, and bare feet revealed her fragility. And yet, when she began to play, head hung over the keys, her mind deep in Scriabin's sound world, Georgy's compelling authority moved the crowd. Her reedy humming was ignored. Glenn Gould used to hum and murmur in a performance and Beat wondered if Georgy knew that. When the final tones sounded, the resonance lingered until silence had devoured the remaining vestige of sound. She bowed graciously in a storm of applause. Garrett grinned. Minutes later, finger to his lips, he uttered superlative praise few musicians will ever hear.

'Magnificent. Sublime.'

~

Beat found Elvira in the kitchen backstage loading a polished silver tray with mouth-watering mini cakes.

Garrett's eyes found the tray. 'As tempting as those look, I can't help thinking there's a price tag attached. Am I right?'

'Maybe,' Elvira sounded coquettish.

Beat had never seen Elvira flirt. A sleek, black dress offset by swanky heels flattered her.

'Shall we?' Beat nodded at the table and chairs.

'Do I have a choice?'

'Georgy's my nominee for the LASO award,' Elvira played her hand.

'Yesterday, she refused to play another Scriabin *Prelude*,' said Garrett. 'Theo told me Dan, her boyfriend, hadn't showed. Naturally, I asked him why that was an issue. Apparently, her guy's a controller and...'

'What has her sex life got to do with this?' Elvira said.

'Georgy plays a brave assortment of music including blockbuster concertos by Schumann, Prokoviev, Rachmaninov, and Saint-Saens. At nineteen, she'd make any orchestra proud,' Beat reasoned.

Garrett selected a chocolate cup cake. 'As you know, talent is only one dimension of the equation.'

'Your scepticism's bizarre,' Elvira scowled at Garrett who looked bemused.

'I'd give her the award in a beat, no pun intended, but she's fooling around with a narc.'

'Don't like where you're going with this, Garrett!' Elvira brushed crumbs off her dress.

'Any hope she'll deep six the chump?' Garrett took a bite of cake.

'I'd say so.' Elvira poured more coffee into his cup.

'Tyson would be a safer bet because that age-old notion still has...'

'Age old what?' Elvira snapped.

Garrett shrugged, head tipped to the side, 'That women can't be soloists. They lack the power, the grit, the courage...

'Clara Schumann,' Elvira's ringleted hair danced. 'Had eight children and a brilliant but unhinged husband yet she toured Europe as a recitalist and composed.

'Well said!' Beat choked on a profiterole.

Elvira slapped her on the back.

'Tyson hasn't Georgy's magnetism,' Beat reached for a drink of water.

'He's male,' said Garrett. 'Without distractions.'

'Codswallop.' Beat rubbed sanitiser into her hands.

'I'd make something of him.'

'Georgy's on the brink of stardom now,' said Beat. She hoped Garrett didn't know Dan was her ex because she couldn't deal with his harsh judgement levelled at her.

'When the girl's used up, he'll seek fresh quarry,' Garrett said.

'Dan isn't a vampire,' Elvira said.

'Ah, but he is.'

'Garrett, listen,' pleaded Beat, 'if, by a certain time frame, Georgy hasn't dumped Dan, we'll move on.'

He fell silent. Elvira tensed. Beat fidgeted. At last, he spoke, 'I'll offer her the scholarship. Give her a few days to decide. How's that?'

'I'm so, so very grateful.' Elvira planted a kiss on Garrett's cheek. When his arm slid around Elvira's waist, Beat could have sworn she heard her friend purr.

44

GROOVE

BEAT struggled to catch her breath as she hurried to the second rehearsal in the concert hall. Matthew caught up with her and begged her to stop. Worrying she'd be late if she did, she quickened her step, it was a brisk twenty-minute walk. She presumed he wanted to apologise for sabotaging her in the performance at the conference centre but that was the last thing she had energy for today.

Matthew pranced along beside her, his precious violin – which no doubt cost as much as a three-bedroom house in a decent suburb – secured under his arm. On her way to the Arts Centre's Concert Hall, she passed massive billboards advertising *West Side Story*, *The Bolshoi Ballet*, and *The Birds of Tokyo*. Melody and Theo were chatting excitedly about the enormous poster for *Beethoven and Sian*. Beat waved. When she reached the Entertainment Centre, Matthew muttered under his breath.

A string quartet of women players, in red, figure-hugging dresses and black Cuban heels, powered tangos by Piazolla, the Argentinian composer near the stairs leading to the ticket office. Matthew waved at them and the players grinned. Deciding to stop and listen to the violinist vent, Beat crossed the floor and headed to the bar to shout him a drink. He followed.

'Sit down, Matthew.' Beat pointed at the bar stool.

Half-heartedly, the young barman polished the granite counter.

'What can I get you?' he said.

'A lemonade please.'

Matthew shook his head and turned his back on the barman.

'Do you want to talk about the Cesar Franck?' She asked.

'Why?' Matthew smirked.

'To say sorry?'

'No. You owe me an apology,' he said.

Swallowing her exasperation she snapped, 'I'm in a rush and...'

'Forcing string players to eke out lengthy notes is...'

'Inhumane.' Beat interrupted.

'And the bowing will trigger tendonitis because they're...'

'Do you remember when Lyrebird performed Penderecki's *Threnody for the Victims of Hiroshima*?'

'Of course,' Matthew clasped his hands together.

'You had no objection to the strings playing those harrowing screams with the bow drawn agonisingly slow across the string.'

Matthew rolled his eyes and licked his lips just as her horses did when they reconciled with something. Recently, she'd found email traffic between him and Steven, in which he'd lambasted the former dean for his exhausting rehearsals. Reading these helped her to put up with Matthew's whining. It wasn't personal. Like Polly had once reminded her. A dog barks. A cat meows. Doomsayers grizzle.

Shrieks of laughter caught Beat's attention as around forty blue-uniformed students stomped up the stairs. Representatives from twelve local high schools were arriving to watch the rehearsal. She sipped on the lemonade, the bubbles fizzed on her tongue and she pulled a face. It tasted sour, like Matthew's conversation.

'Seriously, if you're this concerned, you have my blessing to tweak the string parts to include strategic rests,' Beat conceded.

When he flashed a contemptuous what-would-you-know-you're-just-a-pianist look she lost her patience, 'You're a member of a team,' she raised her voice. 'Your duty is to support this. Remember?'

'I don't see it like you.'

'For the first time, our classical and rock specialists are on stage together.'

'Presenting a dubious happening like this isn't cause for celebration.'

'Rock isn't contagious. Sian's unlikely to trigger a pandemic of populism,' Beat pointed at Matthew's feet. 'You're wearing odd socks?'

He eyed his feet with disinterest, one blue sock, shark patterned, the other, orange with airborne saxophones.

'You're deluded.'

'Moving on. You or Hermione can curate our next event. What would you program?'

'Mahler's *Seventh Symphony.*'

'Good choice,' Beat spoke gently and in an even tone. 'And we will talk about that unfortunate performance soon.'

'You weren't up to it!'

~

Inside the concert hall, rows of bright-eyed, fidgety children were kept in check by strained teachers. Beat sensed a restless energy. There were breakouts, a student ran up and down the aisle flapping a worksheet, pursued by a maddened teacher. A young girl crawled on the floor looking for her phone.

Orchestral players readied their instruments. Sian tapped the live mic, Winton perfected a trumpet fill. Much to the teenagers' delight, the trombonists mimicked hip-hop moves to an imagined groove. Beat's eyes scoured the stage for disengaged musicians, but she couldn't see frustration or mutiny on anyone's faces. Elvira and Hermione hadn't looked this relaxed since the retreat. Connor had his nose in a book. The State Orchestra players positioned their iPads on music stands. Musicians flowed onto the stage from north, south, east, and west and soon, the entire instrumental force, the sixty-strong chorus, Winton's band and Sian were ready.

Garrett raised his arms to begin, held them there for a long time but inexplicably lowered them and marched off stage. The audience booed.

'What was that about?' Beat asked a State Orchestra trombonist standing in the aisle.

'Garrett's not up to it. Rhythmically, he's straight as a spirit level. If we don't swing it we'll be a laughing stock.'

Beat went to find Garrett but only made it to the exit when an indignant Sian sprinted towards her.

'Something wrong?' asked Beat casually.

'Yep.' On stage, Theo as concertmaster stood to tune the orchestra, blissfully unaware of Sian's dissatisfaction.

'Everyone is just great,' said Sian, 'loving, supportive...'

'Spit it out?' Beat prompted, terrified about what she was going to hear, appalled by her use of Dan's expression.

'Garrett's a dud,' Sian said.

Beat's pulse raced, her mouth drier than the Simpson desert. 'Why?'

'He's cool, the skinny jeans, the trainers, the shaggy...'

'Get to the point...' Beat pressed.

Sian shook her head. 'He's a fine conductor.'

'And?' Beat croaked.

'He can't groove, doesn't have the feels.'

'How bad?' Beat said.

'Catastrophic. You didn't hire me to be rhythmically castrated,' Sian reasoned.

'He's a classy—'

'All that and more. But my guess?' Sian stood tall, 'he's never directed a gig of mixed music.'

'I don't know.'

'My rhythm's dirty, funked up. Garrett's hell bent on ironing out the creases.'

'Oh,' Beat gulped.

'Either the orchestra gets behind me or I'm outta here.'

'I'll grab a couple of State Orchestra players. Ask them what they think.'

Sian gripped Beat's arms.

'What for? You know it's not working. I can see it on your face. Here's the thing. The total deck is sitting here reading.'

'Everyone take-up pozzies,' the stage manager bellowed. 'Next session starts in five.'

'Connor?' Beat said.

'That dude flies in any style. Can't believe you didn't use him in the first place. When I studied here, everyone adored him.'

Guilt rattled Beat to the bone. Matthew, Winton, Polly, Thorne, and the managing director of Sounds Best had all tried to persuade her to enlist Connor as conductor. Winton had been tactful but she'd refused to listen. Trouble was she didn't trust any of them: she thought they were out to sabotage not only this project but her every move. She could have spoken to Connor about it. Ironically, for all her deepening regard for Connor, she'd turned her back on his gift like Thorne had on hers.

She raced to Garrett's dressing room. It wasn't the best; the cracked square mirror at the dressing table and the dirty yellow paintwork did nothing to soothe a wired musician. Slumped in the corner, Garrett drank from his hip flask.

'How's it going?' she asked.

'The arrangements are spot on. Each orchestral section gets a workout,' he told her. 'Your audience is gonna love it. The kids already do.'

Now that she'd got to know Garrett, she knew he wasn't as fiercely ego-bound as conductors tended to be.

'You look concerned, Beatrice,' Garrett took another swig. Mopped his face with a towel.

'It's the rhythm,' she spoke gently.

He looked at the floor. Her eyes followed. She looked at his feet. Smiled at his plain grey socks.

Garrett closed his eyes, bunched his lips. 'Rock's not my thing.'

There was a hard knock on the door. 'Maestro, the rehearsal's about to begin.'

'I'm sure the capacity's there,' she said. 'Brass and percussion players can juggle a smorgasbord of styles.'

'Connor's your man. You're lucky we can hand it over to him. I know Hermione, Winton, and Matthew have been urging him to ask you if he could take it on.' Was she really that unapproachable he couldn't have asked her directly?

'Can you take the rehearsal until I find him?' Beat noted the ironic reversal. She had asked Connor to stand in for Garrett in the Tchaikovsky rehearsal.

'He's already on stage,' Garrett said.

Surprised, a little peeved but predominantly relieved Connor had taken the rehearsal over even if she hadn't been consulted about it, she asked herself why she'd stubbornly insisted on his unsuitability. Why had she made this hard on herself and everyone else? She hated the staff's lack of faith in her but then her actions had demonstrated a lack of faith in them. She should have pursued the possibility of Connor directing the show more vigorously.

In future, she'd listen first. Decide later. She'd been doing it all arse about.

45

POCA A POCA

BEAT savoured the sunshine and clear blue sky. She stared at the Botanical Garden's massive lake blanketed by flowering lilies. A small boy trailed a stick on the watery skin at the lake's edge. Beat wondered if he would notice the eels writhing in the shallows.

Crossed-legged, Georgy tugged at tufts of grass. Coffee odours from a refreshment cart clashed with the vile aroma of dog shit.

'You know what they say, it's never the things you did but what you didn't do that you regret,' Garrett observed. 'Georgy, what's it to be? A piano teacher's suburban existence?'

'Not likely,' she said.

'Take up this award. Perform with the best, the Chicago Symphony, Berlin Philharmonic, the London, New York, and Sydney Symphonies. In between concerto engagements you'll give recitals.' Garrett paused.

Was he thinking about which angle to pursue next or whether Georgy was a lost cause? Beat attended to the sounds around her; a yappy dog, squawking cockatoos, squealing children, hit songs from a radio. Her mind jumped. She congratulated herself for being there. Somehow, her professionalism had gained the upper hand and her personal grievance with Georgy wasn't an issue because she'd snapped into her role as dean.

'What d'you say?' He paused for Georgy to speak.

'Your world is way scarier than a suburban one,' Georgy said. Her straightened palm skimmed over the short-cropped grass like a metal detector.

'Nineteen's a pivotal age. You're gifted. Running away from talent like yours is cowardly. Use it, Georgy, or suffer a lifetime of regret.'

Garrett looked to Beat for encouragement. She and Garrett huddled together on the park bench like anxious parents.

Georgy gnawed at her nails because this was the optimal method to keep them acutely short. This way they didn't split during athletic passagework. Now, Georgy examined her hands, palms down, fingers splayed. Elvira had told Beat that Georgy wanted to extend her hand span so she could have a stretch of eleven piano keys. If she succeeded, Rachmaninov's *Second Piano Concerto* and his *Preludes* would be more hospitable for her to play because they required a broad hand like the composer's own. Rachmaninov had a twelve-note stretch. There was a theory he suffered from Marfan, a disease affecting the connective tissue. His exceptional height and huge hands and feet fitted the condition's profile.

'Do you know what a virtuoso's life entails?'

'Yeah,' said Georgy.

'Then you know women are required to glam up. What you're wearing is suitable for a checkout chick in Woolworths or a social worker, but not for the stage, a press conference, or to snag a record label or charm sponsors.'

Beat knew this argument would alienate Georgy. A cluster of ants ferried a dead beetle twenty times their size through a forest of grassy blades. Three men in yellow hi-vis vests chatted companionably as they walked towards a dense grove of shrubs carting a trolley laden with gardening implements.

'Your agent could ask you to model glamorous designer dresses on stage. Even I wear make-up on TV.'

'Ew, how gross.'

Garrett laughed. 'Think of Nicola Benedetti, the pin-up violinist, or Amy Dickson, the Aussie saxophonist who rocks Armani couture.'

'Sounds bullshit.'

'And...' Garrett began.

'There's more?'

He tapped his nose. 'No. Bare. Feet.'

Georgy wrapped her fingers around a bigger clump of grass and pulled hard but couldn't dislodge the roots.

'I can't play in shoes.'

'Can't or won't?' Garrett shrugged.

'Don't.'

Beat caught Garrett's eye, she shook her head. He took the hint.

'I could be marketed as a barefooted virtuoso like the violinist Patricia Kopatchinskaja,' Georgy said. 'She's known as the barefoot fiddler. She's been the guest conductor of the Australian Chamber Orchestra on several occasions.'

Garrett ignored her comment because all heads looked towards the western side of the lake where Winton led a marching troupe of twenty trombonists blasting *When the Saints Go Marching In*. Although the players, with long hair flying in the wind, in frayed jeans and scuffed trainers, looked distinctly unsaintly, they sounded much better than they looked.

'The scholarship is yours for the taking. You'll be in a competitive class and expected to build repertoire rapidly.'

'I'm keen to learn Miriam Hyde's *Piano Concerto No.2 in C sharp minor* and Elena Kats-Chernin's *Piano Concerto no. 3, The Deep and Bitter Flood.*'

Garrett scratched his chin. 'Your concertos will be selected for you.'

Georgy opened up her fist and released grass shoots. She looked distant. Troubled.

'Last year, Evgeny Kissin and Lang Lang gave master classes and...'

'Awesome. But I can't give you a decision,' she paused, 'Not on the spot.' Georgy brushed down her long skirt, picked up her shoes. 'I'm stoked. Truly.' Georgy placed her hand on her heart. 'How much time can I have to decide?'

'Tell me after you've performed Beethoven's *Triple*. If you need more time than that you're not what I'm looking for.'

Beat frowned at Garrett's blunt response.

'Oh... I see.' Georgy's eyes dulled with hurt.

Then Garrett pointed at Georgy imperiously, as if he was cueing the strings' ethereal sonority at the start of Mahler's *First Symphony*. 'I've an alternative pianist should you decline.'

Impulsively, Georgy scrambled up the grassy bank. When she reached the footpath, she looked over her shoulder and waved.

'How will Dan take her news?' Garrett asked.

'Hard to say.' A toddler dropped the final sliver of an ice cream cone. A crow snatched it. Red in the face the outraged child yelled and stamped his feet.

'Did I say too much?' Garrett said, waving his hand to shoo a fly away from his face.

46
SCHERZO

BEAT cleaned the horses' yard and stables vigorously. Weeded Dan's raised flowerbeds planted with zucchini, lettuce, and tomatoes. Could she manage the mortgage, the upkeep of the horses, and pay Dan an adequate allowance? If she rented out the spare bedroom perhaps, but she'd have to guard every cent.

She gouged clumps of alligator grass out of the lawn. She'd promised Cholmley she'd sort her finances over the next couple of days but the paperwork could keep until dusk, because the sunny weather was too inviting to be indoors. Autumn was Queensland's best season. Ideal Mediterranean temperatures during the day then a bite in the air at dusk. She'd hate to leave this rural pocket so close to the sea, nature reserves, and the city. Since it was Saturday, she'd go on a ride and as if to show she meant it she fetched her tack and slung her saddle and bridle over the fence.

She'd promised Cholmley not to speak to Dan. According to him, her ex was a cad, capable of the worst treachery. Bolt whinnied as she approached and pulled at the rope tethering him to the fence. She glanced at her mobile. Nine missed calls. When it rang, she answered.

'Beatrice?' said a familiar voice. 'It's Ellie.'

'How are you doing?'

'We have to talk.'

'I should have told you weeks ago, but Dan and I...' Beat began.

'That's why I'm ringing.'

'Oh...'

'Before the divorce settlement is finalised there's something you have to know.'

'Actually, it's almost done.' Beat picked sticky spider residue off the saddle.

'I'll take an Uber,' Ellie said. 'See you in thirty minutes.'

~

Beat released Bolt's halter and led him back to the paddock. The day was young, she could always ride later. Inside the kitchen, she loaded the dishwasher. After plumping the cushions and giving the couch a few hasty swipes, there was enough time to sort her hair which no doubt would be flecked with hay. The greyhounds' dash to the front door announced Ellie's arrival. Her sister-in-law rushed into the kitchen. Noticing how she shied away from the dogs, Beat reassured her, 'Greyhounds are gentle. I promise.' An uneasiness around canines seemed to be a family trait.

Ellie gazed at the paddocks.

'This is paradise.'

'Yes,' agreed Beat. 'But I may not be living here much longer.'

'Why?'

Had Dan sent Ellie to appraise the property? She couldn't put anything past him.

'Beat, please. Sit down.'

'You're scaring me.'

'Dan lucked out when he found you,' Ellie began. 'I know you've taken care of all the bills.'

'Yes, but that's old news...'

'I'll explain.' She put her finger to her lips. 'Hear me out. I've not come to add to your troubles. Seven years ago, our aunt, my mum's sister, died. When I heard she had cancer I was devastated but it was hard for me to visit because I hadn't yet learned to drive, and she lived on the north-coast.'

'Dan told me he'd spend time with her for both of us. I thought it was unusually considerate of him at the time. Rather than send her to a hospice, we hired a full-time carer.'

'I'm sorry. I know how much you loved her.'

'Yes, I did.' Ellie's voice cracked. 'But during Dan's visits, he painted me as a flake with a gambling addiction. He told her he'd bailed me out with vast sums of money.'

A year ago, Beat would have been wary about Ellie's claim, but now this newly minted unfamiliar Dan seemed capable of anything.

'How nasty. Callous.'

'I stopped going to see her at all, because the carer told me my visits upset her. She told me to stay away.'

Ellie paused, blew her nose.

'I never saw my aunt again.' She struggled to speak.

'Take your time,' Beat said kindly. She didn't know where Ellie's story was leading, but there was no mistaking its significance.

'The other day I came home to find Dan and Georgy in the flat I'm renting. They'd been thrown out of their accommodation because of her piano playing. He didn't have a key, but he'd somehow convinced the landlord to let him in.'

A hot-rod burned up the street. Beat screwed up her eyes. Wongara Road had become a rat run, a week ago a koala and baby had been killed, the week before she'd scraped a dead carpet python from the road.

Beat looked outside. Three black-winged ibis sat on the fence. The temperature had dropped and the sky looked bruised, filled with purply-grey veined clouds.

'Dan did all the talking.'

'Why was he there?' Beat asked.

'He said he needed somewhere to stay. I said no and he got belligerent.' Ellie looked pained. 'Dan inherited my aunt's 10-acre property near Byron Bay. I know he can afford rent.'

'You're kidding me.'

'If only...' Ellie sniffed, blew her nose.

Beat cupped the black and white dog's chin in her hands. 'I'd absolutely no idea.'

'How could you? If he didn't tell you about it.'

'Yes, I know, but...'

'Dan swore me to secrecy.'

'How long has he owned it?'

'Around five years,' Ellie said.

'About the same time, he began his PhD,' said Beat wistfully.

'Dan rented it out.'

'For?'

'Around $900 a week,' said Ellie.

'I've been an idiot. Such a fool.' Beat's phone rang. She switched it off. The relentless buzz of her neighbour's brushcutter shredded her nerves.

'Beat, he's pathological, he'll screw anybody over for money. He's good at it too. Really good. Don't blame yourself.'

'It's hard to take it in.'

'I'm sorry but...'

'There's more?' Beat groaned.

'Dan also has capital in an investment fund.'

'What? Ever since we got together, he's always insisted he hadn't a bean.'

'He's a liar. A scrounger. He squirrels the rental income away. Deposits any interest monies made from his investments into overseas bank accounts.' Ellie sighed.

'Your aunt's property must be worth a few million.'

'And she had intended to divide her assets between us. Dan promised I'd inherit a lump sum held in trust until I turned twenty-one.'

'But it didn't happen,' said Beat.

'No.' Ellie hunched over. 'I had to tell you this.'

'Because?'

'I overheard him on the phone to his lawyer. The call was on loudspeaker. Dan was stalling and being evasive. The lawyer kept repeating Dan had to provide clear details about his assets. I'm here to stop him from fleecing you.'

Beat breathed in and held her breath but the tears rolled anyway.

Ellie held her hand. 'Cry a river if you want but only after you update your lawyer. Think of your dogs and Bolt and Storm.'

PERDENDOSI

SLEEP eluded Beat. When her dogs stirred and pricked their ears, she blamed their agitation on the fox that patrolled the garden under the cloak of darkness. She'd seen it eyeball her neighbour's duck enclosure on many a moonlit night. But when the dogs flew downstairs, she sat up. If it had been the fox, the dogs would have settled by now. She heard a knock on the door and then again but louder. She threw off the covers, pulled on her jeans and ran downstairs.

Looking through her door's peephole, she was surprised to see Connor tramping up and down the path she and Dan had fashioned out of Sally's left-over bricks. He seemed agitated. It was nearly midnight. Far too late for a professional call. His hair and his red and black plaid padded jacket were sopping wet. As soon as she opened the door, he stepped into the kitchen without being asked, unaware his clothes dripped on the terracotta tiles. He sat at the kitchen table. Beat offered him a towel, dry clothes, and a hot drink, but he shook his head with such vehemence droplets freckled the table.

He beckoned for her to sit, as if it were his office, rather than her kitchen. She remembered the day she'd first had lunch with him and he'd been just as high and mighty then. Except it no longer vexed her, because she'd learned there tended to be a legitimate reason behind his curt behaviour.

'What's going on?' She turned the heating on.

'You already know.' Connor grabbed the wooden pepper mill and moved it around like an oversized chess piece.

Beat shrugged. 'If you're here to complain, let me in on it because...'

'Do you have any conception,' he pointed at her, 'any comprehension of the complexities involved in marshalling so many players, artists, and dancers, Winton's band, and Sian in your blasted musical circus?'

'It's huge, I know.'

'Then explain. What possessed you?' Connor unbuttoned his wet jacket.

'To?'

'Cancel tomorrow's rehearsal.' He sliced his hands in the air.

'Hermione told me you were concerned that another rehearsal would be overkill.'

'Did she now?' Connor closed his eyes. Ran his thumb along the table's edge over and over.

'Yes. When Hermione berated me for the umpteenth time about woodwind players missing her performance class and told me you were satisfied, I caved.'

A deafening thunderclap shook the house to its foundations.

'Why didn't you consult me first, Beatrice?'

'I'm sorry, I can't always recall who needs to be consulted, consoled, cosseted, or cooed to. Everybody's precious to a degree that does my head in. And...'

'And?' Connor raised his eyebrows.

'When the shoe is on the other foot I'm not consulted.' Beat clicked the salt and pepper mill side by side in the centre of the table.

'What are you saying?'

'You replacing Garrett warranted my input.'

'So, it wasn't *you* who organised it?' Hurt shadowed Connor's face, his flattened mane-like hair made him look vulnerable.

'No. You said you'd never stand in for a conductor again. Remember?'

'I see. But I wasn't deputising for Garrett. I took over from him which is different.'

'I assumed Hermione had consulted you.'

'You're smart but maddeningly gullible. Absolutely clueless.' Connor planted his elbows on the table and covered his face with his hands.

'Clueless is a bit strong?' Beat stifled a yawn.

'It's a blind spot. Denial.'

Connor's voice ratcheted up in pitch. Outside, the green tree frogs' chorus swelled and shrank in an endless cycle.

'You're not making any sense.'

'You really don't know do you?' Connor twirled his fingers in the air as if he was casting a spell. 'The dissenting voice in Thorne's ear? The one who gave a copy of my letter – intended for your eyes only – to Thorne.'

'I'm done with it.'

'Admirable, but foolish. Think.'

Beat closed her eyes. She waited. Something grated, scratched in the back of her mind and a dark shadow transitioned into the light.

'I played into her hands.' Beat wailed. 'Walked into her trap.'

Connor leant his chair back and then tipped forward with such force his weight slammed up against the table and an orange popped out of the fruit bowl.

'The day after Dan left, Hermione plied you with wine, Mozart and syrupy comfort,' Connor said.

'She was unbelievably kind.'

'How touching.'

Connor's sarcasm rasped. She watched his fingertips rake the table's surface.

'How come you know about it?' Beat said.

'Because the very next morning, she told the entire staff – I wasn't present – she feared for your stability.'

'What a bitch.' Beat's voice was husky with shock. 'And I thought Thorne was the nightmare. Hermione weaselled her way into my house!'

Beat tramped round and round the table.

'She attempted to persuade all and sundry, even Elvira and Polly, to lodge a vote of no confidence in you. Then announced she'd step into the breach.'

'And no one, not even Polly, told me this.'

'You were reeling from Dan's departure.'

'I confided in her.' Beat kicked at a table leg.

'How do you think she knew Dan had left you?'

'Fuck knows. Polly told her? She's a clairvoyant?'

Beat shook her icy hands to get the blood circulating.

'She flattered Dan,' Connor said, 'took him to the pub.'

'How sickening.' Beat sat down and propped her head on her hand.

'She encouraged him to leave you. She knew exactly when Dan moved out because she'd suggested the time and the day. None of us had an inkling about his infatuation with Georgy, not until Hermione put us straight.'

Wearily, Beat hung her head. 'Why has it taken you so long to tell me?'

'Because Hermione and I have history.'

'In what way?'

'We were married.' He scratched his neck.

So that was what Polly wanted to tell her. Shocked and angry she blurted, 'I don't care. You promised to help and then deprived me of this essential...'

'Look, I stuffed up.' He wiped his forehead with the towel Beat had hung over the back of his chair. 'I made the wrong call. I should have told you about Hermione. Thought everybody knew.' Deafening thunder rattled the house. The dogs cowered.

'But I'm from down south.'

'Then there's more you should know. Before you joined us, I was the school's conductor-in-residence, a regular with the State Orchestra. Back then, I had enough arrogance to fill the Queensland Concert Hall. Travelled regularly. Loved every minute...'

'Until?'

Connor's hands inched across the table towards Beat's. 'I'd had weeks of back-to-back engagements all over Europe. Constant travel. Too many scores to prepare. Never enough sleep.'

'And?'

'I froze during the second movement of Beethoven's *Seventh*. I knew this Symphony inside out, I'd never used a score. But I went blank. I gave the nod to the concertmaster for him to lead, but the humiliation as I stood in front of the Berlin Philharmonic, a world-class orchestra, not shaping, not inspiring, but merely marking the beat was intolerable. The shame of it still haunts me.'

Beat took Connor's hand, threaded her fingers through his.

'I stopped conducting. Became phobic about performing.'

'That's why you wanted Hermione to play the Brahms.'

He nodded.

'Did you have regrets?'

'I still do.'

'I'm sorry.'

'Hermione's all het up because I'm conducting again. She suspects I'm angling to be dean,' said Connor.

'Frankly, the lot of you are barking mad.'

'What brought that on?'

'The dean's position is filled.'

'Very true.' Connor forced a smile.

'Do you know why Steven suddenly quit?' Beat asked.

'I wish I did because it was out of character.'

'Yes, agreed. So, are you?'

'What?'

'Angling to be dean?'

'Keep asking if you like, Beatrice, but you should know by now the answer will always be no.'

'I thought you were a right royal pain in the arse.'

Lightning flashed. Thunder echoed inside her head.

'And now?' Connor said.

'How could I?'

'Hermione was gutted when Thorne bypassed her for the deanship.'

'I bet.'

'What pains Hermione the most...'

'Is?'

'You're a natural.'

Beat sighed. Just about everyone, with the exception of Dan, who couldn't get past her elevated salary, had an opinion on why she should or shouldn't continue in the role. She forced the thought of her ex from her mind and wrapped a throw around her quivering faun greyhound.

'It's not in Hermione's interest for this event to succeed.'

'Tsk tsk tsk.' A gecko darted behind a mirror.

Beat picked up the escapee orange popped it back into the fruit bowl.

'She's badgered me to pull out of it and unless you want Sian's show to flop, reinstate the rehearsal.'

'Is that why you came? Couldn't it have waited until tomorrow?'

'Not entirely,' Connor hedged.

'It's a disaster out there,' Beat turned the outside light on and opened the door to the veranda. Saturated, a pygmy possum hunched on the railing. Water sluiced off the guttering, skied off the pipes.

'When there's water gathering under the house, it's a sure sign the roads are flooding.' Beat said.

'Luckily, my place is on higher ground. It never gets this dramatic.'

Outside, a curlew screamed in the frog-throated soundscape. She moved behind Connor, wrapped her arms around his chest and his hands folded over hers. A gesture which lasted well beyond acceptable displays of affection between colleagues.

'I want you to stay.'

When he said nothing, she stepped back and walked away.

'Come here,' Connor whispered, but his hushed tone was a question more than a command. Exhausted from longing, trying not to cross a line, second guessing and doubting she went to him. Shivering, he removed his sweater. Taking off her top she pressed her skin to his and a delicious warmth flooded through her. She felt his desire. Imagined her tongue teasing him, probing, her mouth full. His eyes knew and she was glad. Weeks of awkwardness and uncertainty had been swept aside by a yielding transparency and longing. In her room, she closed her eyes, her body charged until together their urgency peaked and cadenced.

48

PIU

'NOTHING will stop me from flying to England to work on this joint project.' Connor's face was impassive, his eyes clear, he sat still, patient.

Dan's face was flushed, as if he'd just had sex or too many beers. But the heat on his skin that afternoon was because Connor had made him a dream offer.

She felt like an amateur sleuth: ludicrous in her hoodie, not to mention the sunglasses and long skirt Elvira had insisted was a viable if unflattering disguise. Still, it had enabled her to sit, nose in a book, mostly obscured by a convenient overgrown ficus bush and yet within hearing distance.

'I've no dependents,' Dan declared.

Beat's hand jerked as she lifted her full glass and berry juice spilled on the jacket. Now, she'd need to get it dry cleaned. Connor meanwhile twisted a paper napkin in his torturing fingers.

'Dan, that's a big plus. Forgive me, but you and...'

'Finished. We've yet to sort the legals. Beat's a trooper. She'll cope.'

Connor's emotions were breaking loose and beginning to show. By the grim set of his jaw, he was incensed. If he suffered from a surfeit of integrity, Dan had none. Connor stirred his tea and bided his time, but she knew he wasn't going to let Dan shirk his responsibilities.

'I know about you and Beat. I was referring to Georgy.'

'There's no future there. Georgy's great but she's just...'

'A friend with benefits?'

Beat heard the chill in Connor's voice, his face so frosty Dan could get hypothermia just by looking at it. She wished she could prompt him to smile now and then. But her concern was needless because Connor's stern manner and interrogation didn't inhibit Dan.

'She's not a patch on Beat, except she's younger, but not a keeper. Man, that piano thing?' Dan stole a glance at his phone.

'What about it?'

'It's a passion killer,' Dan sighed. 'If Georgy's not within touching distance of one she pines.'

A flute strain caught Beat's ear. Students with portable instruments, violins, cellos, oboes, trumpets and acoustic guitars chalked up practice hours in the park on dry, still days. Often, they'd leave with a handful of gold coins gifted by appreciative listeners.

'Do you want a way out? Will this absence do the trick?'

Dan nodded, 'Timing is perfect.' Dan opened his jacket.

'Good. Our research interests are compatible,' said Connor. 'As long as you're sure about a six-month absence.'

'It suits me fine.'

'How come?'

'When I get back, I'll patch things up with Beat.'

Beat was shocked by Dan's callous disregard of Georgy and his arrogance about her was extraordinary.

'That's your business.' Connor scanned the surroundings.

Beat hoped Connor's phone had captured Dan's every word.

'Who else would want a horse-crazed workaholic?'

Connor clapped his hands at a trio of scavenging ibis, shooing them away with his foot. But other than a half-hearted jump, the birds soon resumed their search for food.

'Pests aren't they?' Dan leaned in conspiratorially.

'Dan please clear this with Georgy. I've been let down before.'

'I give you my word.'

'It's two-thirty now,' Connor stared at his Rolex. 'I want to make the five pm deadline. Also, I need to talk to Georgy about her latest composition.'

Connor handed Dan a form. 'Bring it to my office at four pm. The school's staff room on level three is noisy because of sound leakage but comfortable enough. Hardly anyone uses it.'

~

When Dan ambled into the school's foyer, Beat stood by the noticeboard, pretending to jot down rehearsal dates. At last, Georgy flew towards him, her spiky hair instantly recognisable. Her op shop chic looked shabby these days because she'd lost so much weight. Did she buy second-hand clothes because she was thrifty, or was she trying to reduce her carbon footprint? In her case, probably both. Beat's stomach flipped at Dan's stony expression. No way would he allow Georgy's star to shine brighter than his. It was all about winning where he was concerned.

'Dan, I've got great news.' She bent over, her long fingers splayed on her thighs, while she calmed her breathing.

'Spit it out.' Dan brushed off his jacket's lapel.

Beat approved of this spunky Georgy, the one who'd rocked Tchaikovsky.

'Garrett's offered me a scholarship.'

Dan perked up. Beat supposed he'd be totting up its monetary value. It surprised her he hadn't whipped out a calculator on the spot.

'Lucrative?'

'Fantastic. It pays my fare to Los Angeles, my rent, expenses, and tuition fees.'

Beat could no longer hear the conversation because Dan pointed to the grey armchairs, the *slouchers* the staff called them, outside reception and the pair loped off. She'd been told they often met there in between Georgy's classes and rehearsals. She turned towards her office; she didn't need to hear their conversation because she knew Dan would stomp all over Georgy's exhilaration. He'd lash out because of how gleeful, how prideful she looked, which he'd interpret as a slight and it would spur him on to grind her dream into dust. Polly waited nearby. When Georgy and Dan's tete-a-tete soured, her assistant was primed to interrupt and take Georgy to Beat's office. Beat's hostility towards the youngster had gone – Georgy was as much a victim as she had been.

'Would you like to talk about the scholarship?' Beat asked a glum Georgy. But she shook her head and grabbed a tissue.

'Hey, what's the matter?'

'I thought Dan would be happy for me.'

'He wasn't?'

'No apparently Garrett's gaslighting me. Playing mind games. Luring me into an unobtainable dream.'

Georgy flexed her fingers, then locked her hands together.

Beat waited.

'I've lost my edge.' Tears plopped off Georgy's cheeks onto her shirt.

Beat knew exactly how Dan's you've-lost-your-edge quip would have wound itself tight around Georgy's heart until it strangled her joy.

'Dan's expertise is in art, not music. Why would you trust his judgement?'

'He speaks so authoritatively about it.' Georgy wiped her eyes and blew her nose.

'All of us,' Beat jabbed at her chest, 'Elvira, Hermione, Connor, Matthew, and Garrett, believe you are exceptionally gifted. If you put your mind to it, put the piano first, knock off a few of the big international competitions, such as The Sydney, The Leeds, or the Van Cliburn, you could become a star player.'

'Agents would have to take me on because of the way I play, not because of the way I look, or I won't sign with them.'

'Good you know your own mind. What about the barefoot thing?'

Georgy scrunched up her used paper hanky and tossed it in the wastepaper bin.

'I grew up in Katherine. I was enrolled with School of the Air because our cattle property was in the middle of nowhere. Twice a semester, my teacher came to Katherine for a face-to-face lesson, and she always made her students take their shoes off. She'd say the universe's vibrations travelled through our naked feet into our hearts and made our playing sing. We reckoned it was a ruse to keep the dust down. She vacuumed a lot.' Georgy stopped talking. Subject closed.

'What else did Dan say?'

'I was too old for fairy tales.'

'And you said?'

'I'd never stop pushing to be a soloist.'

'That's the way.' Beat gave her a thumbs up. Georgy evidently didn't know about Dan going to England with Connor, otherwise her distress would have been worse.

'Dan feeds off my energy.'

Beat wondered if Georgy would ever realise how hurtful she'd been in the Botanical Gardens in the first throes of her romance with Dan.

'At the start, he loved my playing. Now he uses ear plugs. Cups his hands over his ears or goes out.'

'Georgy, could you spare a minute?' asked Connor. 'I want to talk about the piano trio you composed. Beatrice, why not come too?'

Inside Connor's office, Beat shut the door and scanned the bookshelves packed with scholarly tomes and biographies. She saw the usual suspects, Chopin, Dvorak, and Bartok biographies. All arranged in alphabetical order.

Connor looked for his phone on his cluttered desk. When he found it, he handed it to Beat gingerly, as if it were a loaded gun.

'Heard you've been offered the LASO scholarship,' Connor said. 'I'm impressed Georgy. I can't think of anyone more deserving. Will you say yes?'

Georgy looked downcast.

'I'm undecided. But I know if I don't, I'll regret it.'

There was a knock on the door. Georgy tensed, folded her arms.

'Hey, can I come in?' Dan asked.

Connor called out 'yes.'

Dan was aghast at the sight of Beat and Georgy.

'What's all this?' Dan placed the completed forms on Connor's desk. 'I thought this was a private meeting?'

Beat and Georgy said nothing. The silence grew and grew until it infiltrated every cavity, every corner. The absence of sound hurt.

'Dan, have you discussed the project with Georgy?'

'What project?' Her eyes sparked with incredulity.

'I looked everywhere for her.'

'And you found me.'

Georgy eased out of her shoes. Beat saw a spark of fury in the young pianist's eyes. 'Well?'

When Dan said nothing, Connor chipped in.

'I've offered Dan the opportunity to work on a research project with me in London. He'll be away for six months.'

Georgy's eyes widened. 'When were you going to tell me Dan?'

'You were excited about Garrett's offer. How could I spoil the moment? Be rational Georgy. Logical.'

The word "rational" had its heyday in the last century and was used as a put down against opinionated women. He had been patronising and blatantly rude. Why didn't Georgy put him in his place? Beat recoiled when Dan shunted his chair besides Georgy and took her hands in his.

'Dan, I'm going to America.'

'Wouldn't it be better to get your playing up to scratch?'

'What would you know about it?' Georgy's tears rolled. 'You haven't heard me play in weeks.'

Beat looked daggers at her ex. How could he make Georgy doubt her gift?

'My absence will give you time to focus on your degree. Then you can train to be a teacher. You'd be gold in any school music program.'

'I'd rather die.'

'But with your fragility, and without Matthew's er... crucial support, the pressure in LA could be overwhelming.'

'I've survived you,' barked Georgy determinedly avoiding Dan's eyes.

'Both of you have tough decisions,' Connor interrupted. 'Dan, what's it to be?'

'London.'

'And you, Georgy?' Beat gently touched the pianist's arm.

'Accommodation is difficult to find these days, I should keep the flat going while Dan's away.'

Georgy's spirit had sunk, and her resolve had weakened yet again. Dan looked smug. Pleased. Exasperated by his behaviour, she gave a signal to Connor, who pressed play on his phone's recording. An amplified crackle preceded Dan's voice.

'There's no future there. Georgy's great but she's just...'

'A friend with benefits?'

'She's not a patch on Beat, except she's younger, but not a keeper. Man, that piano thing?'

'What about it?'

'It's a passion killer.'

Georgy dry-retched, clutched at her throat. Lunging at the door, she grabbed the handle and flew down the corridor. Dan remained seated.

'What the fuck? You've scammed me. There is no overseas project. Watch me blow the whistle on you with the Research Centre.' Dan stood up. 'Then I'm going to the press.'

'Fine,' said Connor. 'You do that.'

'It's vile the way you want to pressure someone as sensitive as Georgy merely to fulfil your own vision for her future. How dare you?'

'Let her go, Dan,' Beat said.

'I bet Georgy's never told you about her dependency?' He gloated.

'What are you talking about?'

'Unless she takes a betablocker she can't perform.'

'That's simply not true,' Beat countered.

'Ask her about it. I'm not the only spoiler in her life. Find out how easy they are to come by in this school.'

'Meaning?'

'Matthew's a supplier. Okay, they're not hard drugs but he sells them at exorbitant cost. Think back to the night Georgy arrived to play the Tchaikovsky, she shuffled along, clutching the banister for support. I saw how you observed her, alarm all over your face. She was petrified until Matthew sold her a pill.'

'If this is true, it's unconscionable. Criminal.'

'Look into it then.'

'Give Georgy your blessing,' Beat said. 'Let her find out for herself if a solo career is what she wants.'

'What's in it for me?'

'It could clear your conscience,' Connor said.

'Conscience for...?'

'Preying on a vulnerable student twenty-two years your junior.'

'Dan,' Beat said, 'I'll push the financial settlement along, providing you don't report Connor and you withdraw from Georgy's life.'

'I'll have to think hard about your second condition because her income pays the rent.'

Connor turned away in disgust. Beat persisted.

'No love bombing: surprise appearances, texts, roomfuls of red roses, or romantic declarations tattooed in the sky.'

'Or?'

'No deal.'

'Are singing telegrams off the table too?' Dan joked.

'Not funny,' Beat said. 'And do *not* come to hear her play Beethoven's *Triple Concerto*.'

'Sure. Too, too easy. But do make sure she pops a couple of betablockers beforehand.'

49
PIANO TRIO

BEAT sat in the middle of the stalls. She stared at Thorne, who wore pearl drop earrings and a floor-length salmon pink taffeta dress. Her precision-cut bob dipped and swung as she squeezed past occupied seats to her reserved spot in front of Beat. Thorne's extravagant frock clashed with the spirit of Beethoven's revolutionary zeal.

Theo, Melody, and Georgy followed Garrett onto the stage. They lined up, held hands, fronted the audience, bowed in unison and then each of them wrenched off their shoes. Beat rolled her eyes at the gesture but in all other ways 1 2 3's stage manners were more professional since the finals of Byron's Chamber Music Competition. All three played from memory. Theo held his violin poised to begin, a seated Melody steadied the cello and waited, bow ready. Georgy's eyes were fixed on the keys. She no longer played with a haunted look and even better didn't stare into the audience. According to Elvira, Georgy had taken a betablocker. Urgently, Beat needed to investigate Dan's claims about Matthew. Now it made sense why Matthews' students had heckled Garrett in his workshop. Of all the issues Beat wanted to reform, Matthew's exploitation of performance students had to be the worst. She couldn't shake off her suspicion he had something to do with Steven's resignation.

Beethoven's *Triple Concerto* could be problematic, because sometimes the violinist, pianist, and cellist compete with each other for the limelight and it's tough to ensure the mellow voiced cello is audible against a powerful orchestra. To combat this, Beethoven plumbed the instrument's higher register, while the piano's bass trill rumbled like a volcanic eruption. Melody introduced the theme after an orchestral introduction, Theo followed and Georgy entered third, each investing the melody with stunning tone.

In the cadenza, Georgy broadened the tempo dramatically, too much for traditionalists no doubt, but to compensate, the music breathed here and there, creating a luxurious feeling of repose. There were beautiful moments when whispered orchestral strings cued Melody, and she spun beautiful lines, her upper body swaying. Melody was a devotee of Jacqueline du Pré, last century's legendary cellist, whose body danced while she played.

The last movement's wild chases, with sparks flying between the players and the orchestra, were exciting. Theo's lyricism expertly intersected with Georgy's piano. Twice, he accidentally eclipsed the cello's voice but appropriate balancing between the three players was such a challenge and between the soloists and orchestra even more so. Centuries after Beethoven was born, the trio's lively interpretation portrayed the composer as cantankerous yet a loveable badass. Georgy called Theo and Melody to arms when the piano's showy contribution started the third movement. When the spirited fourth movement flowed, Elvira leaned back to look up at the organ loft, her loose black hair tumbling over the back of her chair and she pinned her eyes on the elevated spot at the back of the stage, above the choir stalls where singers solo and trumpet fanfares blaze. Elvira raised her purple gloved arm and graciously waved, not just once, but twice.

Time stopped. Beat followed Elvira's eyes. Was she really seeing the glimmer of a grey brocade, silk-lined coat, golden vest, jabot, and lace cuffs? A blurry yet identifiable silhouette of a nineteenth century cultural giant. Beat refocused on the grand sweep of the fourth and final movement, trying to unsee the apparition's chubby hands, which carved the air in a ghostly parody of Garrett's conducting. Glowing brass chaperoned the music's final run.

50
CODA

'IF what you've told me is true, my current expectation for the settlement is out of date.' Cholmley picked up the Daniel Spinner vs Beatrice Snow document on his desk. He peered at her, his glasses slipping down his nose.

'For the better?' ventured Beat.

'You bet. This draft...' Cholmley slapped the papers in his hand, 'was drawn up on the basis that Dan, as your dependent, had no financial assets.'

'Yes.'

'A different settlement is necessary. This man has been your dependant for the last five years when there was no need for him to be. And as infuriating as that must be you will be entitled to fifty percent of the sale of the Byron house and all his assets.'

'Really?' Beat's eyes widened.

'Yes.' Cholmley took off his glasses, held them up to the light, and polished the lenses with his tie.

'It will be a settlement to your advantage. The Byron property Dan inherited with ocean views, could be worth seven million, and that's a conservative guess.'

Cholmley scored out sentences on his previous draft and scribbled in the margin. He scratched his forehead. Sighed. Opened the door and called for his assistant to type up the changes he'd made to the revised document and, bring it in for him to sign.

'I'm stunned.' Beat confessed.

'Dan also has considerable credit.'

'Correct,' confirmed Beat.

'When you leave, I'll ring his lawyer. Because of this timely discovery, you should be able to buy Dan out of Wongara.'

'But the court case is in a few days?' Beat's face flamed. Suddenly too warm, she removed her blue biker's jacket.

'Time enough for us to renegotiate a relevant settlement. A word of caution, I've known dozens of *Dans*. Be prepared. Forewarned is forearmed. Be wary.'

'Because?'

'When Dan discovers he's been sprung, he's likely to make overtures about making things up to you. Do not talk to him. Avoid confiding in relatives, his sister, or any mutual friends. Soon you can build a new life on your terms. Talk to him after the settlement if you have to but not before.'

'Believe me, Dan's the last person I want to talk to.'

Beat grabbed her jacket and her bag, struggling against her urge to race from Cholmley's mahogany swamped office and leap for joy. When her hand reached the doorknob, the lawyer warned, 'It's premature to celebrate. Rulings are unpredictable.'

Beat nodded, but as soon as she'd shut the door behind her, she clattered down the stone stairwell happier than she'd felt in years.

51

BETA BENDER

WHEN Connor stepped on to the podium, the crowd cheered at the spectacle of the performers in bright pink, yellow, and blue tees instead of the classical musician's uniform of black.

'Shout out for Beatrice Snow because this extraordinary beat-bender is her brainchild,' Sian enthused. Beat wasn't happy that Elvira's contribution hadn't been acknowledged but she couldn't do anything about it.

'Make noise for Marilyn Thorne, the CEO of Turalong Arts, the State Orchestra, Winton Thomas and all of Turalong's instrumentalists and singers. Sounds Best for their outstanding support and, last but not least, Connor Perkins our awesome conductor.'

He turned to the audience and bowed his head to the crowd's delight. Mostly youthful, the audience wore white tees with Sian splashed across the front in pink echoing her signature pink sneakers. The majority of tickets had sold, and it meant the school could not only clear the questionable deficit but the profit ought to be enough to seed the rock stream's building project.

Exhilarated, Beat's spirit flew around and around the vast domed ceiling. She was proud of Sian, the school orchestra, the rock chorus and band, and the supportive staff who stood in the wings. The formidable musical force was exciting and when Sian took her position at the front of the stage in her sparkling rainbow-coloured jumpsuit the crowd's excitement soared.

As Connor raised his conducting arm the orchestral players released helium-filled balloons which floated above the stage. Beat was thrilled the ABC was covering the event live. She plugged in her headphones to listen. Gleeful, she slapped her sides when she heard Newton say, 'These days, collaborations between orchestras and other music; rock, funk, pop, hip hop, is a means to ensure a symphony orchestra's survival. Trouble is, it's common to witness grim-lipped players enduring rather than partnering another genre. Like they're swallowing medicine they know is good for them, but the taste is foul. That's not the case here, peeps. I've never, repeat, never seen a keener or more united talent pool.'

'Blast off is imminent. Meaningful looks are passing between Sian, the orchestra, band, and conductor. Yes, yes, it's happening,' Newton raved.

A stomping bass line, duelling guitars, and gnarly percussion underscored Sian's *Don't Lose the Dream*. At each reiteration of the riff, more singers and more players joined in, the sound expanding until its booming theatre made the audience stand. Sian patrolled the stage belting wild narratives on environmental themes offset by Winton's dazzling fills. Beat had laid herself open to criticism by appointing Winton as a soloist, instead of a gifted student, but she'd done so because she wanted Thorne and the audience to hear his superb playing which rivalled the trumpet solos in Billy Joel's *Zanzibar* or *Spinning Wheel* by Blood, Sweat and Tears.

Connor's command was efficient yet bold. Matthew slipped his arm around Beat's shoulder in the heat of the moment, but she bridled, and he swiftly withdrew it. Connor's rapport with the musical cast was productive, ensuring the brass and wind forces expertly flexed the syncopated groove. Flute, clarinet, saxophone, violin solos as well as trumpet sliced clearly through the arrangements. Provocative and persuasive, there was nothing girly or pastel about Sian's scolding reflections on water theft and the extinction crisis.

Georgy's deep engagement was in no doubt as she powered Sian's chord chains from the soloist's latest album on a keyboard and the crowd waved their phones from side to side as they sang along to *Don't Mine the*

Reef. Beat liked the retro scratchy turntable elements which offset the lyrical dimension. But Connor's leadership impressed her most of all. Finally, the massive crowd rose to their feet like a tidal wave and brought tears to her eyes. She could scarcely contain her happiness and relief. And yet, even before the cheers and whistles faded, Beat sensed a shift. Her delight wasn't just sparked by the performance, gladdening though it had been, but from the realisation she was free. In front of thousands of witnesses, she had united the classical and rock musicians. She glowed with pride. No-one could take that away from her and the approval of Marilyn Thorne, the VC, or the school's artistic community she had once so badly craved couldn't heighten the empowerment she already felt. Watching the stage crew pack up equipment and stow the chairs away, she was deep in thought when she heard Matthew's voice. 'If that,' he waved towards the stage, 'doesn't call for a celebration, what does? Why aren't you partying with the others?'

'You and I have to talk Matthew,' Beat said wearily.

'If it's the inevitable betablocker chat, don't bother.'

'Why not?'

'If it goes public it could smash the school's growing reputation you've worked so hard for. My resignation is on your desk. I'm going to be a soloist.'

'But I can't let you get away with it. Simon's psychotic break was caused by the hard-core drugs you sold him.'

'Is this what he told you?' Matthew said.

'Simon was broke. Couldn't afford his rent. Highly anxious. Already on strong prescription medication, the recreational drugs he took on top of them was a dangerous cocktail.'

'You've no proof.'

'Talk to the police about that,' Beat said. 'That drug-fuelled break could have cost him his life. Steven knew what you were doing. Why did he let you get away with it?'

'Because I had him over a barrel,' Matthew smirked. 'Steven had a gambling addiction. Embezzled money from the school's budget to pay for it. That's the real cause of the school's strained economy.'

'I don't believe you.'

'Ask Thorne. She found out about Steven's fraud. But she didn't want a public scandal to smear her professional integrity because she and Steven had been lovers. Even so, she gave him an ultimatum. Resign instantly or she'd involve the police. That's when you came into the picture. She wanted you to be the gullible scapegoat for the overspend.'

Beat's heart raced. Matthew gloated.

'Shall I tell the police to pick you up here?'

'You're bluffing,' Matthew's frown turned into a scowl.

'No, I'm not. They're waiting backstage.'

~

Elvira hugged Beat until she could scarcely breathe. Polly announced the current Box Office takings had already topped the profit she'd anticipated.

'Never knew of an event like this in London,' Winton teased.

Hermione called her a star, Elvira waved and Connor embraced her. Johnny Wood bowed theatrically. Thorne dragged Beat away to greet a beaming VC.

'Exceptional, Beatrice! Unforgettable. And though it pains me to say it, since I've previously detested pop, I want to buy a CD,' he said.

'Now's your chance, Sian's over there, signing.' All she wanted to do was congratulate Connor but couldn't fend off the attentions of the rapt VC.

'I have to hand it to you. The school's future looks significantly brighter.'

Beat thanked him but felt nothing, certainly not the kind of elation she experienced after the Tchaikovsky concert. She was delighted by the truce between the staff. She beamed at Connor, who had stepped out of the way to let Tim Newton, Garrett, and the managing director of Sounds Best approach her. But she couldn't decipher what they were saying, because the faff and the brouhaha and the positive affirmations all sounded like white noise. If the event had generated sufficient funds, and according to Polly it had, she was content. When Connor reached her, he pulled her to him and she bound her arms around his waist.

~

A glum Polly announced, 'I've a message from Professor Thorne. She's having a meeting with the VC and wants you there.'

'Pop it in the diary.'

'But it's on the same day you go to the family court to finalise the divorce.'

'No matter.'

'That's not what you said last time.'

'Let's just say I've had an attitudinal shift, an epiphany, and really what do I have to fear?'

Polly looked concerned. 'Nothing, but you hated the last session remember?'

'That was a world away. Is there something else?'

'Yes.'

'What?'

'Come and see for yourself.'

Beat followed her assistant into the foyer. Distracted by the sight of Theo and Melody kissing, she didn't immediately notice. But her mood crashed when she saw the massive straw basket holding thirty large purple balloons with "I Love You" scribbled across each one.

'What on earth...?'

Polly handed her a card.

'Should I be reading this?'

'It's addressed to you.'

Beat blanched at the words, 'Take me back. Dan xxx'

'I don't care how but this, this abomination has to go.' She kicked the basket hard, and the vibrant helium filled balloons bobbed and swayed and a couple broke free and floated to the ceiling.

'But not now.' Polly's eyes opened wide with alarm.

'Because?'

'Dan's in the dean's studio.'

'Polly, I don't care. Call security to remove this grotesquery. Either Dan leaves or I do.'

'He refuses to budge.'

'Call me when he's gone,' she said and stomped out of the exit door.

~

Connor, primped and jacketed, wore a tie. Beat revelled in her raw informality, her muddy boots. When Thorne's assistant offered the macarons to her boss, Thorne took a purple one. Beat chose three: brown, green, and pink.

The VC cleared his throat. A macaron crumb, like a spot of shaving cream, pimpled his chin. 'We've examined the paperwork and all of us,' he swept a gallant arm around the room, 'believe that the retreat, far from being wasteful, was a great start to a new chapter in the school's history. Anyone care to comment?'

Connor beamed at Beat. Thorne's unfathomable mood no longer bothered her. Despite the VC's upbeat tone, she felt like an outlaw, an outsider. The University's hierarchy was capable of anything, the fake cheer could be hysteria. No one liked to deliver bad news.

'The Committee is impressed by your efforts to gender-proof the school.' The VC pulled back his sleeve to look at his watch.

'Thanks,' mumbled Beat. She was uncomfortably hot in the airless room.

Thorne spoke next. 'I've been hard on you Beatrice.'

'Have you ever,' Beat jumped in and evidently too firmly, if the VC's grimace was anything to go by. He guzzled down some water as if it were a shot of whisky.

'The rock and classical streams were like West Side Story's Jets and Sharks. But to your credit that's no longer the case,' Thorne admitted.

Beat glowed with inner pride.

Connor motioned to speak. 'We've received an unprecedented quantity of student inquiries.'

The VC nodded approval at Connor. Outside, a noisy crow shunted along a magnolia tree's bare branch. Soon it was joined by another three just as rowdy birds.

'Beatrice, the VC and I held private consultations with all of the music staff and several students about your professional input.' Thorne dabbed at the corner of her mouth with a paper napkin.

'Yes, Elvira told me,' Beat managed. She was still furious about it. The invitation to Winton, Hermione, Matthew, Elvira, Connor, Polly, Theo, and Melody and all and sundry to sound off about her performance as dean was too disrespectful. Georgy had refused to say anything.

'It was an arduous undertaking. We spoke to everyone individually, but we were heartened by your colleagues' mostly positive views.' Like a pelican devouring a fish, Thorne knocked back a helping of almonds.

'Winton's bowled over by your building plans,' the VC said.

Beat's hands trembled, she removed her denim jacket, flexed her feet, pressing her boots hard against the wooden floor and sat square on her chair because she had an inkling she was about to be ambushed.

'Beat, we have decided...' The VC paused to whisper in Thorne's ear.

Beat had prepared herself for the worst. If she lost her job she'd weather it, take a few months off, live off her savings while she planned what to do next.

'We are offering you the position of Executive Director of the University's proposed Faculty of Arts,' The VC said.

Momentarily, Beat was swayed by the committee's faith in her. Wasn't that what she'd worked for? She blushed with pride momentarily, but this feeling gave way to deep, deep disappointment. Thorne and the VC didn't care about the school in which she'd invested her heart and soul. She still believed it could have become an internationally and nationally sought after destination for performers. How that would have benefited the University, the music industry, the community and the city. But she had failed to sell the authorities her dream. The VC desired a massive faculty where her precious school would suffocate.

'Beatrice, I'm taking on a broader and greater role,' said Thorne. 'Your brief is to successfully merge the University's creative arts divisions with Turalong Arts.'

'But the music school is performance oriented,' Beat protested.

'Yes,' said the VC kindly, folding his hands on the table. 'There's no wish to alter that emphasis, but the combined University and Turalong schools will become a powerful arts hub.'

'I see,' Beat gave a cursory nod and surrendered to despondency. At last, the school had proved its potential only to be smothered.

'A generous salary will reflect the expanded role, with a suitable executive package and a deluxe concreted parking space under cover.'

Connor looked ecstatic, his face wreathed in smiles. Beat had never seen him so happy. But she couldn't snap her fingers and adjust to a reality where she was suddenly feted and applauded. Beat was supposed to be thrilled about the committee's proposal, but it reminded her of when the reluctant party in an intimate relationship finally agrees to commit, and the other is expected to leap for joy at their partner's long overdue, change of heart.

'Thank you for this offer and, most of all, your belief in me. But I'll need time to consider it.'

~

Beat draped her arms around Connor's neck. 'Johnny must have been impressed to recommend you as the conductor for this European tour. You did a brilliant job in the Sian concert.'

'Thanks.'

'I'd say this European tour is essential.'

'Essential? Why?'

'Because you're going to be a conductor.'

'I'm cautiously pleased at the prospect.' Connor picked eucalypt leaves from an overhanging branch and crushed them between his fingers.

'Cautious, why?'

'My stage fright,' said Connor.

'There wasn't a trace of it the other night,' said Beat.

'What if I miss out on the next staff retreat?'

Beat laughed.

'And Garrett's offer to Georgy?' Connor opened his hand and inhaled the scent of the broken leaves.

'She turned it down.'

'Not because of Dan?'

'No. Thankfully that's over.'

'Why then?'

'Apparently, The Australian National Academy of Music heard about it and made a more attractive offer.'

'Let me guess. ANAM embraces shoeless performance.'

'Along those lines.' Beat laughed. 'I'll miss you when you're in Europe. But we're in a goldfish bowl now and everyone knows about us...'

'For a minute or two. People will get used to it, used to *us*,' Connor said. 'We'll be tactful. I'll back you.'

'Recently, you've given me plenty of support.'

Beat hadn't a clue how she could best explain her decision, her change of heart or how to make him understand the new urgency percolating inside her. Especially, her decision to step back from Turalong Arts entirely.

'Hermione will be a nightmare after being overlooked a second time for the big job,' Connor said.

'I doubt that.'

'How come?'

'I've turned the Executive Directorship down,' her tone was too abrupt, and her eyes welled.

'Excuse me?'

'You heard, Connor. Hermione's accepted the role.'

He snatched his hand away.

'After she did such treacherous things.' He shook his head.

'I knew you wouldn't...'

'Approve? No. How could I?' Connor frowned.

'Who would you suggest then?'

'The role should be advertised and given to a suitable outsider to breathe new life into the place. But my opinion isn't wanted, and neither is yours.'

'Very true.'

'But Hermione of all people.'

'See it from the University's perspective. She approves of the proposed new Faculty. She has super credibility as a performer, she'll toe the line. If there's a clash between what's in the best interests of music performance and a university directive she won't hesitate to back the authorities.'

'She's not you. You sold us your vision,' said Connor.

'And she'll dream up different goals.'

'Like?'

'Festivals, new courses, community programs, a music technology stream. Who knows?'

'Even Winton thinks you're good in the role,' Connor said.

'What I once would have given to hear that.' Beat shrugged. 'But Hermione won't let her professional duties hobble her private life.'

'That, I do know.'

'Music isn't everything. I feel cut off. Stranded. I miss being me.'

'Do you want to teach piano? Or coach 1 2 3?'

Beat swallowed hard. Seeing the love, the hope in Connor's eyes was harder than she'd imagined. Yet, tell him she must. There would never be an ideal time.

'I've resigned.' Silence swirled around her, a moat of impenetrable resolve. She felt dislocated, light-headed. She waited for him to respond.

'Why on earth?'

'I've agonised about it. Dan was right.'

'Surprise me?'

'He said I was besotted with the institution's emotional dramas, the extremes, the conflict, in awe of the colossal talent, and addicted to the all too frequent bouts of bewildering dysfunction. My goal, an obsession really, was to make the school excel. The proposed Faculty structure holds no appeal for me because our school as we know it, will be snuffed out.' She closed her eyes against the sting of tears.

'All of the soul-searching, the politics, the people sorting and finally we turn the corner. What could be as significant as this?'

Beat avoided Connor's wounded eyes. Me, she thought, but couldn't say. 'Nothing, for six months at least.'

Connor shook his head. 'Is this the cliché find-out-who-you are phase?'

'No. I know exactly who I am,' she snapped. 'And you don't know me well enough to dismiss how I feel.'

Gently, Connor asked, 'How will you fill your days?'

'I'll read my box of unread books.'

'You'll soon get over that,' he kicked a stone off the path.

'I'll play the piano. Join a rock band. Record Chopin's *Preludes*. Ride. Renovate the kitchen. Hang with friends. Re-upholster the couch.'

She saw the flicker of a smile in his eyes. 'The sofa goal won't go amiss.'

How she wished she was in Sally's whiter than white house now with her friend holding her until the pain eased, her cat coiling around her ankles as she battles the regret she knows will haunt her.

'And then?' Connor's arch tone cut her to the quick.

'Professionally?' Beat said. 'I haven't a clue.'

'You'll be missed.'

'I'll call, e-mail, skype. Bombard you with reels of Bolt and Storm's training,' she said attempting to be light.

'Not just by me.'

'For a week or two. But the reality that Hermione controls the purse strings will soon kick in.'

'Did the divorce settlement go your way?'

'A fifty-fifty split. I'll get half of Dan's capital, half of his aunt's property, and I'll own half of Wongara. But I plan to buy him out.'

'He must be livid.'

'Ropeable. Rabidly mad.'

'And Ellie?'

'I'll give her a lump sum. Let her stay a while. It's been tough for her to study and work enough hours to meet all her expenses.'

'I'm glad.' He brushed a beetle off his sleeve. 'But what about... us?'

She heard the tremor in his voice. A red stain deepening across his neck.

'We'll be on hold.'

'Tour Europe with me?'

'No, what about my horses? Besides, I've longed to spend more time at Wongara.' Beat spoke in almost a whisper. 'I can't. Not just yet.'

'Ellie will be there. She could look after Bolt and his old buddy.'

'She needs attention too.'

'Mull it over. Please.'

'For as long as I can remember I've wanted...' Beat's words stuck in her throat.

'What?'

'To be free of the expectations of others.'

'You may change your mind.' Connor sounded doubtful.

'Will I see you later?' She liked his casual look of a dark blue sweater and jeans but there was no mistaking the rapidly expanding chasm opening up between them.

'I've got essays to mark. Scores to prepare. I have to find somewhere to keep Stringer.'

'Let me take care of your horse,' Beat said.

'I'd rest easier if you did,' Connor didn't catch her eye.

'That's settled then,' said Beat. 'Tomorrow, we can...'

Connor stood up. Shook his head. 'Thanks. I'll bring him over in a week or so.'

'Surely we can...' her voice broke. Screeching rosellas landed, claws struggling to gain purchase, scratching and skating on the tin roof.

'Call me if you have a change of heart.'

'About Springer, I won't.'

'No. Travelling. I'm in Poland in two months. I've nothing but rehearsals for a week.' Facing her, he rested his hands on her shoulders. 'We could get together there?'

Beat moved in, clung to him, rested her head on his chest. She absorbed his heart's rhythm of distress. She gulped, heavy with loss. She lingered. Gently, he unpeeled her arms.

'No. It's too soon. I wish I could.' Beat shook her head.

He turned his back on her then. Soaring panic mocked her as Connor trod down the garden path, her view of him, as he opened the gate, obscured by the overgrown, orange grevillea. A rush of memories:

him conducting, his touch, his reassurance, his rapport with her horses, playing the viola. She ran down the brick path, hollow inside, her heart burning, tripping in her desperation to reach him.

Fighting for breath, she flung the gate open, tore across the grassy footpath and stood in the middle of the road. Cars drove towards her but she didn't care. She waved wildly, fending off the emptiness, the anguish, every cell in her body willing his return. But there was no point in him turning back, despite her pain, despite her shortage of breath because she couldn't say what he needed to hear. Not yet. Connor waved. Slowed almost to a stop. She ran towards the car but he accelerated, eyes peeled on the road ahead.

ABOUT THE AUTHOR

Gillian Wills is a graduate and an Honorary Associate of the Royal Academy of Music. She is an author, arts writer, and music reviewer who has published with *The Australian, Limelight, Griffith Review, Australian Book Review* and *Inreview*. Her memoir *Elvis and Me: how a world-weary musician and a broken racehorse rescued each other*, Finch Publishing, was released in 2016 in Australia, America, Canada, the United Kingdom, and New Zealand. Gillian has held senior academic positions in the UK and Australia.

ACKNOWLEDGEMENTS

I would like to thank Mostyn Bramley-Moore for his loving support and unwavering belief in this book. Many thanks to Carolyn Martinez for her positivity, encouragement, and commitment to the story and the Hawkeye Publishing team for their excellent input and generous support.

For their astute advice, Kristina Olsson, Peggy Frew, Laura Boon, Sally Piper and James Griffin; for their helpful feedback and special presence in my life, Guido and Seanna Van Helten, Michael, Mira and Alma Baranovic, Mostyn, Imogen and Phoebe Bramley-Moore, Maureen Behan, Phil Brown, Kath Rose, Matthew Bentley, my sister Cathy Joyner, Cecilia and Julian Darker, Deborah Walker, Diane Kirkby, Monica Lloyd-Williams and Phillipa Drynan.

For all of the professional musicians I have worked with and learned from and in particular, Nicholas Braithwaite, Brendan Joyce, Miwako Abe, Robert Constable, Piers Lane AO, Leah Horwitz, Andy Arthurs, Dr Donna Hewitt, Karin Schaupp, Robert Davidson, Dr Donna Coleman, Alex Pertout, Michael Hannan, Jennifer Newcombe, Geoffrey Ashenden, Stewart Kelly, Justin Beere, Katie Stenzel, and a nod to my late father Frederick Scott Wills, a conflicted yet inspirational force.

Gillian